MIKE FOX works in advertising. His previous published
Rolls Royce: The Complete Works (with Steve Smith). At weekends
he runs the largest children's chess club in the Midlands. A former
Warwickshire county player, his tournament record bears comparison
with that of G. D. H. Gossip; and his current grading places him
squarely alongside Colonel Moreau in the list of all-time greats.

RICHARD JAMES, the author of *Move One!*, a chess course for
beginners (Faber 1990), was for a number of years an active tournament and county player. He is the Director of Richmond Junior
Chess Club, (which he founded with Mike Fox in 1975), most of
whose members are both taller and higher graded than he is. He
works in the market research industry.

THE
EVEN MORE COMPLETE
CHESS ADDICT

Mike Fox
Richard James

faber and faber
LONDON · BOSTON

First published as *The Complete Chess Addict* in 1987
by Faber and Faber Limited
3 Queen Square London WCIN 3AU

This revised edition first published in 1993

Typeset by Datix International Limited, Bungay, Suffolk
Printed in England by Clays Ltd, St Ives plc
All rights reserved

Mike Fox and Richard James are hereby identified as authors of
this work in accordance with Section 77 of the Copyright,
Designs and Patents Act 1988.

A CIP record for this book is available from the British Library

ISBN 0–571–17040–4

2 4 6 8 10 9 7 5 3 1

TO BOBBY
May he never cease to amaze us

A problem by Aladdin

(See page 203 for conditions)

Contents

Acknowledgements

So many people helped it would be too space-consuming to acknowledge everyone, but thanks to: Betty and Howard James for their forbearance and hospitality; Janet and Emma Fox for their useful comments on the style, the spelling, the grammar, the content and even the acknowledgements; B. H. Wood for being so generous with his time, memory and pictures; Peter Gibbs for correcting some of the grosser errors; Steve Smith and the Pope for their encouragement; Colin Loose of Birmingham Chess Club for books; Bill Husselby for Napoleon's silk stocking; Laurie Hall for Haroun al-Rashid; Juliet Cook and Amanda Wilmoth for their patience and co-operation; Amy Fox for help with the title; Graham Storey for a desert island; Bernard Levin, Patrick Moore, Art Buchwald, Steve Davis, Michael Foot, Tony Benn, Edmund Dell, Buckingham Palace, the Archbishop of Canterbury, Steve Ovett, A. J. Ayer, Mike Gatting and numerous others for answering our daft questions; Ken Whyld for his help with some of the facts; Hilary Boszko for being a test-market patzer; Robert Maxwell for a book; Paddy Goldring for a joke; Harry Fox for his omniscience in the world of pop music; Niel Anderson for a bare bottom; Ken and Dinah Norman for reading the manuscript, for hospitality and for the loan of books; George Hill for checking some of the game scores; various members of Richmond Chess Club for books and/or information: Chris Baker, Ben Beake, Ray Cannon, Philip Poyser, Gene Veglio, Gavin Wall; Abraham Neviazsky for his part in Chapter IV; Matthew Evans of Faber and Faber for patience and munificence; the ever helpful staff of Birmingham's terrific Central Library; Mike Sheehan of Caïssa Books; Janet and Dave Allen for massive support when they had so much else on their minds; and especially, all those authors whose work we pillaged in our quest for facts; notably Messrs Murray, Hooper, Whyld, Krabbé, Golombek, Chernev, Knight and Twiss.

1987

For this new edition we are happy to record our debt to (in addition to the above): David Pritchard for much unorthodox help; the Ominiscient One for help with more facts and with the longest game; Faye Ainscow for some of our sporting quotes; Hilary Gilmore of the Sick Children's Trust for some celebrities; Juliet Bryant and Caroline Dunkley for easing the production process; Rod McShane for press cuttings; Countrywide Computers for more on the Pope; and, of course, all those readers of Addicts' Corner in *Chess* for their contributions to our monthly column, many of which we have used in this book.

1993

For permission to reprint copyright material the publishers gratefully acknowledge the following: extract from *Abinger Harvest* by E. M. Forster, reprinted by permission of Edward Arnold (Publishers) Ltd; extract from *The Art of Coarse Sport* by Michael Green, reprinted by permission of Century Hutchinson Publishing Group Ltd; *The Ballad of Edward Bray* by A. A. Milne, reprinted by permission of Curtis Brown Ltd, London; lines from *Queer* by William Burroughs, reprinted by permission of Viking Penguin Inc.

For permission to reproduce illustrations the publishers gratefully acknowledge the following: Niel Anderson for the chapter heading illustration for Chapter IV; Associated Press Limited for Pope John Paul II; BBC Hulton Picture Library for Paul Morphy, Emanuel Lasker, José Raúl Capablanca, Alexander Alekhine, Aleister Crowley; Diaz for the cartoon at the start of Chapter VII; Denis O'Regan/ Idols for Phil Lynott; *Liverpool Post and Echo* for William Wallace; The Mansell Collection for engravings of the First World Chess Championship and Chevalier d'Éon; Raduga Publishers, Moscow (from *The Soviet Chess School* by A. Kotov and M. Yudovich (1982)) for Tolstoy and Lenin; David Redfern/David Redfern Photography for Dizzy Gillespie; Graham Storey for the chapter heading illustration for Chapter VI; Steve Tynan and *The Sunday Times*, for Ossie Ardiles, Steve Davis, Terry Marsh; Syndication International Limited for Harold Davidson; The Tate Gallery Archive for Walter Sickert (Sickert 3.4 pb), and Marcel Duchamp (John Banting 779.8.127); Tate Gallery for *The Child's Problem* by Richard Dadd;

Ken Whyld for the engraving of Philidor; and Naomi Sim for the photograph of George Cole and Alastair Sim.

Faber and Faber apologizes for any errors or omissions in the above list and would be grateful to be notified of any corrections that should be incorporated in the next edition of this volume.

Preface to the First Edition

'It's a great game of chess that's being played – all over the world.'
Lewis Carroll, *Through the Looking Glass*

We wanted to call it 'The Monkey's Bum'[1] but Faber thought this lacked *gravitas*. Maybe they were right – but *gravitas* is a commodity you won't find much of in what follows. This is not a deadly serious look at chess.

Our simple intent is to have you say 'Wow!' every couple of pages or so; for *The Complete Chess Addict* is our own private collection of Wow!-inducing facts, anecdotes, legends and quotes about the world's best game.

Somewhere in these pages you'll find: games by Humphrey Bogart, Che Guevara, Yehudi Menuhin, Tolstoy, Patrick Moore, Karl Marx and other notables; Barbra Streisand and Bobby Fischer sharing *MAD* magazine in high school; the awful truth about Pope John Paul II's chess problem; the most depraved team in the history of the universe; the chess-master who ate the pieces; the weirdest chess variants; the most difficult problem of all; the world's oldest game of chess; the world's silliest loss by a grandmaster; the state of the art in computer chess; and what 'bra drag' means in some chess circles.

And just in case you're worrying about investing your hard-earned in something utterly frivolous, we've chucked in for free (as it were) a collection of sixty of the best games ever played. This alone is worth the price of admission.

We also give you, for the first time ever, the results of the matches you've dreamed about: Fischer–Alekhine; Capablanca–Kasparov; and Paul Morphy versus Nigel Short.

What you won't find here is yards of in-depth analysis; the authors[2] aren't qualified to give it. But if you are, as they say, game for a laugh – or at least the occasional wry smile – then you're just the chap we're looking for. Welcome to *The Complete Chess Addict*.

[1] see page 253.
[2] a couple of patzers (see Glossary).

Postscript 1

If you're not a regular player, and you don't know about chess notation, a quick look at the next few pages ('Glossary' and 'Notation') will double the enjoyment you get from this book.

Postscript 2

The quotes at the head of each chapter are mostly by chess-players (including that all-time loser, Anon).

Preface to the Second Edition

(*or, Some Reasons for Buying the Second Edition of This Book*)

If you happen to be Pope John Paul II, you may be induced to lash out on this modest work by the knowledge that you, along with Robert Maxwell, John Wayne, the Amazing Kreskin, and other stars of the first edition, now play a substantially larger role than in our earlier effort.

If, however, your name is Salman Rushdie, Boris Yeltsin, Woody Allen, Jeffrey Archer, Paul Gascoigne, Christine Keeler or Lennox Lewis, welcome to the club. The fact that you are one of the sixty or so new members of our cast ought to be sufficient incentive for you to fork out Faber's extremely reasonable cover price.

Then again, if you're Kasp or Karp or Korch or Kamsk or Kram or any of the other megastars of world chess, you'll be agog to see where (and if) you rank in our new list of the sixty-seven strongest players of all time; or whether one of your *chefs-d'œuvre* has made our collection of the sixty-four greatest games.

If you're Bobby Fischer, then (a) nice to see you again; (b) you'll be delighted, we hope, to see we've chronicled your latest exploits. (If that's not enough to have you stick your hand in your pocket, then a glance at our dedication page should do the trick.)

Finally, if you are like both of us, just a run-of-the-mill blunder-prone patzer,[1] we hope you'll be sufficiently rewarded by the uplifting sight of Gazza K., Tolya, Nige, Vishy and a dozen other superbrains demonstrating that grandmasters can, once in a while, play like absolute berks.

PS
By the way, if you *are* the Pope, we'd be most awfully grateful, Your Holiness, if you could see your way to clearing up the mystery on page 16. Just drop us a line c/o Faber and Faber, and we'll bung you a complimentary copy by return.

[1] Since we last met, our gradings have slumped faster than the property market.

Glossary

BCF: British Chess Federation.

Blindfold simul: An expert plays several opponents without sight of the boards.

Blitz: Lightning chess – usually five minutes each on the clock.

Candidates' Tournament/Match: FIDE-organized event to select World Championship challenger.

Cheapo: A tactical trick.

Draughts: English for what the Americans call 'checkers'.

ELO Rating: Measurement of the comparative strength of a chess player (see page 118).

En Prise: Of a piece, able to be captured.

En Passant: A pawn capture in which a pawn on the fifth rank captures an enemy pawn which has just moved two squares as if it had moved one square.

Exchange (the): Advantage of rook for bishop or knight.

FIDE: Fédération Internationale des Échecs, the international governing body of chess.

Fifty-Move Rule: This states that either player may claim a draw after fifty moves have been played by both sides without a pawn move or capture.

Fish: *See* Patzer.

FM: FIDE master; a title below International Master.

Grandmaster (GM, IGM): Chess title awarded by FIDE to players who have achieved a certain standard in tournaments. (Strictly speaking: International Grandmaster.)

International Master (IM): FIDE-awarded title below that of Grandmaster.

Interzonal Tournament: FIDE-organized event to select participants in Candidates' Tournament or Matches (q.v.).

J'adoube: 'I adjust': warning to opponent that you intend to adjust a piece on its square without moving it.

Lemon: A bad move, frequently played by patzers (q.v.).

Patzer: A bad player (also Rabbit, Fish, Woodpusher etc.).

Rabbit: *See* Patzer.

Sac: A sacrifice.

Sealed Move: Move placed in an envelope by the player whose turn it is to move when a game is adjourned.

Simultaneous Display (Simul): Chess display in which an expert plays a number of opponents at once.

TN: Theoretical novelty.

Woodpusher: *See* Patzer.

Zonal Tournament: Tournament within FIDE zone to select participants in Interzonal Tournaments (q.v.).

Zugzwang: Compulsion to move – a term used when the player doesn't want to.

Notation

If you are unfamiliar with chess notation, or are only familiar with the outmoded Descriptive (or English) notation, don't be put off. The notation used in this book, Algebraic (or Standard) notation, is simple enough to be picked up by young children within five minutes.

Each file (vertical row of squares) is assigned a letter and each rank (horizontal row of squares) a number. Each square has a unique name derived from its file and rank, e.g. a1, e4, h8 (see diagram).

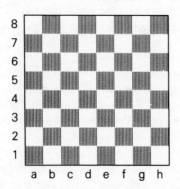

A move by a piece is denoted by the initial letter of the piece (N for knight) followed by the destination square, for instance Qe2, Nf6. For a pawn move only the destination square is given, for example e4 or d5. If two pieces of the same type can move to the same square the starting rank or file of the piece is specified, as in Ngf3.

Other symbols used:

    x : Captures. (Nxe5 is a piece   ! : Good Move
        capture, dxe5 a pawn capture.)   !! : Terrific move.
   + : Check   ? : Poor move.
 O–O : Castles king-side.   ?? : Terrible move.
O–O–O : Castles queen-side.   !? : Interesting move.
                                   ?! : Risky move

Foreword by Dr Patrick Moore

I have no idea when I played my first game of chess. It must have been around 1928 (I am revealing no secrets when I say that I was born in 1923). I have never been more than a very mediocre player, but at least I know that chess – whether you regard it as a game, a challenge or something more – is unique. Luck is eliminated; play a ten-board match, each player having White five times, and there can be no recriminations, as there can be in all other games, notably cricket ('Of course I wasn't lbw. That ball was missing the off-stump by yards!'). Moreover, every game is different. The openings may often be standardized, but after that one is on one's own.

Countless conventional chess books have appeared, but Mike Fox and Richard James have produced something different. Quite apart from discussing the all-time 'greats', ending with Fischer, Kasparov and of course Nigel Short, they have included some really weird encounters – including one of my own. (I have beside me the score of a recent correspondence game between Mike Fox and myself. He has headed it 'Berserk Opening'.) Unexpected people crop up; did you know that Steve Davis was a chess-player? I didn't, though I am not surprised to find Karl Marx and Robert Maxwell!

There have been some tongue-in-cheek criticisms – I once heard it said that chess was racist ('it sets White against Black') and sexist ('the King, not the Queen, is the pivotal figure') – and I also read the apocryphal story of the player who made no move for a long time, and was eventually found to have expired. Yet nobody in their senses can find chess either dull or unexciting. I will go on record as claiming that many people as well as myself will find Short *v.* Kasparov far more gripping than Aston Villa *v.* Manchester United.

Everybody has their own views, and their own pet quirks – mine being that I detest the new notation; P–K4 will do for me! However, in this book every chess enthusiast, from the humble novice (such as myself) through to the Grandmaster, will find something new and something enthralling. Read it, study it, and you will soon find that I am right.

Patrick Moore

What is Chess?

Chefs is a nice and abftrufe game in which two fets of men are moved in oppofition to each other.
  Dr Samuel Johnson's *Dictionary of the English Language*

Chess is a testy, cholericke game, and very offensive to him that looseth the mate *Robert Burton*

Chess is ouer-wise and Philosophicke a folly *James I*

Chess is ludicrously difficult *Stephen Fry*

Chess is an earnest exercise of the minde *Thomas Cogan*

Chess is one long regret *Stephen Leacock*

Chess is a sad waste of brains *Sir Walter Scott*

Chess . . . is a foolish expedient for making idle people believe they are doing something very clever *George Bernard Shaw*

Chess is . . . as elaborate a waste of human intelligence as you could find anywhere outside an advertising agency *Raymond Chandler*

Chess is not a game but a disease *Sir Henry Campbell-Bannerman*

Chess is a cure for diarrhoea and erysipelas *A mistranslation of Herodotus*

Chess is a cure for headaches *John Maynard Keynes*

Chess is an innocent and intellectual amusement after the mind has been engrossed with too much care or study *Hassan of Basra*

Chess, like love, is infectious at any age *Salo Flohr*

Chess is a beautiful mistress *Bent Larsen*

Chess is a very sexy game *Sally Beauman*

(Chess problems are like masturbation but) playing chess is like making love *George Steiner*

Chess is as much a mystery as women *Cecil Purdy*

Chess is a jealous lover *John Healy*

Chess is simply a medium through which concentration and a higher state of mind is achieved ... It is like contemplating your navel, only better. It is perhaps a way of making love *Jon Speelman*

Chess is vanity *Alexander Alekhine*

Chess is one of the sins of pride *John Bromyard*

Chess is life *Bobby Fischer*

Chess is like life *Boris Spassky*

Chess is indeed like life *Stephen Fry*

Chess is my life *Viktor Korchnoi*

Chess is my life – but my life isn't just chess *Anatoly Karpov*

Chess is my job and fills the main part of my life *Alexei Shirov*

Chess is most certainly not my life *Tony Miles*

Chess is life in miniature. Chess is struggle, chess is battles *Gary Kasparov*

Chess is a challenge, a battle *Terry Marsh*

Chess is a fight *Emanuel Lasker*

Chess is a blood sport *Jon Speelman*

Chess is ruthless: you've got to be prepared to kill people *Nigel Short*

Chess is a fighting game which is purely intellectual and excludes chance *Richard Réti*

Chess is a game of courteous aggression *Julian Barnes*

Chess is like war *Attributed to Bobby Fischer*

Chess is a game of war *Anthony Saidy and Norman Lessing*

Chess is a confrontation *Simon Barnes*

Chess is a gladiatorial contest *Ray Keene*

Chess is a test of wills *Paul Keres*

Chess is first of all art *Mikhail Tal*

Chess is the art of battle for the victorious battle of art *Savielly Tartakower*

Chess is the art of analysis *Mikhail Botvinnik*

Chess is the art which expresses the beauty of logic *Mikhail Botvinnik*

Chess is the art of human reason *Gustavus Selenius*

Chess is not only knowledge and logic *Alexander Alekhine*

Chess is an art appearing in the form of a game *Soviet Encyclopaedia*

Chess is an art *Gary Kasparov*

Chess is everything – art, science and sport *Anatoly Karpov*

Chess is just a game *Lajos Portisch*

Chess is a game *Boris Spassky*

Chess is a combination of ten games *Miguel Najdorf*

Chess is only a game and not to be classed with . . . science . . . or the arts *Emanuel Lasker*

Chess is a game of skill and not of genius *William Hazlitt*

Chess is undoubtedly the same sort of art as painting or sculpture *José Raúl Capablanca*

Chess is in its essence a game, in its form an art, and in its execution a science *Baron Tassilo von Heydebrand und der Lasa*

Chess is an almost perfect combination of art, investigative science, knowledge and inspiration *Raymond Keene*

Chess is too difficult to be a game, and not serious enough to be a science or an art *Attributed to Napoleon*

Chess is not just a game; it bears an international significance *Jeremy Hanley MP*

Chess is not a science *Henri Poincaré*

Chess is beautiful enough to waste your life for *Hans Ree*

Chess is the most exciting game in the world *Irving Chernev*

Chess is the most interesting game that exists *Lothar Schmid*

Chess is the most intelligent thing in the universe *David Norwood*

Chess is the game which reflects most honour on human wit *Voltaire*

Chess is one of the noblest inventions of the human mind *Cyril Edwin Mitchinson Joad*

Chess is eminently and emphatically the philosopher's game *Paul Morphy*

Chess is the most beautiful and reasonable of all games *Mme de Sévigné*

Chess is the fairest of all games *Isaac Bashevis Singer*

Chess is challenging (but bridge is the stuff of life) *Lord Lever*

Chess is a fine entertainment *Leo Tolstoy*

Chess is an exercise full of delights *Arthur Saul*

Chess is not merely an idle amusement . . . life is a kind of chess *Ben Franklin*

Chess is a game of intellect and character over the open board . . . chess is a game of life *Frank Marshall*

Chess . . . is a forcing house where the fruits of character can ripen more fully than in life *Edward Morgan Forster*

Chess is a game for strong people with strong character *Mikhail Botvinnik*

Chess is a big time sport *Tony Miles*

Chess is a sport. A violent sport *Marcel Duchamp*

Chess is imagination *David Bronstein*

Chess is work *Walter Browne*

Chess is a cold bath for the mind *Andrew Bonar Law*

Chess is a form of intellectual productiveness *Siegbert Tarrasch*

Chess is the touchstone of the intellect *Johann Wolfgang von Goethe*

Chess is both profoundly trivial and trivially profound . . . a universe simultaneously closed and unbounded *George Steiner*

Chess is not for timid souls *Wilhelm Steinitz*

Chess is . . . a place where I'm going to enjoy myself *John Cage*

Chess is a powerful weapon of intellectual culture *Slogan for 1924 All-Union Congress of Soviet Union*

Chess is the struggle against error *Johannes Zukertort*

Chess is a game of bad moves *Andy Soltis*

Chess is a fairy tale of 1001 blunders *Savielly Tartakower*

Chess is the sublimated fight *par excellence Anthony Saidy and Norman Lessing*

Chess is . . . a mime of the family romance and of the Oedipal drama *Alexander Cockburn*

Chess is a contest between two men in which there is considerable ego involvement *Reuben Fine*

Chess is a pursuit crammed with tension and emotion *Anthony Saidy and Norman Lessing*

Chess is the movement of pieces eating each other *Marcel Duchamp*

Chess is a dromenon *Frank Vigor Morley*

Chess is an international language *Edward Lasker*

Chess is a sea in which a gnat may drink and an elephant may bathe *Indian Proverb*

Chess is me *Salvador Dali*

Chess is fun *Luke McShane*

Chess is a game of skill for two played with figures or men of different kinds which are moved on a chequered board *Chambers 20th Century Dictionary*

I *The Famous*

It will be cheering to know that many people are skilful chess-players, though in many instances their brains, in a general way, compare unfavourably with the cogitative faculties of a rabbit.

James Mortimer

I get my kicks above the waistline, sunshine.

Tim Rice, from Chess, *the musical*

The game of Kings

This is chess from Aladdin to Zatopek. A bouillabaisse of celebrities who made their mark on history as movie stars, musicians, mass murderers, millionaires or marathon runners – and still found time to become adept at the world's best game.

Jostling for your attention you'll find Hollywood's most famous tough guy (he hustled chess on Broadway before becoming a megastar); history's best known transvestite; and the most notorious murderer of modern times.

We've grouped our celebrities by occupation. Since our first edition, the sportsmen have taken over from the musicians as strongest team; and the politicians now rank equal second. These are followed at a distance by the writers, the holy and the baddies (captained by Britain's most famous defrocked vicar).

After you've read this chapter you can make up your own dream matches. Would big Frank Bruno have beaten Albert Einstein? Very possibly. Einstein loathed the game. Megabrain Bertrand Russell versus John (Britain's most wanted man) McVicar? Almost certainly a win for McVicar. He was an Essex boys' champion. Soccer magician Ossie Ardiles versus George Bernard Shaw? Ardiles would have strolled it. GBS was a self-confessed duffer. And Ardiles, as you'll see, is a classy player.

And Aladdin? If you thought he was just a character played by Paul Daniels[1] on the BBC's Christmas Special, think again. In AD 1387 he was the nearest thing they had to a world champion. For the details read on.

The Royals

It's called the royal game; it was invented, says the myth,[2] to please a

---

[1] a non-player, by the way.
[2] For the myth, see 'The Awesome'.

king; and practically every king, queen, emperor, maharajah, shah and tsar you've heard of played it. Some of them played it in the grand manner . . .

The great Mogul emperor Akbar played on a giant board (it still exists, at Fatehpur Sikri) with elephants as pieces, horses as pawns; and Shah Jehan (the chap who built the Taj Mahal) played living chess with thirty-two virgins as pieces. According to some sources, the winner took the thirty-two virgins as prize.[1] The Emperor Ming Huan (712–56) had a similar inspiration – he played living chess against his favourite concubine Yang Kwei-fei, using palace maids. But, for sheer thrill-a-minute stuff we turn to King Muley Hassan of Morocco. His contribution to brighter chess was to use prisoners from the royal dungeons. What made his games prime-time viewing was that captured pieces were beheaded on the spot. And you thought American football was rugged. The prisoners must have taken a keen interest in Muley's opening repertoire. Gruesome (but not necessarily accurate) legend has it that he was particularly fond of the Danish Gambit.[2]

Tamerlane (or Tīmūr the Lame), Emperor of the Mongols, was just as bloodthirsty as Muley, and an even more obsessive chess freak. His favourite occupation was collecting the skulls of his enemies into vast pyramids; but when he wasn't doing that he played chess like an emperor: on a super-board of 112 squares. Tīmūr was so besotted with the game that in 1377 he called one of his sons Knight-fork;[3] but his main claim to a niche in chess history was the fact that he employed Aladdin as his court lawyer. Yes, the same fellow who owned the wonderful lamp.

In the late fourteenth century Aladdin was the best chess-player in the world (his nickname was Ali the chess-player). His speed of play was prodigious; and 400 years before the great Philidor he was

---

[1] The modern equivalent of this would be a year's subscription to the *British Chess Magazine.*

[2] 1. e4 e5 2. d4 exd4 3. c3 dxc3 4. Bc4 cxb2, and so bloodily on.

[3] Well, Shah-rukh actually. At the moment his son's birth was announced, Tīmūr managed to attack his opponent's rook and king simultaneously. He immortalized the instant in his son's name. Which event pleased him more we are not told. (All of this happened, say the history books, on 20 August, which we hereby designate International Knight Fork Day.) A teenager called Ali Shahrukhi was active in Berkshire chess around 1990. Could he be a descendant?

wowing the patzers with blindfold chess – four[1] games at a time, while carrying on a conversation with the spectators, *plus* one more game under normal conditions. He was also an early composer of chess problems (see our frontispiece).

Star of the Arabian Nights was Haroun al-Rashid,[2] Caliph of Baghdad, for whom the slave girl Sheherazade was supposed to have created the thousand and one stories. He flourished about 600 years before Aladdin and Tamerlane – but, says legend, was equally keen on the royal game. Haroun had the girls of his famous harem trained in chess, as well as the more exotic skills of the seraglio; and he spent 10,000 gold pieces on acquiring the world's first woman grandmaster – a slave girl famed for her chess skill.

In their first encounter she beat him, three out of three, and as her reward got a royal pardon for her imprisoned boy-friend. Later, according to Sheherazade's 461st story, the slave girl invented one of the best of all variations on the game: strip chess. Playing a court 'expert' in front of Haroun she beat him twice, then challenged him to a game at odds. She played without her queen, king's rook and queen's knight (he can't have been very good). 'If thou beatest me,' she said, 'take my clothes. If I beat thee, I will take thy clothes.'

Thinking he was on to a sure thing he gleefully grabbed the bait; but further deft sacrifices of material allowed her to queen a pawn and checkmate him. A sadder and wiser chess master left the court in his underpants.

Just as embarrassing is the nightmare come true that happened to a nobleman while playing chess against the first of the Bourbons, King Henry IV, at the French court. François de Bassompierre, Marshal of France, and gambling companion of Henry, shocked the court, himself and his king, by breaking wind loudly and involuntarily while making a knight move. His future as a courtier hanging in shreds, the wretched Bassompierre had enough sang-froid left to

[1] Even Philidor only managed three.
[2] or, more correctly, Hārūn ar-Rashīd. His name translates to Haroun the Pusher – a tribute to his exploits in the harem.

explain: 'Your majesty, my knight will not move if he does not hear the trumpet call.' The king, it is recorded, smiled a wintry smile. But Bassompierre probably wasn't invited back for a while.

The most crushing put-down in chess comes from a royal. When (around AD 905) court favourite al-Māwardī lost his title to the legendary as-Sūlī (the first 'all-time great' of chess history), he got the royal boot from his ruler, the Caliph al-Muktafī, with a line that has come ringing down the ages: 'Your rose-water has turned to urine.' You may be interested to know that this gag is a pun on poor old Māwardī's name: *māward* being ancient Persian for rose-water. Or then again you may not.

If you're a caliph, or a king, whose every whim is law, then losing a game of chess must be a chastening experience. This accounts no doubt for the large number of sore losers in the history of royal chess. There are too many to tell all, but here is a selection of the more interesting.

King Canute, the first king of all England (the one who commanded the tide to stop) was playing Earl Ulf of Denmark, when he blundered away a knight. Imperiously he tried to take the move back, but Ulf wasn't having any. After a vigorous debate, the Earl, fed up at seeing an easy win snatched away, knocked the board over. This was an early example of a fatal chess blunder: Canute had him slain for arguing (the hit-man was called, appropriately, Ivor the White).

William the Conqueror broke a chessboard over a French prince's head when he lost a game. The entente got even less cordiale a generation later: the Dauphin, Louis the Fat,[1] lost a game to William's son Henry, so he threw the pieces at him.

> ... Henry won fo much at Cheffe of Louis the King's eldest fon, as hee growing into Choller, called him the fonne of a Baftard,[2] and threw the cheffe in his face. Henry takes vp the Cheffe-board, and ftrake Louis with that force as drew bloud.
>
> Daniel's *The Collection of the History of England*, 1621.

[1] He became Louis VI.
[2] Pretty strong stuff, since, according to Murray, the French prince was only nine at the time.

It all makes Kasparov–Short seem rather tame.

For more bad language – and more violence – see Chapter III, 'The Frightful'.

As well as Louis the Fat, there was Pepin the Short. His son, choked at losing to a Bavarian nobleman, killed him with a rook.

A timely reminder of the rules, and a spot of off-the-board violence, was exhibited by the aforementioned Louis. On being seized in battle by an English knight, Louis calmly raised his broadsword, and with the words 'Know ye not, a knight cannot take a king?' bisected the unfortunate chevalier.

The award for the best defensive player in this section goes to Prince Valdemar of Denmark. It seems he was playing with King Knut (the fifth of Denmark if you're interested), when they were attacked by a rival king. Knut was killed; Valdemar escaped by employing an early form of king's-side defence: he used his board as a shield.

The Emperor Charlemagne is said to have played chess – and if you go to the Bibliothèque Nationale in Paris you can see the most splendid chess-piece of all, claimed (but modern scholars don't believe this) to have been a present to the emperor from his great contemporary Haroun al-Rashid.

The classiest homicide in chess happened to Charlemagne's nephew, Berthelot. Renaud de Montauban, a French knight, no doubt fed up with losing, chose as his particular blunt instrument a golden chessboard. He smote Berthelot 'so harde that he cloved him to the teeth', says Caxton.

The only known chess instance of someone putting down a king and getting away with it happened in Louis XIV's reign. Louis is playing a courtier, goes the story. There is a disagreement about the game. It gets heated. The members of the court sit frozen in horrified silence.

An old and trusted courtier enters. Angrily Louis asks his opinion. 'You are in the wrong, your majesty,' ventures the old man, without looking at the position. 'How can you possibly know that?' says the outraged monarch. 'If you were in the right, sire, these gentlemen [indicating the silent courtiers] would have been only too eager to tell you so.' He must have been a *very* favourite retainer. Louis also played living chess . . . and subsequently dallied with the queens he captured. His successor, Louis XV, enjoyed the game too. World champ Philidor said he was a pretty duff player.

King Conchubair of Ireland seems to have got his priorities about right. According to Irish legend,[1] he divided his day into three: one third for drinking, one third for fighting, and one third for chess.

It is to a king we owe the idea of travelling chess-sets. Louis XIII of France secures his place in history not merely as the founder of the Académie Française, but as the king whose bright idea it was to travel with a chessboard made of wool, in the form of a cushion. If he wished to play on horseback or in his jolting carriage, he used this board and spiked pieces. Later in history the French nobility used the same idea to play chess on the sand at Dieppe. *Pique-sable* is what they called these pieces and a flourishing business in ivory carving grew up in Dieppe as a result.

King Philip of Spain (the one who sent out the Spanish Armada) organized the first international match, Spain *v.* Italy, at his court. Representing Spain was a priest called Ruy López, after whom they named the opening. To Philip's annoyance, the Italians won easily, but he was big enough to give one of the winners – Leonardo – a thousand crowns.

It's stretching the point a little, but it's conceivable that we owe the

---

[1] There is a fair amount of legend in this section. Many of the early chess stories about the famous and the mighty were written centuries later in the form of medieval romances.

discovery of America to chess. According to the world's first chess magazine, *Le Palamède*, when Columbus was making his pitch for funds to discover a new route to the Indies, King Ferdinand was engaged in a game of chess, which he won. So pleased was the king that he granted the intrepid Christopher's request on the spot.[1] (For the story of how Britain *lost* America through chess see below under 'The Soldiers'.)

Atahualpa, king of the Incas, was taught chess by the Spaniards whilst they pillaged his kingdom. He became expert at the game,[2] playing numberless games with his captors until they treacherously garrotted him in 1533. (And King Montezuma learned chess before he was stoned to death in Mexico thirteen years earlier.)

The Tsars nearly all played chess. Next time you're in St Petersburg, pop into the Hermitage museum and take a look at the chess-sets of Peter the Great and Catherine the Great. Nicholas II played, with an exquisite set fashioned by his royal goldsmith, Fabergé.

Ivan the Terrible, the first of all the Tsars, had an ambivalent attitude to the game. In 1551, in the middle of reforming the clergy, he banned it as an invention of Hellenic devilry. And yet he met his death, dramatically, at the chessboard. Here's how the English ambassador of the time told it. Ivan is playing, would you believe, Boris Godunov. He's just set up the pieces, but mysteriously, his king won't stay upright. Then: 'The Emperor in his lose gown, shirtt and lynen hose, faints and falls backward. Great owtcrie and sturr; one sent for Aqua vita, another to the oppatheke for marigold and rose water, and to call his gostlie father and the phizicions.' But it was all useless. The Tsar of All the Russias was 'strangled and stark dead'.

Charles XII of Sweden (d. 1718), said Voltaire, lost his games because he moved his king far more than any other piece.

[1] Says Edward Lasker in *The Adventure of Chess*.
[2] 'He plays chess very well', said Gaspar de Espinosa in a letter to the Emperor Charles V.

Most of the kings and queens of England played chess. Richard the Lionheart is reputed to have been taught by his great enemy Saladin whilst in captivity.

King John was playing chess when he was supposed to be relieving the siege of Rouen.

Edward III was the king who founded the Order of the Garter. You may recall that the order (instituted to celebrate the battle of Crécy) came about when one of the ladies of the court dropped a blue garter at a court ball. The lady in question was the devastatingly beautiful Princess Joan of Wales, the Fair Maid of Kent. According to Froissart's chronicles, Edward formed a violent passion for Joan (her husband was, conveniently, in prison in France), and as a means of advancing his suit offered to play chess for a hugely valuable ruby ring. Edward, with some difficulty, contrived to lose. He then made what can only be described as overtures to the princess. She, with great dignity, declined. She also declined the ring, and after a certain amount of to-ing and fro-ing with the expensive bauble, she saved everyone's embarrassment by allowing her lady-in-waiting to keep it.

Among the bizarre jobs handed out by Edward III to his courtiers was a cushy number given to the Lord of the Manor of Kingston Russell in Dorset, which involved 'counting the King's chess-pieces every Christmasse'. This was called a serjeantyh of the King. It wasn't the only serjeantyh. Another involved 'holding the King's head when he was seasicke'. At one time, the same individual held both these onerous posts simultaneously.

Henry V (of Agincourt) suffered a rook checkmate while playing John Walcot of Walcot. That's why the Walcot arms bear 'three chessrooks ermine'.[1]

---

[1]If you happen to be called Abelyne, Arthur, Bunbury, Colville, Dawkins, Ormsby-Gore, Pickering, Rockwood, Smart or Walsingham you'll be pleased to know that your family's coat of arms also includes chessrooks (Papworth's *Directory of British Armorials*, 1874, and other sources).

King Henry VIII had a chess-maker on his staff – and his wardrobe lists included 'one bagge of greene velvette with chessmen' and 'a case of black leather conteynynge chestmen'. He was playing chess with Anne Boleyn when the news of Thomas More's execution arrived.

Roger Ascham taught Queen Elizabeth I chess as well as Latin. One of her boards, inlaid with gold, silver and pearls, became Charles I's property – and was sold off by the Roundheads after the Civil War.

Charles's tragic history had a recurring chess theme. During the Bishops' War with Scotland (caused by Archbishop Laud's interference in Scottish church affairs), Charles was playing chess with the Marquess of Winchester. Charles was contemplating a bishop's move when the marquess observed, 'See, sire, how troublesome these bishops are.' Charles got the point.

There is still a Charles I chessboard at Windsor Castle.

It was made just after the outbreak of the Civil War. Around its base is engraved in Latin the poignant legend: *With these, subject and ruler strive without bloodshed.*

And when the beleaguered Charles received the bad news that the Scots were about to hand him over to the pursuing English, he was in the middle of a game of chess. He was philosophical enough to continue the game.

George III lost the American colonies (see below, 'The Soldiers') but was accounted a strong player by his contemporaries.

Victoria was perhaps the most addicted of all British monarchs. In her youth she played a two-game match (the match of four queens) against Queen Louise of the Belgians (1837). For the first game she sought the advice of two prime ministers: Lords Palmerston and Melbourne. She lost, then dispensed with their help for the second game – which she won. According to a contemporary report in the

Hereford Times, chess was the great solace of her widowhood; she seldom travelled without a chess-set. Among Eugene Morphy's collection of Paul Morphy[1] memorabilia was a sheepskin chessboard signed by Queen Victoria. Is it possible that the Empress of India had met the greatest player of the nineteenth century? Maybe: the *New Orleans Times Democrat* for 11 July 1884 carries an account of a Morphy loss to Victoria: 'Morphy gallantly permitted Her Majesty to win' – which is more than he did for Napoleon III.

In the twentieth century chess-playing royals are few – but then there aren't too many twentieth-century monarchs. King Farouk played when he wasn't dallying.[2] King Alfonso of Spain played in a chess tournament in the twenties (and was knocked out by one of his colonels). King Abdullah of Jordan played Atomic chess – a pawn on being promoted became an 'atom-bomb' which destroyed all the pieces around it. And Archduke Ferdinand used to carry a pocket set made of silver on state visits. Whether it was with him on that unfortunate day in Sarajevo, we don't know.

Kaiser Wilhelm II carried on the grand old tradition of assault and battery by chess-playing royals. As a boy, when he lost to his tutor, young Wilhelm hit him over the head with the board.

The Duke of Gloucester, according to B. H. Wood, was a keen player as a boy.

Queen Mary, wife of George V, was taught by Miss Fatima, friend of Sultan Khan (see 'The Greatest') and British Ladies' Champion in 1933 (see our section 'The Politicians' for more on the enigmatic Miss Fatima). Sadly, the chess-playing tradition of English royalty seems to be dying out. Princess Alexandra is reported as saying she finds chess 'too devious', and that she prefers backgammon. The

---

[1] See Chapter II. For more on Morphy and Victoria see *Paul Morphy, the Pride and Sorrow of Chess* by David Lawson.
[2] For the quite revolting details of Farouk's pornographic chess-set, see our chapter 'The Unacceptable' (Chapter IV).

present sovereign, according to Buckingham Palace, currently 'has no interest in the game' – although, they say, she did have Charles, Anne and the other royal children taught in the nursery.

But, according to *Chess* magazine (1956) the Queen, being shown round a working-men's hostel in St Pancras, came across some chess-players. Her comment: 'I play, but I am always losing. I learned my chess the hard way.' Lord Frederick Windsor, rumoured to be a good player, was taught by his mother and Ray Keene.

And, according to our spies, Prince Philip finds time to relax from worrying about the plight of the monarchy by playing against his chess computer.

The Holy

A bad scene. Our saints, popes and religious leaders, with a few notable exceptions, have taken a dim view of the noble game. In the twelfth century you could be excommunicated for what in some circles today would be considered normal club-night behaviour (drunkenness and chess-playing). The fifth chapter of the Koran lists chess among the abominations to be shunned by the faithful (because the pieces are graven images);[1] the Jews banned it in 1322; the Buddha banned it long before chess was invented (he was against games on an eight by eight board);[2] the Christians were always banning it; and, most recently, the Ayatollah Khomeini banned it.[3] He claimed it hurts the memory, can cause brain damage and contributes to warmongering.

St Bernard of Clairvaux, going right over the top, called chess 'a carnal pleasure'; St Louis went even further; he said it was boring. Both of them banned it.

---

[1] Muslim chess freaks got round the ban by carving pieces in abstract designs – echoed in the design, for example, of today's bishops and rooks.
[2] He also banned spillikins and tip-cat.
[3] The Ayatollahs changed their mind in 1988. Chess is now OK provided gambling isn't involved.

In 1061 the Bishop of Florence, poor fellow, was caught playing chess in an inn. He got into all kinds of trouble with his archbishop as a result of this abomination ('shameful, senseless and disgusting'). As a penance he had to wash the feet of twelve paupers.

In 1291 the Prior and Canons of Coxford in Norfolk got it in the neck from the Archbishop of Canterbury[1] for playing chess, 'which heinous vice was to be banished, even if it came to three days and nights on bread and water'. Harsh stuff.

In the fourteenth century John Wycliffe called chess-playing 'ydelnesse and wauntounnesse' and placed it somewhere between lying 'in softe beddis' and 'lecherie' as an example of scandalous behaviour by the priesthood.

During the Inquisition, Savonarola threatened the inhabitants of Florence with eternal damnation if they were caught playing.

There were exceptions though: St Francis Xavier saved a soldier's soul by teaching him chess; St Francis de Sales encouraged it – in moderation; and Thomas à Becket is said to have played chess with Henry II before things turned nasty. But the outstanding chess-player among the saints was a woman: St Teresa of Ávila was keen enough on the game to use it as a means of instruction. She devotes a whole chapter in *The Way of Perfection* to the game, in which she relates the development of the pieces to the development of our faculty for divine love. Her enthusiasm for the game led to her being declared the patron saint of chess-players.

One of her habits, though, would have got her into trouble with FIDE: apparently she was given to involuntary levitation and had to hang on to iron grids to keep herself off the ceiling. This must have been very off-putting for her opponents. Nevertheless, we nominate St Teresa captain of our holy team.

[1] The present Archbishop of Canterbury feels less strongly about it, but doesn't himself play.

St Teresa might have a little difficulty getting a full team together, but she'd have a scorcher on board one. He wasn't a saint, or even a pope, just an ordinary Spanish priest; but Ruy López *was* the first world champion of the modern game.

The church never made Ruy a bishop – but chess had its compensations – a pension from Philip II of Spain (plus a gold rook on a gold chain), a stipend of 2,000 gold crowns a year from an Italian duke, and the income from one of history's most successful chess books, meant that Ruy López was, for a while, a good deal more prosperous than most modern grandmasters.

The rest of the divine team has a curious look: two popes, an American priest, a Brazilian theological student, and a cluster of nineteenth-century English vicars. Strongest of the popes was indubitably Leo XIII, who made it to the throne of St Peter in 1878. Here's one of his brilliancies played when he was just plain old Cardinal Pecci:

Revd Fr Guila–Joachim, Cardinal Pecci, Perugia, *c.* 1875.
Giuoco Piano

1. e4 e5	6. e5 d5	11. N x d4 B x d4	16. K x g2 Qg6 +
2. Nf3 Nc6	7. e x f6 d x c4	12. Qh5 Qf6	17. Kh1 Bd5 +
3. Bc4 Bc5	8. Qe2 + Be6	13. O–O R x g7	18. f3 B x f3 +
4. c3 Nf6	9. f x g7 Rg8	14. Qb5 + c6	19. R x f3 Qg1
5. d4 e x d4	10. c x d4 N x d4	15. Q x b7 R x g2 + !	mate

Innocent III was another chess-playing pope. How good he was isn't clear, but he's worth a mention for a ruling which even the British Chess Federation would have difficulty making stick – killing after a game of chess is not a crime. '. . . If any clerk plays at chess and should quarrel in consequence of so playing, and kill his man, such homicide shall be accounted casual and not voluntary . . . the reason is: he employeth himself in a lawful work' (quoted by Dr Salvio in 1634).

And now we come to a tale of the most appalling duplicity. Take a look at this:

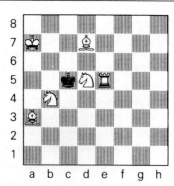

Mate in 2.

It appeared in that respected publication, *The Problemist*, in March 1987. Accompanying it was this astonishing letter:

Dear Sir
You will please forgive the few syntax mistakes that I surely did in this fast written letter.

My friend the Cardinal Hume claims *The Problemist* is the best international publication devoted to chess problems (contrary to the French ones, narrow minded and sectarian). Consequently, I would like to take out a subscription. Could you either send me a specimen of your review or specify me the price of a yearly subscription.

I still happen to compose some problems, from time to time, and I believe it is a kind of healthy relaxation. I send to you three of my recent and unpublished problems, because until today the Polish specialised review never edited them (my pontifical duty must embarrass them . . .) If you are interested, please be kind enough when they are published, to signed them Karol Wojtyła instead of John Paul II.

Please accept all my thanks. I send you my fatherly benediction if you are a Roman Catholic. If you are part of the Anglican Church, believe in my brotherly feelings of

Joannes Paulus P.P. II

P.S. John Nunn's *Solving in Style* was my bedside book the whole last summer. Teaching how to resolve, the author reveals in a remarkable way the art of composing.

The authors got very excited about all this. Hitherto there had only been rumours about the chess-playing ability of God's supreme representative on earth. Could it be that John Paul II (one of the few popes who has also been a soccer goalie) was a demon on the chessboard? Alas, a phone call to *The Problemist* revealed that the whole thing was a hoax on Vatican City notepaper. Our maledictions on the perpetrator (a Frenchman). Chess-players have been excommunicated for less.

A papal game, Zartobliwy *v.* Wojtyła, was published in Mensa's chess magazine, *Kingfisher*, and was quoted in the first edition of Batsford's *Chess Openings* (p. 51) as a line in the Veresov opening. Sadly, this too was a hoax by the Frenchman; and, it turns out, *zartobliwy* is Polish for facetious, or jokey.

We wrote to the Pope asking for enlightenment. He blessed us and our work, but didn't add to our knowledge. Then, in 1992, Grandmaster Najdorf, a fellow Pole, gave an interview to *New in Chess*, in which he swore that the Pope did play, and that he'd published a book of problems.

And as we go to press, another clue lands on our desk, in the shape of a letter from Countrywide Computers. Countrywide were asked by an Italian customer to supply a Mephisto Almeria to a Signor X in Vatican City. No address, just the name. In response to Countrywide's query about the lack of postal information, their Italian contact chortled, and said anyone going to Vatican City and asking for X would have no delivery problems whatsoever, the implication being that X was very close to Il Papa. Countrywide say that subsequent conversations confirmed their suspicions. They are 'Ninety-nine per cent certain' that the Almeria (shouldn't it have been a Roma?) was going to the Top Man. Your guess is as good as ours.

For amusement only, here is the opening of the fake game between Wanda Zartobliwy (wife of the ambassador of the Malta Knights) and the future pope, Karol Wojtyła (Poland, 1946): 1. d4 d5 2. Nc3 Nf6 3. Bg5 Nbd7 4. Nf3 h6 5. Bh4 e6.

♟

A very strong board three for the holy team is the American priest, William Lombardy. Father William is an international grandmaster, has twice been US Open Champion and in 1972 he was Bobby Fischer's second in his match against Boris Spassky.

In 1957 Lombardy won the World Junior Championship with a 100 per cent score, a feat which may never be equalled. Here's how he demolished the West German representative.

M. Gerusel–W. Lombardy, Toronto, 1957. Nimzo-Indian Defence

1. d4 Nf6	6. a3 Bxc3+	11. Be3 d4	16. Qb3 Nc5
2. c4 e6	7. Qxc3 Ne4	12. Rd1 dxe3	17. Qc3 Na5
3. Nc3 Bb4	8. Qc2 e5	13. Rxd8 exf2+	18. e4 Nab3+
4. Qc2 Nc6	9. dxe5 Bf5	14. Kd1 Rfxd8+	White resigns
5. Nf3 d5	10. Qa4 O–O	15. Kc1 a6	

The English parsons were a talented mob; presumably quiet country parishes in the nineteenth century gave one the leisure needed to become a star. Most of them played under an alias so that their parishioners couldn't know what they were up to on those long weekends in London. They're too numerous to mention all, but here are a few.

The Reverend George Alcock MacDonnell[1] played under the name 'Hiber' and was perhaps the strongest Revd of the lot. The following game was dubbed the 'Koh-i-Noor' of chess.

G. A. MacDonnell–S. S. Boden, London, 1861 (Casual game?).
Evans Gambit Declined

1. e4 e5	9. Be3 Nxb4	17. f4 Nd5	25. Re2 Qxd1
2. Nf3 Nc6	10. Ne2 Nc6	18. Qh5 f6	26. Nh5 Rg8
3. Bc4 Bc5	11. Ng3 d5	19. Ng6 Qe3+	27. Nxg8 Rxg8
4. b4 Bb6	12. Bb5 dxe4	20. Kh2 Rd8	28. Re8 Black
5. O–O d6	13. Bxc6 bxc6	21. Rfe1 Qxd3	resigns
6. h3 Nf6	14. Nxe5 exd3	22. Rad1 Qc2	
7. d3 O–O	15. cxd3 Qe8	23. Ne7+ Kh8	
8. Nc3 h6	16. Bxb6 axb6	24. Qf7 Bxh3	

MacDonnell caused a flutter in clerical circles in 1872 by carrying out the marriage ceremony for a divorcee, so they took his curacy off him. This did wonders for his chess; he achieved his best result six months later: third equal at London.

[1]He seems to have been the John Virgo of chess: he was celebrated for his impressions of other famous players.

The Revd John Owen played as 'Alter'. He was strong enough to play matches with Morphy and Zukertort, and to beat Anderssen in their game at London, 1862. Owen's Defence (1. . . . b6), which was trendy a few years ago, was named after him.

The Revd C. E. Ranken[1] was a friend of Winston Churchill's father, Randolph,[2] with whom he founded Oxford University Chess Club (of which Ranken was the first president). Not as strong as the other two, his best result was first at Malvern in 1872 (followed by the Revd Thorold and the Revd Wayte).

Since our first edition, we have had to demote St Thomas à Becket to first reserve on our holy team, to make place for a new board two. Henrique da Costa Mecking, one of the strongest players of the seventies, dropped out of chess after contracting a serious muscle disease. He studied to become a Catholic priest, then joined a sect called Charismatic Renovation. Miraculously his disease was cured, a fact he attributes to divine intervention. Mecking has taken up chess once more and in 1991 claimed that God had helped him convert a loss (against Predrag Nikolić) into a draw.

Here's a Mecking win:

Mecking–Agdamus, Buenos Aires, 1970. King's Indian Defence

1. d4 Nf6	10. d5 c5	19. fxe5 dxe5	28. Bxb7+ Kb8
2. c4 d6	11. O–O h5	20. Nxe5 Qe8	29. Bxa8 Kxa8
3. Nc3 e5	12. Ne1 Nb6	21. Qd2 Kd8	30. Qa5+ Qa7
4. Nf3 Nbd7	13. b3 Bd7	22. Nd3 Qxe4	31. Qxa7+ Kxa7
5. e4 g6	14. a3 Qc8	23. Bf2 bxc4	32. Nxd7
6. Be2 Bg7	15. Nb5 Ke7	24. Nxc5 Qxd5	Black resigns
7. Be3 Ng4	16. h3 Nh6	25. Qb4 Kc8	
8. Bg5 f6	17. Nd3 a6	26. Bf3 Qd6	
9. Bh4 c6	18. f4! axb5	27. Rad1 Qc7	

[1]His claim to chess fame was *Chess Openings Ancient and Modern* – a nineteenth-century precursor of *Modern Chess Openings*.
[2]Randolph lost a King's Gambit to Steinitz when the world champ gave a simul in Oxford (1870).

For the record (and because it's so impressive) here is the most devout team of all time. If there is anything in the efficacy of prayer they'd be tough to stop:

1. Fr Ruy López
2. Henrique Mecking
3. Fr William Lombardy
4. Revd G. A. MacDonnell
5. Revd J. Owen
6. His Holiness Pope Leo XIII
7. His Holiness Pope Innocent III
8. St Teresa of Ávila (capt.)

Among the reserves would be: Luther (M) (his recurring dream was of owning an ornate gold and silver chess-set); Cardinal Richelieu (an enthusiastic player); two more popes, Gregory VI and Leo X; Archbishop Cranmer (who played chess every day after dinner); Sir Thomas More, who said chess would be played in Utopia; Cardinal Wolsey, who had a cake made in the shape of a chessboard for the French ambassador; Nicholas Ridley (the bishop and martyr); Terry Waite, who played while in captivity and chose a chess computer as his luxury on *Desert Island Discs*; and, when he is not saving souls, Billy Graham.

Somewhere in there would be a Dominican monk who had the sinister task of running the Inquisition in Genoa. Jacopo da Cessole found time to spare from the rack and the stake to write the first of all European chess books. William Caxton published a translation in 1481 – the second book printed in English. Cessole called his book *Liber de moribus Hominum et officiis Nobilium ac Popularium super ludo scacchorum*. Caxton gave it a snappier title: *The Game and Playe of the Chesse*.

St Charles Borromeo, a leader of the Counter-Reformation, had the right idea. As cardinal he was rebuked for his devotion to chess: 'What would you do if you were playing and the world came to an

end?' 'Carry on playing,' replied Charles. He deserved to be canon-
ized.

If you go to the Musée de Cluny in Paris you can see one of the most
beautiful chess-sets ever made. It's in rock crystal and smoky topaz
set in gold, and it is said to have been a gift from the legendary
Rashīd al-Din as-Sinān, the Old Man of the Mountains (leader of the
Assassins) to King (later Saint) Louis IX in the thirteenth century.
(Not everyone agrees – Murray says the set is at least fourteenth
century.)[1]

Solution to papal problem: 1. Bb5

The Sinners

One of the strongest of all teams and a threat to anyone (including as
it does four of Britain's best-known murderers, a g.b.h. specialist, the
most famous assassin of all time and a magician in league with the
devil).

As captain we select the late, great, Harold Davidson, one of the
most colourful characters in a section teeming with them. Harold
was the rector who became a geek.[2] In 1932, the year of the yo-yo, he
cheered up Britain and pushed the rise of Hitler off the front pages
with headlines like 'Rector's midnight call on waitress', 'The rector
and the nude model' and 'Rector's black eye'. To tell it briefly,
Harold went to the quiet parish of Stiffkey in Norfolk as rector in
the late twenties. Finding rural life a little slow, he spent his weekends
in Soho, saving young girls from sin. At his trial the prosecution
maintained that what he was saving them for was himself. Anyway,
after much eloquence from Harold and a number of salacious photo-
graphs in evidence, he was defrocked.

---

[1] And we know that St Louis is supposed to have banned the game (see above).
[2] A geek (US slang): a side-show exhibit in fairgrounds; originally one who performed
bizarre acts such as biting the heads off live animals. With Harold, as you'll see,
almost the reverse happened.

The scene shifts (uneasily, as S. J. Perelman once said) to Blackpool's Golden Mile where the Rector of Stiffkey became a star attraction, exhibited in a barrel (with a chimney for his cigar smoke) to crowds of Lancashire holidaymakers.

As a variation, he also appeared before the pleasure-seekers in a glass oven while a mechanical demon prodded his bottom with a pitchfork. For a while, Harold was in the big money, easily the most popular spectacle on the Golden Mile (completely eclipsing such contemporary attractions as the Starving Woman of Haslingden, and the Genuine Pacific Mermaid). He was also a master of showbiz. On emerging from gaol (for non-payment of rent) he made a triumphant ride along Blackpool's promenade in a horse-drawn carriage, attended by two statuesque African girls who threw flowers to the enthusiastic crowds.

Our story stops abruptly on 28 July 1937, in Skegness Amusement Park. The ex-pillar of the church was now appearing in a cage with Toto and Freddy, two hitherto docile lions. Freddy didn't take kindly to this intrusion (presumably feeling that his new companion lowered the tone somewhat) and after a little injudicious whip cracking, there was a growl, a gulp, and one of the more fascinating footnotes in British social history came to a messy end.

What, you are patiently wondering, has all this to do with chess? Well, the surprising Harold, in the early years of the century, was one of the strongest young players in the country. He was President of Oxford Chess Club and captain of the Combined Universities team that beat American Universities in 1903. In that year, Harold was cheered by the onlookers for a spectacular win on top board that decided the match; and after he'd come down from university he was strong enough to take on five opponents simultaneously, blindfold.

(Freddy, incidentally, achieved fleeting celebrity, drawing thousands as 'the Lion that ate the Rector'. He didn't, as far as we know, play chess.)

♖

Just as strange was the career of bad old Aleister Crowley a.k.a. the wickedest man in the world, the King of Depravity; Alastor the Destroyer; the Wanderer of the Wasteland; the ipsissimus; the Great

Beast; 666; Brother Perdurabo; Master Thereon et cetera. In view of his proclivities, we nominate Aleister Vice-captain.

Crowley was hell-bent from an early age. As a youth he poisoned, gassed, hanged, drowned, bashed, chloroformed, defenestrated and sliced up a family moggy to check the theory that cats have nine lives (they don't, it transpired). He went on to become the most notorious practitioner of black magic of the twentieth century, a prolific author on the subject, and the greatest poet since Shakespeare (according to Aleister). Shocking stories of his life-style filtered into the popular press: nameless orgies in a Sicilian abbey; his habit of filing his teeth to a point so he could give women the mark of the beast on their wrists on being introduced (most didn't like it – but enough did to make it seem a good idea); the mountaineering expedition from which his companions inexplicably failed to return; and his watch-word: 'Do what thou wilt shall be the whole of the Law.'

Between the cat episode and the Sicilian orgies, Aleister found time to become at least as strong a player as Davidson. Around 1896 he represented Trinity College, Cambridge, and the combined Oxford/Cambridge team, and he rarely lost. (The exception: an Oxford–Cambridge match when Spencer Churchill beat him on top board in a Petroff Defence.)

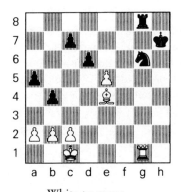

White to move

In this position in the 1896 inter-varsity match, *v.* Robbins, Aleister (black) was clearly dead lost, yet won. Witchcraft? Possibly. The fact that his opponent ran out of time probably helped.

More interestingly, a Crowley problem. White (it should perhaps, since it's Crowley, be black[1]) to play and mate in 3:

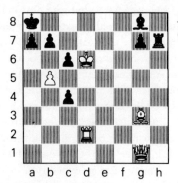

British Chess Magazine, 1894
(Solution at end of section)

We turn (with a slight *moue* of distaste) from witchcraft to mucky books, and another colourful member of our sinners' team. John Mansfield is the name on the passport; he is currently a resident of Amsterdam, and he's a keen chess-player. He's better known to the police however, as Porny John, the prince of European porn. In May 1986 he appeared on Central TV fondling a rather splendid marble chess-set.

Depressingly, the ringleader of the unspeakable Chelsea Headhunters, a gang of soccer hooligans, is a chess-player. He had a BCF grade of 128 and played in the London Legal League before he was put away for ten years in May 1987 for causing an affray. We don't want to give him further publicity, so we shan't publish his name.

One of the strongest sinners of all was Norman Tweed Whitaker, the lawyer who became a conman. Whitaker reached international master strength in the twenties. He was placed well in several American tournaments (1st San Francisco 1923, 1st Kalamazoo 1927) and he beat former American champ Jackson Showalter in a match (+ 4, = 3, − 1). But neither chess nor law provided the kind of income

[1] In all problems in this book it is white to move.

Norman needed – so he turned to crime. His most famous scam was extracting $100,000 from the Lindbergh parents on a promise that he could return the kidnapped Lindbergh infant. Needless to say, Whitaker had never set eyes on the child. The cops caught up with him, Norm was sent down for a five-stretch, but the $100,000 was never seen again.

Norman had a long (eighty-five years) and interesting life. In the latter half of it he supplemented his precarious income by the skilful use of a screwdriver on car odometers. He made enough money from this and other confidence tricks to finance several tours of Europe. But it all concluded rather shabbily: the one-time high-flyer ended his days in a disused army hut on some waste ground. We make him board two for the sinners.

Here's a game between International Master Norm and the Sportsmen's board two. For once Norman's swindling ability failed him.

N. T. Whitaker–Sir G. A. Thomas, USA–GB Cable Match, 1930.
Evans Gambit Declined

1. e4 e5	7. d4 d6	13. Nc3 cxd4	19. Kf1 Nd2 +
2. Nf3 Nc6	8. Bxh6 dxe5	14. Nd5 Qe8	20. Qxd2 Qxb5 +
3. Bc4 Bc5	9. Bxg7 Rg8	15. Qg3 Nc4	21. Kg1 Bxd2
4. b4 Bb6	10. Bxf7 + Kxf7	16. Qf4 + Ke6	22. Nc7 + Kxe5
5. b5 Na5	11. Bxe5 Bg4	17. h3 Ba5 +	23. Nxb5 Bf3
6. Nxe5 Nh6	12. Qd3 c5	18. c3 Bxc3 +	White resigns

♜

Next, the murderers. If you believe the Warren Report (half of us do), The Man Who Killed Kennedy was a keen player. In *The Trial of Lee Harvey Oswald*, shown on British TV in 1986, Nelson Delgado, Oswald's squad leader in the Marines, said, 'Chess was Lee's favourite game.'

♜

Board one for the sinners would be Raymond Weinstein, who, last time we heard, was doing life in an American gaol for a razor murder. He was an International Master and an opponent of Bobby

Fischer. According to an article in the *British Chess Magazine, before* the crime, he 'had a ruthless killer instinct' for the game.

♖

The euphoniously named Claude Bloodgood wrote a well-known opening textbook, *The Tactical Grob*, while in the Virginia State slammer for matricide. Prison did not dull his tactical brilliance: in the course of a chess match he improvised a successful escape; but was subsequently recaptured.

Here's Claude using his favourite opening to blitz a patzer.

C. Bloodgood–J. Boothe, Correspondence, 1972. Grob's Opening

1. g4 d5	4. Qb3 Qc7	7. Nb5 Qb6	10 Qxb7
2. Bg2 Bxg4	5. cxd5 cxd5	8. Bxb7 Qxb7??	Black resigns
3. c4 c6	6. Nc3 d4?	9. Nd6+ exd6	

For another game with this opening turn to 'The Artists' where we reveal the identity of the eponymous Grob.

♖

Patrick Magee, the Brighton bomber, a keen player, is now looking for opponents in Wandsworth prison; and the infamous Moors Murderer, Ian Brady, played chess during his stay at Wormwood Scrubs. Among his opponents was former Postmaster-General John Stonehouse (see below).

♖

If he did it (and the pundits can't agree) then William Herbert Wallace was much better at murder than chess. William was at the centre of what Raymond Chandler and many others called the most fascinating murder case of all. The story is too well documented to retell in detail, but *en bref*: in January 1931, Wallace, an insurance agent and chess-player, was telephoned at Liverpool Central Chess Club about a business appointment. He didn't take the call himself, and his appointment turned out to be a hoax to lure him to a distant part of Liverpool. While he was out, someone eliminated his wife. Wallace was held on a murder charge (the prosecution's case being that he made the call himself to establish an alibi). Much was made at the trial of Wallace's 'scheming chess-player's mind'. In fact, his fellow club-members said he was a really awful player.[1] His solicitor however, Hector Munro, was a strong county player – and Wallace was acquitted on appeal.[2]

♖

John Reginald Halliday Christie was a goodish chess-player – and the most celebrated serial killer of the forties. Whilst awaiting the ultimate punishment in Brixton, he passed the time thrashing his warders at chess (Chris the chess champion, they nicknamed him).

♖

The Podola case made the front pages in 1959. Günther Fritz Podola, a German immigrant living opposite South Kensington tube station, shot a Detective Sergeant while resisting arrest. Podola pleaded guilty but insane, claiming total loss of memory. The prosecution attacked this defence on the grounds that he'd played numerous games of chess with his warders, so couldn't have lost his memory. Defence experts argued that the ability to play chess, like the ability to tie your shoelaces, was a skill that didn't get lost through trauma, but the judge and jury didn't buy it. Podola appealed, but the appeal judges, latching on to the chess theory, rejected his claim of insanity. Podola met his maker on 5 November 1959.

♖

The last on our roster of murderers is the most famous of all. According to a well-argued book by Stephen Knight,[3] Jack the Ripper (who gave London an autumn of terror in 1888) was in fact the painter Walter Sickert as part of a three-man team. One of the things we know about Sickert was that he was a keen chess-player. If Knight's theory is correct, then we must place Jack on a high board in our macabre team, if only for his ability to scare the hell out of the opposition.

♖

In the first edition of this book, Robert Maxwell was on our

[1] One of them said: 'The murder of his wife apart, I think Wallace ought to be hanged for being such a bad chess-player.'
[2] For more on this fascinating case see a very good book: *The Killing of Julia Wallace* by Jonathan Goodman (Harrap, 1969).
[3] *Jack the Ripper: The Final Solution.* Incidentally, Ripper addicts will know that another of the numerous suggestions as to the true identity of the real Jack the R. was Lord Randolph Churchill, who, as we saw in our previous section, once played Steinitz.

businessmen's team; but since the unfolding of the *Mirror* pension fund scam, we've moved him into the Sinners. He may not be the last businessman to make such a move.

Maxwell, a keen player in his youth, was later responsible for numerous excellent chess books through Pergamon, his technical publishing house. In his office at the *Mirror* building he always kept a splendid ivory and marble chess-set. According to one biographer, Maxwell's megalomania took on a bizarre form when it came to chess. He would set up critical positions from great games of the past, and then astonish visitors by casually making (as if it were his own) the brilliant queen sac that Zukertort (or whoever) had sweated on all those years ago. The effect on us was diminished by the fact that when we last visited the great conman in his office, he had the board the wrong way round.

The only person we know of who played Maxwell was Rodney Leach of Rothschild. He decided to call it a day when he observed that after they'd emerged from the opening Cap'n Bob had somehow got two bishops on the same-coloured squares.

The bouncing Czech's egomania would scarcely permit him to serve under anyone else as captain, but he's not strong enough to replace Davidson; so we elect Maxwell chairman of the Sinners' chess club (and Norm Whitaker treasurer).

♖

A well-known former British champion and supplier of chess equipment has been on the run from the West Yorkshire police for the last couple of years for (allegedly) various chess-related crimes. Whether he makes the Sinners' team (he'd be a strong board three) depends on the outcome of his trial (if ever there is one). Last time we heard, he was frequenting chess cafés in Amsterdam.

♖

Rounding off this section: three men who've paid their debt to society.

H. R. Haldeman was the most senior of that frightful bunch of (expletives deleted) who fouled up American history by assisting President Nixon in the Watergate episode. His hobby when he wasn't organizing dirty tricks was chess.

John McVicar, gang boss and for a while Britain's most wanted man, was an Essex boys' champion before he turned to crime and subsequent stardom. He resumed his chess career in HM prisons, where it is said he met another strong player: John Stonehouse, ex-MP, ex-Postmaster-General and (following a financial imbroglio) mastermind of a well-publicized fake suicide disappearing act. After the Old Bill caught up with John in Australia, he and McVicar were finalists, legend has it, in the Wormwood Scrubs chess championships. Certainly (because one of the authors played there) the Scrubs had a flourishing and strong chess team in the sixties. And so did Broadmoor and Wandsworth prison. In 1990, Julian Simpole played a simul at the Scrubs.

Postscript

If he were available for selection, an excellent addition to the Sinners' team would be the devil himself. A good friend of Aleister Crowley, he is currently endorsing a well-known make of chess computer.[1] According to legend and several short stories Old Nick is practically unbeatable. Club secretaries willing to stake their soul on an infernally strong top board could try lighting thirteen candles and reciting the Lord's Prayer backwards while looking in a mirror . . .

(For more sinners, see 'The Politicians'.)

Solution to Crowley problem: Qb6.

The Musicians

In the championship of the professions, the musicians beat most other teams out of sight. Indeed if the players below could be reincarnated, they'd look pretty good in the European club championship (and even better at the post-match concert).

No argument about board one: the French composer François-André Danican Philidor (1726–95). When he wasn't composing (twenty-one musical comedies and a grand opera that netted him a

---

[1] The Mephisto.

pension from Louis XV), Philidor found time to become the strongest player of the eighteenth century, the wonder of the age at blindfold play, and author of the most successful chess textbook in history. Grandmaster Larsen rated him as all-time number one. We think this is pushing it a bit, but Phil was certainly world championship standard. As a musician, his compositions lasted less well than his chess, but in 1976 there was a 250th anniversary performance of one of his operas (*Blaise le Savetier*) in London. Here's a Philidor game:

Capt. Smith–Philidor, London, 1790. Bishop's Opening

1. e4 e5	10. Qd2 Be6	19. c3 Rag8	28. Kh1 Rxh3
2. Bc4 Nf6	11. Bxe6 fxe6	20. d4 Bb6	29. Rg1 Rxh2+
3. d3 c6	12. O–O g5	21. dxe5 Qxe5	30. Kxh2 Rh8+
4. Bg5 h6	13. h3 Nd7	22. Nd4 Kd7	31. Nh5 Rxh5+
5. Bxf6 Qxf6	14. Nh2 h5	23. Rae1 h4	32. Kg3 Nh3+
6. Nc3 b5	15. g3 Ke7	24. Qf2 Bc7	33. Kg4 Rh4
7. Bb3 a5	16. Kg2 d5	25. Ne2 hxg3	mate.
8. a3 Bc5	17. f3 Nf8	26. Qxg3 Qxg3+	
9. Nf3 d6	18. Ne2 Ng6	27. Nxg3 Nf4+	

Board two, the Viennese concert pianist Moriz Rosenthal, the last surviving pupil of Liszt, and the strongest musician that US master Ed Lasker (who also played our boards four and five) ever met.

Fighting it out for board three, below the pianist, would be composer Sergey Prokofiev and violin virtuosi Mischa Elman and David Oistrakh. Prokofiev was chess crazy, and played well enough to beat Lasker, Capablanca and Rubinstein in simultaneous exhibitions. Here's his win against Capablanca:

Capablanca–Prokofiev, Simultaneous Display, St Petersburg, 1914. Queen's Gambit

1. d4 d5	6. Qa6 Nxc4	11. g4 Bg6	16. gxh5 Bxh5
2. Nf3 Nf6	7. Nc3 e6	12. Bg5 Be7	17. Nb5 Kf8
3. c4 Bf5	8. e4 dxe4	13. Bxe7 Kxe7	18. d5 Qf6
4. Qb3 Nc6	9. Bxc4 exf3	14. O–O–O Re8	19. dxe6 Ne5
5. Qxb7 Na5	10. Qc6+ Nd7	15. h4 h5	20. Qc5+ Kg8

21. exf7 + Bxf7	27. Rxc7 Qxc7	33. Qf5 Ne4	39. Ra6 Nb3 +
22. Bxf7 + Qxf7	28. Qe6 + Kh8	34. Qxf3 Nd2	40. Ka2 Ra5
23. Kb1 Rab8	29. a3 Qc2 +	35. Qxc6 Rxc6	41. Rxa5 Nxa5
24. Nxc7 Rbc8	30. Ka1 Nd3	36. Rd1 Rc2	42. b4 g5
25. Rc1 Re7	31. Rb1 Nxf2	37. Rg1 Rc5	43. Kb2 g4
26. Qd6 Rexc7	32. h5 Qc6	38. Rg6 Rxh5	White resigns

Prok described Capa as the 'Bach of the chessboard' and Lask as the 'chess Mozart'. He also played against Alekhine, Tartakower and Botvinnik. Tartakower said that P. was master strength: Botvinnik described him as a 'pre-revolutionary King's Gambiteer'.

In 1937 a match Prokofiev *v.* Oistrakh was arranged in the USSR. The violinist beat the composer: four draws and a win (so we'll make Oistrakh board three). Oistrakh was rated a USSR category one player – approximately a 190–200 grading. Here's how he fiddled a draw when two pawns down to Prokofiev:

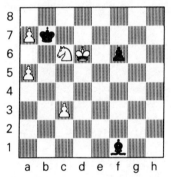

60. . . . f5	64. Nb4 Kxa7	68. Nd5 Bd3!	72. Nxc6 Kb7
61. Ke5 Bd3	65. c4 Kb6	69. Nb4 Be4	Draw
62. Kd4 Be4	66. c5 + Ka7	70. c6 Kc7	
63. a6 + Ka8	67. Ke5 Kb8	71. a7 Bxc6!	

Mischa Elman (board five) played in style: with a hundred-year-old Staunton pattern set handed down from world champion Paul Morphy. Elman was strong enough to play regularly with US master Edward Lasker, who rated him 'very good'. While Prokofiev was in

31

the USA, Lasker arranged a couple of Prokofiev–Elman games. The result: a win apiece.

♛

A very strong board six (and maybe higher) would be a former Master of the King's Musick:[1] Sir Walter Parratt, organist at St George's Chapel Windsor, who won on top board for Oxford in the first Oxford–Cambridge match, 1873. Well after his eightieth birthday, Sir Walter was still good enough to beat Bonar Law (easily the strongest of British prime ministers) while the latter was staying at Windsor Castle. Parratt's party trick was to play Bach fugues while conducting two games simultaneously, blindfold.

♛

On board seven, another master of the violin: Yehudi Menuhin. Yehudi was a strong child player (after a recital at the Paris Opera, the twelve-year-old Menuhin surprised journalists by giving interviews while playing chess). In later life (1944) he played this casual game on a train against Aird Thomson, who was Scottish champion in 1951:

Y. Menuhin–A. A. Thomson, 1944. Four Knights' Opening

1. e4 e5	12. h3 Rg8	23. Bxf5 Ne7	34. Kd5 Bg3
2. Nf3 Nc6	13. c3 Bxh3	24. g4 Nxf5	35. c4 h3
3. Nc3 Nf6	14. Nh4 f5	25. gxf5 Kd7	36. c5 dxc5
4. Bc4 Bb4	15. Qh5 Qg5	26. Kg2 Rf8	37. Kxc5 + Ke7
5. Nd5 Nxe4	16. Nxc7 + Bxc7	27. Kf3 Rxf5 +	38. a4 Bf2 +
6. a3 Bc5	17. Qxf7 + Kd8	28. Ke3 Bb6 +	39. Kb5 h2
7. O–O d6	18. Qxg8 + Qxg8	29. Kd3 Bxf2	40. a5 Bg1
8. d3 Nf6	19. Bxg8 Bg4	30. Re4 h5	White resigns
9. Bg5 h6	20. Be6 Be2	31. Rd1 h4	
10. Bxf6 gxf6	21. Rfe1 Bxd3	32. Kc4 Rf4	
11. b4 Bb6	22. Nxf5 Bxf5	33. Rxf4 exf4	

♛

And board eight, a good player and phenomenal violinist: Fritz Kreisler. Once, while he was staying with some musical friends, dinner interrupted his game. When he returned, the pianist Paderewski

[1]A master of the Queen's Musick, Sir Arthur Bliss, composed the music for the chess ballet, *Checkmate*.

had set up the adjourned position on the chequered floor of the drawing-room, with human pieces instead of chessmen.

Jostling for a place among the reserves would be Schumann, who took a chess book as solace into the asylum at Endenich; Mendelssohn (a strong player), Richard Strauss (who also played against Ed Lasker), Mussorgsky, Shostakovich (who adored chess because it linked art and science), Rimsky-Korsakov, Verdi, Borodin, Villa-Lobos, Dvořák, Rossini, Arthur Rubinstein, Sviatoslav Richter, Sir Thomas Beecham,[1] Adolf Brodsky (first to perform the Tchaikovsky violin concerto, and a strong player), Isaac Stern, Ruggiero Ricci, Pablo Casals, Gregor Piatigorsky (the cellist, whose wife sponsored two legendary tournaments in the sixties), Lorin Maazel, who asked for a chess-set and books as his luxury on *Desert Island Discs*, John Lill (he picked *Modern Chess Openings* as his book to take to that overpopulated desert island),[2] Steve Race (he asked for a chess-set), and Aaron Copland. And, according to the *Polish History of Chess*, Chopin and Beethoven. Nina Milkina, classical pianist, on chess: 'I find it absorbing and relaxing like a good book.'

John Cage, the modern musician responsible for 4′ 33″ (which, if you haven't heard it, consists of four minutes and thirty-three seconds of absolute silence)[3] was a keen player of 3D chess. He also constructed a board in which each square produced a different musical note (amplified for the audience). In 1968, at the University of Toronto he gave his first performance of musical chess. It was played in almost total darkness, against a very famous artistic opponent: the founder of surrealism, Marcel Duchamp. Duchamp gave Cage knight odds, but still crushed him quickly. Cage then took on Duchamp's wife, Teeny, with no better luck.

---

[1] Described by the lady manager of the Berlin Philharmonic as 'a passionate player'.
[2] Lill, who claims to be in psychic contact with all the composers he performs, also played against Tim Rice when they shared a room in the Lloyd Webber residence.
[3] It's in three movements. Cage also composed a piece, 'Imaginary Landscape No. 4' in which 24 performers randomly twiddle the knobs on 12 radios. One of his disciples, Anna Lockwood, wrote a piece called 'Piano Burning' which is exactly that.

33

For more on the great Duchamp, see 'The Artists'.

One composer who might be surprised to find himself in the above company is Johnny Marks, a member of the board of governors of New York's Marshall Chess Club. His claim to musical immortality: 'Rudolph the Red-Nosed Reindeer'.

From the great vocal virtuosi, we can only track down Feodor Chaliapin and Paul Robeson, who used to play with his son.

Among jazz musicians we have the doyen of British jazz and master of the one-liner,[2] Ronnie Scott; Dizzy Gillespie (who played against Ronnie on a British gig); Paul Whiteman; and drumming phenomenon Gene Krupa (if you haven't heard his drum solo on Benny Goodman's 'Sing, sing, sing' you haven't lived). Ray Charles plays on a specially made chess-set for the blind. His views on how to improve are much the same as Capablanca's: 'I learned by people beating me. You get tired of losing, then you learn what ya' doin' wrong.'

Rudolf Willmers, concert pianist (1821–78), was pretty obsessive about chess problems: in the middle of a recital in Copenhagen he stopped to write down on his cuff the solution to a problem that had been troubling him.

The composer of 'Sussex by the Sea' was W. Ward Higgs, a keen player and donor of the Ward Higgs trophy for correspondence chess.

The founder of the Hallé orchestra, Charles Hallé, was a member of Manchester Chess Club; Ferenc Erkel, creator of the Hungarian National Opera, was president of Budapest Chess Club.

---

[1] Addressing a more than usually small audience: 'I should've stayed in bed – there were more people there.'

Postscript

Not that the musicians need it, but if we stretched a point, we could considerably strengthen even the above team by adding in a few musicians (Smyslov, Taimanov, du Mont) who are more famous for their chess than their music. (After his terrible 6–0 defeat by Fischer, Taimanov consoled himself: 'At least I still have my music.') See Chapter VI for more on chess-playing musicians; and 'The Entertainers' for rock musicians.

The Artists

Not as strong as the musicians, but on the top two boards players of master strength. Captain and board two is one of the most influential artists of the twentieth century: Marcel Duchamp.

Duchamp was one of the founders of Dadaism, surrealism and cubism, but became so obsessed with chess he gave up art.[1] He won tournaments in Paris (1932, ahead of Znosko-Borovsky) and New York, played for France in four Olympiads, and co-authored one of the most obscure of all books on the endgame: *L'Opposition et les Cases conjugées sont réconciliées*. ('The positions discussed in it will occur about once in a lifetime,' he said proudly.) Duchamp also won the first International Olympiad for correspondence chess; and translated Znosko-Borovsky's well-known book on the openings into French.

High spot of Duchamp's chess career was probably Hamburg 1930 when, Alekhine being indisposed, he had to face one of the all-time greats, Frank Marshall, in a France–USA match. To France's surprise and delight, Duchamp snatched a draw from the grandmaster.

Marcel's passion for the game was overwhelming. On his honeymoon in 1927, he spent the days studying chess problems and most of the nights sleeping off his chess jags. After a week of disappointment, his enraged bride, Lydie, crept downstairs one night and glued

---

[1] 'My attention is so completely absorbed by chess. I play night and day ... I like painting less and less.' Duchamp in a letter, 1919.

all the pieces to the board.[1] Surprisingly, the marriage lasted three months.[2]

Here is one of Marcel's games against one of the all-time great soccer players (see our 'Sportsmen' section):

M. Duchamp–C. Wreford Brown, Paris, 1924. English Opening

1. Nf3 Nc6	9. O–O Qd7	17. Nf3 f4	25. Qc3 Qg5
2. c4 e5	10. Kh2 Nce7	18. Ng5 Qe7	26. Ba3 fxg3 +
3. d3 Nf6	11. b3 Ng6	19. Qc4 + Nd5	27. fxg3 Rxf1
4. Nbd2 Bc5	12. Bb2 f5	20. Bxd5 + cxd5	28. Rxf1 Rf6
5. h3 O–O	13. Qc2 Bd6	21. Qxd5 + Kh8	29. Qc8 + Nf8
6. g3 d5	14. Ng5 Nb4	22. Ne4 Rad8	and Black
7. cxd5 Nxd5	15. Qc1 c6	23. Nxd6 Rxd6	resigned
8. Bg2 Be6	16. Nxe6 Qxe6	24. Qc5 b6	

'When you play a game of chess, it is like designing something or constructing some mechanism of some kind by which you win or lose. The competitive side of it has no importance. The thing itself is very very plastic. That is probably what attracted me to the game.' In 1963 at a retrospective exhibition of his work Duchamp played chess against a nude young lady. She was described as 'well developed'. It's not clear whether this applied to the lady or her pieces.

The opening of the Candidates' Quarter-finals match (1991) was attended by Duchamp's widow, Teeny, and John Cage, the musician and weirdo (see 'The Musicians'). The draw for colours was surreal. It was made by selecting black and white urinals.

♟

René Magritte was another great surrealist who was absorbed by chess. Not in the same league as Duchamp though; his friends said it was just as well his paintings were better than his Sicilian Defence.

♟

Just beating Duchamp for board one: Henry Grob, portrait painter and International Master. He won the Swiss Championship twice, beat Grandmaster Mieses in a match (1934), and at Ostend 1937 he won games from two of the strongest players in the world, Keres and

---

[1] Another glue gag: German master Carl Carls was famous for never playing anything but 1. c4 for white. Some jokester once glued his c-pawn to the board.
[2] 'He needs a good game of chess like a baby needs a bottle' – Roche (a friend of his).

Fine (and shared first place with them). His artistic works include portraits of Alekhine and Fischer. Here's a strange game with the obscure opening he made his own.

H. Grob–H. Sperling, Correspondence. Grob's Opening

1. g4 d5	5. d3 d4	9. Nfd2 (threat:	12. Ned6 Black
2. Bg2 c6	6. Nf3 Qd6	Nf6+) Ke7	resigns (if
3. g5 e5	7. Nbd2 Be6	10. Kf1 Bb6	12... Qc5 13.
4. h4 Bc5	8. Ne4 Qd5	11. Nc4 Nd7	b4 Qxb4 14.
			c3 dxc3 15.
			Ba3)

♟

The exotically named Maximilian Mopp[1] was, like Duchamp, one of the founders of Dadaism, and was reckoned to be in the Duchamp class as a chess-player, so we put him on board three. As for the rest, you choose.

Max Ernst and Man Ray both played chess with Duchamp: but they were more famous for their chess-set designs than for the quality of their play.

♟

If you go to the Tate you can see a very strange painting by artist/chess-player Richard Dadd. It's called *The Child's Problem*. The chess problem is indeed simple; what makes the painting disturbing is the sinister expression on the child's face – and the knowledge that Dadd killed his own father. In his journals he raved about the Ruy López.

♟

Other chess-playing artists: Rembrandt (who, according to one biographer, learned from Ruy López's textbook), Gustav Doré (he played against Ajeeb the automaton – see Chapter VIII), Paul Klee, Georges Braque, Vicky the cartoonist,[2] Yves Tanguy (he designed a

---

[1] né Max Oppenheim.
[2] Here's a fragment from a game against British champion Alexander in a simultaneous display:

Alexander–Vicky. French Defence

1. e4 e6	5. a3 Bxc3+	9. Qf4 Qc7	13. Nxh7 Nxg4
2. d4 d5	6. bxc3 Nc6	10. Qf6 Rg8	14. Qh4 Rg7
3. Nc3 Bb4	7. Qg4 g6	11. Ng5 Nf5	and White
4. e5 c5	8. Nf3 Nge7	12. g4 Nh6	won

set from broom handles); Maurice Vlaminck, Walter Sickert (see 'The Sinners') and Salvador Dali, who designed a surreal set made up of solid silver fingers and thumbs, and whose only known dictum on the game is the characteristic: 'Les échecs, c'est moi' (in a book on Duchamp).

♟

Among modern British artists, Barry Martin and Patrick Hughes play at the Chelsea Arts Club (Barry became club champ in 1990 and was presented with his trophy by G. Kasparov). Roger Fry and Clive Bell played with Desmond McCarthy and Leonard Woolf, and Alexander Calder not only plays, but designed a modern-art set.

♟

Not strictly an artist, but he fits in here as well as anywhere, is Edwin Lutyens, a keen player and the designer of New Delhi, the Cenotaph and much else.

The Writers

This is the biggest, and one of the strongest teams of all (with, as we shall see, an extraordinary number of Nobel Prize winners).

Here, first, are the top ten in ascending order of strength.

♟

The best excuse anyone ever had for losing a chess game happened to the writers' board ten, William Golding. In 1983 the author of *Lord of the Flies* was in the middle of a difficult Evans Gambit with the Literary Editor of the *Financial Times* when the news of his Nobel Prize came through. Understandably agitated, the author mailed off an inaccuracy. The Nobel Prize cost him the game. You win some, you lose some. Here's the disaster:

William Golding–Anthony Curtis. Evans Gambit

1. e4 e5	5. c3 Bc5	9. Bxf7+ Kf8	13. Ng5+ Ke8
2. Nf3 Nc6	6. d4 exd4	10. Ba3+ d6	14. Qf4 Qf6
3. Bc4 Bc5	7. cxd4 Bb4+	11. Rc1 Bxd2+	15. Qxf6 Nxf6
4. b4 Bxb4	8. Nbd2 Bc3	12. Qxd2 Kxf7	16. d5 Nd4

At this point, the good news from Sweden came through, followed by a Golding blunder:

17. R x c7?? Nb5
18. R x g7

(Golding's annotation, according to Curtis: 'Fork it!!!!')

A few moves later the 1983 Nobel Laureate resigned. Golding, incidentally, also played correspondence chess against Richard Adams of *Watership Down* fame. Who usually won we don't know.

♟

On board nine, a biggie. Count Leo Nikolayevich Tolstoy learned chess as a boy. When he was fifteen he played against Turgenev, about whom more in a minute. Tolstoy must have been pretty keen: as a young officer he was gaoled for playing chess when he should have been on guard duty; but he wasted the early part of his life losing money at cards and writing *War and Peace*. Later on he took up the game again, most enthusiastically, and according to *Z Szachami Przez Wieki i Kraje*[1] became an ingenious tactical player. In his diary, he gave himself a piece of bad advice: 'One's main concern should be not to win at all costs, but to go in for interesting combinations.'

Tolstoy's skill at the game was honed in games with a really outstanding player: Prince Sergey S. Urusov (for *his* exploits, see 'The Aristocrats'). During the siege of Sebastopol, when he wasn't losing most of his roubles at cards with his fellow officers, he had dozens of games against the prince, one of the strongest Russian players of the nineteenth century.

♟

Here's a Tolstoy game (played in his eighties!)[2] against his biographer:

---

[1]A Polish history of chess by Jerzy Gizycki, translated by Wojciechowski, Ronowicz and Bartoszewski. (We read the translation.)
[2]Sprightly is the word to describe old Tolstoy: at sixty-seven he learned to ride the bicycle.

Count L. Tolstoy–Aylmer Maude, Yasnaya Polyana, 1906. King's Gambit

1. e4 e5	6. Kf1 d5	11. Rg1 Qh4+	16. Qe1 Qe7
2. f4 exf4	7. Bxd5 f3	12. Ke2 Nh6	17. Nc3 f6
3. Nf3 g5	8. gxf3 Qh3+	13. Rxg2 c6	18. Nxd5 Qd6
4. Bc4 g4	9. Ke1 g3	14. Bxh6 cxd5	19. Qg3
5. Ne5 Qh4+	10. d4 g2	15. Bxf8 Kxf8	Black resigns

Art Buchwald is our board eight. Art, long-time columnist for the *New York Herald Tribune* and one of America's funniest writers, was good enough to beat Humphrey Bogart (see below 'The Entertainers') regularly. In Paris, Art lost to Marcel Duchamp ('he was broke, so I bought one of his famous cigar boxes for $250') but then he moved to Washington and knocked over a string of celebrity chess players: Henry Kissinger ('I used the Kremlin defense'), Secretary of Defense Zbigniew Brzezinski ('Very tough. He won't let you smoke cigars in his office') and Vice-President Spiro T. Agnew, when he was governor of Maryland (a pretty good player, but Buchwald reckons he had the better of him).

Board seven is one of the best-loved of all children's authors. Arthur Ransome was a good player and gets a place in chess history for a weird juxtaposition: the author of *Swallows and Amazons* once played chess with Lenin, not to mention a number of other Russian notables.

Next, the French romanticist, Alfred de Musset, a strong café player. He would have been placed higher than board six were it not for his determined attempts to combine chess with absinthe-drinking. When he wasn't falling off his chair, Alfred was pretty good: you can get some idea of his powers from this, his most famous contribution to chess. It's a clever demonstration of the impossible: you can't force mate with two knights.

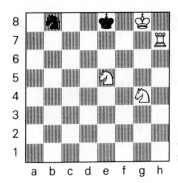

A. de Musset, La Régence, 1849

Mate in 3. (Solution at end of this section.)

Board five is yet another Nobel Laureate: Samuel Beckett. The author of *Waiting for Godot* played for Trinity College Dublin as a student; later, in Paris, he met Marcel Duchamp with whom he played many games (lost forever, unfortunately). They were both obsessed with endings and the Beckett–Duchamp encounters ('some of the most stimulating of Beckett's life,' says his biographer) are supposed to have inspired the Beckett play *Endgame*.

This 'game' is from Beckett's *Murphy*, annotations translated by Ken Whyld.

Murphy–Endon. Opening: Affense Endon, or Zweispringerspott

1. e4 (*The basic cause of White's subsequent problems*) 1... Nh6 2. Nh3 Rg8 3. Rg1 Nc6 4. Nc3 Ne5 5. Nd5 (*Bad, but there seems to be nothing better*) 5... Rh8 6. Rh1 Nc6 7. Nc3 Ng8 8. Nb1 Nb8 (*Fine and ingenious opening, sometimes called* bol d'air) 9. Ng1 e6 10. g3 (*Ill-judged*) 10... Ne7 11. Ne2 Ng6 12. g4 Be7 13. Ng3 d6 14. Be2 Qd7 15. d3 Kd8 (*Never seen at the Café de la Régence, rarely at Simpson's Divan*) 16. Qd2 Qe8 17. Kd1 Nd7 18. Nc3 (*Distress signal*) 18... Rb8 19. Rb1 Nb6 20. Na4 Bd7 21. b3 Rg8 22. Rg1 Kc8 (*Exquisitely played*) 23. Bb2 Qf8 24. Kc1 Be8 25. Bc3 (*It is hard to imagine a more deplorable situation than that of the unhappy White here*) 25... Nh8 26. b4 Bd8 27. Qh6 (*The ingenuity of desperation*) 27... Na8 (*Black now has an irresistible game*) 28. Qf6 Ng6 29. Be5 Be7 30. Nc5 (*The obstinacy with which White is set on losing a piece merits all praise*) 30... Kd8 (*At this point, without even taking the trouble to say*

41

'J'adoube', M. *Endon turned his king and queen's rook upside down, and tried to maintain them thus until the end of the game*) 31. Nh1 (*Somewhat late waiting move*) 31. . . Bd7 32. Kb2!! Rh8 33. Kb3 Bc8 34. Ka4 Qe8 (*M. Endon not giving check aloud, or otherwise showing the least sign of knowing he was attacking the king of his adversary, or rather opposite, Murphy, in accordance with law 18, was spared from bothing about it. But that would be to admit the escape was adventitious*) 35. Ka5 Nb6 36. Bf4 Nd7 37. Qc3 Ra8 38. Na6 (*The written word is unable to express the anguish of the soul that inspired in White this abject attack*) 38. . . Bf8 39. Kb5 Ne7 40. Ka5 Nb8 41. Qc6 Ng8 42. Kb5 Ke7 (*This brilliancy's ending is admirably played by M. Endon*) 43. Ka5 Qd8 (*To persist further would be frivolous and vexations and Murphy resigned*).

White resigns.

One of the great short-story writers, Lord Dunsany[1] is board four. Dunsany was a strong player (he played in the Irish championship), an ingenious problemist, and was elected president of the Irish Chess Union and the Kent County Chess Association. In this game from a simultaneous display Dunsany holds the great Capa to a draw.

[1]If you can get your hands on it, try the collection *Jorkens has a Large Whiskey*. Brilliant. Or if you like chess stories, 'The Three Sailors' Gambit'.

J. R. Capablanca–Lord Dunsany, London, 1929. Ruy López

1. e4 e5	9. dxc7 Qxc7	17. Re1 Qd6	25. Nd4 Rc5
2. Nf3 Nc6	10. Nc3 Bb7	18. Ne4 Qc6	26. Nb3 Rd5
3. Bb5 a6	11. a4 b4	19. Bg5 Bxg5	27. Rae1 Nd7
4. Ba4 b5	12. Nxd5 Bxd5	20. Nxg5 Rac8	28. Re4 Nb6
5. Bb3 Nf6	13. Bxd5 Nxd5	21. Qf3 Nf6	29. Re5 Rfd8
6. Ng5 d5	14. O–O Be7	22. Re2 h6	30. Rxd5 Rxd5
7. exd5 Ne7	15. d4 O–O	23. Qxc6 Rxc6	31. Kf1 Nxa4
8. d6 Ned5	16. dxe5 Qxe5	24. Nf3 a5	Draw agreed

This Dunsany problem is as strange as some of his stories.

Mate in 4. (Solution at end of this section.)

Board three belongs to Sir Richard Burton (no, not *that* one), explorer, soldier, author and, the way the Victorians saw it, pornographer (he translated the much banned *Arabian Nights Entertainment*[1] from the Persian). Burton played chess, like he did most things, pretty well. He could manage two games simultaneously, blindfold. Whilst an intelligence officer in Sind, he disguised himself as a native and played chess with likely sources of information.

Board two on the writers' team is the Russian novelist Ivan Sergeyevich Turgenev (who had the largest brain ever recorded). He was strong enough to play a match in Paris against a Polish professional, Maczuski (+1, =2, −3) in 1861. A year later he finished

---

[1]Plus that positional masterpiece the *Kama Sutra*; and the *The Perfumed Garden* (which recommends monkey dung as an aphrodisiac. The authors cannot endorse this).

second of sixty in a tournament at the Café de la Régence (Rivière, a strong French master, won it). In 1870 he was elected vice-chairman of the Baden-Baden tournament. Here's a game extract:

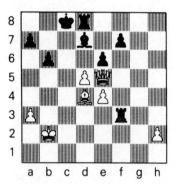

Conclusion of a game Maczuski–Turgenev, Paris, 1861.

33. . . . Rg8	37. h4 Rff2	41. exd5 Rxd5	45. Ka4 Rc7
34. Bc3 Ba4	38. Kc3 Rxd2	42. h6 Bf5	46. Kb3 Rb5 +
35. Qd4 Rg2 +	39. Qh8 + Kb7	43. Qf6 Rc2 +	47. Ka4 Bd7! and
36. Bd2 Bd7!	40. h5 exd5	44. Kb4 a5 +	White resigns

A tremendous number one for the writers is the polyglot[1] Henry Buckle, author of the influential masterwork *The History of Civilisation in England*. Buckle was one of the strongest players of the mid-nineteenth century (he won the first modern chess tournament: London 1849). Two world-class players, Anderssen and Steinitz, rated him as among the best they'd ever met. Certainly he would thrash most of the other top boards in this chapter. Here's a brief sample of his skill from 1847. He's giving the other chap the odds of queen's rook (i.e. remove White's QR from the initial line-up):

Buckle–Brown, London, 1849. Petroff Defence

1. e4 e5	5. Bd3 Nc5	9. exd6 Qxd6	13. Nd6 + Kf8
2. Nf3 Nf6	6. O–O Nxd3	10. Na3 c5	14. Ng5 Qd8
3. d4 exd4	7. Qxd3 d6	11. Nb5 Qb6	15. Qc4 Be6
4. e5 Ne4	8. Re1 Be7	12. Bf4 Na6	

[1]He spoke or wrote nineteen languages.

16. Rxe6! Bxd6   18. Bxd6 + Kg8   20. Rg6 mate
17. Nxf7! Qd7   19. Nh6 +! gxh6

Buckle died of fever in Damascus; his famous last words are appropriate for the writers' top board: 'My book, my book! I shall never finish my book!' We know the feeling.

The remaining chess-playing writers are numerous enough to make up a second team. Among the contenders for a place is another Nobel Prize winner (1981), Elias Canetti, a keen player, and, according to Anthony Curtis, an expert problem composer. He is especially interesting because of his novel *Auto da Fé*. One of the characters in *Auto da Fé* is an obsessive chess-player called Fischerle (which he shortens to Fischer). Like the great Bobby, Canetti's Fischer is a chess phenomenon: like Bobby, he lives, sleeps, breathes the game; like Bobby, he dreams of the day when chess will bring him enough money to buy hundreds of hand-made suits, and to live in a chess palace modelled on the pieces (a Bobby fantasy, see Chapter VI); and he imagines making (like Bobby) huge financial demands for his services. The spooky thing is that *Auto da Fé* was published eight years before the real Bobby Fischer was born.

Yet more Nobel Prize winners: Sinclair Lewis, who took lessons in chess from US star Al Horowitz; W. B. Yeats who, a member of the same weird circle as Aleister Crowley (see 'The Sinners'), played chess against a ghost at a house in Paris;[1] Henryk Sienkiewicz (who wrote *Quo Vadis* and played a lot of café chess in Warsaw); Gabriel García Márquez (who wrote a true short story, 'The Long Chess Night of Paul Badura-Škoda'); Isaac Bashevis Singer ('I consider chess the fairest of games because the opponents can hide nothing from each other'); and Boris Pasternak. Bertrand Russell was a Nobel Laureate too, but we've put him in with the philosophers, who need all the help they can get. And so was Churchill – he's in with the politicians.

i

One Nobel Prize winner who would never be picked is George Bernard Shaw. He deserves a FIDE life ban for his acid observation, 'Chess . . . is a foolish expedient for making idle people believe they are doing something very clever, when they are only wasting their time.' GBS was a rotten player anyway: 'I am hopeless . . . my genius did not point in that direction,' he once said. Sir Walter Scott, who played as a boy, was on Shaw's side: 'Surely chess is a sad waste of brains.' A ban in perpetuity too, for the king of hard-boiled fiction (and a chess player), Raymond Chandler, for: '. . . as elaborate a waste of human intelligence as you could find anywhere outside an advertising agency' (*The Long Goodbye*).

i

Apart from Tolstoy, Turgenev and Pasternak some other Russians are worth a mention. The Russian national poet Alexander Pushkin (*Eugene Onegin* and *Boris Godunov*) was a chess fanatic. He wrote to his beautiful wife Natalia, 'Thank you darling, for learning to play chess. It is an absolute necessity in any well-organized family' (and quite right too). But chess wasn't enough to occupy Natalia; as a result of her flirtations, poor old Pushkin got involved in a fatal duel; the night before he met his doom he passed the time playing chess.[2]

---

[1] It was four-sided chess, Yeats and a Mrs Mathers versus Mr Mathers and a spirit partner. Mr Mathers would 'shade his eyes and gaze earnestly at the spirit's empty chair' when it was its move.

[2] When his rival, d'Anthès, appeared, Pushkin removed a knight from the board, saying, 'This officer threatens to checkmate me. I shall have to kill him.' Unfortunately for literature (and chess) it didn't work out like that.

Dostoevsky was a member of the St Petersburg chess club; Maxim Gorky was a chess addict; so was Lermontov – and he too met his end in a duel.

Vladimir Nabokov might well make the first team; apart from writing one of the best novels about chess (*The Defence*) he was apparently quite a good player and a published problemist.

Nabokov considered this his best problem and discussed its composition in his autobiography, *Speak, Memory*. It's mate in 2.

(Solution at end of this section.)

The co-author of *White Horse Inn*, Oscar Blumenthal, is better known to problemists as a composer of miniatures like this:

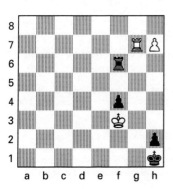

Deutsches Wochenschach, 1905

To J. Kohtz and C. Kockelkorn

Mate in 4.

47

‡

One man who deserves an entry into the 'not a lot of people know that' section is Peter Mark Roget, the writers' friend. Most writers in English owe him a debt for devising the thesaurus; the bit you didn't know is that chess-players also owe him a debt for inventing the truly pocket[1] chess-set (1845). He called it 'The Economic Chess Board'.[2]

‡

King James II gave Samuel Pepys a magnificent chess-table and men for his services to the Crown.

‡

Some short stories about the remaining British writers/players:

Lord Tennyson was President of the British Chess Association; Charles Dickens loved social chess, and was especially fond of problems – he called them, facetiously, 'chess-nuts'; Lord Alfred Douglas (or 'Bosie'), friend of Oscar Wilde, was a Muzio Gambit player; Guy Bellamy, author of the novel *The Secret Lemonade Drinker* is a self-confessed lousy player – the book itself contains a pretty awful chess game that he himself played:

NN–Bellamy. Pirc Defence

1. e4 g6	5. d3 h6	9. O–O c6	13. Ng5
2. Nf3 d6	6. Bf4 O–O	10. Qd2 Nh5	Black resigns
3. Nc3 Bg7	7. e5 Nh5	11. h3 Bh8	
4. Bc4 Nf6	8. d4 Nxf4	12. Qxh6 b5	

David Benedictus, contemporary author (*The Fourth of June* was his first novel) plays for the BBC; the author of *A Passage to India*, E. M. Forster, gave the best-ever analysis of the Evans Gambit;[3] and

[1] i.e. two-dimensional
[2] And doubtless told his friends it was ingenious, imaginative, brilliant, clever, felicitous, apt, slick, well contrived. He also published solutions to the Knight's Tour. See our section on 'Desert Island Chess'.
[3] 'I play the Evans.
'The invention of a naval officer, the Evans Gambit is noted for its liquidity. A heavy current rapidly sets in from the South-West and laps against the foundations of Black's King's Bishop's Pawn. The whole surface of the board breaks into whirlpools. But sooner or later out of this marine display there rises a familiar corpse. It is mine. Oh, what have I been doing, what have I been doing? The usual thing. Premature attack, followed by timidity. Oh, why didn't I move out my Rook's Pawn? Because as always I was misled by superficial emotion. No, not as always. It must be that the Evans doesn't suit my style. Henceforward I play Old Stodge.' (*The Game of Life*)

R. D. Blackmore of *Lorna Doone* fame was a friend of world champion Steinitz: ('the only game worth playing,' Blackmore said, 'think of the genius who invented the knight's move'). Dr Johnson called chessmen 'puppets' in his dictionary and wrote the dedication to the first English textbook on draughts.

George Eliot, Oliver Goldsmith, Robert Louis Stevenson (he took a set on his journey to the South Seas, and claimed to be a strong player), A. A. Milne, H. G. Wells, John Ruskin (a lifelong patzer), Lewis Carroll (who solved chess problems as a cure for insomnia), Enid Blyton, Doris Lessing, A. P. Herbert, Evelyn Waugh, Salman Rushdie (though since the fatwa he's taken up Nintendo games), George Orwell, Thomas Hardy, Martin Amis (his novel *Money* contains (p. 373) an excellent description of a chess game, featuring the Nimzo-Larsen opening), Julian Barnes (who lost a five-game match against Arthur Koestler and, in a celebrity simul, lost to Matthew Sadler), Malcolm Muggeridge (who played chess with his wife for sixty years), and Bernard Levin, were, or are, all addicts. Levin, a self-confessed woodpusher, has lost to some stars: Michael Foot; former *New Statesman* editor Kingsley Martin (a strong Cambridge University player); Captain Liddell Hart (see 'The Soldiers'); and *The Times* former editor, William Rees-Mogg. Levin's most painful loss though, was to fellow journalist Tim Jones, who 'not only beat me but broke one of my Sheraton chairs while doing so'.

Harold Evans, former editor of *The Times*, lists chess amongst his recreations in *Who's Who*.

The best poem about chess by a patzer:

The Ballad of Edward Bray

'The author cannot lay claim to any technical knowledge of chess,[1] but he fancies that he understands the spirit of the game. He feels that, after the many poems on the Boat Race, a few bracing lines on the Inter-University Chess Match would be a welcome change.' (A. A. Milne)

---

[1]Milne was too modest. He was champion of his house at school. He thought chess must have been invented by a woman, because the queen was the strongest piece.

THIS IS THE BALLAD of Edward Bray.
  Captain of Catherine's, Cambridge Blue –
Oh, no one ever had just his way
    Of huffing a bishop with KB2.

The day breaks fine, and the evening brings
    A worthy foe in the Oxford man –
A great finesser with pawns and things,
    But quick in the loose when the game began.

The board was set, and the rivals tossed,
    But Fortune (alas!) was Oxford's friend,
'Tail' cried Edward, and Edward lost:
    So Oxford played from the fireplace end.

We hold our breath, for the game's begun –
    Oh, who so gallant as Edward Bray!
He's taken a bishop from KQ1
    And ruffed it just in the Cambridge way!

Then Oxford castles his QBKnight
    (He follows the old, old Oxford groove;
Though never a gambit saw the light
    That's able to cope with Edward's move.)

The game went on, and the game was fast,
    Oh, Oxford huffed and his King was crowned,
The exchange was lost, and a pawn was passed,
    And under the table a knight was found!

Then Oxford chuckled; but Edward swore,
    A horrible, horrible oath swore he;
And landed him one on the QB4,
    And followed it up with an RQ3.

Time was called; with an air of pride
    Up to his feet rose Edward Bray.
'Marker, what of the score?' he cried,
    'What of the battle I've won this day?'

The score was counted; and Bray had won
    By two in honours, and four by tricks,

And half of a bishop that came undone,
   And all of a bishop on KQ6.

Then here's to Chess: and a cheer again
   For the man who fought on an April day
With never a thought of sordid gain!
   England's proud of you, Edward Bray!   A. A. Milne

The best bit of chess analysis by a patzer:

. . . a hoarse voice called from the corner of the lounge.
   'Pssst!' cried the voice. 'Honoured Grand Master Mr Green!'
   I turned and saw the gnome-like figure of Globovitch, the
world chess champion, crouched malevolently at a table.
   'Just one game,' he begged. 'Just one game, before you go to
bed. I have never forgiven you for that thrashing in Moscow.'
   I strolled over and pushing aside the Russian's hand, casually
moved forward my King's Pawn. Sweat broke out on the Russian's
forehead. Half an hour later he desperately moved his own King's
Pawn. I shrugged and brought out my Knight. He gave an
hysterical cry and buried his face in his hands.
   'I resign,' he sobbed. 'In thirteen moves your Queen will take
my undefended Rook on the back line and all will be lost.'
   'That's the way the cookie crumbles, Globovitch.'
   I grinned and moved away. He bored me.
   Slowly I walked up the broad central staircase of the hotel.
Behind me came the sound of a shot. Poor fellow. These Russians
can't stand being beaten.

Michael Green, *The Art of Coarse Sport*

♟

The remaining Americans include Walter Tevis (*The Hustler* and
The Queen's Gambit); James (*From Here to Eternity*) Jones, a keen
student of the game; Edgar Allan Poe (who preferred draughts
because he thought it was deeper); L. Frank Baum (*The Wizard of
Oz*); Charles MacArthur (co-author of that terrific play *The Front
Page*); Henry Miller (*Tropic of Cancer, Nexus, Sexus, Plexus*); John
Steinbeck; O. Henry, master of the short story, who played against
Ajeeb (see Chapter VIII); the Canadian humorist and economics

professor, Stephen Leacock; and the great Argentinian author, Jorge Luis Borges (he wrote a poem about the game). US novelist Jerzy Kosinski was on the 1990 World Championship organizing committee.

Among the Europeans we haven't yet mentioned are: Rabelais (probably the first great writer to play modern chess; his scatological masterpiece *Gargantua and Pantagruel* contains – book five – the first description in literature of castling), Balzac, Goethe ('Chess is the touchstone of the intellect'), Ionesco,[1] Joseph Conrad, Henrik Ibsen, Tristan Tzara (he was one of the founders of Dadaism and might well, like Arthur Ransome, have played with Lenin), Boccaccio, Cervantes, half the brothers Grimm (Jakob), Antoine de Saint-Exupéry, Schiller, Montaigne, Bertolt Brecht – who tried to invent a chess variant in which the pieces changed their powers during the game – and Stefan Zweig, who wrote the best-ever story about chess: *The Royal Game.*

The one-legged alcoholic Belgian poet, Arthur Rimbaud, when he wasn't fighting in Parisian brothels, consuming absinthe by the bucketful and generally annoying the hell out of the gendarmerie, played café chess with his mate, fellow poet and hell raiser, Paul Verlaine. Here's the beginning of a rather nice poem (Prelude LVI) about it all, by Conrad Aiken:

> Rimbaud and Verlaine, precious pair of poets,
> Genius in both (but what is genius?) playing
> Chess on a marble table at an inn
> With chestnut blossom falling in blond beer
> And on their hair and between knight and bishop –
> Sunlight squared between them on the chess-board
> Cirrus in heaven, and a squeal of music
> Blown from the leathern door of Ste Sulpice –

(It ended in tears: Paul, awash with the green firewater, shot Art in the wrist. The Belgian teenager packed in poetry, Paris, Verlaine and possibly chess, for good.)

[1] See 'Desert Island Chess' for more about him, Sartre and others.

♟

Omar Khayyám played Shaṭranj (see Chapter VII) and gave us (via Edward FitzGerald) the best known lines about the game.[1]

♟

Then there's the fascinating case of Jeffrey Archer. A short story in *A Twist in the Tale* features a game of chess; but in answer to our query he claimed not to play. Then we discovered the following game, played against former financier and writer of children's books Jim Slater, who challenged Jeffrey to a game, having read in an Archer publicity blurb that J.A. did play. Perhaps he gave up after this débâcle:

J. Slater–J. Archer. Italian Game

1. e4 e5	4. Nc3 Bg4	7. Bxf7+ Ke7
2. Nf3 Nc6	5. O–O Nd4	8. Nd5 mate
3. Bc4 d6	6. Nxe5 Bxd1	(cf. page 115).

♟

One name that hasn't come up yet is that of William Shakespeare (or as US boxing impresario Don King recently and unnecessarily dubbed him: 'the late, great, William Shakespeare').

Nobody knows for sure whether the Swan of Avon played chess. The only evidence we have is a painting by Karel van Mander of him (we think) launching a queen's-side attack against Ben Jonson. It is *circa* 1603. This is around the time he wrote *King Lear*, which contains one of only four[2] references to the game in his plays.

Our bet is that as an educated Elizabethan he probably knew the moves, but the scant number of references to the game in his oeuvre suggest he wasn't addicted. So regrettably, the Bard doesn't make our dream team.

♟

A strong player who would have been chucked off the writers' team

---

[1] 'Tis all a chequer board of Nights and Days
  Where Destiny with Men for Pieces plays;
  Hither and thither moves and mates and slays,
  And one by one back in the closet lays.
[2] If you care to track them down they are: *The Tempest*, Act V Scene 1; *King John*, Act II Scene 1; *King Lear*, Act I Scene 1; *The Taming of the Shrew*, Act I Scene 1.

53

by a unanimous vote of its members is the infamous Dr Thomas Bowdler, the expletive-deleter of Shakespeare. Bowdler's *Family Shakespeare* was the Bard without the dirty bits – or as Bowdler expressed it, a version of Shakespeare which would 'no longer raise a blush on the cheek of modest innocence' for Dr Thomas had expunged all those passages 'which cannot with propriety be read aloud to the family'. The result was abysmal. He did the same thing to Gibbon's *Decline and Fall of the Roman Empire*, to similar effect. (Gibbon, by the way, was a chess-player.) Still, his chess was sparkling enough. Here's Bowdler, with the first double rook sacrifice on record, beating the daylights out of a member of parliament:

Bowdler–General Conway, London, 1796. Bishop's Opening

1. e4 e5	7. Qf3 Qxb2	13. Qg4+ Kc7	19. d4 b4
2. Bc4 Bc5	8. Bxf7+ Kd7	14. Qxg7 Nd7	20. Bxb4 Kb5
3. d3 c6	9. Ne2 Qxa1	15. Qg3 b6	21. c4+ Kxb4
4. Qe2 d6	10. Kd2 Bb4+	16. Nb5+! cxb5	22. Qb3+ Ka5
5. f4 exf4	11. Nbc3 Bxc3+	17. Bxd6+ Kb7	23. Qb5
6. Bxf4 Qb6	12. Nxc3 Qxh1	18. Bd5+ Ka6	mate

Dr Bowdler also beat the great Philidor[1] (but he had a pawn and two moves start).

♟

To balance the Bowdler entry, we conclude with a quotation from a terrific writer whose work must have the good Dr Bowdler spinning in his grave:

> During the Baroque period of chess the practice of harrying your opponent with some annoying mannerism came into general use. Some players used dental floss, others cracked their joints or blew saliva bubbles. The method was constantly developed. In the 1917 match at Baghdad, the Arab Arachnid Khayam defeated the German master Kurt Schlemiel by humming 'I'll Be Around When You're Gone' forty thousand times, and each time reaching his hand towards the board as if he intended to make a move. Schlemiel went into convulsions finally.
>
> *Queer*, William Burroughs

[1] See 'The Musicians'. And for much more on literature and chess, see Norman Knight's superb books (Bibliography).

♟

Solution to Alfred de Musset problem:

1. Rd7 Nxd7   3. Nf6 mate
2. Nc6 any

Solution to Dunsany problem: the position as it stands is impossible so rotate the board by 180 degrees. Then

1. Nc6 Nf3   3. Qxe5 any
2. Nb4 Ne5   4. Nd3 mate

Solution to Nabokov problem:

1. Bc2 (not b8 = N? c2!)

Solution to Blumenthal problem:

1. Ra7 Rg6   3. h8 = Q and mate
2. Ra1 + Rg1

The Entertainers

The movie buffs amongst you will recall that in *Casablanca*, our first view of Rick (Humphrey Bogart) shows him playing solitaire chess.[1] The scene was suggested to the director, Mike Curtiz, by the actor himself, for Bogie was an addict.

Probably the strongest of all the major movie stars, Bogart was obsessed by the game from his student days onwards; and in the depths of the great depression, when struggling young actors were earning even less than they do in normal years, he found a novel way of adding to the family income. Bogart lived near a New York chess café, with a resident 'expert' who hustled customers for dimes. The actor beat the expert so often that the café owner offered him the job. Humphrey declined, but chess hustling up and down Broadway made an appreciable difference to the Bogarts' standard of living.

Decades later, when he'd become box-office magic, he still hustled

[1]Movie buffs will also recall that Ronald Reagan was the first choice for the part. Just imagine.

chess, in Hollywood and for much larger sums. One of his biographers says he rated his friends on their ability to play chess and hold liquor. Bogart was adept at both. We know that he beat GM Sammy Reshevsky, in a simul. Unfortunately the only Bogie games we have are losses against masters. Here's Humphrey (black), on location for *The African Queen*, losing to Belgian master Limbos, watched by Lauren Bacall and Katharine Hepburn (who was also a chess-player):

P. Limbos–H. Bogart, Stanleyville, 1951. French Defence

1. e4 e6	7. O–O c6	13. Rfe1 Nb6	19. Re1 Qd6
2. d4 d5	8. Bg5 Nbd7	14. Re2 Bd7	20. g4 Rd8
3. Nc3 Bb4	9. Ng3 Qc7	15. Be7 Bxe7	21. f4 g5
4. exd5 exd5	10. Nh5 Nxh5	16. Rxe7 Rf7	22. h4 Black
5. Bd3 Nf6	11. Qxh5 g6	17. Rxf7 Kxf7	resigns
6. Ne2 O–O	12. Qh6 f5	18. Qxh7+ Kf6	

The star of *Casablanca* didn't have it all his own way. Art Buchwald (columnist for the *Herald Tribune* – you read of him above, under 'The Writers') beat Bogie regularly. And so did Hollywood's most famous restaurateur – Mike Romanoff. Indeed so one-sided were the matches that Romanoff once bet Bogart $100 that he could win twenty consecutive games. Humphrey lost – and planned a terrible revenge. He called up Romanoff and challenged him to just one more game, by phone, for a similar stake. Mike jumped at the easy money and was thunderstruck when the actor blitzed him in twenty moves. What he didn't know was that sitting at Bogart's elbow was Herman Steiner, US chess champion (and organizer of the Hollywood Chess Club).

♖

Marlon Brando played chess on the set of *Julius Caesar*. Whilst filming, he gave an interview to a Hollywood reporter on condition they played chess. The reporter thrashed him. Brando's comment: 'That was the worst interview I ever gave.'

♖

John Wayne – you wouldn't have thought it – was a chess-player, too. According to his agent Wayne was 'a good country player', whatever that means. He did play a series of games against William Windom, a lesser-known actor (*To Kill a Mockingbird*) who was rated about 1600 US. Big John, showing true grit, lost the match 6–0. At the conclusion of the sixth game, the Duke, losing his cool, gave board and men the old left hook. A shaken Windom retrieved all but two of the pieces from the floor, and kept the incomplete set as a souvenir.

♜

Charles Boyer, the archetypal French lover, was in the Bogart league as a chess-player.

♜

Steve Martin was among the audience at the 1990 Kasparov–Karpov match.

♜

An unlikely pair of opponents: George Sanders and Zsa Zsa ('I never hated a man enough to give him his diamonds back') Gabor. They played incessantly on their honeymoon, for want of better things to do, reports George in his autobiography.

♜

Al Jolson, after he became the first movie actor of the talkies, was keen enough to form a chess club of radio stars called Knight Riders of the Air.

♜

Nigel Havers, on the set of *A Passage to India*, played chess pretty incessantly. He, being a kind-hearted chap, decided to teach some Indian children the game. Annoyingly for Nigel, they beat him easily.

♜

Other chess-playing film stars: Shirley Temple, Marlene Dietrich, Lionel Barrymore, Charlie Chaplin (who was taught by the wonder-kid Sammy Reshevsky), Douglas Fairbanks Jnr, Errol Flynn (when he wasn't raising hell), Leo Genn, Peter Lorre (another star of *Casablanca*), Belinda Lee (British sex symbol of the fifties), Ray Milland, Yves Montand (with Simone Signoret), Anthony (*Zorba*) Quinn, Walter Pidgeon, George Peppard, George C. Scott, Walter Matthau, Alan Alda (of *MASH*, a computer chess freak), José Ferrer (a frequent Fischer opponent), Henry Fonda, Nigel Bruce, Woody Allen ('I was too small for my school chess team'; he wrote a short story with a chess theme), Basil Rathbone, Mae West, Franchot

Tone, Conrad Veidt, Myrna Loy, Maureen O'Sullivan, Linda Dar-
nell, and Alastair Sim. Ralph Morgan (*Charlie Chan's Last Chance*,
The Power and the Glory) had one of the world's smallest chess-sets:
carved from date stones, the kings were less than half an inch high
(but if the *Guinness Book of Records* is reading this, the smallest
ever is probably that made by five engineering students from Geneva.
The board dimensions are 8 mm by 8 mm, the pawns are 1.5 mm
high and the king is 2.5 mm, says *Chess Notes*).[1]

♜

Probably the strongest player in Hollywood nowadays is Henry
Darrow (if you're a *High Chaparral* fan, you'll know him as the
perpetually grinning Manolito). Henry once drew with Spassky in a
simul, and won a tournament of stars in Mexico in 1989. The runner-
up, Jesse Vint (*Little Big Man*), hurled himself fully clothed into an
adjacent swimming-pool after losing the crucial last-round game.
Also competing: Morgan Fairchild, the exquisite star of *Flamingo
Road* and other soaps.

♜

In 1988, the star of *White Mischief*, Greta Scacchi, played quite
adequately (with some help from British ladies' champ Sheila Jackson) against International Master Matthew Sadler in a celebrity
simul (alongside Patrick Moore and Julian Barnes *q.v.*).

♜

Bing Crosby didn't[2] ('I have worries enough already,' he said in one
of his films), but Sinatra does, occasionally. Bob Hope played once,
and memorably. On a TV spectacular in 1972 he became one of the
handful of people who have beaten Bobby Fischer. It is just possible
that Bobby, for once in his life, wasn't entirely serious. (Hope won
the game by jumping several pieces in succession as in checkers, and
declaring 'That's gin' as in gin rummy.)

♜

A nicely balanced match would be movie stars versus directors. The
directors' team: Stanley Kubrick (who featured HAL, a chess-playing

---

[1]Another contender – a chess-set on sale in Ciudadela, Menorca in 1987 was small
enough to fit into a match box.
[2]One of the authors asked him, on Turnberry Golf Course.

robot in *2001*,[1] and who likes to play his stars before filming); Roger 'Mr Bardot' Vadim who chose a computer chess-set as his one luxury on *Desert Island Discs*; Ingmar Bergman; Billy Wilder; John Huston; Milos Forman; Roberto Rossellini; Sergei Bondarchuk, Eisenstein, and Vsevolod Pudovkin (who made *Chess Fever*, a film starring Capablanca). In Rome's Cinecittà in the fifties, Vadim played against Rossellini and Bondarchuk. The Frenchman won both games.

♖

The ten best films with chess scenes

1. *A Matter of Life and Death*	Michael Powell and Emeric Pressburger	
2. *The Seventh Seal*	Ingmar Bergman	
3. *Casablanca*	Michael Curtiz	
4. *2001*	Stanley Kubrick	
5. *Ivan the Terrible*	Sergei Eisenstein	
6. *The Chess Players*	Satyajit Ray	
7. *Blazing Saddles*	Mel Brooks	
8. *Blade Runner*	Ridley Scott	
9. *The Thomas Crown Affair*	Norman Jewison	
10. *From Russia with Love*	Terence Young	

(plus some very soft porn: a *Betty Boop* cartoon in which Betty is captured by a black king and rescued by white pawns).

♖

In the film *8 × 8* by the Dadaist Hans Richter, Jean Cocteau plays a pawn that is promoted to a queen.

♖

Of stage actors, we know that Sarah Bernhardt played; and from the BBC TV programme *My Favourite Things* that the divine Felicity Kendal likes playing with her son; Jessie Matthews (Mrs Dale) played; Patrick McGoohan (star of that terrific TV series *The Prisoner*) is a keen player; so is Anthony Andrews, of *Brideshead Revisited*; John Sessions (*Whose Line Is It Anyway?*) played Nigel

---

[1] And a Russian called Smyslov.

Short in a simul; so did Ian Holm; Jennifer Saunders; and ballet star Mikhail Baryshnikov, who with Milos Forman, was a keen spectator at the USSR *v.* Rest of World match (1984).

♖

Kate Jackson of *Charlie's Angels* said in a TV interview she would rather play with her Sargon chess computer than watch television.

♖

The logorrhoeaic Tony Blackburn used to play against other ship-bound DJs in the golden days of Radio Caroline.

♖

Robert Lindsey (star of *G.B.H.*) asked for a chess-set as his luxury on *Desert Island Discs* (while Leslie Phillips, on the same prog., asked for a jade chess-set).

♖

One of the funniest men on TV, Stephen Fry, of *Jeeves and Wooster* and much else, is a chess freak. His entertaining novel *The Liar* includes a chess master among its characters. He has a superb board of bird's-eye maple and Moluccan ebony, edged in sycamore, an 1871 boxwood and ebony Staunton set, plus a chess clock by Grant's of Stamford. Dolefully he confesses that what he brings to this wonderful equipment is the playing talent of a dead rat.

♖

Magicians seem particularly addicted to chess. Houdini, the wizard of escape played (how well we don't know). And David Nixon, the TV star, was a keen and capable player. One of the authors helped him beat an early chess computer at an Islington chess congress in the seventies. But the prize for chess cheek goes to magician, hypnotist and showman, The Great Romark. Towards the end of the Fischer–Spassky 'Match of the Century', a cable arrived from Romark challenging the two superstars to a simultaneous match. Romark, blindfold, would take on Boris and Bobby together for a $50,000 stake. Spassky declined, but Fischer expressed enough interest in it to have Romark's financial status checked out. Nothing came of it though.

How it's done

If you'd like to do a Romark, and play, say Kasparov and Karpov (or merely two of your club stars) together and guarantee to come out even, here's how. After agreeing suitably high stakes, and after placing the boards some distance apart, you take white against Kasparov and, generously, black against Karpov. You then await Karpov's first move. 'd4' says the wizard of Zlatoust. 'd4' you say to Kasparov. 'Nf6' replies the world champion; which of course is your reply to Anatoly. And so on. If you can pull it off before they tumble, it should do wonders for your grading.

The last we read of Romark was in the *Book of Heroic Failures*. In a memorable demonstration of blindfold driving he, eyes tightly bandaged, blundered along the main street of Ilford and wrecked a police van.

♖

Another magician, The Amazing Kreskin, whilst appearing in a mental magic act at Reno, Nevada, went one further. He (having played less than a dozen games in his life) challenged Fischer, Karpov or Korchnoi to play him for $50,000. The Amazing K. would be blindfold, and the grandmasters needn't announce their moves. Larry Evans (not quite in the Karpov class, although still a grandmaster) took up the challenge but Kreskin, pleading a hectic business schedule, chickened out. Some years later, however, Kreskin got up the nerve to tackle a couple of GMs, Korchnoi and R. Byrne, and was crushed horribly (in the Korchnoi game, the Amazing amazingly castled illegally).

Korchnoi–Kreskin, New York, 1979. Kreskin-Indian Defence

1. d4 Nf6	5. e4 Qd8	9. Bb5 + Nc6	13. Qg3 Qe8
2. c4 b6	6. Nc3 e5	10. Bxc6 + Bd7	14. Qxg7 mate
3. f3 d5	7. dxe5 c5	11. Qxd6 O–O!?	
4. cxd5 Qxd5	8. exf6 Bd6	12. Bxa8 Qxa8	

After Korch's 11th move he scribbled a note saying that if Kresk castled illegally it should be allowed.

Kreskin–Byrne, New York, 1979. Slav Defence

1. d4 Nf6	7. dxe5 Nxe5	13. Rg1 Bh3	19. Kd4 O–O
2. c4 c6	8. a3 Bd6	14. Rg3 Bxg3 +	20. Qe2 Qg6
3. f3 d5	9. Bb5 + Nc6	15. hxg3 Qd6	21. Re1 Rfe8
4. cxd5 cxd5	10. Bxc6 + bxc6	16. b4 Qxg3 +	22. a4 Nd7
5. e3 Nc6	11. Nh3 Bxh3	17. Ke2 Qg2 +	23. b5 Qf6
6. Nc3 e5	12. Bd2 Bxg2	18. Kd3 Bf5 +	mate

♜

If you're an *Only Fools and Horses* fan you'll be interested to know that Trigger (or more accurately, actor Roger Lloyd Pack) is an enthusiastic player. His comment: 'It's 100 per cent skill; there's no element of chance like the sun in your eyes.'

♜

Alistair Cooke, doyen of British broadcasters from America (who might also represent the writers) lists chess amongst his hobbies in *Who's Who*.

♜

From the world of pop we have the following (maybe they should be among the musicians, but the classical virtuosi have a strong enough team already): Bobby Darin; one quarter of Abba (Björn Ulvaeus); Phil Lynott of Thin Lizzy; Country and Western star Willie Nelson; folk singers Leon Rosselson (who played for Cambridge University in the fifties) and Nic Jones (who recorded *The Noah's Ark Trap*, an album named after a trap in the Ruy López); Adam Faith; Sting (of The Police); Bono, of U2; Dr Robert of the Blow Monkeys; and at least two of the Fab Four – John Lennon, who on the promo film accompanying the song 'Imagine' played chess with Yoko (they both used white pieces to symbolize peace and love);[1] and Ringo,[2] who after the split-up, designed a chess-set in the shape of human hands. The royal jewellers made two copies of it in gold and silver. In the sixties Jefferson Airplane had a song about getting stoned which included the line (sung by Grace Slick) '. . . when the chess pieces start to tell you where to go'. We don't know if they themselves played.

[1] They played an English Opening. Yoko introduced a t.n.: she stuffed the captured pieces down her blouse; Lennon's ingenious response was to eat both the kings.
[2] He learned (from Lennon?) while they were making *Sgt Pepper*.

♖

Apart from Ulvaeus, other people involved with the musical *Chess* play; Tim Rice is an addict; and last time we heard, Elaine Paige was learning.

♖

French singing legends Charles Aznavour and Charles Trenet were supposed to be in a France *v.* USSR celebs match in 1990 – but perhaps it was yet another French hoax.

♖

Mystifyingly, Michael Jackson's girl friend Brooke Shields was a member of the 1990 World Championship organizing committee (and comedian Gary Shandling performed at the opening ceremony). Only in America . . .

♖

Our showbiz allstars team is:

1. Humphrey Bogart
2. Al Jolson
3. John Wayne
4. Sir Charles Chaplin
5. John Lennon
6. Frank Sinatra
7. Harry Houdini
8. Marlon Brando

This lot would pull in the crowds like no other chess team in the history of the universe. But if you're looking for board strength make room for: William Windom;[1] Henry Darrow; Fritz Feld (dapper

---

[1] Here's Windom beating a Greek master in a simul:
Windom–Kourkounakis, 1972. Queen's Pawn Game

1. Nf3 d5	5. d4 Bd6	9. Bxh7+ Kxh7	13. Nf3 Be7
2. e3 Nf6	6. Bd3 O–O	10. Qh5+ Kg8	14. Qh8+ Kf7
3. Ne5 Nbd7	7. Nd2 Ne8	11. Ng6 c5	
4. f4 e6	8. O–O f6	12. c3 f5	

Now Nfe5+ is mate in 4, but instead Windom played Nxf8 and won on move 58.

cameo actor of dozens of films[1] and organizer of the Hollywood Chess Club in the forties); Mike Romanoff (almost an entertainer in his own right); Roger Vadim; and Stanley Kubrick (who beat George C. Scott on the set of *Dr Strangelove*).

Here's a Vadim game:

R. Vadim–CHESS 4.6 Simultaneous Display, Paris, 1977. Queen's Pawn Game

1. d4 d5	10. Rd1 h6	19. Rc1 Bd3	28. Qg4 Be5
2. e3 Nf6	11. c4 dxc4	20. Qe1 exd5	29. e4 Bxa1
3. h3 Nc6	12. Bxc4 Ng5	21. Nc3 c6	30. Bxh6 f5
4. Nf3 Bf5	13. d5 Nxf3+	22. Na4 Bf5	31. exf5 Qxa3
5. Bd3 Ne4	14. Qxf3 Ne5	23. Kh1 Bxh3	32. Re1 Qxb4
6. c3 e6	15. Qe2 Nxc4	24. gxh3 Qe4+	33. Re7 Qxe7
7. O–O Bd6	16. Qxc4 Qg6	25. Kg1 Qxa4	White resigns
8. Qe2 O–O	17. Bd2 Be4	26. b4 f6	
9. a3 Qf6	18. Qf1 Bc2	27. Qe2 a5	

The Sportsmen

If you watched Norwegian football more often than you do, you might be aware of a talented young midfield player called Simen Agdestein. He was once the world's youngest grandmaster and is top board for our sportsmen's team. The multi-faceted Simen played under-21 football for his country around the same time he was becoming Nordic chess champion. He has since represented his country in full internationals versus Italy and Czechoslovakia (against whom he scored a goal). He's currently in the top twenty grandmasters in the world, rated alongside Adams.

Other chess/football wizards: Danish GM Lars Bo Hansen (board two for the sportsmen) has represented his country at soccer; IM Béla Şooş (board four) was a Romanian soccer international; Torkil Nielsen

---

[1] *The Secret Life of Walter Mitty, Hello Dolly, Silent Movie, The Sunshine Boys*, et cetera.

(board six), chess champion of the Faeroe Islands, was a key figure in the soccer upset of the decade: he scored the Faeroes' winning goal against the much fancied Austrian side in the 1990 European Championships. Here's board one versus board two:

Agdestein–L. B. Hansen, Ostersund, 1992 Slav Defence

1. c4 c6	10. Qb3 Qb6	19. Rxd4 Nb8	28. Rxa7 Nc3
2. d4 d5	11. Nc4 Qa6	20. Rad1 Nc6	29. Bf3 Ned5
3. Nf3 Nf6	12. Bf4 Be4	21. R4d2 Rfe8	30. b6 Nb5
4. Qc2 dxc4	13. Bd6 Bxd6	22. Qb5 Rb8	31. Bxd5 exd5
5. Qxc4 Bf5	14. Nxd6 Bxf3	23. e3 Qxb5	32. Rxd5 Nc3
6. g3 e6	15. Bxf3 c5	24. axb5 Nce7	33. Rd7 Black
7. Bg2 Nbd7	16. Nc4 Nd5	25. Ra1 Rec8	resigns
8. O–O Be7	17. Rfd1 Rad8	26. Be2 Nb6	
9. Nbd2 O–O	18. a4 cxd4	27. b3 Nbd5	

On board three, the Daley Thompson of ball games, the amazing Sir George Thomas. Sir George played hockey for Hampshire, tennis for England (he reached the last eight at Wimbledon) and was All-England badminton champion in 1920, 21, 22 and 23. In this last year he scored a remarkable double: he was also British chess champion. (Another unique double: he captained England at badminton and chess.)

Sir George did pretty well for an amateur; at the Hastings Tournament of 1934–5 he came ahead of two all-time greats (Capablanca and Botvinnik) and first equal with a future world champion (Euwe). He played for England in seven Olympiads, and at his best approached grandmaster strength. Here's a sample of his play – a lightning (ten minutes) game against a master when he was nearly seventy.

Sir G. A. Thomas–E. Klein, London, 1946. Ruy López

1. e4 e5	7. Bb3 d5	13. Nd4! Nxd4	19. f6 g6
2. Nf3 Nc6	8. dxe5 Be6	14. cxd4 Ng5	20. Qh6 Ne6
3. Bb5 a6	9. c3 Bc5	15. f3 Bc8	21. Bc2 Kh8
4. Ba4 Nf6	10. Qe2 Bg4	16. Nd2 c6	22. Rf5 Rg8
5. O–O Nxe4	11. Be3 Bxe3	17. f4 Ne6	23. Qxh7+ Black
6. d4 b5	12. Qxe3 O–O	18. f5 Nc7	resigns

On board five another soccer star. Time's ever-rolling stream has wiped out most people's memory of C. Wreford Brown, but in the early part of the century he played for Old Carthusians, and was rated by C. B. Fry as the best centre-half of his day, playing until he was fifty-nine. He was good enough to represent England at chess. He also played in the British championships, 1933, scored a win and a draw, then withdrew through illness. His claim to immortality: he coined the word 'soccer'. He was also an ancestor of the man who, in the Falklands conflict, commanded the ship that sank the *Belgrano*.

C. Wreford Brown–P. R. Gibbs, London, 1918 (Casual Game). Giuoco Piano (Max Lange Attack)

1. e4 e5	5. d4 exd4	9. Bg5 gxf6	13. Qe2 Ne5
2. Nf3 Nc6	6. e5 d5	10. Bh6+ Kg8	14. Nxe5 Bxe2
3. Bc4 Bc5	7. exf6 dxc4	11. Nc3 Bb6	15. Nd7
4. O–O Nf6	8. Re1+ Kf8	12. Ne4 Bg4	Black resigns

For another Wreford Brown game, see 'The Artists'.

Board seven goes to bridge pro Alan Truscott. Alan now makes a living out of bridge in the USA, but before taking the wrong path, he was a strong Cambridge University player.

If you're not American you may not have heard of our board eight, Ron Guidry. If you have, you'll know he's the pitcher with one of the highest lifetime winning percentages in major league baseball. 'Rapid' Ron is a strong player – good enough to take US master Bruce Pandolfini to the endgame before losing.

First reserve is a surprise: the former world light welterweight boxing champion, Terry Marsh. Before he took up boxing Terry was a chess star: at eleven, he was a London schools champion. He now plays computer chess. He likens boxing to chess: 'It's all about nullifying your opponent's strengths, and exploiting their weakness.'

Second reserve, yet another footballer, and a very famous one: Ossie Ardiles, world cup wizard, Spurs idol, and now their manager, had played correspondence chess with former England international Michael Franklin. He is also a friend of GM Quinteros. Ossie says he devotes ten to twelve hours a week to studying or playing chess: 'I'm probably more competitive in chess than in football.' In an interview with Anthea Hall for the *Sunday Telegraph* he volunteered: 'The satisfaction of chess is, like football, beautiful – an intellectual beauty. But football comes first.' He also echoed Lasker on the absence of hypocrisy in the game of chess: 'You and the game, and nothing else. It's like being with God. Just you and – I know it's a bad word – no bullshit, nobody else.'

As third reserve, another former world champion and (according to the TV series *The Greatest*) the greatest snooker player who ever drew breath: Steve Davis. Steve gave up Space Invaders to concentrate on the more difficult game, and is now a dedicated computer chess player.

Steve learned to play chess before he could play snooker (his father taught him when he was three years old). In an interview with Faye Ainscow he said of his prowess: 'I know I'm bad, but by most standards I'm OK.' Several years ago he threw out a chess challenge to his fellow snooker stars, but there were no takers.

Steve's proudest chess moment: after he won the world title in 1987, he received a telegram of congratulations from Anatoly Karpov. (Karpov, you'll be surprised to hear, is a snooker fan. More than once, keen entrepreneurs have tried to arrange a chess/snooker match between the two ex-champs; both are keen, but their respective tournament schedules have never allowed it. Pity.)

We agonized for a long time about fourth reserve; in the end world heavyweight title contender Frank Bruno got the nod. He listed chess among his hobbies in his autobiography and on a TV interview. How good he is we're not sure, but the mere sight of him standing in the wings should be worth a couple of points. Know what I mean, Harry?

♞

Competing for (but not quite catching) the judge's eye for big Frank's place were such superstars as:

– world heavyweight champ (at least, according to the World Boxing Council) Lennox Lewis. In the run-up to his battle with Donovan 'Razor' Ruddock, Sky television showed him defending against a dangerous-looking king-side attack. If, as seems likely, he gets it on with Frank Bruno for the title, it will be the first time two chess-players have fought for the richest prize in sport. Unsurprisingly, his manager said, 'He fights every fight like it's a game of chess';[1]

– former heavyweight contender Joe Bugner, who chose a chess-set for his luxury on *Desert Island Discs*;

– *Playboy*'s 'Woman of Steel', world female boxing champion (bantamweight), and world karate champion, Graciella Casillas. Among her less macho accomplishments is a modest skill at chess. In 1989 she played in a tournament in Mexico and lost to Henry Darrow (see 'The Entertainers');

– Prince of milers and Olympic hero, Steve Ovett, who took a chess computer with him on those long flights between meets (Seb Coe doesn't play, incidentally);

– the first sub-3.50 miler, John Walker, a frequent Ovett opponent on the track;

– Harry (Butch) Reynolds, who broke the world 400 metres record (43.29 seconds), and was subsequently and controversially banned for drug-taking;

– the daddy of all distance runners, Emil Zatopek, a goodish player. In *Das Spiel der Könige* by Diel, there's a picture of him defending a

---

[1] This cliché has been applied to just about every sporting activity you can think of. The prize goes to the commentator on *The World's Strongest Man* programme, who said, of the fairly uncerebral process of lifting a chunk of rock as big as a Škoda, then dropping it: 'It's a game of chess out there.'

Caro-Kann advance variation against no less a grandmaster than Salo Flohr;

– David Hemery, who won gold in the 400 metres hurdles at the Mexico Olympics. Before the finals at the next Olympics (Munich) he played a two-hour game with fellow finalist and eventual silver medallist Ralph Mann. David finished third;

– Sevvy Ballesteros, who takes a chess computer to every golf tournament, and plays about twice a week;

– Paul Gascoigne, the tearful England soccer star, alleged to have drawn a speed game with GM Jon Speelman. This is about as plausible as Speelman being selected as striker for the next World Cup;

– Anton Geesink. When Hans Böhm broke the European simul record, the last game to finish was resigned by this genial giant. Geesink secured his spot among the immortals at the Tokyo Olympics. He crushed Japanese champ Kaminaga to become the first judo superheavyweight champion (and the whole of Japan went into mourning);

– Chris Bonnington, Britain's most famous climber, who played chess four miles up a Himalayan mountain called Changabang;

– the formidable father of English cricket, W. G. Grace; the *British Chess Magazine* once published a poem celebrating his chess-playing ability;

– tennis ace, Ivan Lendl, a keen player and son of a Czech junior chess champion;

– winter sports champ, Tony Kastner, who swapped ski lessons for chess lessons with Bobby Fischer;

– the most cultured former heavyweight champion of the world, Gene Tunney, who was rumoured to have played George Bernard Shaw;

– the robust (to put it mildly) Rugby Union international Gareth Chilcott (England's answer to The Refrigerator) who claims to thrash all his Oxbridge-educated team mates (at chess, that is);

– the greatest bridge publicist of all time, Ely Culbertson, friend of world champion Emanuel Lasker, and a grateful recipient of chess master Janowsky's money over the card table;

– Jimmy Greaves, soccer wizard and TV sage, who challenged Terry Marsh to a game on *This is Your Life*;

– another multi-talented sportsman, Lord Brabazon of Tara – first Englishman down the Cresta run, first Briton to hold a pilot's licence, and a county standard chess-player (there's now a Brabazon trophy for chess);

– someone else who, like Agdestein and Thomas, scored a strange double is Othmar Egger – he was champion of Birmingham at wrestling and chess at the turn of the century;

– and England's former cricket captain, the man who brought back the Ashes, Mike Gatting, is a chess-player.

Plus Alfredo di Stefano (football); Wally Hammond (cricket); Bobby Jones (golf); Lord Burleigh (track); Mike Powell (long jump); Valery Brumel (high jump); Sergei Bubka (the pole-vault wizard who uses the same psychological coach as Kasparov); Steve Lawson (speed-way); Boris Becker (tennis); Lothar Matthäus, Alan Ball, Rodney Marsh (soccer); Dave Whitcombe (darts); Spurs goalie Erik Thorstvedt, a keen player; Willi Trepp (cycling); Terence Reese and Tobias Stone (bridge) and the whole of the Zurich football team in the sixties, for whom chess was made a compulsory part of their training. (It didn't catch on.)

In 1993 two members of the Oxford United team, Gary Smart and Ceri Evans, took on Kasparov in a charity simul. Guess which Gary won.

♞

Of the commentators, BBC's Mr Boxing, Harry Carpenter, played a World Series of games against his computer. The computer won. Desmond Lynam was a keen schoolboy player and taught his son to play by the time he was four.

Postscript

An outstanding challenger for a high board among the sportsmen is the astonishing Newell M. Banks.

Banks was a draughts (checkers) champion, but embarrassed several chess stars in his career, among them grandmaster Frank Marshall (US champion), and Isaac Kashdan, one of the world's ten best grandmasters in the thirties. Banks was also stunning in simultaneous displays. A typical effort would be 25 games of chess, plus 25 games of draughts, plus 6 blindfold games of draughts.[1] And occasionally he'd have a game of billiards on the side.

But since he was a professional board-games player, we think it wouldn't be fair to include him. The athletes' team is good enough without Banks anyway.[2] For similar reasons we disqualify the legendary Marion Tinsley, probably the greatest draughts-player of all time. Marion once represented the USA at chess, in a fifty-board match against Canada.

The Thinkers

Surprisingly the thinkers (philosophers and mathematicians) have one of the weakest teams of all. Presumably if you spend your time thinking up the General Theory of Relativity or writing *Principia Mathematica* you don't have much time left for rook and pawn endgames.

---

[1] It's nothing to do with chess but in a *45-day* blindfold splurge he took on 1,187 draughts games without sight of the board, and lost only two.
[2] For similar reasons, we exclude the prodigious whist-player, billiards champ and gardener, A. L. H. L. Deschapelles. See page 265.

Certainly Einstein for one was a self-confessed duffer: 'I am no chess-player . . . indeed I have to confess I have always disliked the fierce competitive spirit embodied in that highly intellectual game.' Bertrand Russell gave up chess at eighteen, the better to concentrate on whatever mathematical philosophers concentrate on. Henri Poincaré (1854–1912), one of the most brilliant of all mathematicians, confessed himself a hopeless chess-player.

The father of computer chess and pioneer of machine intelligence, Alan Turing, was so bad that Harry Golombek used to give him a queen start and still beat him.[1] And Ken Thompson, the brain who programmed BELLE, the outstanding chess computer of the early eighties, confessed (shock, horror) he doesn't play chess at all!

Nor, as far as we know, were the great philosophers of history much better. The men whose brains helped bring about the French Revolution for example, were rabbits.

Jean-Jacques Rousseau (who played in a fur hat and cape) determined to master the game by hard study. After months of solitary toil he returned to his favourite café – and one of the finest minds of eighteenth-century France was slaughtered by a humble patzer. It is said that when Jean-Jacques played at the Café de la Régence, crowds used to press up against the windows to watch. It certainly wasn't the quality of his games that attracted them (perhaps it was the fur hat).[2]

Rousseau's fellow encyclopaedist, Denis Diderot, gave up playing and took up watching when he figured he'd never master the game; and Voltaire (who played correspondence chess with Frederick the Great) complained when a 'donkey' called Father Adam beat him

---

[1] Turing merits a place in our First Adjournment for his invention 'round-the-houses' chess, which he played with David Champernowne (an expert on the computer composition of music). After you've made your move, run around the house; if you get back before your opponent has moved, you get another move. Turing was a better runner than a chess-player.
[2] A frequently published brilliancy by Rousseau against the Prince de Conti is believed to be a fake.

ceaselessly. (Voltaire gets on our long list of people who used to knock the pieces over when they lost – see Chapter IV).

So, to boost this sorry lot, we've chucked in the scientists. This makes the thinkers' team respectable, though not unbeatable.

Board one: good old Karl Marx, the strongest philosopher. He played a lot of his chess in London (Holborn and Covent Garden) while writing *Das Kapital*. He was a bad loser (Liebknecht, the German revolutionary, tells how Karl tried to detain him by force when Liebknecht wanted to quit while he was winning) but a good player. Here's a sample:

Karl Marx–Meyer. King's Gambit

1. e4 e5	9. Nc3 Ne7	17. Qe4 d6	25. Qxe6 Ra6
2. f4 exf4	10. Bd2 Nbc6	18. h4 Qg4	26. Rf1 Qg7
3. Nf3 g5	11. Rae1 Qf5	19. Bxf7 Rf8	27. Bg4 Nb8
4. Bc4 g4	12. Nd5 Kd8	20. Bh5 Qg7	28. Rf7
5. O–O gxf3	13. Bc3 Rg8	21. d4 N5c6	Black resigns
6. Qxf3 Qf6	14. Bf6 Bg5	22. c3 a5	
7. e5 Qxe5	15. Bxg5 Qxg5	23. Ne6+ Bxe6	
8. d3 Bh6	16. Nxf4 Ne5	24. Rxf8+ Qxf8	

Next a couple of Nobel Prize winners for chemistry.

Board two, Professor John Cornforth,[1] who in his youth was one of the strongest players in Australia. He once held the Australian blindfold simultaneous record (twelve). When he moved to England he was on the strong Hampstead team of the sixties (with British champ Jonathan Penrose) and regularly played for Middlesex. Here's one of the games from the simul:

J. W. Cornforth–F. F. Kelly, Perth, 1937. Damiano's Defence

1. e4 e5	4. Nf3 d5	7. dxe4 Qxe4	10. Re1 Qg4
2. Nf3 f6	5. d3 Bf5	8. O–O Bd6	11. h3 Qh5
3. Nxe5 Qe7	6. Be2 dxe4	9. Bb5+ Kf8	12. Re8+ Qxe8

[1]His Nobel Prize, if you're interested, was for work on the stereo-chemistry of enzyme-catalysed reactions.

13. Bxe8 Kxe8	16. Bd2 Ne7	19. Nxd6+ cxd6
14. Nc3 a6	17. Re1 Nd7	20. Qxd6
15. Qd5 Bc8	18. Ne4 Rf8	Black resigns

Board three, Sir Robert Robinson, Nobel Prize winner in 1947, Order of Merit 1949, and one of Britain's greatest scientists: Sir Robert was also a chess author, twice Oxfordshire champion and the man who taught Professor Cornforth.

Board four – television star Jacob Bronowski. Bronowski was Yorkshire champion (1936), a published problemist, and a noted player in the London Commercial League. His name is commemorated in the Bronowski Cup, an inter-league competition. Here's Jacob in action:

Dr J. Bronowski–E. W. Harrison, London Commercial League, 1962. Réti Opening

1. Nf3 Nf6	11. Nd5 Nxd5	22. Qxd7+ Kxd7	33. Bg7 Rc8
2. c4 d6	12. cxd5 Nb8	23. dxc6+ bxc6	34. Bc4 Bd2
3. b3 e5	13. Qe3 a6	24. Rxc6 a5	35. d4 Bc3
4. Bb2 Bg4	14. Rc1 Qb5	25. Ra6 Rc8	36. e5 Ke8
5. h3 Bh5	15. O–O f5	26. Ra7+ Rc7	37. d5 Rd8
6. g4 Bg6	16. gxf5 Bxf5	27. Rxc7+ Kxc7	38. Bf6 Rb8
7. Bg2 Nc6	17. Nxe5 dxe5	28. Bd5 Rd8	39. d6
8. Nc3 Be7	18. Qxe5 Qd7	29. e4 g6	Black resigns
9. d3 Qd7	19. Rxc7+ Qxc7	30. f4 Rf8	
10. Qd2	20. Rc1 Nc6	31. Kg2 Kd7	
O–O–O	21. Qxf5+ Qd7	32. Kg3 Bb4	

And here's a Bronowski problem:

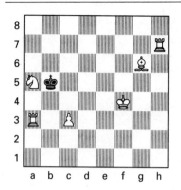

British Chess Magazine, 1970
(Solution at end of section.)

Mate in 3.

Professor Lionel Penrose, who gets in at board five, played board one for Cambridge University and on a high board for Essex and was a skilled problemist. To scientists he's the world-famous geneticist: but chess-players know him best as the father of Jonathan Penrose, ten times British champion.

The only pure mathematician to make the thinkers' team goes in at board six. Abraham de Moivre was a seventeenth-century pioneer in probability theory, and the man called in to settle the Leibniz–Newton squabble about who invented differential calculus. But mathematics didn't pay enough; so de Moivre became a chess professional.[1] Like Roget, and that much greater mathematician, Leonard Euler, he published solutions to the Knight's Tour (see our section, 'Desert Island Chess').

Erich Ernest Zepler arrived in England with practically nothing in 1935, a refugee from the Nazis. By 1949 he had become a leading international expert on electronics, and Britain's first professor of electronics (at Southampton). He also found time to become one of the world's most eminent problemists (International Master of Composition, 1973). A Hampshire county player, he gets into the team on board seven.

---

[1]Irrelevant but interesting is how de Moivre met his death. He vowed to sleep a quarter of an hour more each successive night. This worked fine until he'd got up to $23\frac{3}{4}$ hours – after which, you guessed it, he died in his sleep.

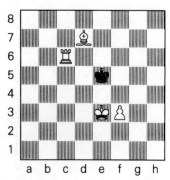

On board eight, another problemist. Wolfgang Pauly was one of the greatest problem composers who ever lived. In private life he was an actuary and an astronomer (he discovered comet 1898VII). If you're feeling sharp, have a go at this:

W. Pauly, *Deutsche Schachblätter*, 1924

Mate in 5.

See end of section for solution.

That's the thinkers' team. You may be thinking we've put Karl Marx on too high a board – but we imagine the thinkers would be cute enough to juggle the board order to give them wins over stronger teams.

First reserve might well be TV supernova, starwatcher Patrick Moore. Not a lot of people know it, but Patrick was a founder of the East Grinstead Chess Club and represented Sussex at chess. Here's a game:

Revd C. Dinwoodie–P. Moore, 1960. Nimzo-Larsen Attack

1. b3 e5	10. e3 Qe5	19. Kg3 Be2	29. a4 Re4
2. Bb2 Nc6	11. d4 Bxc3 +	20. Bxe2 Qxe2	29. Rf3 Rhe8
3. Nf3 e4	12. Ke2 Qb5 +	21. Rh3 Qg4 +	30. f5 Rxh4 +
4. Nd4 Nxd4	13. Kf3 Qf5 +	22. Kh2 O–O–O	31. Kg3 g5
5. Bxd4 Nf6	14. Ke2 Bxa1	23. Qc3 Qd7	32. f6 Rhe4
6. Nc3 c6	15. Qxa1 Qxc2 +	24. Qc5 Qd6 +	33. Kf2 g4
7. Bxf6 Qxf6	16. Kf3 d5	25. f4 Qxc5	34. Rf5 h4
8. Nxe4 Qd4	17. a3 h5	26. dxc5 Rde8	White resigns
9. Nc3 Bb4	18. h4 Bg4 +	27. Rg3 g6	

As we write this, Patrick is winning a postal game from one of the authors of this book. Perhaps we should promote him in the thinkers' board order.

Alongside Patrick, we place one of Russia's greatest scientists. Dmitri Mendeleyev, when he wasn't busy discovering the periodicity of the elements, was an avid player and student of the game. He claimed it refreshed his mind after hard study.

Among the other reserves we have: astonomer Fred Hoyle (he played for Cambridge in the inter-varsity match – maybe he should be on the team); Erasmus (who played chess while standing up and wisecracking); Newton; Gauss; Machiavelli (after he was banished by the Medici, chess was his solace); Wittgenstein (his writings are spattered with chess analogies); Lord Keynes (his father was a strong Cambridge player); Francis Bacon; the great mathematicians Leibniz ('People's ingenuity is best revealed at chess') and Euler; philosopher A. J. Ayer (who once won a friendly match with Tony Benn); Professor C. E. M. Joad, nationally famous in the forties on the BBC's *Brains Trust,* was a county player, and once won a game of living chess against a bus conductor; and one of the men who first split the atom, another Nobel Prize winner: Sir Frederick Soddy. Soddy played in the Oxford–Cambridge match around the same time as those two reprobates Aleister Crowley and Harold Davidson (see 'The Sinners'). Professor Robin Matthews, formerly Master of Clare College and economic guru of the SDP, is one of the world's leading three-move problemists. Professor Hans Eysenck loses regularly to his nine-year-old grandson, William (but William suspects his grandad may be throwing the odd game); Stephen Hawking plays chess with his sons. And George Steiner, philosopher and chess writer, may have been overstating the case when he said (in an article in the *Independent*): 'The poets lie about the orgasm, compared to the crescendo of triumph in chess.'

Finally, hats off to the sixteenth-century physicist Girolamo Cardano, gambler and founder of probability theory. He may have invented the Cardan transmission in mechanics, but what earns him a place in the chess Hall of Fame is that he was the bloke who invented the method of shading the black squares in chess diagrams.

Solution to the Bronowski problem:

1. Nb7 Kc4 2. Rh6 *or* 1. . . . Kb6 2. c4 *or* 1. . . . Kc6 2. Ra6 +

Solution to the Pauly problem:

1. Bc8 Kd5	3. Rg6 Kf5	5. f4 mate
2. Bb7 Ke5	4. Be4 + Ke5	

The Politicians

The squabbling over board order would be endless, but if you could get them to stop talking and start playing, the politicians would have a pretty good team.

Here's a future British prime minister (playing white) knocking off a sparkling miniature against the chess editor of the *Observer*:

11 Downing Street, *c.* 1920. Ruy López

1. e4 e5	6. Nxd4 Nd6	11. Bh6 d5	15. Bf8)
2. Nf3 Nc6	7. Re1 + Be7	12. Qxf8 + Kd7	
3. Bb5 Nf6	8. Qg4 Nxd4	13. Qxf7 Kd6	
4. O–O Nxe4	9. Qxd4 Nxb5	14. Rxe7 Black	
5. d4 exd4	10. Qxg7 Rf8	resigns (if Qxe7	

That was Andrew Bonar Law, throwing off the cares of office, against Brian Harley. Bonar Law was easily the best of our prime ministers. There's a Capablanca versus Bonar Law (and friends) game in Dale Brandreth's *The Unknown Capablanca*. In its obituary, the *British Chess Magazine* described Law as 'an attacking player full of energy and resource'. Lady Thatcher doesn't play at all (though she opened the Kasparov–Karpov world championship in 1986), but Lord Callaghan (who closed it) does. Jim, a computer chess addict, was zapped in ten moves by Gazza Kasparov in 1993. The Marquess of Rockingham, Sir Robert Peel, the younger Pitt, Gladstone, Disraeli, Balfour, Asquith, Churchill and Attlee all did. Prime Minister Campbell-Bannerman called chess 'not a game, but a disease'. John Major was taught by his father (the now celebrated tightrope-walker and garden-gnome manufacturer).

♖

Churchill is one of the great might-have-beens of chess. He learned at prep school in Hove: 'Dear Mamma . . . do not forget to get the set of chess for me. I should like the board to be red and white, not black and white . . .' said a letter from the twelve-year-old Winston. By the time he was twenty-one he was beginning to show signs of addiction. A letter from Bombay told how he'd reached the semi-finals of a shipboard tournament and continued . . . 'I shall try and get really good when I am in India.' But other distractions occupied the great man and he never fulfilled his early promise. We do know that Winston played a game against the most mysterious of British Ladies' champions, Miss Fatima. She was unimpressed. After Fatima won the title, she returned to India, retired from chess and virtually disappeared. In 1989, in her eighties, she was rediscovered by a British television crew working in the Punjab. The only later record of Churchill we have is of a game with Asquith before which Winston gave vent to his bizarre battle cry: 'Marshal your Baldwins!' (Churchillian slang for pawns.)

♖

The American presidents are less well represented. Washington played. And Thomas Jefferson was keen enough to copy down the whole of Philidor's analysis of rook versus rook and bishop, in a notebook. The fifth president, James Monroe, kept an English fine bone china set on display in his office. President Harding played a bit (but preferred draughts) and Teddy Roosevelt played the automaton, Ajeeb. Abe Lincoln (according to the *American Chess Magazine*, 1898) was 'a really skilful devotee'. Evidence of Abe's superhuman good nature is that when, in the middle of a serious game with a judge, his young son, Tad, kicked the board over, Lincoln calmly remarked, 'I guess that's Tad's game.' Jimmy Carter and his wife Rosalynn played; Jimmy taught his son, who became quite a good player.

Here's a game by Woodrow Wilson.

W. Wilson–S. Langleben, Buffalo, 1898. Queen's Gambit

1. Nf3 d5	5. Nc3 Nc6	9. Be2 Bd6	13. d5 Nd4
2. d4 Bf5	6. a3 a6	10. Nh4 Bg6	14. Nxg6 Nxf3+
3. e3 Nf6	7. b4 dxc4	11. Bf3 Qd7	15. Qxf3 fxg6
4. c4 e6	8. Bxc4 b5	12. e4 e5	16. Bb2 O–O

17. O–O? Nxd5	25. Rxd2 Rb8	33. Qd2 Rc8	41. Qb6+ Ne6
18. Qg3 Nf4	26. Rd7 Bb6	34. Ne3 Bxe3	42. Qg1 Rb3
19. Rad1 Qe7	27. Qd2 Be3	35. Qxe3 Rc2	43. Qd1 Nd4
20. Rd2 c6	28. Qc2 Nh3!	36. Bd2 Rb2	44. f4 Rxg3
21. Rfd1 Rad8	29. Nd1 Bb6	37. g3 Rb1+	45. fxe5+ Kxe5
22. f3 Bc7	30. Qxc6 Nf4	38. Bc1 Qh3	White resigns
23. Qf2 Qg5	31. Qc2 h6	39. Rxg7+! Kxg7	
24. Kh1 Rxd2	32. Bc1 Qh4	40. Qa7+ Kf6	

♖

Lenin, like Marx, was a keen player but a bad loser.[1] He didn't play much after the Revolution but whilst in exile he was so preoccupied with correspondence chess that he raved about it in his sleep. If you're in Paris, check Metro Alésia – that's where Lenin used to play, at a café on the corner of the Avenue d'Orléans and the Place Montrouge.

♖

Boris Yeltsin was the founder of Sverdlovsk Chess Club; he persuaded his friend Anatoly Karpov to open it. And one of his main opponents, Ruslan Khasbulatov, the speaker of the Russian parliament, is an enthusiastic player.

♖

Here's our team. We elect J. Stalin (a non-player[2] but a world-class disciplinarian) captain of an ill-assorted bunch in which the forces of the left have the edge over those of the right:

Board one, one of the strongest players of the 1850s, Marmaduke Wyvill, Tory MP for Richmond, Yorkshire. He was good enough to take two games off the great Adolf Anderssen in the London 1851 tournament (Wyvill was second to Adolf). Here he is, carving up the world's best player:

---

[1] Maxim Gorky records, 'He got peeved and depressed when he lost.' Don't we all?
[2] A Stalin game featured in various publications is a hoax. 'Comrade Stalin is a very busy man, but if he ever found time to play he would reveal strategic judgement of the very highest order' was what Soviet diplomats used to say of their boss.

A. Anderssen–M. Wyvill, London, 1851. Sicilian Defence

1. e4 c5	12. Rf3 c5	23. Qh4 Qd7	34. Bc4 Rc2
2. d4 cxd4	13. Rh3 Rf7	24. Rd1 Rc8	35. Ke1 Rxd2
3. Nf3 Nc6	14. b3 g6	25. Be2 h5	36. Rxd2 Qg1+
4. Nxd4 e6	15. Nf3 Nb6	26. Rg3 Qe8	37. Bf1 Rc7
5. Be3 Nf6	16. Bf2 d4	27. Rd2 Rg7	38. Rd1 Rc2
6. Bd3 Be7	17. Bh4 Nd5	28. c3 Ne3	39. Qg3 Ba6
7. O-O O-O-O	18. Qd2 a5	29. cxd4 cxd4	40. Qf3 Bxf1
8. Nd2 d5	19. Bxe7 Rxe7	30. Rxd4 Rc1+	White resigns
9. Nxc6 bxc6	20. Ng5 Ne3	31. Kf2 Nd5	
10. e5 Nd7	21. Qf2 Bb7	32. Rgd3 Qc6	
11. f4 f5	22. Bf1 Ng4	33. Rd2 Qb6	

♟

Board two, Lithuanian President Vitautis Landsbergis, was master strength. Before he gave up chess for politics Landsbergis scored draws against Soviet stars Simagin, Mikenas, Suetin and, notably, future world champion Petrosian. Here's his game against Suetin from the Soviet team championship:

V. Landsbergis–A. Suetin, Lvov, 1951. Sicilian Defence

1. e4 c5	12. Qg3 Rfd8	23. Bb6 Rc8	34. Ke1 Bxc3+
2. Nf3 d6	13. Nxc6 bxc6	24. Bxa6 Rc6	35. Kxf2 Bxa1
3. d4 cxd4	14. e5 Nd5	25. Rfb1 Rh6+	36. Bxd5 Bxd5
4. Nxd4 Nf6	15. Nxd5 cxd5	26. Kg1 Rbxb6	37. Rxd5 Kxf7
5. Nc3 a6	16. Bd3 Rab8	27. axb6 Bc5+	38. Kf3 Ke6
6. Be2 e6	17. Kh1 dxe5	28. Kf1 Bxb6	39. Ke4 h5
7. O-O Be7	18. fxe5 f5	29. Bb7 Rf6+	40. Ra5 Bd4
8. f4 Qc7	19. exf6 Qxg3	30. Ke1 Bf2+	41. Ra6+ Kf7
9. Be3 O-O	20. f7+ Kf8	31. Kd2 Be6	42. Kf3 Bc5
10. a4 Nc6	21. hxg3 Rxb2	32. Rb5 Bd4	Draw agreed
11. Qe1 Bd7	22. a5 e5	33. c3 Rf2+	

♟

Board three, Josip Broz Tito. Tito learned chess as a boy, and found time, whilst raising hell against the Nazis as a Yugoslav partisan, to play the occasional game. He rose to Yugoslav candidate master standard. When the Russians queried his prowess at chess, he offered to take on the whole of the Soviet Praesidium in a simul. Nothing further was heard from the USSR. At the 1950 Dubrovnik Olympiad, the Marshal played a game *hors concours*.

♜

Board four, János Kádár, leader of the Hungarian Communist Party, and also a candidate master.

♜

Board five, former Birmingham MP Julius Silverman. Julius, the man who carried out the investigations into the Birmingham riots, was for many years the strongest chess-playing MP. He played in international tournaments in the thirties and won (among others) a spectacular game against Eliskases, who at the time was one of the world's best players:

J. Silverman–E. Eliskases, Birmingham, 1937. King's Gambit

1. e4 e5	7. Bb3 Bd6	13. Qe2 d4	19. Bxf7+ Kh8
2. f4 exf4	8. O–O O–O	14. Nd5 Bxd5	20. Qxh7+
3. Bc4 Nf6	9. d4 Be6	15. Bxd5 Ne3	Black resigns
4. Nc3 c6	10. Ne5 Bxe5	16. Bxe3 dxe3	
5. Nf3 d5	11. dxe5 Qb6+	17. Rxf4 Nc6	
6. exd5 cxd5	12. Kh1 Ng4	18. Qh5 Qxb2	

♜

Board six, Bonar Law, an example of whose play we saw above. Law was good at most indoor games but brilliant at chess. Grandmaster Mieses rated him as one of the best amateur players he'd met. (But we saw in 'The Musicians' how he met his match against old Walter Parratt.)

♜

Board seven, at the opposite end of the political spectrum: Che Guevara. Che and Fidel Castro played together in the mountains during the revolution, but Che was by far the better player. He played in Cuban tournaments and had a number of casual games against British IM Bob Wade. Bob rates him highly: 'about 180 to 200 grading' he says – which would get him into most English county sides. This is Che drawing a simultaneous game against Grandmaster Najdorf:

M. Najdorf–Che Guevara, Havana, 1962. Ruy López

1. e4 e5	6. Re1 b5	11. Nbd2 Bf8	16. Be3 Be6
2. Nf3 Nc6	7. Bb3 d6	12. d5 Ne7	Draw agreed
3. Bb5 a6	8. c3 O–O	13. c4 bxc4	(but Ba4 is
4. Ba4 Nf6	9. h3 h6	14. Nxc4 c6	winning for
5. O–O Be7	10. d4 Re8	15. dxc6 Nxc6	White)

Board eight, Edmund Dell, Secretary of State for Trade and Industry under Harold Wilson, former chairman of Channel Four and 1937 London under-eighteen champion (at fifteen). Dell played individual games against grandmaster Tartakower, and drew a game in a twenty-five board simul against grandmaster Reshevsky (the other twenty-four lost). After beating the University of Oxford captain 2–0 Dell quit chess until, in 1977, he was challenged to a game whilst leading a British government trade delegation in Moscow. His opponent: Deputy Prime Minister Kirillin, Head of the Soviet Academy of Sciences and friend of Smyslov and Petrosian. The result, an honourable 1–1 draw. Here's the young Dell *en route* to the London under-eighteen title:

E. Dell–N. A. Phillips, 1937. Queen's Gambit Declined

1. d4 e6	12. Qb3 dxc4	23. Qb3 Kf7	34. Rxd7 Rxd7
2. c4 Nf6	13. Qxc4 Nd5	24. Qxb5 Rab8	35. Qg4 Re7
3. Nc3 c6	14. b4 Nxb4	25. Qd3 Qxa2	36. Qg6+ Ke6
4. Bg5 d5	15. O–O Nxd3	26. Rbc1 Re7	37. Qxe4+ Kf7
5. e3 Be7	16. Rxd3 Bd7	27. h3 Rd8	38. Qg6+ Ke6
6. Nf3 h6	17. Rb1 b5	28. Rc7 Rdd7	39. Qg4+ Kf7
7. Bh4 Bb4	18. Qc2 O–O	29. Rc8 Rd6	40. Rc6 Qb1+
8. Rc1 Bxc3+	19. Ne5 Be8	30. h4 e5	41. Kh2 Qe4
9. Rxc3 Nbd7	20. Rc3 f6	31. h5 e4	42. Qxe4
10. Bd3 Qa5	21. Nxc6 Bxc6	32. Qd1 Rd5	and White
11. Bxf6 Nxf6	22. Rxc6 Rfe8	33. R1c7 Rdd7	won

First reserve, the man who's probably done more for world chess than anyone: Nikolai Krylenko, first Bolshevik Commissar for War. A much feared man, his one contribution to civilization was to persuade the new Soviet state to popularize chess. He once played a game against Arthur Ransome – we don't know who won – and wrote a book on the 1935 Moscow tournament.

♖

Other political contenders: Michael Foot, once one of the strongest players in the House of Commons, Charles James Fox (like Lenin he couldn't sleep for thinking about chess), Willy Brandt, Johannes Vorster (he learned as a Second World War detainee, and was an avid collector of chess sets); Cyrus Vance (who was on the 1990 world championship organizing committee), Lord (Douglas) Jay (who played in a 1991 simul at Longleat), MP Stan Orme (played at Hastings), Cory Aquino (scored a diplomatic three-move draw against Kasparov in 1992), Armenian President Levon Ter-Petrosian, Angela Eagle (joint British Girls' under-eighteen champion in 1976, she's now replaced Foot as the strongest player in the House of Commons), Armithalingam Thileepan (who, in case you didn't know, led the Liberation Tigers of Tamil and was once champion of Jaffna), David, Lord Owen (a visitor to the Fischer–Spassky match in Yugoslavia), Michel Noir, the charismatic Mayor of Lyons (he used to be 170 strength), Yasser Arafat (who, according to the *Independent*, loves jogging, chess and Mickey Mouse), Jan Masaryk, Robespierre, Rowland Hill (who gave us the penny post), Ho Chi Minh (who wrote a poem about chess and played in the jungle when he wasn't fighting the Americans), four times Mayor of New York Fiorello La Guardia (he played Tito, but said 'I am absolutely the worst player in the world. Nobody approaches me.'), Leon Trotsky, Vice-President Spiro T. Agnew (not a bad player apparently), Henry Kissinger, Sir Clement Freud, Valéry Giscard d'Estaing, Gamal Abdul Nasser, Fidel Castro (to whom grandmaster Petrosian ceded a diplomatic draw); and President Marcos of the Philippines (ditto against Bobby Fischer). Tony Benn once won a game off philosopher A. J. Ayer (but lost several more). Harold Lever, Cabinet Minister under Wilson, played Korchnoi in a simul. Enoch Powell went to the same school as British champions Hugh Alexander and Tony Miles, but it didn't catch – he played as a boy, then gave up.

Here's an unimpressive Castro game:

Filiberto Terrazas–Fidel Castro, Havana, 1966. King's Gambit

1. e4 e5	6. c3 Ba5	11. Qa4+ Nc6	16. c7+ Bd7
2. f4 exf4	7. Bxf4 g5	12. d5 Bd8	17. c8=Q Rxc8
3. Nf3 Bd6	8. Bg3 Qe7	13. dxc6 b5	18. Qd4 gxf3
4. d4 h6	9. Be2 d6	14. Qxb5 a6	19. Qxh8 Qxe2
5. e5 Bb4+	10. exd6 cxd6	15. Qa4 g4	mate

♖

Here's a game between Czech president and playwright Vaclav Havel and Bessel Kok, Chairman of the G.M.A. (Grandmaster's Association):

Havel–Kok, Prague, 1990. Queen's Pawn Game

1. d4 d5	7. Qe2 Bb4	13. a3 Ba5	19. Bc4 Qf5
2. e3 Nf6	8. Bd2 O–O	14. e4 dxe4	20. Rd4 c5
3. Nf3 Bg4	9. O–O–O e5	15. Nxe4 Nxe4	21. Rg5 Black
4. h3 Bxf3	10. dxe5 Nxe5	16. Bxa5 Qxa5	resigns
5. gxf3 Nc6	11. f4 Ned7	17. Qxe4 Nf6	
6. Nc3 e6	12. Rg1 c6	18. Qe7 Rab8	

Both players received expert help: Kok was seconded by Kavalek (now Short's second) and Havel by Krizan, one of his advisers and an avid player.

♖

For coolness under fire, we give a special mention to Israeli prime minister Menachem Begin. In September 1940 he was playing chess with his wife, when Russian soldiers burst into his house to arrest him. As they dragged him away, he shouted back to Mrs Begin: 'I resign! I resign!'

♖

In 1992 Kasparov played a simul in the House of Commons against, among others, Tam Dalyell, Michael Fallon, Lord (Christopher) Mayhew, Emma Nicholson and Jeremy Hanley. Here's the Hanley game:

Hanley–Kasparov, Simultaneous Display, London, 1989. Sicilian Defence

1. e4 c5	3. Qxd4 Nc6	5. Nf3 Bg7	7. Nbd2 Nf6
2. d4 cxd4	4. Qd1 g6	6. Bd3 d6	8. O–O O–O

9. h3 d5	17. Qxd3 Bxd3	25. Rxb7 a6	33. Rd6 Ra2
10. exd5 Nxd5	18. Rfd1 Rfd8	26. a4 h5	34. Kf1 Rxa4
11. Ne4 Ndb4	19. Rd2 Bc4	27. Bc5 e6	35. g4 a5
12. Nc3 Nxd3	20. Rad1 Rxd2	28. Rb6 h4	36. Rc6 Ra1 +
13. cxd3 Bf5	21. Rxd2 Be6	29. g4 hxg3	37. Be1 Bh4
14. Ne1 Nb4	22. Nd5 Bxd5	30. fxg3 Rc8	White resigns
15. Be3 Nxd3	23. Rxd5 Bxb2	31. Bf2 Rc1 +	
16. Nxd3 Qxd3	24. Rd7 Bf6	32. Kg2 Rc2	

♜

Former German Chancellor Helmut Schmidt's sixtieth birthday presents included: a chess computer from the Friedrich-Ebert Institute, a porcelain chess-set from Giscard d'Estaing, and some antiquarian chess books from Foreign Minister Hans-Dietrich Genscher.

♜

Ben Franklin, co-author of the Declaration of Independence, was an addict. He, author of an essay on chess morals, used his skill at the game to gain access to the boudoirs of numerous French ladies while he was American Ambassador in Paris. Among his conquests was Madame Brillon de Juoy, the thirty-year-old wife of the Receiver-General of Trusts of the French parliament. He beat her six–nil. Next day they played a return match of several hours' duration while she soaked in her bath-tub (at least, that's what they told her husband).

Another female adversary was the Duchess of Bourbon. She missed a check; so Franklin captured her king. 'We do not take kings like that,' she protested. 'We do in America,' replied Ben.

In 1781 Franklin visited the Café de la Régence and secured the autograph of the then world champion, André Philidor. 'Never knew he was a chess player,' was Phil's comment.

♜

We couldn't find much about the leading Nazi politicians and chess. Hitler made a reference to 'dog lovers and members of chess clubs' in a 1933 speech: and in 1941 he was presented with a chess set, filched from the Croat National History Museum, by Ante Pavelić, the Croat Quisling. We know Adolf was a dog-lover; was he perhaps a chess-player?

♖

The unspeakable Hans Frank, Governor-General of Poland after 1939, was a chess-player. He founded a chess college, and in 1941 played four games against former world championship contender Bogoljubow and a partner. We don't know how good Frank's chess was, but he certainly knew how to pick allies: *his* consultation partner was the world champion, Alekhine.

Bogoljubow and Stolzyk (?)–Alekhine & Frank, Warsaw, 1941. Queen's Gambit Declined

1. d4 d5	13. dxe5 Ne4	25. gxf5 dxe3	37. Bd3 g5
2. c4 e6	14. Bxe7 Qxe7	26. Bh5 b5	38. Kc3 h5
3. Nf3 Nf6	15. f4 Nxc3	27. Kf1 Be4	39. Kd4 h4
4. Bg5 Nbd7	16. bxc3 f6	28. Ke2 Bxf5	40. Ke3 Kf8
5. e3 Be7	17. Qh5 fxe5	29. a3 a5	41. Kd4 Kg7
6. Nc3 O–O	18. fxe5 Rxf1+	30. Kxe3 b4	42. Kc3 Be6
7. Rc1 h6	19. Rxf1 Rf8	31. axb4 axb4	43. Kd4 g4
8. Bh4 b6	20. Rxf8+ Kxf8	32. Kd4 Be6	44. Kc3 Kh6
9. cxd5 exd5	21. Bg6 Qe6	33. Bg6 Ke7	45. Kd4 Kg5
10. Bd3 Bb7	22. g4 d4	34. Kc5 b3	46. Be4 Bf5
11. O–O c5	23. cxd4 cxd4	35. Kb4 Bf7	White resigns
12. Ne5 Nxe5	24. Qf5+ Qxf5	36. Bf5 g6	

Alekhine said that Frank had one of the best chess libraries he'd ever seen.

Four years after this game Frank was still playing chess – while in captivity at Mondorf, awaiting his trial and eventual execution by the Allies.

♖

The traitor William Joyce (Lord Haw-Haw) played chess in his cell in Wandsworth to take his mind off his impending execution. 'He concentrated on his moves without the least sign of strain,' said an observer.

Postscript

For a century, the only game permitted in the Palace of Westminster was chess. But, alas, on 17 April 1987, *The Times* reported that 'because of the diminishing number of MPs with the time or inclination for chess' the hallowed chess room was to be thrown open for games of chance 'from mah-jong to poker'. Ghastly.

The Soldiers

In the Café de la Régence, for a hundred years, there was a table with a brass plaque saying 'Napoleon Bonaparte used to play chess at this table'. What it didn't say is that the greatest military tactician in history was a pretty rotten player. George Walker, the chess historian, reckons he could have given Bonaparte a rook start (and George was no grandmaster). His contemporaries said Napoleon was too impatient, too given to impetuous attacks. But he did love the game. Even at the height of his great campaigns, when he was making mincemeat of the best generals in Europe, he took time off to get thrashed by his own generals[1] over the chessboard.

Later, after his coronation, he started to win more games. But that's because his opponents had become, shall we say, more tactful;[2] the Emperor was getting a reputation as a bad-tempered loser. Walker reports that he was 'sore and irritable' after a defeat; and as you'll see in Chapter VIII, when Maelzel's automaton beat him, Napoleon knocked the pieces to the floor.

Another annoying habit he picked up around this time was a rabid insistence on the touch and move rule – for his opponents only. When *he* wanted to take a move back, Napoleon acted like an emperor.

Here's a game that Napoleon is supposed to have won against a good player, the beautiful Madame de Rémusat. The historically minded will be interested to know that the game happened the night before the young Duc d'Enghien was executed.

[1] Murat, Berthier, Beauharnais.
[2] All except his foreign minister Talleyrand. He regularly beat the Emperor. Perhaps that's why Napoleon once described him as a silk stocking full of dung.

'Mme de Rémusat'–'Napoleon Bonaparte', Paris, 1802. Alekhine's
Defence

1. e4 Nf6	5. Nc3 Nfg4	9. Ke2 Nxd4+	13. Kd5 Qd6
2. d3 Nc6	6. d4 Qh4+	10. Kd3 Ne5+	mate
3. f4 e5	7. g3 Qf6	11. Kxd4 Bc5+	
4. fxe5 Nxe5	8. Nh3 Nf3+	12. Kxc5 Qb6+	

You will have noticed the use of the word 'supposed' in the above
paragraph: modern authorities reckon that all published Napoleon
victories are fakes.

After Waterloo, Bonaparte continued his chessboard battles in
exile; and his loyal staff still continued to let the ex-emperor win.

What neither he nor they knew was that his chess-pieces may have
hidden a most poignant secret. According to an article in the
London *Morning Post* of 1928 (about an exhibition of Napoleonic
relics) a French officer was despatched to St Helena with a chess-set
in ivory and mother-of-pearl. He was to tell Napoleon that inside
some of the pieces were secret compartments containing an escape
plan. The officer was killed by a falling spar on board ship; Napoleon
accepted the set, played with it to the end of his days – but never
discovered the plans.

The next most famous chess-playing general was the hero of Alamein,
Viscount Montgomery. He gave up the game on being beaten by his
nine-year-old son. Another World War Two hero, General Sir Claude
Auchinleck, was also a keen player.

The British colonel, Rall, played chess. Perhaps it cost us the American
colonies.

On Christmas Day, 1776, George Washington was preparing his
troops to attack the British at Trenton across the Delaware River.
An Englishman who lived nearby sent his son with a note to Colonel
Rall, warning him of the danger. Rall, immersed in a game of chess,
took the note and put it, unopened, in his pocket.

Next day Washington attacked, and the Americans won their first
great victory. Colonel Rall was killed, and the note discovered in his
pocket. His game of chess marked the turning in the tide of the
colonists' fortunes.

That brilliant tactician Robert E. Lee, commander of the Confederate armies, had his own travelling chess-set and was an enthusiastic player. So was one of his most formidable opponents, General McClellan.

Field Marshal von Moltke, the renowned Prussian military strategist, was an excellent player. He recorded his best games in his diary.

America's General Pershing carried a pocket chess-set with him during the First World War.

Captain Sir Basil Liddell Hart was perhaps Britain's greatest military historian and strategist; his chess strategy was poor though. Arthur Ransome said of him, 'He dashes into attack in a Churchill manner with insufficient concentration of forces.' Another of his opponents (and a friend of Montgomery) was Bernard Levin (see 'The Writers').

Not a soldier, but a chess-playing sailor was the unfortunate[1] Admiral Byng. All we know of his prowess is a loss to the exquisitely named Don Scipione del Grotto, champion of the Naples Academy.

The Aristocrats

Sergei Semyenevich Urusov was a Russian prince and one of the strongest players of the mid-nineteenth century. He invented a gambit (1. e4 e5 2. Bc4 Nf6 3. d4 exd4 4. Nf3), played innumerable games with Tolstoy, and during the siege of Sebastopol tried to win a battle by chess. The Russians and the English had been disputing the same ridge of ground for weeks with great losses and no result. Prince Sergei went to his commanding officer with a novel suggestion: let

[1] He was the chap who got shot, *'pour encourager les autres'*, for failing to take Minorca in 1756.

the English pick their best player and the two of them would play for the ridge. The general was entranced by the romantic idea but turned it down on the reasonable grounds that even if Urusov won, they couldn't be sure the English would keep their bargain.

The exotically named Prince Dadian of Mingrelia (it's between the Black Sea and the Caucasus, if you didn't know) belongs, strictly speaking, in the chapter on unacceptable behaviour.

Dadian decided early on that rather than spend his life flogging serfs and looking after the family estates, he'd much rather hang out on the Riviera and become a famous chess-player. The only flaw in this plan was a lack of genius for the game. But when your family owns most of Mingrelia there's always a way. Dadian's ingenious solution to the problem was to pay impecunious chess-masters (in those days, they mostly were) for brilliancies which he'd publish as his own. Here's a very brief brevity which he may or may not have sired.

Dadian–Doubrava, Kiev, 1896. Modern Defence (?)

1. e4 d6	5. Bxf7+ Nxf7
2. Bc4 Nd7	6. Ne6 Black
3. Nf3 g6	resigns
4. Ng5 Nh6	

In 1903 the prince helped create a memorable piece of chess history. Miffed by Chigorin's refusal to sell him a sparkler, he banned the great master from the Monte Carlo tournament of that year. This left him a man short; so the Prince persuaded one of his mates, Colonel Moreau, to make up the numbers. For the appalling details of how the Colonel staggered from anonymity to immortality in one tournament see our chapter 'The Frightful'.

There are lots more aristocrats in early chess history.[1] But since most of them got famous for aggro with a chessboard, and since you read enough about that under 'The Royals', we'll mention just a few more.

---

[1] E.g. Charles d'Orléans, who spent twenty-five years after the Battle of Agincourt in captivity, playing chess and writing poetry about it.

The Duke of Brunswick and Count Isouard de Vauvenargue get into the history books for just one game – and that they lost. It's the best-known game in all chess history, and it was played against the tragic American genius Paul Morphy in 1858. The conditions of play were unusual: Morphy had been invited to the Paris Opera to see a performance (*Norma*, say most authorities).[1] The game was played in a box. Whether the opera was being performed at the time is not clear, but the game itself is a sizzler. It's in every collection of great games, but just in case you've missed it, see our Chapter II.

♛

Duke Huon of Bordeaux played for one night of love with a princess. Huon was a guest at the court of a Muslim ruler (King Ivoryn), and, boasting of his prowess at chess and love-making, was challenged to play the king's daughter. If he won he got the daughter for a night, plus a hundred marks. If he lost, he lost his head. The game must have been pretty exciting, although the princess seems not to have been trying too hard ('I wolde this game were at an end, so that I were in bed with him all nyght'). Huon won the game, and chivalrously declined the girl – much to her intense annoyance ('Yf I had knowne that thou woldest a refused my company, I wold have mated the'). (From a thirteenth-century French romance.)

The Businessmen

You'd think life was too short for anyone to become both a chess-master and a millionaire, but a couple of bright sparks managed it.

Ignac Kolisch, one of the best players in the world in the 1860s, always had an eye peeled for the green stuff; when he won the great Paris tournament of 1867, his prize, from Napoleon III, was a magnificent Sevres vase; he sold it instantly for 4,000 francs which he invested in property. The year after that he met Baron Albert

---

[1] But not all. David Lawson, Morphy's biographer, was certain it was *The Barber of Seville*.

Rothschild – himself a strong player.[1] Rothschild, impressed with Ignac's financial wizardry, found a novel way of helping him. The baron played the chess-master a match for a thousand pounds. Kolisch won of course, and was off on a dazzling financial career. Helped by the Rothschilds, he set up as a banker. Within nine years he'd made his first million, and a year after that became a baron. Perhaps the moral is, if you want to become a millionaire, give up chess.[2] Here's Kolisch beating the writers' board two, Turgenev:

Turgenev–Kolisch, *c.* 1870. Two Knights' Defence

1. e4 e5	7. Nf3 e4	13. Kd1 Re8	19. Bc1 Qxg2
2. Nf3 Nc6	8. Qe2 Nxc4	14. Qf3 Bxd2	20. Rf1 and Black
3. Bc4 Nf6	9. dxc4 Bc5	15. Nxd2 c6	mates in 2
4. Ng5 d5	10. Nfd2 O–O	16. b3 cxd5	
5. exd5 Na5	11. h3 e3	17. Bb2 Ne4	
6. d3 h6	12. fxe3 Bxe3	18. c5 Qg5	

♟

Someone who didn't give up chess and managed nevertheless to be a millionaire is German grandmaster Lothar Schmid. Lothar was chief arbiter at the Fischer–Spassky match (1972) and at the 1986 Kasparov–Karpov match. Herr Schmid made a fortune in publishing[3] and yet managed to become one of Western Europe's best players in the sixties. He used his money to create the largest private chess library in the world.

[1]He was a pupil of world champion Steinitz. Here's a Rothschild game against a player of master strength:

A. Clerc–Rothschild, Paris (Casual Game), 1884. King's Gambit

1. e4 e5	8. h4 g4	15. Kh3 g2	21. Qxf6+ Ne7
2. f4 exf4	9. Nh2 f3	16. Rg1 h5	22. Be3 Rxh6+!
3. Nf3 g5	10. gxf3 g3	17. g5 Nh6!!	23. Qxh6 Qh1+
4. Bc4 Bg7	11. Ng4 Qxh4	18. gxh6 Bf6	24. Kg3 Qxh6
5. d4 d6	12. Kg2 Bxg4	19. Qxh5? Qxg1	25. Bxh6 g1=Q+
6. O–O h6	13. Rh1 Qf6	20. Qxf7+ Kd8	White resigns
7. c3 Nc6	14. fxg4 Qf2+		

Incidentally, Meyer Amschel Rothschild, the founder of the dynasty, was the best player in Frankfurt.

[2]Kolisch didn't quite give up; he was a generous patron of many tournaments – and hence gave much financial assistance to impoverished former colleagues.

[3]His speciality: Westerns.

Here's a Lothar brevity against a player from Hong Kong: the shortest game in the 1968 Olympics.

Gibbs–L. Schmid, Lugano, 1968. Alekhine's Defence

1. e4 Nf6	4. Nge2 Nc6	7. Bxd5 Qxd5!	9. Rf1 Qg2 White
2. Nc3 d5	5. g3? Bg4	8. f3 (if Nxd5 it's	resigns
3. exd5 Nxd5	6. Bg2 Nd4	mate) Qxf3	

Jim Slater, the financier and children's author, was a strong school-boy player. He gave up chess for finance. This turned out a very good thing for chess, since he was able to tempt Bobby Fischer (with a £50,000 increase in stake-money) into playing Boris Spassky for the world title in 1972. Here's what the young Slater was capable of:

J. D. Slater–P. C. Tomlin, West London Chess Club, 1947. Orang Utan opening

1. b4 Nf6	8. h4 d6	15. Nb5! cxb5	22. Rg1 Rc8
2. Bb2 g6	9. Nc3 Be6	16. Bxa8 bxc4	23. Rb3 Nf5
3. g4 Bg7	10. d3 Qb6	17. e4 c3	24. Rxc3 Nd4!
4. g5 Nh5	11. Qd2 Bf5	18. Qc2 O–O	Draw agreed
5. Bxg7 Nxg7	12. Rb1 Nbd7	19. exf5 Rxa8	
6. Bg2 c6	13. b5 Qc7	20. fxg6 hxg6	
7. c4 e5	14. bxc6 bxc6	21. Ne2 Qc6	

John Spedan Lewis founded the John Lewis chain of stores and was a great benefactor of British chess:

L. Vine–J. S. Lewis, Philidor Defence

1. e4 e5	5. Bc4 Nh6	9. f5 gxf5	13. Rxf6 Bxg4
2. Nf3 d6	6. O–O Ng4	10. Qxg4 Qf6	14. Nxg4 Bxb2
3. d4 exd4	7. f4 Bh6	11. Nxf5 Bxc1	White resigns
4. Nxd4 g6	8. Bxf7+ Kxf7	12. Nh6+ Ke7	

Sir Jeremy Morse, chairman of Lloyds Bank (who do much for chess), is an accomplished problemist. A sample of his work:

First Prize, the *Observer*, 1964

Mate in 2. Solution at end of section.

Other chess-playing businessmen: Charles Saatchi[1] (head of the world's largest advertising agency and according to *Chess* magazine, a garrulous lunchtime player); Rosser Reeves (former chairman of the Ted Bates agency, founder of the USP[2] school of advertising and non-playing captain of the US Olympic chess team); Richard Branson; publisher André Deutsch; Aristotle Onassis (who in 1969 paid $65,000 for a gold chessboard encrusted with emeralds); Cecil King, newspaper magnate ('I have always felt that chess should be a part of every business executive's training'); and Leslie Waddington, managing director of London's most influential private art dealers (who was, as a young man, an enthusiastic and good player).

Solution to the Morse problem: Qc4

The Rest

First, some twentieth-century names who don't quite fit into any of the above teams; and then a collection of exotica who defy categorization.

Brian Walden[3] said he was giving up TV to become a chess-

---

[1]According to the *Observer*, he rarely takes longer than ten seconds over a move. This doesn't necessarily mean he's any good.
[2]Unique Selling Proposition.
[3]We couldn't make our minds up whether he was a writer, politician or entertainer – hence his inclusion here.

master. We think he was joking – but he was once strong enough to play in the British Boys' Championship (1948), and in the Junior World Championship Qualifying Tournament (1951). He was equal fifth.

Ninth in the same tournament was Walter Marshall, who became Lord Marshall of the Central Electricity Generating Board, a Welsh Junior International who won a brilliancy prize on top board for his country in 1949. He scored 50 per cent in a Junior International Tournament (Birmingham 1950), including a draw with future World Championship Candidate, Fridrik Olafsson. Nowadays all he has time for is computer chess.

Christine Keeler, star of the Profumo affair, learned to play chess as a young girl; in her autobiography *Scandal!* she says, 'The first time I discovered boys was when we played chess together.'

From the world of espionage and counter-espionage, Graham Mitchell who was deputy director of MI5.[1] He was also an inter-national master of correspondence chess, and in the time he wasn't dealing with real-life James Bonds, he found the time for such entertaining games as this:

Mitchell–Riley, Correspondence, 1964–5. Sicilian Defence

1. e4 c5	8. Qd2 Qxb2	15. Bxe6 Bxd4	22. Bh6 Rfd8
2. Nf3 d6	9. Rb1 Qa3	16. Bxd7+ Nxd7	23. Rxg6 fxg6
3. d4 cxd4	10. e5 dxe5	17. Qxd4 O-O	24. Bxg7+ Kxg7
4. Nxd4 Nf6	11. fxe5 Nfd7	18. O-O Nxe5	25. Ne8+ Kh6
5. Nc3 a6	12. Bc4 Bb4	19. Ne4 Be6	26. Qf4+ Black
6. Bg5 e6	13. Rb3 Qa5	20. Rg3 Kh8	resigns
7. f4 Qb6	14. a3 Bc5	21. Nf6 Ng6	

There has been speculation that Mitchell may have been the mysterious 'fifth man'; it was suggested (inanely) that he used his correspondence games as a code to communicate with the Eastern bloc.

[1] Another spymaster/chess-player was Fouché, head of Napoleon's secret police.

✿

Captain Robert Falcon Scott, the explorer, was an addict. According to Edward Wilson's diaries Scott played every evening on one of his Antarctic expeditions; and got 'in a cantanker' if he lost.

✿

The cosmonaut Vitaly Sevastianov became president of the USSR Chess Federation. He played in the first game between space and earth (Soyuz-9, represented by Sevastianov and A. Nikolayev; earth by Air Force Colonel General N. Kamanin and cosmonaut V. Gorbatko).

Soyuz-9–Earth, 1970. Queen's Gambit Accepted

1. d4 d5	10. h3 Bf5	19. bxc3 Be4	28. g5 Qd6
2. c4 dxc4	11. Nh4 Qd7	20. Qg3 c6	29. Nxd5 cxd5
3. e3 e5	12. Qf3 Ne7	21. f3 Bd5	30. Bf4 Qd8
4. Bxc4 exd4	13. g4 Bg6	22. Bd3 b5	31. Be5+ f6
5. exd4 Nc6	14. Rae1 Kh8	23. Qh4 g6	32. gxf6 Nxf6
6. Be3 Bd6	15. Bg5 Neg8!	24. Nf4 Bc4!	33. Bxf6 Rxf6
7. Nc3 Nf6	16. Ng2 Rae8	25. Bxc4 bxc4	34. Re8+ Qxe8
8. Nf3 O–O	17. Be3 Bb4	26. Bd2 Rxe1	35. Qxf6+ Kg8
9. O–O Bg4	18. a3 Bxc3	27. Rxe1 Nd5	Draw

✿

Dominic Lawson, editor of *The Spectator,* is a county standard player; and Donald Trelford, ex-editor of the *Observer,* co-wrote *Child of Change*, Kasparov's (auto)biography.

✿

Further miscellaneous chess-players: Gerd Heidemann, the gullible loon who bought the Hitler diaries for *Stern* magazine; chat-show hosts Clive Anderson, who played against Short in a simul, and Jonathan Ross who, in the *Radio Times*, was pictured in his dressing-room with a chess-set among the props; Loyd Grossman, another Kasparov victim; political hostages Daphne Parish, John McCarthy, Terry Anderson and Thomas Sutherland, all of whom played chess while in captivity; fashion designers Mary Quant (who played in Keene's Longleat simul) and Betty Jackson, who first met her husband playing chess; G. S. A. Wheatcroft the inventor of

VAT, and an English chess international; and, a very keen player, journalist Donald Woods, the co-hero of the film *Cry Freedom*. Woods feigned a chess game against a friend to cover his absence from home while escaping from the South African secret police. He now plays for Surbiton.

♟

The Chevalier d'Éon was history's most famous transvestite. Charles Geneviève Louis Auguste André Timothée d'Éon de Beaumont (1728–1810) had a most colourful career as a diplomat, swordsman, chess-player, nun and Lady-in-Waiting to the Empress of Russia. He disguised himself as a woman when acting as a spy for Louis XV, became attached to the idea, and spent half his life dressed as a woman (the rest of the time he masqueraded as her – or rather his – own brother). So convincing was he that when he showed up at the court of Versailles dressed as a man, he was ordered to change into women's clothes; and became Lady-in-Waiting to Marie Antoinette.

Later on he spent several years in London, where he became a noted chess-player (a member of the St George's Club), good enough to beat Philidor in a simul.

The Chevalier was a celebrity – mainly on account of the large wagers placed on the question of his gender. In 1810 all bets were settled when the gallant Chevalier died, and a post-mortem established his masculinity.

♟

Dr Charles Stanley Hunter of Rochdale was joint British Correspondence Chess Champion in 1961. What gets him into this collection of oddballs is that in 1968 he became the world's fastest speaker (Hamlet's best-known soliloquy in forty-one seconds. His fastest burst was fifty words in 7.2 seconds).

♟

General Tom Thumb – star attraction of Barnum's American Museum – was born Charles S. Stratton. A normal baby, he stopped growing at twenty-five inches. At this point fate, in the shape of the great showman, Phineas T. Barnum, stepped in, and Charles became the most famous midget of all time. First New York, then Europe went wild about the little chap. He was granted an audience with

Queen Victoria, swapped jokes with President Lincoln, and was Barnum's greatest ever crowd-puller.[1]

Tom was, according to contemporary reports 'an excellent chess-player for his size', and won many games from his fans (because, it was said, his opponents couldn't distinguish between him and the pieces). This game was attributed to him:

Scotch Gambit

1. e4 e5	3. d4 exd4	5. Ng5 d5	7. Nxf7 Kxf7
2. Nf3 Nc6	4. Bc4 Nf6	6. exd5 Nxd5	8. Qf3 + Kg8,

and the world's smallest adult chess-player announced mate in three.

But it was probably all a Barnum publicity stunt.

This has nothing to do with chess, but you may be interested to know that Tom Thumb was married to Mercy Bumpus, over whom he came to blows with the equally diminutive Commodore Nutt.[2]

♟

Madame Tussaud was a chess-player: among her possessions, a chess-set in green and white ivory.

♟

Casanova played chess – but not well. We learn from his memoirs that he played a girl called Pauline as part of the process of seduction. He lost the first game in four moves, the second in five. But almost certainly his mind was on lower things.

♟

Finally, if you believe fifteenth-century French romances, we have the great Merlin. In addition to all that stuff with the sword and the stone, King Arthur's wizard was a whizz at chess: he found time to build the world's first chess computer – a wonderful board of gold and ivory that, without so much as a silicon chip to help it, could beat any opponent in the world. (Incidentally, Merlin was not the only member of King Arthur's court to play chess: Lancelot used the game as a cover when he wooed Guinevere.)

---

[1] When the crowds stayed too long for profit, the ingenious Barnum had a sign erected saying, accurately, 'This way to the Giant Egress!' It worked like a charm.

[2] Freaky footnote: Alekhine once won two consultation games off an American problemist, W. K. Wimsatt Jnr, who, said the press, stood seven foot in his stockinged feet.

II *The Greatest*

Genius is pain   *John Lennon*

The Greatest?

American Chess Bulletin
(ISSUED BI-MONTHLY; $2.00 A YEAR)
ESTABLISHED IN 1904

CHESS PARAPHERNALIA
OF EVERY DESCRIPTION

Cable Address: CHESS, New York
Publisher: H. HELMS

150 NASSAU STREET
Telephone: BEekman 3-3761

New York 7, N. Y.

January 13, 1951

Mrs. R. Fischer,
1059 Union St.,
Brooklyn, N. Y.

Dear Madam:

Your postcard of Nov. 14th, mislaid in The Eagle
office, has just reached me.

If you can bring your little chess-playing boy to
the Brooklyn Public Library, Grand Army Plaza, next Wednesday
evening at eight o'clock, he might find someone there about
his own age. If he should care to take a board and play against
Mr. Pavey, who is to give an exhibition of simultaneous play at
that time, just have him bring along his own set of chessmen with
which to play. The boards, I understand, are to be provided.

I will also bring your request to the attention of Mr.
Henry Spinner, secretary of the Brooklyn Chess Club, which meets
Tuesday, Friday and Saturday evenings on the third floor of the
Brooklyn Academy of Music. It is quite possible that Mr. Spinner
may know a boy or two of that age.

Yours respectfully,

H. Helms

Chess Editor.

This is chess at the summit. The strongest grandmasters, the most gifted prodigies, the most formidable geriatrics, the most phenomenal blindfold performances, the toughest tournaments – and our modest attempt to answer the unanswerables: would Capa have beaten Kasparov? Or Fischer, Alekhine? Who *was* the greatest?

Here, too, is our favourite section: a shot at the sixty-four greatest games ever played. It would be unbecoming for players of our modest attainments to add notes to such masterworks; but we suggest that if you, dear reader, were to devote your leisure hours to annotating them yourself, it would do your grading no harm whatsoever.

The Great Prodigies

Meet first the megabrats of the chequered board: the kids who made the headlines by duffing up their elders and (supposedly) betters at an age when most of us preferred ludo or Lego to bad bishops and smothered mates.

A January 1987 report in *The Times* featured ten-year-old Adragon Eastwood DeMello (distantly related to Clint), from (where else?) California. Modestly described by his father as 'probably the most gifted scholar this century has ever seen', Adragon had, we are told, mastered chess by the age of two and a half. To the best of our knowledge he has now abandoned chess in favour of nuclear physics, brain surgery or whatever it is ten-year-old geniuses study. But Adragon wins our nomination for the world's strongest-ever two-year-old chess-player.

The last we heard of Adragon, he was living in a foster home. After an apparent suicide pact between father and son had been discovered, his father was arrested on a charge of 'child endangerment'.

With the world's best four-year-old we reach one of the all-time greats. José Raúl Capablanca learned chess, so he told us, at the age of four by watching his father play. Having thrashed his astonished father, Capa was taken along to Havana Chess Club where an unsuspecting opponent offered him queen odds. This is what happened:

R. Iglesias–J. R. Capablanca, Havana, 1893 (Remove White's Queen).
Petroff Defence

1. e4 e5	11. O–O–O Bd7	21. Bxc4 Bxg4	31. Rcg2 Rxg2
2. Nf3 Nf6	12. Kb1 Na5	22. Bd3 Bf3	32. Rxg2 Qf6
3. Nxe5 Nxe4	13. Rc1 Nb3	23. Rh3 Bxd5	33. Bg7+ Qxg7
4. d4 d6	14. Rc2 c5	24. h5 Be6	34. Rxg7 Kxg7
5. Nf3 Be7	15. d5 Re8	25. Rg3 g6	35. Kc2 Kf6
6. Bd3 Nf6	16. h4 b5	26. f4 Bh4	36. Kd3 Ke5
7. c4 O–O	17. g4 Nd4	27. Rg1 Kh8	37. h6 f4
8. Nc3 Nc6	18. Nxd4 cxd4	28. f5 Bxf5	38. Ke2 White
9. a3 a6	19. Ne4 bxc4	29. Bxf5 gxf5	resigns
10. Bd2 b6	20. Nxf6+ Bxf6	30. Bh6 Rg8	

The infant Capa hardly needed the queen start.

The next few awards all go to the same player. Sammy Reshevsky, the boy wonder of the early 1920s, was wowing the crowds with simuls and blindfold games across two continents between the ages of six and eleven.[1] Here's an example of his play, from a simul in Hanover when he was eight years old.

S. Reshevsky–Dr H. Traube, Hanover, 1920. Bird's Opening

1. f4 e6	4. Bg2 Bd6	7. Be3 c6	10. c4 b6
2. Nf3 d5	5. d4 Nc6	8. a3 h6	11. b4 f6
3. g3 Nf6	6. Ne5 Ne7	9. Nd2 Nd7	12. Nxc6 Nxc6

---

[1] After Reshevsky's death in 1992 it was claimed that the diminutive GM told his friends he was born in 1909 rather than 1911. If this is true it makes his childhood performances slightly less remarkable but his achievements in old age more so.

13. cxd5 exd5	15. Qc2 Rc8	17. Qf7	
14. Bxd5 Bb7	16. Qg6+ Ke7	mate	

Sammy is also the youngest player to have beaten a grandmaster in a tournament game. At the age of ten he took a game off David Janowsky, who had been good enough to play a World Championship match against Lasker twelve years earlier. Shortly afterwards, Reshevsky all but gave up chess for nearly ten years to pursue a more conventional education. Here's the historic game:

D. Janowsky–S. Reshevsky, New York, 1922. Queen's Gambit Declined

1. d4 Nf6	19. Reb1 Qd6	37. d6 Qb7	53. Kf3 Rf8
2. Nf3 d5	20. Qe2 a5	38. h4 (Ng5+	54. Qf6+ Kg8
3. c4 e6	21. Bb5 Rd8	would have	55. d7 Rxf6+
4. Nc3 Nbd7	22. h3 Qc7	won) Qc6	56. gxf6 (exf6
5. Bg5 Be7	23. e4 Nf8	39. h5 Nh8	would have
6. e3 c6	24. Qe3 Bd7	40. Ng5+ hxg5	led to a draw)
7. Bd3 a6	25. Ne5 Be8	41. fxg5 Ng6	Qd2
8. O–O dxc4	26. Bxe8 Rxe8	42. Rg3 Kg7	57. Rh1 Qd3+
9. Bxc4 Nb6	27. f4 f6	43. Rh3 Rh8	58. Kg2 Qxg6+
10. Bd3 Nfd5	28. Nf3 Nd7	44. hxg6 Rxh3+	59. Kf2 Qf5+
11. Bxe7 Qxe7	29. e5 f5	45. Kxh3 Rh8+	60. Kg2 Qg4+
12. Qd2 Nxc3	30. g4 g6	46. Kg3 Qxa4	61. Kh2 Qe2+
13. bxc3 c5	31. gxf5 gxf5	47. Qf3 f4+	62. Kh3 Qd3+
14. Rab1 Nd7	32. d5 Nf8	48. Kg4 Qc2	63. Kh4 Qxd7
15. a4 O–O	33. Rg2+ Kh7	49. Qxf4 Qe2+	64. Rg1+ Kf8
16. Qc2 h6	34. c4 Qf7	50. Kg3 Qd3+	65. Kg5 Qd4
17. Rfe1 b6	35. Kh2 Ng6	51. Kg2 Qe2+	White resigns
18. Rb2 Rb8	36. Rbg1 Rg8	52. Kg3 Qh2	

♚

For the strongest twelve-year-old of all time we turn the clock back to 1850. The location: New Orleans, where young Paul Morphy had already proved himself the best player around. Johann Löwenthal, a political refugee from Hungary and one of the world's strongest players was in town and condescended to play the young lad. Paul won twice and generously agreed a draw in the third game following a Löwenthal lemon.

Here's an example of Morphy at the age of twelve, surprising local champ Eugène Rousseau.

P. Morphy–E. Rousseau, New Orleans, 1849. King's Gambit

1. e4 e5	6. Nxf7 Kxf7	11. Kd1 Kd8	16. Nxd5+ Kd6
2. f4 exf4	7. Qxg4 Qf6	12. Re1 Qc5	17. Qc7
3. Nf3 g5	8. Bc4+ Ke7	13. Bxg8 d5	mate
4. h4 g4	9. Nc3 c6	14. Re8+ Kxe8	
5. Ng5 h6	10. e5 Qxe5+	15. Qxc8+ Ke7	

For the world's strongest fifteen-year-old we turn yet again to the New World, and the supreme megabrat of chess, Bobby Fischer. US Junior Champion at thirteen, US Open and Closed Champion at fourteen, grandmaster and World Championship candidate at fifteen – truly phenomenal achievements. At only thirteen he played one of the greatest games of all time (against Donald Byrne), dubbed 'The Game of the Century'. You'll find it later in this chapter.

Fischer's results at the age of fifteen have now, no doubt to his horror, been almost equalled by Judith Polgár, who, in December 1991, broke Bobby's record as the world's youngest ever grandmaster.

Another near miss is accredited to Gata Kamsky, a Tartar who emigrated with his father from Leningrad to New York. In July 1990, when he was sixteen, his rating soared from 2510 to 2650. For more on Gata and his pugnacious father turn to Chapter IV.

But Bobby can no longer claim to have been the World's Strongest Teenager. That honour now rests with Gary Kasparov, who reached the Number Two spot in the International Rating List at the age of nineteen.

And what, you may ask, about the girls? Well, there was Elaine Saunders (now Pritchard), from England, British and International Girls' Champion at ten and British Ladies' Champion at thirteen. And Jutta Hempel, born in West Germany in 1960, was, it was claimed, a female Reshevsky. She learned the moves at three, and two years later she was giving simuls. She beat the local champion at the age of six, and scored 1–1 against Danish International Master Jens Enevoldsen at nine. She gave up chess on leaving school at eighteen.[1]

But the most remarkable girl prodigies are the Polgár sisters from Budapest. Zsuzsa (Susan), born in 1969, won the Budapest Under-eleven Championship at the age of four and a half with a 100 per cent score. At the age of fourteen only Fischer up to that time had been significantly stronger. In 1984 she qualified as an International Master, one of the youngest ever, but since then progress has been slower and it was not until 1991 that she became a grandmaster.

The second and third sisters, Zsofia (Sofia) and Judit (Judith), were born in 1974 and 1976. From an early age they were performing even better than their big sister. As early as spring 1984, at the ages of nine and seven, they were beating masters, IMs and, at least in the case of Judith, GMs in blitz and blindfold games. Sofia's results were more erratic than those of her sisters, but at the age of fourteen in February 1989 she stunned the chess world by winning the Rome Open with a score of 8½/9 and a tournament performance against her rated opponents of 2930, one of the highest ever recorded. So far she has not been able to repeat this, and her rating lags some way behind those of her sisters.

But the real star of the family is Judith. Her first win over an IM under tournament conditions was at the age of ten, and at eleven she took her first GM scalp in non-blitz tournament play, Lev Gutman of Israel. Given the doubt over Reshevsky's date of birth, this may be considered a world record. She qualified as an International Master just after her twelfth birthday and became a grandmaster at the age of fifteen.

The three sisters have all been educated at home, learning chess at the age of four and spending eight to ten hours a day on the game. Here are three of their earliest published games, one from each sister.

[1] The scores of two games against Elaine Pritchard played in a BBC Radio match in 1967 cast some doubt on her prowess. The second, with Jutta black, went 1. e4 e5 2. d4 f6 3. dxe5 fxe5 4. Qh5+ g6 5. Qxe5+ Kf7 6. Bc4+ resigns.

Pataky–Susan Polgár (aged nine), Budapest, 1978. From Gambit

1. f4 e5	6. c3 g4	11. Rxh2 gxh2	16. Qd4 Bxc6
2. fxe5 d6	7. Qa4+ Nc6	12. Nxc6 h1=Q	17. Qxh8 O-O-O
3. Nf3 dxe5	8. Nd4 Qh4+	13. Ke2 Qh5+	18. Qg7 Be5
4. Nxe5 Bd6	9. Kd1 g3	14. Kf2 Qf5+	19. g4 Bh2+
5. Nf3 g5	10. e3 Qxh2!	15. Kg1 Bd7	White resigns

Sofia Polgár (age seven)–Kontra, Budapest, 1982. Ruy López

1. e4 e5	7. Bxd7+ Qxd7	13. Rhe1 Rhe8	19. Nc4 Rxd2
2. Nf3 Nc6	8. Qxd4 Ne7	14. Nd5 Bf8	20. Nxb6 Rxd1+
3. Bb5 d6	9. Be3 Nc6	15. Bb6! Ne7	21. Rxd1
4. d4 exd4	10. Qd2 Be7	16. Nxc7 Qc6	Black resigns
5. Nxd4 Bd7	11. f4 a6	17. Nxe8 Qxb6	
6. Nc3 Nxd4	12. O-O-O O-O-O	18. Nxd6+ Kb8	

Judith Polgár (age seven)–Szendrei, Budapest, 1984. Sicilian Defence

1. e4 c5	8. f4 O-O	15. Nd5 Qd8	Black resigns
2. Nf3 d6	9. Qf3 Nbd7	16. Rg1 b6	(if 21. .... Rg8,
3. d4 cxd4	10. g4 e5	17. Rg4 Nxb3	22. Qxh7+!
4. Nxd4 Nf6	11. Nf5 Nc5	18. axb3 Nc5	Kxh7
5. Nc3 a6	12. Nxe7+ Qxe7	19. Nf6+! gxf6	23. Rh4 mate).
6. Bc4 e6	13. g5 Nfd7	20. gxf6+ Kh8	
7. Bb3 Be7	14. f5 a5	21. Qh3	

Cathy Forbes's book *The Polgár Sisters* is recommended to those readers seeking more information on the Polgár phenomenon.

Over the last few years, considerable effort has gone into developing junior chess in Britain; so it is not surprising that many contemporary prodigies are British.

The best known and most successful (so far) of the new generation of English boy wonders is Nigel Short. Nigel rocketed to megastardom in 1976 when he took a simul game off Viktor (The Leningrad Lip) Korchnoi. He qualified for the British Championship three days before his twelfth birthday, and at the age of fourteen shared first place in the same event, breaking the record for the youngest IM norm. A few months later, at Hastings, he secured the title.

The next English prodigy to emerge, Michael Adams, from Cornwall, born in 1971, became an IM at fifteen and a GM at seventeen. In 1988, Kent's Matthew Sadler emulated Nigel by gaining the IM title at fourteen, while London's Dharshan Kumaran is a double World Junior Champion.

England's most recent junior sensation, Luke McShane, a member of Richmond Junior Chess Club in London, was born in January 1984. He learned the moves from his grandfather at the age of five, and within six months was regularly winning junior tournaments. His win in the 1992 World Under-Ten Boys' Championship against players up to two years older made him the world's youngest ever FIDE Master. And younger players than Luke are already making a name for themselves, such as Siobhan O'Neill from Cambridgeshire, doing well against strong adult opposition at the age of seven, and John Pike, of Hampshire, who won two tournaments in early 1992 at the age of four.

On the international scene, the leading prodigy in 1993 is another Hungarian, Peter Lékó. Like the Polgár sisters, Peter is educated at home, only going to school to take exams. In 1992 he became an IM at the age of twelve.

The Americans have been guilty of over-hyping their young talents in recent years, but perhaps Jorge Zamora is the real thing. Jorge comes originally from El Salvador, but moved to New York in 1990 at the age of eleven, where he has been compared with Bobby Fischer. 'If God wants, I will be champion at twenty,' says Jorge.

With the successes of Vishy Anand and Xie Jun, the Chinese Women's World Champion, it will be no surprise to see a wave of prodigies from Asia. Perhaps, then, it was not entirely unexpected when the erudite Dr John Nunn, one of England's top GMs, lost to a twelve-year-old Vietnamese girl with the white pieces in only twenty-one moves. To be fair to the doctor, it was a rapid-play game (forty-five minutes each).

J. Nunn–Hoang Trang, Oviedo, 1992. French Defence

1. e4 e6	7. Be3 Qb6	13. Nxd2 g5	19. Qxd4 Rc8
2. d4 d5	8. Na4 Qa5+	14. Nb2 b6	20. Bd3? Bxd3
3. Nc3 Nf6	9. c3 cxd4	15. Kf2 gxf4	21. Nxd3 Rc4!
4. e5 Nfd7	10. b4 Nxb4	16. Nd3 Ba6	White resigns
5. f4 c5	11. cxb4 Bxb4+	17. Nb3 Qa4	
6. Nf3 Nc6	12. Bd2 Bxd2+	18. Nb2 Qa3	

Briefly, a few other kiddie records. The youngest-ever national champion is Niaz Murshed, champion of Bangladesh in 1982 at the age of twelve. To prove it was no fluke he did it again at thirteen and fourteen. Jimmy Goloboy, aged eight, from Massachusetts, beat US Master Larry Lavigne in a tournament game in 1987. At the age of only six in 1990, Londoner George Hassabis[1] beat US Life Master Orest Popovych. The game was a quickie on a giant board at London's Marble Arch to publicize the Lloyds Bank Masters' Tournament, but even so . . .

O. Popovych–G. Hassabis, London, 1990. Sicilian Defence

1. e4 c5	6. c4 Be7	11. O–O Rc8	16. Bb6 Qe8
2. Nf3 Nc6	7. N1c3 a6	12. Rc1 Na5	17. f3? Ra8!
3. d4 cxd4	8. Na3 Be6	13. Qa4 Nxc4	18. Qb5 Qxb5
4. Nxd4 e5	9. Be3 Nf6	14. Nxc4 b5	19. Nxb5 Rab8
5. Nb5 d6	10. Be2 O–O	15. Qxa6 bxc4	White resigns

The Golden Oldies

Now we pay our respects to those who achieved excellence at chess in their sixties or above.

First, we have two candidates for the best performance by players in their sixties. Vasily Smyslov, World Champion 1957/8, celebrated his sixty-third birthday during his Candidates' Final match against Gary Kasparov. For a delightful game from his semi-final match

---

[1] At the time of the game he spelled his name Hassapis.

against Hungarian GM Zoltán Ribli, see the Games Section at the end of this chapter.

At the age of seventy Smyslov won the inaugural Senior World Championship in November 1991, so future editions of this book may see a new nominee in the next category.

Smyslov's only rival in the over-sixties stakes was the great Emanuel Lasker. Driven by financial hardship to make a come-back in his mid-sixties, nine years after his retirement, his best result in later years was at Moscow in 1935. At the age of sixty-six he finished third, half a point behind the coming men Botvinnik and Flohr, and the same distance in front of no less a player than Capablanca.

Our nomination for the strongest septuagenarian is a familiar name: the amazing Sammy Reshevsky. Yes, the same player who won our vote as the strongest six- (or possibly eight-)year-old. Right up to his death in 1992 at the age of eighty (eighty-two?) and following two heart attacks, he was still playing strong grandmaster chess. In 1991 he travelled to Moscow to compete in a tournament in honour of Smyslov's seventieth birthday. In the last round Smyslov needed a win against Reshevsky for an outright victory or a draw for shared first place. Did Sammy show his old rival any mercy? Not likely.

S. Reshevsky–V. Smyslov, Moscow, 1991. Slav Defence

1. d4 d5	16. bxc3 Nxc1	31. Rc7 gxf5	46. Rxb6 Bd6+
2. c4 c6	17. Raxc1 Rfxd8	32. gxf5 exf5	47. Ke4 Rxa4
3. Nc3 Nf6	18. f4 Rac8	33. Ke2 Rf6	48. Rb7+ Bc7
4. e3 g6	19. c4 dxc4	34. Bd3 Rh8	49. Kd5 Ra1
5. Nf3 Bg7	20. Bxc4 a5	35. Bxf5 Rh2+	50. Ra8 Ra2
6. Be2 O–O	21. a4 e6	36. Kd3 Ra2	51. Raa7 Rc2
7. O–O Bg4	22. Ba6 Ra8	37. Rg1+ Kf8	52. Rxa5 Kc8
8. cxd5 cxd5	23. Bb7 Rab8	38. Bh7 Ra3+	53. Rab5 f5
9. Qb3 b6	24. Rc7 Bf8	39. Ke4 Re6+	54. Ra7 f4
10. h3 Be6	25. Ba6 Bd6	40. Kf5 Ke8	55. Rc5 Rxc5+
11. Ne5 Ne4	26. Rc6 Bb4	41. Rg8+ Bf8	56. Kxc5 Kb8
12. Nd3 Nc6	27. Kf2 h5	42. Kf4 Rexe3	57. Ra3 Kb7
13. Nf4 Na5	28. g4 hxg4	43. Be4 Rec3	58. Rb3+ Kc8
14. Nxe6 Nxb3	29. hxg4 Kg7	44. Bc6+ Rxc6	59. Kc6 Black
15. Nxd8 Nxc3	30. f5! Rd6	45. Rxc6 Kd7	resigns

If Reshevsky was really born in 1909, he would certainly win our nomination as the strongest octogenarian. But as his date of birth must be open to doubt, we have to look elsewhere.

♚

Here's a simple question that's sure to win you a lot of bets at your local club. Who was the first English grandmaster? The surprising answer is Jacques Mieses, a German Jew born in 1865. He fled his homeland in the thirties and settled in England, becoming a naturalized British citizen shortly before being chosen as one of the first FIDE grandmasters in 1950. He played in his last grandmaster event in 1948, gaining our nomination as the strongest octogenarian. Here's the sprightly veteran in action at the age of eighty-three:

J. Mieses–Dr H. G. Schenk, Oxford, 1948. Nimzowitsch Defence

1. e4 Nc6	8. O–O Qa5	15. Rfb1 c6	22. Qxg7 Rc8
2. d4 d5	9. Nxe5 Bxe2	16. c3 axb5	23. Qf6 Rxd1+
3. exd5 Qxd5	10. Qxe2 Nxe5	17. cxb4 Qa6	24. Rxd1 Nd5
4. Nf3 e5	11. dxe5 Nh6	18. a5 Nf5	25. Qd6+ Ka8
5. Nc3 Bb4	12. Nb5 a6	19. Bb6 Rd5	26. Rxd5 cxd5
6. Be3 Bg4	13. a4 Be7	20. Rd1 Ne7	27. g3 Black
7. Be2 O–O–O	14. b4 Bxb4	21. Qg4+ Kb8	resigns

♚

We have four candidates for the nonagenarian award. For quality of play, though, the vote goes to Edward Lasker (1885–1981), a very distant relation of Emanuel, who at the age of ninety in 1976 played for New York on the Board of Honour in a telex match against London. His game lasted nine hours! His last tournament was in 1980 when he finished fourth in a veterans' event. Here's how he played at eighty-nine, against another old-timer:

Ed. Lasker–S. Bernstein, New York, 1975. Ruy López

1. e4 e5	7. Bb3 O–O	13. Qc2 Bf6	19. Ne3 Qe8
2. Nf3 Nc6	8. h3 d6	14. Nf1 Ne6	20. Nf5 Bd8
3. Bb5 a6	9. c3 Be6	15. Ne3 Ne7	21. h4 Rf7
4. Ba4 Nf6	10. d3 Bxb3	16. Ng4 Ng6	22. a4 Rb8
5. O–O Be7	11. Qxb3 Nd7	17. g3 Be7	23. axb5 axb5
6. Re1 b5	12. Nbd2 Nc5	18. d4 f6	24. Be3 Ne7

25. Qb3 Nxf5	34. Ne6 Qxd4	43. dxc5 dxc5	52. Kxd4 Ra1
26. exf5 Nf8	35. cxd4 Nb6	44. Rxc5 Rb7	53. Kc4 Rg1
27. h5 Kh8	36. Rac1 Nd5	45. Bd2 Nd3	54. g5 fxg5
28. Qd1 Re7	37. Kg2 Ra8	46. Rd5 Rd7	55. fxg5 Rg4 +
29. dxe5 Qxh5	38. Kf3 Rd7	47. Rxd7 Ne5 +	56. Kb3 Ne5
30. exf6 gxf6	39. Rh1 Ne7	48. Ke4 Nxd7	57. Rh6 Nf7
31. Qd5 Qf7	40. g4 Nd5	49. Bc3 b4	58. Rf6 and
32. Qd4 Nd7	41. Bh6 Nb4	50. Bd4 Bb6	White soon
33. Ng5 Qc4	42. Rh5 c5	51. f4 Bxd4	won

We must also mention Joseph Blake, who achieved his lifetime best result at Weston-super-Mare at sixty-three and was champion of Kingston, Surrey, at the grand age of ninety.

Spare a thought for George Peck, champion of Rugby (the place, not the game) in 1965 when a mere ninety-seven years of age.

At the time of his ninety-eighth birthday in May 1991 US enthusiast Jared B. Moore had, optimistically, thirty correspondence games on the go. It was also reported that he conducted an orchestra, played the oboe and transcribed books into Braille.

We have still to come across a centenarian active in tournament or match chess. If you know of, or are, one we'd love to hear from you.

The longest lived master was the Hungarian, György Négyesy (1893–1992), who died shortly before his ninety-ninth birthday. We'd welcome information from any Hungarian readers as to when he retired from active play.

Our award for the best female geriatric achievement goes to Edith Price, British Ladies' Champion in 1946 at seventy-six. A close runner-up is Mary Houlding, seventy-eight years old when champion of Newport, Monmouthshire, in 1928.

Lady Jane Carew ('a strong player' says Whyld) lived in three centuries, from 1797 to 1901. We don't know how long she carried on playing. Violet Kemp (a.k.a. Violet Nesbitt), who died towards the end of 1991 at the tremendous age of one hundred and three, attended Richmond, Surrey, Chess Club regularly until her late nineties.

The Greats

Before we examine the achievements of the all-time greats, let us mention briefly a player who, though not quite reaching that level, was perhaps the most phenomenal of all grandmasters. His name was Mir Sultan Khan and he was born in the Punjab in 1905. As a boy he learned the Indian form of chess and by the age of twenty-one was the best player in the state. In 1926 he was discovered by Sir Umar Hayat Khan, who took the young man into his household, taught him the Western game and brought him to England in 1929. That year he won the British championship, a feat which he repeated in 1932 and 1933, and in other tournaments proved himself not far short of the world's best. And this despite the handicap of being unable to read Western chess literature and suffering frequent bouts of malaria. At the end of 1933 he returned to his homeland and retired from chess, apart from a match against another Indian player in 1935. He died of tuberculosis in 1966. To see how he beat the chess machine Capablanca turn to page 146.

Unofficial World Champions

(You may be interested to know that history's first Number One – according to our list – was black; the third, Chinese. Don't write and complain if you disagree with what follows; it is highly speculative.)

(a) Shatranj Champions

Name	Dates	Nationality	Champion
Sa'id bin Jubair	665–714	Africa/Persia	c.700–714
Jābīr al-Kūfī		Persia	Early 9th C.
Rabrab Khatā'ī		China/Persia	Early 9th C.
Abū'n Na'ām		Persia	Early 9th C.
al-'Adlī ar-Rumi		Turkey/Persia	c.835–c.848
al-Rāzī		Persia	c.848–?
al-Māwardī		Persia	?–c.905
as-Sūlī[1]	c.880–946	Turkey/Persia	c.905–c.940
al-Lajlāj[2] (The Stammerer)	d. c.970	Persia	c.940–c.970
Abū'l-Fath Ahmad		Persia	11th/12th C.
'Alā'Addin at-Tabrīzī (Aladdin)		Persia	late 14th C.

[1] His full name was Abū-Bakr Muhammed Ben Yahyā as-Sūlī.
[2] In full, Abu'l-Faraj bin al-Muzaffar bin Sa'-īd al-Lajlāj. See Chapter VI for some equally impressive names.

(b) Chess Champions

Name	Dates	Nationality	Champion
Ruy López	c.1530–c.80	Spain	c.1560–75
Giovanni Leonardo di Bona da Cutri	1542–87	Italy	1575–87
Paolo Boi	1528–98	Italy	1575–98
Alessandro Salvio	c.1570–c.1640	Italy	1598–c.1621 c.1634–40
Gioacchino Greco	c.1600–c.34	Italy	c.1621–34
Legall de Kermeur[1]	1702–92	France	c.1730–47
François-André Philidor	1726–95	France	1747–95
Alexandre Deschapelles	1780–1847	France	c.1798–1824
Louis de la Bourdonnais	1795–1840	France	c.1824–40

[1] His only surviving game runs as follows: Legall–St Brie, Paris 1750. Philidor's Defence. 1. e4 e5 2. Bc4 d6 3. Nf3 Bg4 4. Nc3 g6 5. Nxe5 Bxd1 6. Bxf7 + Ke7 7. Nd5 mate: the famous Legall's Mate.

Name	Dates	Nationality	Champion
Howard Staunton	1810–74	England	1843–51
Adolf Anderssen	1818–79	Germany	1851–58
			1859–66
Paul Morphy	1837–84	USA	1858–59
Wilhelm Steinitz	1836–1900	Bohemia/USA	1866–86

The Official World Champions

	Name	Dates	Nationality	Champion
1.	Wilhelm Steinitz	1836–1900	Bohemia/USA	1886–94
2.	Emanuel Lasker	1868–1941	Germany	1894–1921
3.	José Raúl Capablanca	1888–1942	Cuba	1921–27
4.	Alexander Alekhine	1892–1946	Russia/France	1927–35
				1937–46
5.	Machgielis (Max) Euwe	1901–81	Holland	1935–37
6.	Mikhail Botvinnik	1911–	USSR	1948–57
				1958–60
				1961–63
7.	Vasily Smyslov	1921–	USSR	1957–58
8.	Mikhail Tal	1936–92	USSR	1960–61
9.	Tigran Petrosian	1929–84	USSR	1963–69
10.	Boris Spassky	1937–	USSR (now France)	1969–72
11.	Robert (Bobby) Fischer	1943–	USA	1972–75
12.	Anatoly Karpov	1951–	USSR	1975–85
13.	Gary Kasparov	1963–	USSR	1985–93[1]

[1] On 23 March 1993, FIDE announced that, by agreeing to play their match under the auspices of the newly formed Professional Chess Association, Gary Kasparov and Nigel Short had forfeited their rights as World Champion and challenger. Anatoly Karpov, the loser of the previous World Championship match, and Jan Timman, the runner-up in the Candidates Matches, would contest a match for the title of World Champion. At the time of writing, it looks as if, at least in the short term, chess will, like boxing, find itself with several world champions: the winner of the PCA World Championship, the FIDE World Champion, and self-proclaimed champ Bobby Fischer.

The World Championship Matches

Champion	Challenger	+	=	−	Date
1. Steinitz	Zukertort	10	5	5	1886
2. Steinitz	Chigorin	10	1	6	1889
3. Steinitz	Gunsberg	6	9	4	1890/91
4. Steinitz	Chigorin	10	5	8	1892
5. Steinitz	Lasker	5	4	10	1894
6. Lasker	Steinitz	10	5	2	1896/7
7. Lasker	Marshall	8	7	0	1907
8. Lasker	Tarrasch	8	5	3	1908
9. Lasker	Schlechter	1	8	1	1910
10. Lasker	Janowsky	8	3	0	1910
11. Lasker	Capablanca	0	10	4	1921
12. Capablanca	Alekhine	3	25	6	1927
13. Alekhine	Bogoljubow	11	9	5	1929
14. Alekhine	Bogoljubow	8	15	3	1934
15. Alekhine	Euwe	8	13	9	1935
16. Euwe	Alekhine	4	11	10	1937

World Championship Match-Tournament 1948:
Botvinnik 14, Smyslov 11, Keres & Reshevsky 10½, Euwe 4

17. Botvinnik	Bronstein	5	14	5	1951
18. Botvinnik	Smyslov	7	10	7	1954
19. Botvinnik	Smyslov	3	13	6	1957
20. Smyslov	Botvinnik	5	11	7	1958
21. Botvinnik	Tal	2	13	6	1960
22. Tal	Botvinnik	5	6	10	1961
23. Botvinnik	Petrosian	2	15	5	1963
24. Petrosian	Spassky	4	17	3	1966
25. Petrosian	Spassky	4	13	6	1969
26. Spassky	Fischer[1]	3	11	7	1972

Karpov became champion in 1975, Fischer refusing to defend his title

---

[1] 'This little thing between me and Spassky is bigger than Frazier and Ali. It's the free world against the lying, cheating, hypocritical Russians,' said Bobby.

Champion	Challenger	+	=	−	Date
27. Karpov	Korchnoi	6	21	5	1978
28. Karpov	Korchnoi	6	10	2	1981
29. Karpov	Kasparov	5	40	3	1984/5
Match abandoned with no decision					
30. Karpov	Kasparov	3	16	5	1985
31. Kasparov	Karpov	5	15	4	1986
32. Kasparov	Karpov	4	16	4	1987
33. Kasparov	Karpov	4	17	3	1990

The Sixty-four[1] Strongest Players

Since 1972 FIDE has published a regular rating list, first annually, now twice a year. Two attempts have been made to grade retrospectively tournament and match results before 1972, one by Professor Elo, inventor of the FIDE rating system, and one by English civil servant and grading expert Sir Richard Clarke. These two, in many cases, produced very different results.

The following lists are largely subjective and make no claim to statistical accuracy. For a few young players, their average over the three years up to January 1993, or in one case (Kramnik) the year up to January 1993, have been used. For other players who have reached their peak since 1972 their best five-year average has been used, and for earlier players a combination of Elo's and Clarke's figures. Two young players, Joël Lautier (France, 2645) and Veselin Topalov (Bulgaria, 2635), who achieved a high rating for the first time in January 1993, have been omitted from the list.

All the players on the list have achieved a rating of 2610 which, until the last few years, would have been equivalent to that of a credible challenger for the world title. In the January 1987 rating list nine players had a rating of 2610 +: in January 1993 the figure was

[1] Because of the tie for last place, we have sixty-seven players in our list.

forty-five. There is some evidence of slight inflation in the ELO lists (this has not been taken into account in our calculations) but the main reason for this increase is the explosion of new talent appearing on the chess scene in the last five years. As a result of this, a credible world championship challenger would now be expected to have a rating of at least 2650.[1]

The top sixty-four

Grade		Name	Dates	Nationality/affiliation
1. =	2785	Robert Fischer	1943–	USA
		Gary Kasparov	1963–	USSR/Russia
3.	2765	José Raúl Capablanca	1888–1942	Cuba
4.	2745	Emanuel Lasker	1868–1941	Germany
5.	2735	Alexander Alekhine	1892–1946	Russia/France
6. =	2730	Mikhail Botvinnik	1911–	USSR
		Anatoly Karpov	1951–	USSR/Russia
8. =	2710	Vasily Ivanchuk	1969–	USSR/Ukraine
		Mikhail Tal	1936–92	USSR/Latvia
10.	2700	Vasily Smyslov	1921–	USSR/Russia
11. =	2690	Paul Morphy	1837–84	USA
		Tigran Petrosian	1929–84	USSR
13.	2685	Paul Keres	1916–75	Estonia/USSR
14. =	2680	Boris Gelfand	1968–	USSR/Belarus
		Viktor Korchnoi	1931–	USSR/Switzerland
		Samuel Reshevsky	1911–92	USA
		Boris Spassky	1937–	USSR/France
18.	2670	David Bronstein	1924–	USSR/Russia
19. =	2665	Akiva Rubinstein	1882–1961	Poland
		Siegbert Tarrasch	1862–1934	Germany
21. =	2660	Viswanathan Anand	1969–	India
		Reuben Fine	1914–93	USA
		Harry Pillsbury	1872–1906	USA
		Wilhelm Steinitz	1836–1900	Bohemia/USA

[1] As a guide, a good club player would have a rating of 1800–2000. To convert to BCF grading subtract 600 and divide by 8.

The top sixty-four (continued)

Grade		Name	Dates	Nationality/affiliation
25. =	2655	Max Euwe	1901–81	Holland
		Efim Geller	1925–	USSR/Russia
		Vladimir Kramnik	1975–	Russia
		Nigel Short	1965–	England
29. =	2650	Evgeny Bareev	1966–	USSR/Russia
		Efim Bogoljubow	1889–1952	USSR/Germany
		Isaak Boleslavsky	1919–77	USSR
		Géza Maróczy	1870–1951	Hungary
		Aron Nimzowitsch	1886–1935	Latvia/Denmark
		Valery Salov	1964–	USSR/Russia
35.	2645	Jan Timman	1951–	Holland
36. =	2640	Gata Kamsky	1974–	USA
		Bent Larsen	1935–	Denmark
		Lajos Portisch	1937–	Hungary
		Alexei Shirov	1973–	Latvia
		Leonid Stein	1934–73	USSR
41. =	2635	Alexander Beliavsky	1953–	USSR/Ukraine
		Salomon Flohr	1908–83	Czechoslovakia/USSR
		Miguel Najdorf	1910–	Poland/Argentina
		Lev Polugayevsky	1934–	USSR/Russia
45. =	2630	Mikhail Gurevich	1959–	USSR/Belgium
		Alexander Khalifman	1966–	USSR/Russia
47. =	2625	Ulf Andersson	1951–	Sweden
		Robert Hübner	1948–	(West) Germany
		Alexander Kotov	1913–81	USSR
		Jonathan Speelman	1956–	England
		Artur Yusupov	1960–	USSR/Russia
		Johannes Zukertort	1842–88	Prussia/England
53. =	2620	Mikhail Chigorin	1850–1908	Russia
		Jaan Ehlvest	1962–	USSR/Estonia
		Svetozar Gligorić	1923–	Yugoslavia
		Ratmir Kholmov	1925–	USSR
		Ljubomir Ljubojević	1950–	Yugoslavia
		Rafael Vaganian	1951–	USSR/Armenia
		Milan Vidmar	1885–1962	Yugoslavia

The top sixty-four (continued)

Grade		Name	Dates	Nationality/affiliation
60. =	2615	Yuri Averbakh	1922–	USSR
		Henrique Mecking	1952–	Brazil
		Predrag Nikolić	1960–	Yugoslavia/Bosnia
63. =	2610	Semen Furman	1920–78	USSR
		Zoltan Ribli	1951–	Hungary
		Carl Schlechter	1874–1918	Austria
		Gideon Ståhlberg	1908–67	Sweden
		László Szabó	1917–	Hungary

Just missing out on 2600 are those nineteenth-century greats Anderssen and Von der Lasa.[1] Other notable absentees are Marshall, Tartakower, Réti and Spielmann, whom Elo rated between 2550 and 2570. Clarke's figures are slightly higher. In their controversial 1989 book *Warriors of the Mind*, Raymond Keene and Nathan Divinsky produced their own list of the top sixty-four players, based on complicated mathematics which neither of us pretends to understand. Professor Divinsky's computer whirred, coughed, spluttered and came up with the following top twenty (note that the numbers are not ELO ratings):

1.	Kasparov	3096	*11.*	Morphy	2305
2.	Karpov	2876	*12.*	Polugayevsky	2290
3.	Fischer	2690	*13.*	Geller	2282
4.	Botvinnik	2616	*14.*	Tal	2255
5.	Capablanca	2552	*15.*	Stein	2247
6.	Lasker	2550	*16.*	Keres	2233
7.	Korchnoi	2535	*17.*	Bronstein	2177
8.	Spassky	2480	*18.*	Alekhine	2170
9.	Smyslov	2413	*19.*	Sokolov	2151
10.	Petrosian	2363	*20.*	Boleslavsky	2142

[1]For his full name see Chapter VI.

On our list Andrei Sokolov (1963–, USSR/Russia) would have shared sixty-eighth place with a rating of 2605.

Poor old Alekhine relegated to eighteenth! Steinitz was forty-seventh and Short fifty-second. Readers may judge for themselves whether they prefer our gut feelings or Divinsky's mathematics.

The Dream Matches
According to the ELO system, our ratings suggest the following dream match scores:

Fischer	17,	Alekhine	13;
Kasparov	16,	Capablanca	14;
Lasker	15½,	Botvinnik	14½;
Karpov	18,	Steinitz	12;
Morphy	16½,	Short	13½;
Adams	15½,	Anderssen	14½

and the one you've all been waiting for:

Fischer	15,	Kasparov	15

The Top British Players

1.	2655	Nigel Short	1965–
2.	2625	Jonathan Speelman	1956–
3. =	2605	Michael Adams	1971–
		John Nunn	1955–
5.	2590	Murray Chandler	1960–
6.	2580	Tony Miles	1955–
7.	2570	Joseph Blackburne	1841–1924
8.	2560	Isidor Gunsberg	1854–1930
9.	2550	Julian Hodgson	1963–
10.	2540	Henry Atkins	1872–1955

11. =	2530	Amos Burn	1848–1925
		Mir Sultan Khan	1905–66
13.	2525	Jonathan Mestel	1957–
14. =	2520	Michael Stean	1953–
		Howard Staunton	1810–74
16. =	2515	Daniel King	1963–
		William Watson	1962–

We have not included the Romanian émigré Mihai Şuba, who represented England briefly, but was last heard of in Spain.

Two other outstanding British players were C. H. O'D Alexander (2475), who beat, amongst others, Botvinnik and Bronstein; and Jonathan Penrose (2470), ten times British Champion in the fifties and sixties. These ELO ratings seem rather low to us.

The Top Women (at 1 January 1993)

1.	2595	Judith Polgár[1]	Hungary
2.	2560	Susan Polgár	Hungary
3.	2525	Pia Cramling	Sweden
4.	2510	Maia Chiburdanidze	Georgia
5.	2470	Xie Jun	China
6.	2460	Nana Ioseliani	Georgia
7.	2445	Alisa Galliamova	Ukraine
8.	2440	Ketevan Arakhamia	Georgia

Alisa Galliamova is married to Vasily Ivanchuk, making them the strongest married couple of all time.

Vera Menchik-Stevenson (1906–44), Russian-born but a representative of England, who dominated women's chess in the thirties, had a best five-year average of 2350. Judith Polgár, on her current form, would swamp Vera in a match: 24–6.

[1] Stop press: in the 1 July 1993 Rating List, Judith's grade has risen to 2630, equal to Michael Adams.

The world's strongest tournaments

The FIDE rating system categorizes tournaments according to the average ELO rating of the participants. The highest category tournament seen to date is category 18 (average ELO 2676–2700) and thereon down in bands of twenty-five points.

Since 1979 it has become fashionable for tournament organizers to vie with each other to run stronger and stronger tournaments. This, combined with the massive increase in 2600 + -rated players, has led to a huge increase in category 15 + tournaments.

The two strongest tournaments held up to 1979 were undoubtedly the AVRO tournament held in Holland in 1938, consisting of the eight strongest players in the world at the time, and the 1948 World Championship tournament (The Hague and Moscow) to decide the World Championship, which had fallen vacant on Alekhine's death. The former event had an average rating of about 2658 and the latter a phenomenal 2665 (both category 17).

The following tables give the winners of all tournaments of category 15 or higher (2600 +). The ratings of tournaments before 1971 are taken from articles in *BCM*, January 1978 (Ken Whyld) and November 1987 (Romelio Milian Gonzalez), and are based on Clarke's ratings.

Category 18

Reggio Emilia	1991/2	Anand	6/9	67%
Moscow	1992	Anand/ Gelfand	$4\frac{1}{2}$/7	64%
Linares	1993	Kasparov	10/13	77%

Category 17

AVRO	1938	Fine Keres	$8\frac{1}{2}$/14	61%
World Championship	1948	Botvinnik	14/29	70%
Amsterdam (Euwe Memorial)	1988	Short	4/6	67%
Amsterdam	1988	Kasparov	9/12	75%
Linares	1991	Ivanchuk	$9\frac{1}{2}$/13	73%
Tilburg	1991	Kasparov	10/14	71%
Linares	1992	Kasparov	10/13	77%
Dortmund	1992	Kasparov Ivanchuk	6/9	67%
Amsterdam (Euwe Memorial)	1993	Anand Kramnik Short	$3\frac{1}{2}$/6	58%

Category 16

St Petersburg Final	1914	Lasker	7/8	88%
Candidates' Tournament	1950	Boleslavsky Bronstein	12/18	67%
Candidates' Tournament	1953	Smyslov	18/28	64%
Candidates' Tournament	1962	Petrosian	$17\frac{1}{2}$/27	65%
Johannesburg	1981	Andersson	7/12	58%
Turin	1982	Karpov Andersson	6/11[1]	55%
Bugojno	1986	Karpov	$8\frac{1}{2}$/14	61%
OHRA Brussels	1986	Kasparov	$7\frac{1}{2}$/10	75%
Amsterdam	1987	Karpov Timman	4/6	67%
Tilburg	1988	Karpov	$10\frac{1}{2}$/14	75%
Linares	1989	Ivanchuk	$7\frac{1}{2}$/10	75%
Amsterdam	1989	Timman	$4\frac{1}{2}$/6	75%
Skelleftea World Cup	1989	Karpov Kasparov	$9\frac{1}{2}$/15	63%
Tilburg	1989	Kasparov	12/14	86%

[1] Plus one win by default.

Reggio Emilia	1989/90 Ehlvest	7/10	70%
Linares	1990 Kasparov	8/11	73%
Tilburg	1990 Kamsky Ivanchuk	8½/14	61%
Reggio Emilia A1	1990/1 Karpov	7½/12	63%
Amsterdam	1991 Salov Short	6/9	67%
Reykjavik World Cup	1991 Ivanchuk Karpov	10½/15	70%
Amsterdam	1992 Anand Short	3½/6	58%
Biel	1992 Karpov	10½/14	75%
Dortmund	1993 Karpov	5½/7	79%
Munich	1993 Shirov	8/11	73%
Las Palmas	1993 Morović	6/9	67%

Category 15

St Petersburg	1895/6 Lasker	11½/18	64%
New York	1927 Capablanca	14/20	70%
Nauheim, Stuttgart, Garmisch	1937 Euwe	4/6	67%
USSR Absolute Championship	1941 Botvinnik	13½/20	68%
Candidates' Tournament	1956 Smyslov	11½/18	64%
Candidates' Tournament	1959 Tal	20/28	71%
Piatigorsky Cup (Los Angeles)	1963 Keres Petrosian	8½/14	61%
USSR Zonal Tournament	1964 Spassky	7/12	58%
Piatigorsky Cup (Santa Monica)	1966 Spassky	11½/18	64%
Leiden	1970 Spassky	7/12	58%
Milan (Preliminary)	1975 Portisch	7/11	64%
Montreal	1979 Karpov Tal	12/18	67%
Waddinxveen	1979 Karpov	5/6	83%

Tilburg	1979	Karpov	$7\frac{1}{2}/11$	68%
Bad Kissingen	1980	Karpov	$4\frac{1}{2}/6$	75%
Bugojno	1980	Karpov	8/11	73%
Tilburg	1980	Karpov	$7\frac{1}{2}/11$	68%
Moscow	1981	Karpov	9/13	69%
Tilburg	1981	Beliavsky	$7\frac{1}{2}/11$	68%
Tilburg	1983	Karpov	7/11	64%
Tilburg	1985	Hübner	$8\frac{1}{2}/14$	61%
		Miles		
		Korchnoi		
Tilburg	1986	Beliavsky	$8\frac{1}{2}/14$	61%
Tilburg	1987	Timman	$8\frac{1}{2}/14$	61%
Reggio Emilia	1987/8	Tukmakov	6/9	67%
Linares	1988	Timman	$8\frac{1}{2}/11$	77%
Brussels World Cup	1988	Karpov	11/16	69%
Belfort World Cup	1988	Kasparov	$11\frac{1}{2}/15$	77%
Reykjavik World Cup	1988	Kasparov	11/17	65%
Barcelona World Cup	1989	Kasparov/	11/16	69%
		Ljubojević		
Rotterdam World Cup	1989	Timman	$10\frac{1}{2}/15$	70%
Belgrade	1989	Kasparov	$9\frac{1}{2}/11$	86%
Reggio Emilia A2	1990/1	Ljubojević	7/12	58%
Biel	1991	Shirov	$9\frac{1}{2}/14$	68%
Belgrade	1991	Gelfand	$7\frac{1}{2}/11$	68%
Munich	1992	M. Gurevich	7/11	64%
Madrid	1993	Anand	$6\frac{1}{2}/9$	72%
		Kramnik		
		Topalov		

Other Major Tournaments

Baden-Baden	1870	Anderssen	11/16	66%	Cat. 9
Vienna	1882	Steinitz	24/34	71%	Cat. 10
		Winawer			
London	1883	Zukertort	$24\frac{1}{2}/32$	77%	Cat. 10
Hastings	1895	Pillsbury	$16\frac{1}{2}/21$	79%	Cat. 10
Nuremberg	1896	Lasker	$13\frac{1}{2}/18$	75%	Cat. 11
Budapest	1896	Charousek	$8\frac{1}{2}/12$	71%	Cat. 11
		Chigorin			

London	1899	Lasker	21½/26 83%	Cat. 11
San Sebastián	1911	Capablanca 9½/14	68%	Cat. 13
San Sebastián	1912	Rubinstein 12½/19	66%	Cat. 13
St Petersburg	1914	Lasker	13½/18 75%	Cat. 13
New York	1924	Lasker	16/20 80%	Cat. 13
Berlin	1928	Capablanca 8½/12	71%	Cat. 14
Bled	1931	Alekhine	20½/26 79%	Cat. 13
Moscow	1936	Capablanca 13/18	72%	Cat. 13
Nottingham	1936	Botvinnik	10/14 71%	Cat. 14
		Capablanca		
Semmering-Baden	1937	Keres	9/14 64%	Cat. 14
Saltsjöbaden	1948	Bronstein	13½/19 71%	Cat. 14

Notes:
1. Games won by default are not included.
2. At London 1883 the first two drawn games played between opponents were discounted and replayed. These drawn games are included in Zukertort's result.

The longest winning run of all time is held by the first World Champion, Wilhelm Steinitz. He won his last 14 games at Vienna 1873, beat Blackburne 2–0 in the play-off, blitzed the same opponent 7–0 in an 1876 match and won his first two games at Vienna 1882, making a total of 25 consecutive wins in just under nine years.

You might think that in the highly competitive world of modern chess such a performance would be unrepeatable, but Bobby Fischer came pretty close in 1970–1. A run of 20 wins included the last seven rounds of the 1970 Interzonal, 6–0 shutouts of Mark Taimanov and Bent Larsen in the 1971 Candidates' Matches and the first game of the Candidates' Final match against Tigran Petrosian. (Turn to Chapter III for Bobby's win against Panno from the last round of the Interzonal, and to Chapter IV for how Taimanov qualified for the Candidates' Matches.)

Capablanca was undefeated over 63 games (+ 40, = 23) between 10 February 1916 and 21 March 1924.

But the longest unbeaten run in terms of number of games is, surprisingly, held by that combinational genius Mikhail Tal. He played 86 games without defeat between 15 July 1972 and 26 April 1973 (+ 47, = 39).[1]

A 100 per cent score in a tournament is a rather special achievement attained by only a select few at master level. Pride of place here must go to Gustav Neumann, with 34/34 at Berlin back in 1865.

Other 100 per cent scores include:

– *New York 1893:* Emanuel Lasker wins all his 13 games.

– *Amsterdam 1899:* Englishman Henry Atkins scores 15/15.

– *New York 1913:* 13 straight wins for the young Capablanca (including one by default).

– *New York 1963/4:* Bobby Fischer's greatest ever result. 11/11 against some pretty formidable opposition.

The best all-play-all tournament result ever is Kasparov's 12/14 at Tilburg (1989), a 2913 performance. The previous record-holder was Alekhine, whose 14/15 at San Remo (1930), a category 11 tournament with such superstars as Nimzowitsch, Rubinstein, Bogoljubow, Vidmar and Maróczy, was estimated at about 2900. (Fischer's 1971 Candidates' Matches work out at an astronomical 2950.)

The greatest of all

Faced with this barrage of information we now have to think the unthinkable: who was (or is) the greatest of them all?

– 'Philidor,' said Larsen back in 1967, 'because he was so far ahead of his peers.'

---

[1] But compare: *Sugar Ray Robinson* (USA), 91 consecutive fights without a loss; *Ed Moses* (USA), 122 400 metre hurdles wins in a row; *Iolanda Balas* (Romania), 140 high jump wins in a row; *Osamu Watanabe* (Japan), unbeaten in 187 consecutive free-style wrestling bouts; *Jahangir Khan* (Pakistan), over 500 consecutive wins at squash; *Heather McKay* (Australia), unbeaten from 1962 to 1980 in innumerable squash games; and *Asa Long* (USA), former world chequers champion, who has held his place in the top six for over seventy years (since 1922).

- 'Morphy,' wrote Bobby Fischer in 1964. 'In a set match he would beat anyone alive today.'
- 'Morphy,' said Max Euwe, the author of several books about the all-time greats.
- 'Morphy,' said Gligorić, who has beaten more world champions than most.

Then we come to the three players who between them dominated chess for the first forty years of the century: Lasker, Capablanca and Alekhine.

- Lasker's opinion: 'I have known many chess players but only one genius, Capablanca.'
- Alekhine on Capa: 'The greatest genius of chess.'
- Botvinnik on Capa: 'I think Capablanca had the greatest natural talent.'
- Spassky on Capa: 'Personally, I think the best chess-player of all time was Capablanca.'

Tartakower, when asked who was the greatest, replied: 'If chess is an art, Alekhine, if chess is a science, Capablanca, if chess is a struggle, Lasker.' But this was before Fischer, not to mention Karpov and Kasparov.

In our search for the greatest player of all time we must regretfully disqualify Philidor and Morphy on the gounds of insufficient evidence, but we feel that a valid case could be made for any of the top seven[1] on our grading list. The word 'greatest', we feel, implies rather more than simply 'strongest', so we choose to award accolades in a number of categories.

The strongest players: Fischer and Kasparov.

The greatest natural genius: Capablanca.[2]

The greatest practical player: Lasker.

The greatest tournament players: Lasker and Karpov.

---

[1] The phenomenal Tal would have been a contender were it not for ill health.
[2] Paul Morphy rivals even Capa in this category. By the age of twenty-one (1858) he was streets ahead of his contemporaries. Tragically, he gave it all up after two years at the top. His rating at this point was about the same as the twenty-two-year-old Fischer's. (And see, above, Sultan Khan.)

The greatest match players: Steinitz[1] and Fischer.

The greatest positional player: Capablanca.

The greatest strategist: Botvinnik.

The greatest attacking players: Alekhine, Tal and Kasparov.

The greatest player of all time? Well . . .

Botvinnik's overall record is perhaps not quite as good as the others'. Alekhine's record suffers slightly when compared with Capa's or Lasker's. Karpov's record since 1975 has been tremendous but he lacks something in popular appeal and has three times been bested by Kasparov. Capablanca, towering genius though he was, was too lazy to make full use of his talent. Fischer, though sharing first place with Kasparov as the strongest player ever according to our ratings, ruled himself out of contention for the title of 'the greatest' by abdicating. If it's any compensation, his amazing 1992 match against Spassky must be considered the greatest sporting comeback of all time. This leaves us with Lasker and Kasparov. Lasker, if you discount his loss to Capa in 1921,[2] did virtually nothing wrong in a career spanning over forty years. Kasparov has been an outstanding champion since 1985, scaling peaks previously only reached by Fischer. If he stays at the top into the next century, he'll be able to call himself the greatest ever, but for now we're happy to split the award between Emanuel Lasker (see illustration at the start of the chapter) and Gary Kasparov.

A popular diversion amongst the chess fraternity is the simultaneous display (or simul), in which a master or expert takes on a number of players at the same time. Here are our claims for record simultaneous displays:

The largest display: Havana 1966 (during the Chess Olympics): 6840 boards with over 300 experts taking on 20 players each. One of the participants was Fidel Castro, who scored a diplomatic draw against

[1] Steinitz was only twenty-first on our rating list – but he was world number one for over twenty years. His match record was terrific.
[2] After the match he spent several months in hospital.

World Champion Tigran Petrosian. The display was held outdoors. The final result: rain stopped play after two hours.

The most impressive performance:[1] Capablanca at Cleveland, Ohio, 4 February 1922. Played 103, + 102 = 1. This was the first chess event for fourteen months and his opponents included the State Champion amongst other strong players. This display lasted seven hours without a break.

The greatest number of opponents: Canadian Branimir Bebrich played 575 games on 21 boards in Edmonton in 1978, making over 800 circuits and scoring + 533, = 27, − 15 (95.04%). An honourable mention to Vlastimil Hort, who played 550 opponents (200 simultaneously, then 50 simultaneously seven times) at Seltjarnes, Iceland, on 23–24 April 1977. His score was + 477, = 63, − 10. This event took place immediately after what he described as 'the blackest day of my life', for which see the next chapter.

The greatest number of games: also held by Hort. 663 games over 32.5 hours at Porz, West Germany, 5–6 October 1984. He played between 60 and 100 games at a time, winning over 80 per cent of the games.

The greatest number of games at one time: this one's held by Yugoslav chess journalist Dimitrije Bjelica, who took on 301 opponents at Sarajevo on 18 September 1982. The display lasted nine hours and the final score was + 258, = 36, − 7.

The largest number of games played simultaneously blindfold: a controversial one, this. The Hungarian János Flesch played 52 games blindfold at Budapest in 1960 (+ 31, = 18, − 3), but rumour has it that some of his opponents were persuaded to resign after only a few moves. This takes us back to Miguel Najdorf, who took on 45 opponents with a score of + 39, = 4, − 2, in 1947. It is claimed, however, that his moves were written down for him, which disqualifies him from the record books. So the record is still held by George

[1] Other contenders: George Koltanowski, the Belgian–American wizard of blindfold play, is reputed to have beaten the rest of the Belgian national team in a simul. Capablanca (again) beat a Swedish team 5–2 in a clock simul in 1928. Kasparov has been making a habit of beating national teams in clock simuls in recent years. The Swiss, French, German and Argentine teams have all fallen victim to the great Gazza.

Koltanoswki (then Belgium, now USA) who played 34 games, winning 24 and drawing 10, back in 1934.

The most remarkable simultaneous player: this must be the great American Harry Nelson Pillsbury. Pillsbury would play up to 22 simultaneous games of chess and draughts blindfold while taking part in a game of whist. Before the display he would ask the audience for lists of words or objects, and repeat them at the end of the display. On one famous occasion in London two professors came up with the following curious list of words:

Antiphlogistine	micrococcus	Etchenberg	Bangmanvate
periosteum	plasmodium	American	Schlechter's Nek
takadiastase	Mississippi	Russian	Manzinyama
plasmon	Freiheit	philosophy	theosophy
ambrosia	Philadelphia	Piet Potgelter's	catechism
Threlkeld	Cincinnati	Rost	Madjesoomalops
streptococcus	athletics	Salamagundi	
staphylococcus	no war	Oomisellecootsi	

Pillsbury looked at the list, repeated the words, and then again in reverse order. The next day he recited them again. Here's Pillsbury doing his scintillating stuff. The game was one of twelve chess and four draughts simultaneously *blindfold*, plus a game of whist on the side!

H. N. Pillsbury–Amateur, Toronto, 1899. Queen's Pawn Game.

1. d4 d5	7. e4 dxe4	13. Rfe1 Rc6	19. Rxe6+ fxe6
2. Nf3 e6	8. Nxe4 Bb7	14. Ba3 a5	20. Qg6+ hxg6
3. e3 Nf6	9. Nxd6+ cxd6	15. c4 Ne4	21. Bxg6 mate
4. Bd3 Nbd7	10. Bf4 Bxf3	16. cxd5 Ng5	Wow!
5. O–O b6	11. Qxf3 d5	17. Qg3 Rc8	
6. Nbd2 Bd6	12. Bd6 Rc8	18. dxe6 Nxe6	

♚

The individual chess marathon record (a 75 per cent score against opponents with an average rating of at least 1800 is required) is currently held by Dutchman Erik Knoppert, who, in London between 9.19 on 13 September and 5.17 on 16 September 1985 scored 82.6 per cent in 500 games against opponents averaging ELO 2000.

The chess marathon record as authorized by *The Guinness Book of Records* stands to Roger Long and Graham Croft, who played for 200 hours at Dingles, Bristol, between 11 and 19 May 1984.

The Sixty-four Greatest Games

To conclude this chapter we offer the reader a selection of sixty-four of the best, most famous and most significant games of all time. To those of our readers who have seen them before we can only apologize and suggest they amuse themselves by compiling their own list. For the rest of you, stand by to be amazed, thrilled and, dare we say it, educated.

♛

1. Bourdonnais–McDonnell, 50th Match Game, 1834. Queen's Gambit Accepted
From a series of games between the two best players of their day, the beginnings of modern international chess.

1. d4 d5	11. Rd1 Bg4	21. Bxb5 Bxf3	31. Qa2 Nc4+
2. c4 dxc4	12. d6 cxd6	22. gxf3 Nd4	32. Kg4 Rg8
3. e4 e5	13. Nd5 Nxd5	23. Bc4 Nxf3+	33. Rxb6 axb6
4. d5 f5	14. Bxe7 Ne3+	24. Kf2 Nxd2	34. Kh4 Kf6
5. Nc3 Nf6	15. Ke1 Kxe7	25. Rxg7+ Kf6	35. Qe2 Rg6
6. Bxc4 Bc5	16. Qd3 Rd8	26. Rf7+ Kg6	36. Qh5 Ne3
7. Nf3 Qe7	17. Rd2 Nc6	27. Rb7 Ndxc4	White resigns
8. Bg5 Bxf2+	18. b3 Ba5	28. bxc4 Rxc4	
9. Kf1 Bb6	19. a3 Rac8	29. Qb1 Bb6	
10. Qe2 f4	20. Rg1 b5	30. Kf3 Rc3	

2. McDonnell–Bourdonnais, 62nd Match Game, 1834. Sicilian Defence
The Frenchman's most famous win in the match (really a series of six matches) in which he came out ahead of his Irish opponent by a score believed to be +45, =13, −27.

1. e4 c5	4. Nxd4 e5	7. Bg5 Be7	10. Bb3 O–O
2. Nf3 Nc6	5. Nxc6 bxc6	8. Qe2 d5	11. O–O a5
3. d4 cxd4	6. Bc4 Nf6	9. Bxf6 Bxf6	12. exd5 cxd5

13. Rd1 d4	20. Rac1 f5	27. Bd7 f2	34. Qc5 Rg8
14. c4 Qb6	21. Qc4+ Kh8	28. Rf1 d3	35. Rd1 e3
15. Bc2 Bb7	22. Ba4 Qh6	29. Rc3 Bxd7	36. Qc3 Qxd1
16. Nd2 Rae8	23. Bxe8 fxe4	30. cxd7 e4	37. Rxd1 e2
17. Ne4 Bd8	24. c6 exf3	31. Qc8 Bd8	White resigns
18. c5 Qc6	25. Rc2 Qe3+	32. Qc4 Qe1	
19. f3 Be7	26. Kh1 Bc8	33. Rc1 d2	

Final Position

3. Anderssen–Kieseritzky, Casual Game, London, 1851, King's Gambit

Nicknamed the 'Immortal Game', a classic example of sacrificial attack against an opponent who neglects his development.

1. e4 e5	7. d3 Nh5	13. h5 Qg5	19. Ke2 Bxg1
2. f4 exf4	8. Nh4 Qg5	14. Qf3 Ng8	20. e5 Na6
3. Bc4 Qh4+	9. Nf5 c6	15. Bxf4 Qf6	21. Nxg7+ Kd8
4. Kf1 b5	10. Rg1 cxb5	16. Nc3 Bc5	22. Qf6+ Nxf6
5. Bxb5 Nf6	11. g4 Nf6	17. Nd5 Qxb2	23. Be7 mate
6. Nf3 Qh6	12. h4 Qg6	18. Bd6 Qxa1+	

4. Anderssen–Dufresne, Casual Game, Berlin, 1852. Evans Gambit

Anderssen's other legendary masterpiece, the 'Evergreen game'; White's nineteenth move was described by Lasker as one of the most subtle on record.

1. e4 e5	5. c3 Ba5	9. e5 Qg6	13. Qa4 Bb6
2. Nf3 Nc6	6. d4 exd4	10. Re1 Nge7	14. Nbd2 Bb7
3. Bc4 Bc5	7. O–O d3	11. Ba3 b5	15. Ne4 Qf5
4. b4 Bxb4	8. Qb3 Qf6	12. Qxb5 Rb8	16. Bxd3 Qh5

IMPOSSIBLE

17. Nf6+ gxf6	20. Rxe7+ Nxe7	23. Bd7+ Kf8
18. exf6 Rg8	21. Qxd7+ Kxd7	24. Bxe7
19. Rad1 Qxf3	22. Bf5+ Ke8	mate

5. *L. Paulsen–Morphy, New York, 1857. Four Knights' Opening*
From Morphy's only tournament, featuring a stunning queen sacrifice.

1. e4 e5	9. Be2 Nxe4	17. Qa6 Qxf3	25. Qf1 Bxf1
2. Nf3 Nc6	10. Nxe4 Rxe4	18. gxf3 Rg6+	26. Rxf1 Re2
3. Nc3 Nf6	11. Bf3 Re6	19. Kh1 Bh3	27. Ra1 Rh6
4. Bb5 Bc5	12. c3 Qd3	20. Rd1 Bg2+	28. d4 Be3
5. O–O O–O	13. b4 Bb6	21. Kg1 Bxf3+	White resigns
6. Nxe5 Re8	14. a4 bxa4	22. Kf1 Bg2+	
7. Nxc6 dxc6	15. Qxa4 Bd7	23. Kg1 Bh3+	
8. Bc4 b5	16. Ra2 Rae8	24. Kh1 Bxf2	

6. *Morphy–Duke of Brunswick and Count Isouard, Paris Opera House, 1858. Philidor Defence*
Perhaps the most famous, most published game of all time, frequently used by chess teachers to exemplify the value of rapid development.

1. e4 e5	6. Bc4 Nf6	11. Bxb5+ Nbd7	16. Qb8+ Nxb8
2. Nf3 d6	7. Qb3 Qe7	12. O–O–O Rd8	17. Rd8
3. d4 Bg4	8. Nc3 c6	13. Rxd7 Rxd7	mate
4. dxe5 Bxf3	9. Bg5 b5	14. Rd1 Qe6	
5. Qxf3 dxe5	10. Nxb5 cxb5	15. Bxd7+ Nxd7	

7. *Zukertort–Blackburne, London, 1883. Queen's Gambit Declined (by transposition)*
A combination by a man who, with better health, might conceivably have become World Champion; it was said to have 'literally electrified the lookers-on'.

1. c4 e6	8. b3 Nbd7	15. Bxc4 d5	22. exf6 Nxf6
2. e3 Nf6	9. Bb2 Qe7	16. Bd3 Rfc8	23. f5 Ne4
3. Nf3 b6	10. Nb5 Ne4	17. Rae1 Rc7	24. Bxe4 dxe4
4. Be2 Bb7	11. Nxd6 cxd6	18. e4 Rac8	25. fxg6 Rc2
5. O–O d5	12. Nd2 Ndf6	19. e5 Ne8	26. gxh7+ Kh8
6. d4 Bd6	13. f3 Nxd2	20. f4 g6	27. d5+ e5
7. Nc3 O–O	14. Qxd2 dxc4	21. Re3 f5	

28. Qb4 R8c5	31. Bxe5+ Kxf8	33. Qxe7 Black
29. Rf8+ Kxh7	32. Bg7+ Kg8	resigns
30. Qxe4+ Kg7		

8. Em Lasker–Bauer, Amsterdam, 1889. Bird's Opening
The first example of the famous double bishop sacrifice.

1. f4 d5	10. Ng3 Qc7	19. Rf3 e5	28. e6 Rb7
2. Nf3 e6	11. Ne5 Nxe5	20. Rh3+ Qh6	29. Qg6 f6
3. e3 Nf6	12. Bxe5 Qc6	21. Rxh6+ Kxh6	30. Rxf6+ Bxf6
4. b3 Be7	13. Qe2 a6	22. Qd7 Bf6	31. Qxf6+ Ke8
5. Bb2 b6	14. Nh5 Nxh5	23. Qxb7 Kg7	32. Qh8+ Ke7
6. Bd3 Bb7	15. Bxh7+ Kxh7	24. Rf1 Rab8	33. Qg7+ Black
7. Nc3 O–O	16. Qxh5+ Kg8	25. Qd7 Rfd8	resigns
8. O–O Nbd7	17. Bxg7 Kxg7	26. Qg4+ Kf8	
9. Ne2 c5	18. Qg4+ Kh7	27. fxe5 Bg7	

9. Pillsbury–Tarrasch, Hastings, 1895. Queen's Gambit Declined
A tremendous struggle which signalled the emergence of the previously unknown Pillsbury as a great master.

1. d4 d5	9. Bd3 Bb7	17. Bxe7 Rxe7	25. Nc3 Bd5
2. c4 e6	10. O–O c5	18. Bxe4 dxe4	26. Nf2 Qc6
3. Nc3 Nf6	11. Re1 c4	19. Qg3 f6	27. Rf1 b4
4. Bg5 Be7	12. Bb1 a6	20. Ng4 Kh8	28. Ne2 Qa4
5. Nf3 Nbd7	13. Ne5 b5	21. f5 Qd7	29. Ng4 Nd7
6. Rc1 O–O	14. f4 Re8	22. Rf1 Rd8	30. R4f2 Kg8
7. e3 b6	15. Qf3 Nf8	23. Rf4 Qd6	31. Nc1 c3
8. cxd5 exd5	16. Ne2 Ne4	24. Qh4 Rde8	32. b3 Qc6

33. h3 a5	39. Rg2 Kh8	45. Kh1 Qd5	51. Qxd7 c2
34. Nh2 a4	40. gxf6 gxf6	46. Rg1 Qxf5	52. Qxh7
35. g4 axb3	41. Nxb3 Rxb3	47. Qh4+ Qh5	
36. axb3 Ra8	42. Nh6 Rg7	48. Qf4+ Qg5	
37. g5 Ra3	43. Rxg7 Kxg7	49. Rxg5 fxg5	
38. Ng4 Bxb3	44. Qg3+ Kxh6	50. Qd6+ Kh5	

10. Steinitz–von Bardeleben, Hastings, 1895. Giuoco Piano
From the same tournament, Steinitz's immortal game.

1. e4 e5	8. exd5 Nxd5	15. Qe2 Qd7	22. Rxe7+ Kf8
2. Nf3 Nc6	9. O–O Be6	16. Rac1 c6	23. Rf7+ Kg8
3. Bc4 Bc5	10. Bg5 Be7	17. d5 cxd5	24. Rg7+ Kh8
4. c3 Nf6	11. Bxd5 Bxd5	18. Nd4 Kf7	25. Rxh7+
5. d4 exd4	12. Nxd5 Qxd5	19. Ne6 Rhc8	Black resigns
6. cxd4 Bb4+	13. Bxe7 Nxe7	20. Qg4 g6	
7. Nc3 d5	14. Re1 f6	21. Ng5+ Ke8	

11. Pillsbury–Em Lasker, St Petersburg, 1895–6. Queen's Gambit Declined
Every one of the games between these two players is full of interest, this one featuring a superb Lasker attack.

1. d4 d5	9. e3 Bd7	18. fxe6 Ra3	27. Qe6+ Kh7
2. c4 e6	10. Kb1 h6	19. exf7+ Rxf7	28. Kxa3 Qc3+
3. Nc3 Nf6	11. cxd5 exd5	20. bxa3 Qb6+	29. Ka4 b5+
4. Nf3 c5	12. Nd4 O–O	21. Bb5 Qxb5+	30. Kxb5 Qc4+
5. Bg5 cxd4	13. Bxf6 Bxf6	22. Ka1 Rc7	31. Ka5 Bd8+
6. Qxd4 Nc6	14. Qh5 Nxd4	23. Rd2 Rc4	32. Qb6 axb6
7. Qh4 Be7	15. exd4 Be6	24. Rhd1 Rc3	mate
8. O–O–O	16. f4 Rac8	25. Qf5 Qc4	
Qa5	17. f5 Rxc3	26. Kb2 Rxa3	

12. Capablanca–Corzo, 11th Match Game, Havana, 1901. Queen's Pawn Game
Capa at the age of thirteen: the decisive game in a match against the Cuban champion and one of the best ever played by a prodigy.

1. d4 d5	4. b3 e6	7. exd4 Bd6	10. g3 f5
2. Nf3 c5	5. Bb2 Nf6	8. Bd3 O–O	11. Ne5 Nf6
3. e3 Nc6	6. Nbd2 cxd4	9. O–O Nh5	12. f4 Bxe5

13. fxe5 Ng4	26. c4 Qe6	39. hxg4 hxg4	52. b4 Ke4
14. Qe2 Qb6	27. cxd5 Qxd5	40. Be5 Kh6	53. Bb6 Kd5
15. Nf3 Bd7	28. e6 Bb5	41. d7 Rd8	54. Kd3 Kc6
16. a3 Kh8	29. Qxb5 Qxb5	42. Ng8+ Rxg8	55. Bg1 Kd5
17. h3 Nh6	30. d5+ Rg7	43. Bf6 Kg6	56. Bh2 Kc6
18. Qf2 Nf7	31. exf7 h6	44. d8=Q Rxd8	57. Kd4 a4
19. Kg2 g5	32. Nd4 Qxf1	45. Bxd8 b5	58. Ke5 Kb6
20. g4 Ne7	33. Rxf1 Rxf7	46. Kf2 Kf5	59. Kd5 Ka6
21. Qe3 Rg8	34. Rxf5 Rxf5	47. Ke3 Ke5	60. Kc5
22. Rae1 Ng6	35. Nxf5 Kh7	48. Kd3 Kd5	Black resigns
23. gxf5 Nf4+	36. Ne7 Rf8	49. Kc3 g3	
24. Kh2 Nxd3	37. Kg2 h5	50. Bh4 g2	
25. Qxd3 exf5	38. d6 g4	51. Bf2 a5	

13. Em Lasker–Napier, Cambridge Springs, 1904. Sicilian Defence
A terrific slugfest which the loser rated his best-ever game.

1. e4 c5	10. h4 Nc7	19. Bc5 gxh5	28. Rxb7 a5
2. Nc3 Nc6	11. f4 e5	20. Bc4 exf4	29. Rb3 Bg7
3. Nf3 g6	12. Nde2 d5	21. Bxf7 Ne4	30. Rh3 Ng3
4. d4 cxd4	13. exd5 Nd4	22. Bxe8 Bxb2	31. Kf3 Ra6
5. Nxd4 Bg7	14. Nxd4 Nxd5	23. Rb1 Bc3+	32. Kxf4 Ne2+
6. Be3 d6	15. Nf5 Nxc3	24. Kf1 Bg4	33. Kf5 Nc3
7. f3 Nf6	16. Qxd8 Rxd8	25. Bxh5 Bxh5	34. a3 Na4
8. g4 O–O	17. Ne7+ Kh8	26. Rxh5 Ng3+	35. Be3
9. g5 Ne8	18. h5 Re8	27. Kg2 Nxh5	Black resigns

14. Rotlewi–Rubinstein, Łódź, 1907. Queen's Gambit Declined
Rubinstein's most famous game – another all-time great combination.

1. d4 d5	9. Bb2 O–O	17. f4 Bc7	25. Qg2 Rh3
2. Nf3 e6	10. Qd2 Qe7	18. e4 Rac8	26. Bd4 Bxd4
3. e3 c5	11. Bd3 dxc4	19. e5 Bb6+	27. Rf2 Bxf2
4. c4 Nc6	12. Bxc4 b5	20. Kh1 Ng4	and mate next
5. Nc3 Nf6	13. Bd3 Rd8	21. Be4 Qh4	move
6. dxc5 Bxc5	14. Qe2 Bb7	22. g3 Rxc3	
7. a3 a6	15. O–O Ne5	23. gxh4 Rd2	
8. b4 Bd6	16. Nxe5 Bxe5	24. Qxd2 Bxe4+	

15. Levitsky–Marshall, Breslau, 1912. French Defence

The brilliant American's last move has been described as the most beautiful ever – Marshall said that the spectators showered the board with gold coins[1] after he played it; and we're not surprised.

1. e4 e6	7. O–O Be7	13. Bh3 Rae8	19. Rxd5 Nd4
2. d4 d5	8. Bg5 O–O	14. Qd2 Bb4	20. Qh5 Ref8
3. Nc3 c5	9. dxc5 Be6	15. Bxf6 Rxf6	21. Re5 Rh6
4. Nf3 Nc6	10. Nd4 Bxc5	16. Rad1 Qc5	22. Qg5 Rxh3
5. exd5 exd5	11. Nxe6 fxe6	17. Qe2 Bxc3	23. Rc5 Qg3
6. Be2 Nf6	12. Bg4 Qd6	18. bxc3 Qxc3	White resigns

16. Bernstein–Capablanca, Exhibition Game, Moscow, 1914. Queen's Gambit Declined

Capa's last move is one of the most famous in chess history.

1. d4 d5	9. Qa4 Bb7	17. Nd4 Bb4	25. Nd4 Rc7
2. c4 e6	10. Ba6 Bxa6	18. b3 Rac8	26. Nb5 Rc5
3. Nc3 Nf6	11. Qxa6 c5	19. bxc4 dxc4	27. Nxc3 Nxc3
4. Nf3 Be7	12. Bxf6 Nxf6	20. Rc2 Bxc3	28. Rxc3 Rxc3
5. Bg5 O–O	13. dxc5 bxc5	21. Rxc3 Nd5	29. Rxc3 Qb2
6. e3 Nbd7	14. O–O Qb6	22. Rc2 c3	White resigns
7. Rc1 b6	15. Qe2 c4	23. Rdc1 Rc5	
8. cxd5 exd5	16. Rfd1 Rfd8	24. Nb3 Rc6	

17. Em Lasker–Capablanca, St Petersburg, 1914. Ruy López

A much-quoted example of Lasker's psychological approach: needing to win at all costs he chooses a drawish variation and his opponent drops his guard.

1. e4 e5	8. Nc3 Ne7	15. Nd4 Rad8	22. Kf2 Ra7
2. Nf3 Nc6	9. O–O O–O	16. Ne6 Rd7	23. g4 h6
3. Bb5 a6	10. f4 Re8	17. Rad1 Nc8	24. Rd3 a5
4. Bxc6 dxc6	11. Nb3 f6	18. Rf2 b5	25. h4 axb4
5. d4 exd4	12. f5 b6	19. Rfd2 Rde7	26. axb4 Rae7
6. Qxd4 Qxd4	13. Bf4 Bb7	20. b4 Kf7	27. Kf3 Rg8
7. Nxd4 Bd6	14. Bxd6 cxd6	21. a3 Ba8	28. Kf4 g6

[1] According to Walter Korn, these were payoffs by Russians who'd backed Levitsky with gold roubles, marks and Austrian crowns.

29. Rg3 g5 +	33. Kg3 Ke8	37. N6c5 Bc8	41. Ra8 + Bc8
30. Kf3 Nb6	34. Rdh1 Bb7	38. N×d7 B×d7	42. Nc5
31. h×g5 h×g5	35. e5 d×e5	39. Rh7 Rf8	Black resigns
32. Rh3 Rd7	36. Ne4 Nd5	40. Ra1 Kd8	

18. Nimzowitsch–Tarrasch, St Petersburg, 1914. Queen's Gambit Declined

Perhaps Tarrasch's best-known game, and another example of the double bishop sacrifice.

1. d4 d5	10. Rc1 Qe7	19. e×d4 B×h2 +	28. f×e4 f4 +
2. Nf3 c5	11. c×d5 e×d5	20. K×h2 Qh4 +	29. K×f4 Rf8 +
3. c4 e6	12. Nh4 g6	21. Kg1 B×g2	30. Ke5 Qh2 +
4. e3 Nf6	13. Nhf3 Rad8	22. f3 Rfe8	31. Ke6 Re8 +
5. Bd3 Nc6	14. d×c5 b×c5	23. Ne4 Qh1 +	32. Kd7 Bb5
6. O–O Bd6	15. Bb5 Ne4	24. Kf2 B×f1	mate
7. b3 O–O	16. B×c6 B×c6	25. d5 f5	
8. Bb2 b6	17. Qc2 N×d2	26. Qc3 Qg2 +	
9. Nbd2 Bb7	18. N×d2 d4	27. Ke3 R×e4 +	

19. Bogoljubow–Alekhine, Hastings, 1922. Dutch Defence

'The greatest masterpiece ever created on a chessboard,' according to Irving Chernev.

1. d4 f5	15. Ng5 Bd7	29. R×a5 b4	43. e4 N×e4
2. c4 Nf6	16. f3 Nf6	30. R×a8 d×c3	44. N×e4 Q×e4
3. g3 e6	17. f4 e4	31. R×e8 c2	45. d6 c×d6
4. Bg2 Bb4 +	18. Rfd1 h6	32. R×f8 + Kh7	46. f6 g×f6
5. Bd2 B×d2 +	19. Nh3 d5	33. Nf2 c1 = Q +	47. Rd2 Qe2
6. N×d2 Nc6	20. Nf1 Ne7	34. Nf1 Ne1	48. R×e2 f×e2
7. Ngf3 O–O	21. a4 Nc6	35. Rh2 Q×c4	49. Kf2
8. O–O d6	22. Rd2 Nb4	36. Rb8 Bb5	e×f1 = Q +
9. Qb3 Kh8	23. Bh1 Qe8	37. R×b5 Q×b5	50. K×f1 Kg7
10. Qc3 e5	24. Rg2 d×c4	38. g4 Nf3 +	51. Kf2 Kf7
11. e3 a5	25. b×c4 B×a4	39. B×f3 e×f3	52. Ke3 Ke6
12. b3 Qe8	26. Nf2 Bd7	40. g×f5 Qe2	53. Ke4 d5 +
13. a3 Qh5	27. Nd2 b5	41. d5 Kg8	White resigns
14. h4 Ng4	28. Nd1 Nd3	42. h5 Kh7	

20. Alekhine–Yates, London, 1922. Queen's Gambit Declined
Alekhine in positional style: seize the open file, rooks on the seventh rank and wham!

1. d4 Nf6	11. Ne4 f5	21. Ne5 Reb8	31. h5 Bf1
2. c4 e6	12. Bxe7 Qxe7	22. f3 b3	32. g3 Ba6
3. Nf3 d5	13. Ned2 b5	23. a3 h6	33. Rf7 Kh7
4. Nc3 Be7	14. Bxd5 cxd5	24. Kf2 Kh7	34. Rcc7 Rg8
5. Bg5 O–O	15. O–O a5	25. h4 Rf8	35. Nd7 Kh8
6. e3 Nbd7	16. Nb3 a4	26. Kg3 Rfb8	36. Nf6 Rgf8
7. Rc1 c6	17. Nc5 Nxc5	27. Rc7 Bb5	37. Rxg7 Rxf6
8. Qc2 Re8	18. Qxc5 Qxc5	28. R1c5 Ba6	38. Ke5
9. Bd3 dxc4	19. Rxc5 b4	29. R5c6 Re8	Black resigns
10. Bxc4 Nd5	20. Rfc1 Ba6	30. Kf4 Kg8	

21. Maróczy–Tartakower, Teplitz-Schönau, 1922. Dutch Defence
A marvellous intuitive sacrifice by one of the most imaginative players of his time.

1. d4 e6	10. b3 Nd7	19. Kh1 Nf6	28. Be1 Rxf1+
2. c4 f5	11. Bb2 Rf6	20. Re2 Qxg3	29. Kxf1 e5
3. Nc3 Nf6	12. Rfe1 Rh6	21. Nb1 Nh5	30. Kg1 Bg4
4. a3 Be7	13. g3 Qf6	22. Qd2 Bd7	31. Bxg3 Nxg3
5. e3 O–O	14. Bf1 g5	23. Rf2 Qh4+	32. Re1 Nf5
6. Bd3 d5	15. Rad1 g4	24. Kg1 Bg3	33. Qf2 Qg5
7. Nf3 c6	16. Nxe4 fxe4	25. Bc3 Bxf2+	34. dxe5 Bf3+
8. O–O Ne4	17. Nd2 Rxh2	26. Qxf2 g3	35. Kf1 Ng3+
9. Qc2 Bd6	18. Kxh2 Qxf2+	27. Qg2 Rf8	White resigns

22. Grünfeld–Alekhine, Carlsbad, 1923. Queen's Gambit Declined
Another Alekhine special, concluding with a great combination.

1. d4 Nf6	10. Bh4 Re8	19. Bxf6 Bxf6	28. Na2 Nd3
2. c4 e6	11. Bd3 dxc4	20. Qc2 g6	29. Rxc8 Qxc8
3. Nf3 d5	12. Bxc4 b5	21. Qe2 Nc4	30. f3 Rxd4
4. Nc3 Be7	13. Ba2 c5	22. Be4 Bg7	31. fxe4 Nf4
5. Bg5 Nbd7	14. Rd1 cxd4	23. Bxb7 Qxb7	32. exf4 Qc4
6. e3 O–O	15. Nxd4 Qb6	24. Rc1 e5	33. Qxc4 Rxd1+
7. Rc1 c6	16. Bb1 Bb7	25. Nb3 e4	34. Qf1 Bd4+
8. Qc2 a6	17. O–O Rac8	26. Nd4 Red8	and mate next
9. a3 h6	18. Qd2 Ne5	27. Rfd1 Ne5	move

23. *Sämisch–Nimzowitsch, Copenhagen, 1923. Queen's Indian Defence*
'The Immortal Zugzwang Game' – a modest pawn advance reduces White to complete impotence: he has only a few pawn moves that do not lose material.

1. d4 Nf6	8. Ne5 c6	15. Kh2 Nh5	22. Qg5 Raf8
2. c4 e6	9. cxd5 cxd5	16. Bd2 f5	23. Kh1 R8f5
3. Nf3 b6	10. Bf4 a6	17. Qd1 b4	24. Qe3 Bd3
4. g3 Bb7	11. Rc1 b5	18. Nb1 Bb5	25. Rce1 h6
5. Bg2 Be7	12. Qb3 Nc6	19. Rg1 Bd6	White resigns
6. Nc3 O–O	13. Nxc6 Bxc6	20. e4 fxe4	
7. O–O d5	14. h3 Qd7	21. Qxh5 Rxf2	

Final Position

24. *Capablanca–Tartakower, New York, 1924. Dutch Defence*
Capa's most famous ending, a classic example of a rook and pawn endgame.

1. d4 f5	11. bxc3 Qxe7	21. g3 Kf8	31. g4 Nc4
2. Nf3 e6	12. a4 Bxf3	22. Kg2 Rf7	32. g5 Ne3+
3. c4 Nf6	13. Qxf3 Nc6	23. h4 d5	33. Kf3 Nf5
4. Bg5 Be7	14. Rfb1 Rae8	24. cxd5 exd5	34. Bxf5 gxf5
5. Nc3 O–O	15. Qh3 Rf6	25. Qxe8+ Qxe8	35. Kg3 Rxc3+
6. e3 b6	16. f4 Na5	26. Rxe8+ Kxe8	36. Kh4 Rf3
7. Bd3 Bb7	17. Qf3 d6	27. h5 Rf6	37. g6 Rxf4+
8. O–O Qe8	18. Re1 Qd7	28. hxg6 hxg6	38. Kg5 Re4
9. Qe2 Ne4	19. e4 fxe4	29. Rh1 Kf8	39. Kf6 Kg8
10. Bxe7 Nxc3	20. Qxe4 g6	30. Rh7 Rc6	40. Rg7+ Kh8

41. Rxc7 Re8	45. g7+ Kg8	49. d5 Rc1	Black resigns
42. Kxf5 Re4	46. Rxa7 Rg1	50. Rc7 Ra1	
43. Kf6 Rf4+	47. Kxd5 Rc1	51. Kc6 Rxa4	
44. Ke5 Rg4	48. Kd6 Rc2	52. d6	

A footnote to this game: in 1987, Capa's widow, Olga Capablanca Clark, offered for sale the manuscript of a hitherto unpublished Capablanca–Tartakower game. The reserve price, a very reasonable $10,000. Sadly, no bids were received by the closing date.

25. Réti–Bogoljubow, New York, 1924. Réti Opening

The first brilliancy prize game in one of the greatest tournaments of all time, and voted top of the pops by BCM readers in the sixties.

1. Nf3 Nf6	8. d4 c6	15. e4 e5	22. Qxf5 Rxd4
2. c4 e6	9. Nbd2 Ne4	16. c5 Bf8	23. Rf1 Rd8
3. g3 d5	10. Nxe4 dxe4	17. Qc2 exd4	24. Bf7+ Kh8
4. Bg2 Bd6	11. Ne5 f5	18. exf5 Rad8	25. Be8
5. O–O O–O	12. f3 exf3	19. Bh5 Re5	Black resigns
6. b3 Re8	13. Bxf3 Qc7	20. Bxd4 Rxf5	
7. Bb2 Nbd7	14. Nxd7 Bxd7	21. Rxf5 Bxf5	

26. Réti–Alekhine, Baden-Baden, 1925. King's Fianchetto

One of the most remarkable combinations of all time, lasting from Black's twenty-sixth move to the end of the game.

1. g3 e5	8. Nxd2 O–O	15. Rd2 Qc8	22. Rc1 h4
2. Nf3 e4	9. c4 Na6	16. Nc5 Bh3	23. a4 hxg3
3. Nd4 d5	10. cxd5 Nb4	17. Bf3 Bg4	24. hxg3 Qc7
4. d3 exd3	11. Qc4 Nbxd5	18. Bg2 Bh3	25. b5 axb5
5. Qxd3 Nf6	12. N2b3 c6	19. Bf3 Bg4	26. axb5
6. Bg2 Bb4+	13. O–O Re8	20. Bh1 h5	
7. Bd2 Bxd2+	14. Rfd1 Bg4	21. b4 a6	

26. .... Re3	30. Nxb7 Nxe2+	34. Rcc2 Ng4+	38. Kh3 Ne3+
27. Nf3 cxb5	31. Kh2 Ne4	35. Kh3 Ne5+	39. Kh2 Nxc2
28. Qxb5 Nc3	32. Rc4 Nxf2	36. Kh2 Rxf3	40. Bxf3 Nd4
29. Qxb7 Qxb7	33. Bg2 Be6	37. Rxe2 Ng4+	White resigns

27. C. Torre–Em Lasker, Moscow, 1925. Torre Attack
Lasker's most famous loss – his Mexican opponent, whose career was tragically cut short by a mental breakdown, wins with an amusing 'windmill' combination.

1. d4 Nf6	12. Rfe1 Rfe8	23. Nc4 Qd5	34. Rxh6+ Kg5
2. Nf3 e6	13. Rad1 Nf8	24. Ne3 Qb5	35. Rh3 Reb8
3. Bg5 c5	14. Bc1 Nd5	25. Bf6 Qxh5	36. Rg3+ Kf6
4. e3 cxd4	15. Ng5 b5	26. Rxg7+ Kh8	37. Rf3+ Kg6
5. exd4 Be7	16. Na3 b4	27. Rxf7+ Kg8	38. a3 a5
6. Nbd2 d6	17. cxb4 Nxb4	28. Rg7+ Kh8	39. bxa5 Rxa5
7. c3 Nbd7	18. Qh5 Bxg5	29. Rxb7+ Kg8	40. Nc4 Rd5
8. Bd3 b6	19. Bxg5 Nxd3	30. Rg7+ Kh8	41. Rf4 Nd7
9. Nc4 Bb7	20. Rxd3 Qa5	31. Rg5+ Kh7	42. Rxe6+ Kg5
10. Qe2 Qc7	21. b4 Qf5	32. Rxh5 Kg6	43. g3
11. O–O O–O	22. Rg3 h6	33. Rh3 Kxf6	Black resigns

28. P. Johner–Nimzowitsch, Dresden, 1926. Nimzo-Indian Defence
Another profound effort by one of the leaders of the Hypermodern School, providing a practical illustration of his theory of the blockade.

1. d4 Nf6	12. Be2 Qd7	23. Nd2 Rg8	34. Bxe4 Bf5
2. c4 e6	13. h3 Ne7	24. Bg2 g5	35. Bxf5 Nxf5
3. Nc3 Bb4	14. Qe1 h5	25. Nf1 Rg7	36. Re2 h4
4. e3 O–O	15. Bd2 Qf5	26. Ra2 Nf5	37. Rgg2 hxg3+
5. Bd3 c5	16. Kh2 Qh7	27. Bh1 Rcg8	38. Kg1 Qh3
6. Nf3 Nc6	17. a4 Nf5	28. Qd1 gxf4	39. Ne3 Nh4
7. O–O Bxc3	18. g3 a5	29. exf4 Bc8	40. Kf1 Re8
8. bxc3 d6	19. Rg1 Nh6	30. Qb3 Ba6	White resigns
9. Nd2 b6	20. Bf1 Bd7	31. Re2 Nh4	
10. Nb3 e5	21. Bc1 Rac8	32. Re3 Bc8	
11. f4 e4	22. d5 Kh8	33. Qc2 Bxh3	

29. Nimzowitsch–Capablanca, New York, 1927. Caro-Kann Defence
Capablanca wins in the style of Nimzowitsch(!) by running his opponent out of moves.

1. e4 c6	13. f4 Nf5	25. Red2 Rec8	37. cxd4 Qc4
2. d4 d5	14. c3 Nc6	26. Re2 Ne7	38. Kg2 b5
3. e5 Bf5	15. Rad1 g6	27. Red2 Rc4	39. Kg1 b4
4. Bd3 Bxd3	16. g4 Nxe3	28. Qh3 Kg7	40. axb4 axb4
5. Qxd3 e6	17. Qxe3 h5	29. Rf2 a5	41. Kg2 Qc1
6. Nc3 Qb6	18. g5 O–O	30. Re2 Nf5	42. Kg3 Qh1
7. Nge2 c5	19. Nd4 Qb6	31. Nxf5+ gxf5	43. Rd3 Re1
8. dxc5 Bxc5	20. Rf2 Rfc8	32. Qf3 Kg6	44. Rf3 Rd1
9. O–O Ne7	21. a3 Rc7	33. Red2 Re4	45. b3 Rc1
10. Na4 Qc6	22. Rd3 Na5	34. Rd4 Rc4	46. Re3 Rf1
11. Nxc5 Qxc5	23. Re2 Re8	35. Qf2 Qb5	White resigns.
12. Be3 Qc7	24. Kg2 Nc6	36. Kg3 Rcxd4	

30. Sultan Khan–Capablanca, Hastings, 1930–31. Queen's Indian Defence
The extraordinary Indian genius inexorably manoeuvres his way to victory – and what an opponent!

1. Nf3 Nf6	8. e3 O–O	15. Qb3 Qe7	22. Kd2 R8c2+
2. d4 b6	9. Bd3 Ne4	16. Nd2 Ndf6	23. Qxc2 Rxc2+
3. c4 Bb7	10. Bf4 Nd7	17. Nxe4 fxe4	24. Kxc2 Qc7+
4. Nc3 e6	11. Qc2 f5	18. Be2 Rc6	25. Kd2 Qc4
5. a3 d5	12. Nb5 Bd6	19. g4 Rfc8	26. Be2 Qb3
6. cxd5 exd5	13. Nxd6 cxd6	20. g5 Ne8	27. Rab1 Kf7
7. Bg5 Be7	14. h4 Rc8	21. Bg4 Rc1+	28. Rhc1 Ke7

29. Rc3 Qa4	39. R3c2 Qh3	49. Kb1 Qh3	59. Bg3 Qxg5
30. b4 Qd7	40. a4 Qh4	50. Ka1 Qg2	60. Kd2 Qf5
31. Rbc1 a6	41. Ka3 Qh3	51. Kb2 Qh3	61. Rxb6 Ke7
32. Rg1 Qh3	42. Bg3 Qf5	52. Rg1 Bc8	62. Rb7+ Ke6
33. Rgc1 Qd7	43. Bh4 g6	53. Rc6 Qh4	63. b6 Nf6
34. h5 Kd8	44. h6 Qd7	54. Rgc1 Bg4	64. Bb5 Qf3
35. R1c2 Qh3	45. b5 a5	55. Bf1 Qh5	65. Rb1
36. Kc1 Qh4	46. Bg3 Qf5	56. Re1 Qh1	Black resigns
37. Kb2 Qh3	47. Bf4 Qh3	57. Rec1 Qh5	
38. Rc1 Qh4	48. Kb2 Qg2	58. Kc3 Qh4	

31. Botvinnik–Chekover, Moscow, 1935. Réti Opening
A stirring, if untypical, king hunt from the first great Soviet player.

1. Nf3 d5	12. Nf3 Rd8	23. fxg5 N8d7	34. Re1 Be5
2. c4 e6	13. Qc2 Ncd7	24. Nxf7 Kxf7	35. Qh8+ Ke7
3. b3 Nf6	14. d4 c5	25. g6+ Kg8	36. Qxg7+ Kd6
4. Bb2 Be7	15. Ne5 b6	26. Qxe6+ Kh8	37. Qxe5+ Kd7
5. e3 O–O	16. Bd3 cxd4	27. Qh3+ Kg8	38. Qf5+ Kc6
6. Be2 c6	17. exd4 Bb7	28. Bf5 Nf8	39. d5+ Kc5
7. O–O Nbd7	18. Qe2 Nf8	29. Be6+ Nxe6	40. Ba3+ Kxc4
8. Nc3 a6	19. Nd1 Ra7	30. Qxe6+ Kh8	41. Qe4+ Kc3
9. Nd4 dxc4	20. Nf2 Qb8	31. Qh3+ Kg8	42. Bb4+ Kb2
10. bxc4 Nc5	21. Nh3 h6	32. Rxf6 Bxf6	43. Qb1 mate
11. f4 Qc7	22. Ng5 hxg5	33. Qh7+ Kf8	

32. Euwe–Alekhine, 26th Game, World Championship Match, 1935.
Dutch Defence
The popular Dutchman's most famous game, 'The Pearl of Zandvoort', which helped him towards a sensational match victory.

1. d4 e6	10. Ne5 Nxc3	19. Nc2 Nd7	28. e6 Rg8
2. c4 f5	11. Bxc3 Bxg2	20. Ne3 Bf6	29. Nf3 Qg6
3. g3 Bb4+	12. Kxg2 Qc8	21. Nxf5 Bxc3	30. Rg1 Bxg1
4. Bd2 Be7	13. d5 d6	22. Nxd6 Qb8	31. Rxg1 Qf6
5. Bg2 Nf6	14. Nd3 e5	23. Nxe4 Bf6	32. Ng5 Rg7
6. Nc3 O–O	15. Kh1 c6	24. Nd2 g5	33. exd7 Rxd7
7. Nf3 Ne4	16. Qb3 Kh8	25. e4 gxf4	34. Qe3 Re7
8. O–O b6	17. f4 e4	26. gxf4 Bd4	35. Ne6 Rf8
9. Qc2 Bb7	18. Nb4 c5	27. e5 Qe8	36. Qe5 Qxe5

37. fxe5 Rf5	40. e6 Rd2	43. Nd8 Kg7	46. Nd6 Rxe7
38. Re1 h6	41. Nc6 Re8	44. Nb7 Kf6	47. Ne4+
39. Nd8 Rf2	42. e7 b5	45. Re6+ Kg5	Black resigns

33. Keres–Alekhine, Margate, 1937. Ruy López

A miniature against a formidable opponent demonstrates why the young Estonian was considered a future World Champion.

1. e4 e5	7. d4 Bg7	13. e5 g5	19. Nxg5 O–O–O
2. Nf3 Nc6	8. Be3 Nf6	14. Qd5 Bf8	20. Nf3 f6
3. Bb5 a6	9. dxe5 dxe5	15. Bxf8 Rxf8	21. exf6 Rxf6
4. Ba4 d6	10. Bc5 Nh5	16. O–O–O Qe7	22. Rhe1 Qb4
5. c4 Bd7	11. Nd5 Nf4	17. Bxc6 Bxc6	23. Qxd7+
6. Nc3 g6	12. Nxf4 exf4	18. Qd3 Bd7	Black resigns

34. Fine–Flohr, AVRO, 1938. French Defence

Reuben Fine gave up chess for a career in psychoanalysis, but he showed what he was capable of by sharing first place in one of the strongest tournaments of all time.

1. e4 e6	9. O–O Nc6	17. Rd4 g6	25. Bxe7 Rxe7
2. d4 d5	10. Re1 h6	18. Qf3 Qc7	26. Qf6 a6
3. Nc3 Bb4	11. Na4 Bf8	19. Nc3 Nf5	27. Rd1 axb5
4. e5 c5	12. Rc1 Bd7	20. Nb5 Qb6	28. Be4+
5. Bd2 Ne7	13. Nxh4 Qxh4	21. Rxd7 Kxd7	Black resigns
6. Nf3 Nf5	14. c4 dxc4	22. g4 Nh4	
7. dxc5 Bxc5	15. Rxc4 Qd8	23. Qxf7+ Be7	
8. Bd3 Nh4	16. Qh5 Ne7	24. Bb4 Rae8	

35. Botvinnik–Capablanca, AVRO, 1938. Nimzo-Indian Defence

Botvinnik's greatest, and a popular choice for the best game of all: a strategic masterpiece crowned with a fine combination.

1. d4 Nf6	9. Ne2 b6	17. Ng3 Na5	25. Rxe1 Re8
2. c4 e6	10. O–O Ba6	18. f3 Nb3	26. Re6 Rxe6
3. Nc3 Bb4	11. Bxa6 Nxa6	19. e4 Qxa4	27. fxe6 Kg7
4. e3 d5	12. Bb2 Qd7	20. e5 Nd7	28. Qf4 Qe8
5. a3 Bxc3+	13. a4 Rfe8	21. Qf2 g6	29. Qe5 Qe7
6. bxc3 c5	14. Qd3 c4	22. f4 f5	
7. cxd5 exd5	15. Qc2 Nb8	23. exf6 Nxf6	
8. Bd3 O–O	16. Rae1 Nc6	24. f5 Rxe1	

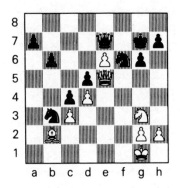

30. Ba3 Qxa3	34. e7 Qc1 +	38. Kxh5 Qe2 +	Black resigns
31. Nh5 + gxh5	35. Kf2 Qc2 +	39. Kh4 Qe4 +	
32. Qg5 + Kf8	36. Kg3 Qd3 +	40. g4 Qe1 +	
33. Qxf6 + Kg8	37. Kh4 Qe4 +	41. Kh5	

36. Botvinnik–Reshevsky, World Championship Tournament, 1948.
Nimzo-Indian Defence
The former prodigy, here shown defeating the tournament winner in
excellent style, was perhaps the world's strongest player in the early
fifties.

1. d4 Nf6	12. Ng3 Ba6	23. Ne3 Qa4	34. Red1 h4
2. c4 e6	13. Qe2 Qd7	24. Qa2 Nxg3	35. Ke1 Nb3
3. Nc3 Bb4	14. f4 f5	25. hxg3 h5	36. Nd5 + exd5
4. e3 c5	15. Rae1 g6	26. Be2 Kf7	37. Bxf5 Nxd2
5. a3 Bxc3 +	16. Rd1 Qf7	27. Kf2 Qb3	38. Rxd2 dxc4
6. bxc3 Nc6	17. e5 Rc8	28. Qxb3 Nxb3	39. Bxd7 Rxd7
7. Bd3 O–O	18. Rfe1 dxe5	29. Bd3 Ke7	40. Rf2 Ke6
8. Ne2 b6	19. dxe5 Ng7	30. Ke2 Na5	41. Rf3 Rd3
9. e4 Ne8	20. Nf1 Rfd8	31. Rd2 Rc7	42. Ke2 and
10. Be3 d6	21. Bf2 Nh5	32. g4 Rcd7	White resigns
11. O–O Na5	22. Bg3 Qe8	33. gxf5 gxf5	

37. Averbakh–Kotov, Candidates' Tournament, Neuhausen/Zurich,
1953. Old Indian Defence
An amazing queen sacrifice wins the first brilliancy prize in a
tournament immortalized by Bronstein's superb tournament book.

1. d4 Nf6	14. Rbc1 g6	27. gxf5 gxf5	40. Kf5 Ng8+
2. c4 d6	15. Nd2 Rab8	28. Rg2 f4	41. Kg4 Nf6+
3. Nf3 Nbd7	16. Nb3 Nxb3	29. Bf2 Rf6	42. Kf5 Ng8+
4. Nc3 e5	17. Qxb3 c5	30. Ne2 Qxh3+	43. Kg4 Bxg5
5. e4 Be7	18. Kh2 Kh8	31. Kxh3 Rh6+	44. Kxg5 Rf7
6. Be2 O–O	19. Qc2 Ng8	32. Kg4 Nf6+	45. Bh4 Rg6+
7. O–O c6	20. Bg4 Nh6	33. Kf5 Nd7	46. Kh5 Rfg7
8. Qc2 Re8	21. Bxd7 Qxd7	34. Rg5 Rf8+	47. Bg5 Rxg5+
9. Rd1 Bf8	22. Qd2 Ng8	35. Kg4 Nf6+	48. Kh4 Nf6
10. Rb1 a5	23. g4 f5	36. Kf5 Ng8+	49. Ng3 Rxg3
11. d5 Nc5	24. f3 Be7	37. Kg4 Nf6+	50. Qxd6 R3g6
12. Be3 Qc7	25. Rg1 Rf8	38. Kf5 Nxd5+	51. Qb8+ Rg8
13. h3 Bd7	26. Rcf1 Rf7	39. Kg4 Nf6+	White resigns

38. Bronstein–Keres, Interzonal Tournament, Göteborg, 1955.
Nimzo-Indian Defence
A modern masterpiece, considered one of the most profound games ever played.

1. d4 Nf6	11. Nb5 exd5	21. Nd6 Bc6	31. h3 Qe2
2. c4 e6	12. a3 Be7	22. Qg4 Kh8	32. Ng3 Qe3+
3. Nc3 Bb4	13. Ng3 dxc4	23. Be4 Bh6	33. Kh2 Nd4
4. e3 c5	14. Bxh6 gxh6	24. Bxc6 dxc6	34. Qd5 Re8
5. Bd3 b6	15. Qd2 Nh7	25. Qxc4 Nc5	35. Nh5 Ne2
6. Ne2 Bb7	16. Qxh6 f5	26. b4 Ne6	36. Nxg7 Qg3+
7. O–O cxd4	17. Nxf5 Rxf5	27. Qxc6 Rb8	37. Kh1 Nxf4
8. exd4 O–O	18. Bxf5 Nf8	28. Ne4 Qg6	38. Qf3 Ne2
9. d5 h6	19. Rad1 Bg5	29. Rd6 Bg7	39. Rh6+
10. Bc2 Na6	20. Qh5 Qf6	30. f4 Qg4	Black resigns

39. D. Byrne–Fischer, Rosenwald Tournament, New York, 1956.
Grünfeld Defence
Billed as 'The Game of the Century', in which the thirteen-year-old boy wonder hits the world's headlines for the first time with a remarkable queen sacrifice.

1. Nf3 Nf6	6. Qb3 dxc4	11. Bg5 Na4	16. Bc5 Rfe8+
2. c4 g6	7. Qxc4 c6	12. Qa3 Nxc3	17. Kf1
3. Nc3 Bg7	8. e4 Nbd7	13. bxc3 Nxe4	
4. d4 O–O	9. Rd1 Nb6	14. Bxe7 Qb6	
5. Bf4 d5	10. Qc5 Bg4	15. Bc4 Nxc3	

17. .... Be6	24. Qb4 Ra4	31. Nf3 Ne4	38. Kd1 Bb3 +
18. Bxb6 Bxc4 +	25. Qxb6 Nxd1	32. Qb8 b5	39. Kc1 Ne2 +
19. Kg1 Ne2 +	26. h3 Rxa2	33. h4 h5	40. Kb1 Nc3 +
20. Kf1 Nxd4 +	27. Kh2 Nxf2	34. Ne5 Kg7	41. Kc1 Rc2
21. Kg1 Ne2 +	28. Re1 Rxe1	35. Kg1 Bc5 +	mate
22. Kf1 Nc3 +	29. Qd8 + Bf8	36. Kf1 Ng3 +	
23. Kg1 axb6	30. Nxe1 Bd5	37. Ke1 Bb4 +	

40. Spassky–Bronstein, Leningrad, 1959, King's Gambit
In one sense *the* most famous game of all – the final position was
used in the film *From Russia With Love* – and just look at white's
fifteenth move.

1. e4 e5	8. O–O h6	15. Nd6 Nf8	21. Bb3 Bxe5
2. f4 exf4	9. Ne4 Nxd5	16. Nxf7	22. Nxe5 + Kh7
3. Nf3 d5	10. c4 Ne3	exf1 = Q +	23. Qe4 +
4. exd5 Bd6	11. Bxe3 fxe3	17. Rxf1 Bf5	Black resigns
5. Nc3 Ne7	12. c5 Be7	18. Qxf5 Qd7	
6. d4 O–O	13. Bc2 Re8	19. Qf4 Bf6	
7. Bd3 Nd7	14. Qd3 e2	20. N3e5 Qe7	

*41. Tal–Smyslov, Candidates' Tournament, Bled, 1959. Caro-Kann
Defence*
The Latvian genius in sparkling form on his way to an appointment
with Botvinnik.

1. e4 c6	3. Nd2 e5	5. d4 dxe4	7. Qxd4 Ngf6
2. d3 d5	4. Ngf3 Nd7	6. Nxe4 exd4	8. Bg5 Be7

9. O–O–O O–O	14. Qh4 bxc4	19. Qxf7 Qa1 +	24. Nxc6 Ne4 +
10. Nd6 Qa5	15. Qg5 Nh5	20. Kd2 Rxf7	25. Ke3 Bb6 +
11. Bc4 b5	16. Nh6 + Kh8	21. Nxf7 + Kg8	26. Bd4 Black
12. Bd2 Qa6	17. Qxh5 Qxa2	22. Rxa1 Kxf7	resigns
13. Nf5 Bd8	18. Bc3 Nf6	23. Ne5 + Ke6	

42. Tal–Botvinnik, 1st Game, World Championship Match, 1960. French Defence

Highly original and imaginative play gives Tal a great start in the world title match.

1. e4 e6	10. Qxh7 cxd4	19. Rh3 Qf7	28. fxe3 Kc7
2. d4 d5	11. Kd1 Bd7	20. dxe5 Ncxe5	29. c4 dxc4
3. Nc3 Bb4	12. Qh5 + Ng6	21. Re3 Kd7	30. Bxc4 Qg7
4. e5 c5	13. Ne2 d3	22. Rb1 b6	31. Bxg8 Qxg8
5. a3 Bxc3 +	14. cxd3 Ba4 +	23. Nf4 Rae8	32. h5 Black
6. bxc3 Qc7	15. Ke1 Qxe5	24. Rb4 Bc6	resigns
7. Qg4 f5	16. Bg5 Nc6	25. Qd1 Nxf4	
8. Qg3 Ne7	17. d4 Qc7	26. Rxf4 Ng6	
9. Qxg7 Rg8	18. h4 e5	27. Rd4 Rxe3 +	

43. Korchnoi–Tal, USSR Championship, 1962. Modern Benoni

One of Korchnoi's greatest games, his defusion of his opponent's favourite defence bears the hallmark of true mastery.

1. d4 Nf6	15. a4 a6	29. Bc4 Bc8	43. g4 a5
2. c4 c5	16. Bf1 Qe7	30. Rf1 Rb4	44. Kg3 Rb8
3. d5 e6	17. Nd2 Nc7	31. Bxe6 Bxe6	45. Kh4 Qf7
4. Nc3 exd5	18. f4 b5	32. Bh6 Re8	46. Kg5 fxg4
5. cxd5 d6	19. e5 dxe5	33. Qg5 Re4	47. hxg4 Bd7
6. Nf3 g6	20. Nde4 Qd8	34. Rf2 f5	48. Rc4 a4
7. g3 Bg7	21. Nxf6 + Nxf6	35. Qf6 Qd7	49. Rc7 a3
8. Bg2 O–O	22. d6 Ne6	36. Rxc5 Rc4	50. Rxd7 Qxd7
9. O–O Na6	23. fxe5 b4	37. Rxc4 Bxc4	51. e6 Qa7
10. h3 Nc7	24. Nd5 Nxd5	38. Rd2 Be6	52. Qe5 axb2
11. e4 Nd7	25. Qxd5 Bb7	39. Rd1 Qa7	53. e7 Kf7
12. Re1 Ne8	26. Qd2 Qd7	40. Rd2 Qd7	54. d7 Black
13. Bg5 Bf6	27. Kh2 b3	41. Rd1 Qa7	resigns
14. Be3 Rb8	28. Rac1 Qxa4	42. Rd4 Qd7	

44. *R. Byrne–Fischer, US Championship, 1963–4. Grünfeld Defence*
A masterpiece in miniature from Bobby's 100 per cent tournament
leaves the spectators astonished.

1. d4 Nf6	7. e3 O–O	13. dxe5 Nxe5	19. Kxg2 d4
2. c4 g6	8. Nge2 Nc6	14. Rfd1 Nd3	20. Nxd4 Bb7 +
3. g3 c6	9. O–O b6	15. Qc2 Nxf2	21. Kf1 Qd7
4. Bg2 d5	10. b3 Ba6	16. Kxf2 Ng4 +	White resigns
5. cxd5 cxd5	11. Ba3 Re8	17. Kg1 Nxe3	
6. Nc3 Bg7	12. Qd2 e5	18. Qd2 Nxg2	

45. *Petrosian–Spassky, 10th Game, World Championship Match,
1966. King's Indian Defence*
Exchange sacrifices are often said to be the trademark of Soviet
players – here Petrosian does it twice.

1. Nf3 Nf6	9. Nd2 c5	17. Bxf3 Bxb2	25. Be6 + Rf7
2. g3 g6	10. Qc2 e5	18. Qxb2 Ne5	26. Ne4 Qh4
3. c4 Bg7	11. b3 Ng4	19. Be2 f4	27. Nxd6 Qg5 +
4. Bg2 O–O	12. e4 f5	20. gxf4 Bh3	28. Kh1 Ra7
5. O–O Nc6	13. exf5 gxf5	21. Ne3 Bxf1	29. Bxf7 + Rxf7
6. Nc3 d6	14. Nd1 b5	22. Rxf1 Ng6	30. Qh8 + Black
7. d4 a6	15. f3 e4	23. Bg4 Nxf4	resigns
8. d5 Na5	16. Bb2 exf3	24. Rxf4 Rxf4	

46. *Botvinnik–Portisch, Monte Carlo, 1968. English Opening*
Even in his late fifties Botvinnik could still play with youthful vigour,
here producing one of the games of the decade.

1. c4 e5	8. d3 Be7	15. Rac1 Nb8	22. Ng6 + Kh7
2. Nc3 Nf6	9. a3 a5	16. Rxc7 Bc6	23. Be4 Bd6
3. g3 d5	10. Be3 O–O	17. R1xc6 bxc6	24. Nxe5 + g6
4. cxd5 Nxd5	11. Na4 Nxa4	18. Rxf7 h6	25. Bxg6 + Kg7
5. Bg2 Be6	12. Qxa4 Bd5	19. Rb7 Qc8	26. Bxh6 + Black
6. Nf3 Nc6	13. Rfc1 Re8	20. Qc4 + Kh8	resigns
7. O–O Nb6	14. Rc2 Bf8	21. Nh4 Qxb7	

47. *Larsen–Spassky, USSR v. Rest of World, 1969. Nimzo–Larsen Attack*
A scintillating quickie from the 'Match of the Century' and one of
the best-known games of recent years.

1. b3 e5	6. Nxc6 dxc6	11. g3 h5	16. Rf1 Qh4+
2. Bb2 Nc6	7. e3 Bf5	12. h3 h4	17. Kd1
3. c4 Nf6	8. Qc2 Qe7	13. hxg4 hxg3	gxf1 = Q+
4. Nf3 e4	9. Be2 O–O–O	14. Rg1 Rh1	White resigns
5. Nd4 Bc5	10. f4 Ng4	15. Rxh1 g2	

48. Fischer–Petrosian, 7th Game, Candidates' Final Match, 1971. Sicilian Defence

An instructive positional masterpiece against a redoubtable opponent.

1. e4 c5	10. exd5 exd5	19. Nc5 Bc8	28. Kf3 f5
2. Nf3 e6	11. Nc3 Be7	20. f3 Rea7	29. Ke3 d4+
3. d4 cxd4	12. Qa4+ Qd7	21. Re5 Bd7	30. Kd2 Nb6
4. Nxd4 a6	13. Re1 Qxa4	22. Nxd7+ Rxd7	31. Ree7 Nd5
5. Bd3 Nc6	14. Nxa4 Be6	23. Rc1 Rd6	32. Rf7+ Ke8
6. Nxc6 bxc6	15. Be3 O–O	24. Rc7 Nd7	33. Rb7 Nxb4
7. O–O d5	16. Bc5 Rfe8	25. Re2 g6	34. Bc4 Black
8. c4 Nf6	17. Bxe7 Rxe7	26. Kf2 h5	resigns
9. cxd5 cxd5	18. b4 Kf8	27. f4 h4	

49. Fischer–Spassky, 6th Game, World Championship Match, 1972. Queen's Gambit Declined

Perhaps the best game of the now legendary Fischer–Spassky match, Bobby proving that e4 is not the only way he knows to start a game.

1. c4 e6	12. Qa4 c5	23. Bc4 Kh8	34. R1f2 Qe8
2. Nf3 d5	13. Qa3 Rc8	24. Qh3 Nf8	35. R2f3 Qd8
3. d4 Nf6	14. Bb5 a6	25. b3 a5	36. Bd3 Qe8
4. Nc3 Be7	15. dxc5 bxc5	26. f5 exf5	37. Qe4 Nf6
5. Bg5 O–O	16. O–O Ra7	27. Rxf5 Nh7	38. Rxf6 gxf6
6. e3 h6	17. Be2 Nd7	28. Rcf1 Qd8	39. Rxf6 Kg8
7. Bh4 b6	18. Nd4 Qf8	29. Qg3 Re7	40. Bc4 Kh8
8. cxd5 Nxd5	19. Nxe6 fxe6	30. h4 Rbb7	41. Qf4 Black
9. Bxe7 Qxe7	20. e4 d4	31. e6 Rbc7	resigns
10. Nxd5 exd5	21. f4 Qe7	32. Qe5 Qe8	
11. Rc1 Be6	22. e5 Rb8	33. a4 Qd8	

50. Karpov–Spassky, 9th Game, Candidates' Semi-Final, 1974. Sicilian Defence

Look out for Karpov's twenty-fourth, the sort of move that only a truly great player would find, quiet yet deadly.

1. e4 c5	7. O–O O–O	13. Nd4 g6	19. Bg4 h5
2. Nf3 e6	8. f4 Nc6	14. Rf2 e5	20. Bxd7 Qxd7
3. d4 cxd4	9. Be3 Bd7	15. Nxc6 bxc6	21. Qc4 Bh4
4. Nxd4 Nf6	10. Nb3 a5	16. fxe5 dxe5	22. Rd2 Qe7
5. Nc3 d6	11. a4 Nb4	17. Qf1 Qc8	23. Rf1 Rfd8
6. Be2 Be7	12. Bf3 Bc6	18. h3 Nd7	

24. Nb1 Qb7	28. Nd2 Bd8	32. Rxd8 Bxd8	Black resigns
25. Kh2 Kg7	29. Nf3 f6	33. Rd1 Nb8	
26. c3 Na6	30. Rd2 Be7	34. Bc5 Rh8	
27. Re2 Rf8	31. Qe6 Rad8	35. Rxd8	

51. Karpov–Korchnoi, 2nd Game, Candidates' Final, 1974. Sicilian Defence
Superior opening preparation helps Karpov on his way to a brilliant victory and, by default, the World Championship.

1. e4 c5	8. Qd2 O–O	15. g4 Nf6	22. Nxd5 Re8
2. Nf3 d6	9. Bc4 Bd7	16. Nde2 Qa5	23. Nef4 Bc6
3. d4 cxd4	10. h4 Rc8	17. Bh6 Bxh6	24. e5 Bxd5
4. Nxd4 Nf6	11. Bb3 Ne5	18. Qxh6 Rfc8	25. exf6 exf6
5. Nc3 g6	12. O–O–O Nc4	19. Rd3 R4c5	26. Qxh7+ Kf8
6. Be3 Bg7	13. Bxc4 Rxc4	20. g5 Rxg5	27. Qh8+ Black
7. f3 Nc6	14. h5 Nxh5	21. Rd5 Rxd5	resigns

52. Karpov–Dorfman, Soviet Championship, Moscow, 1976. Sicilian Defence
One of Karpov's best games, a long-term piece sacrifice belies his reputation for dull play.

1. e4 c5	14. Nd5 exd5	27. Rxe3 Qxh4	40. Rg1 Rxe5
2. Nf3 d6	15. Bxg7 Rg8	28. Qf3 Qxg5	41. Rg8+ Ke7
3. d4 cxd4	16. exd5 Qc7	29. Re1 Qg2	42. Qh4+ Kd7
4. Nxd4 Nf6	17. Bf6 Ne5	30. Qf5 Rg6	43. Qf6 Re7
5. Nc3 e6	18. Bxe5 dxe5	31. Rf1 Qd5	44. Qf5+ Kd6
6. g4 Be7	19. f4 Bf5	32. dxe7 Kxe7	45. Qxa5 Re5
7. g5 Nfd7	20. Bh3 Bxh3	33. Qf4 a5	46. Qd8+ Ke6
8. h4 Nc6	21. Rxh3 Rc8	34. Qh4+ Ke8	47. Kb2 f6
9. Be3 a6	22. fxe5 Qc4	35. Qxh7 Qf3	48. Rf8 Qg7
10. Qe2 Qc7	23. R1d3 Qf4+	36. Qh8+ Ke7	49. Qc8+ Kd5
11. O–O–O b5	24. Kb1 Rc4	37. Qh4+ Ke8	50. Qc4+ Black
12. Nxc6 Qxc6	25. d6 Re4	38. Qc4 Qb7	resigns
13. Bd4 b4	26. Rhe3 Rxe3	39. b3 Re6	

53. Karpov–Miles, European Team Championship, Skara, 1980. St George Defence
England's Number One bamboozles the champ with an eccentric choice of opening.

1. e4 a6	13. c4 bxc3	25. Re1 Qxe5	37. Ke1 Rh8
2. d4 b5	14. Nxc3 Nxc3	26. Qxd7 Bb4	38. f4 gxf4
3. Nf3 Bb7	15. Bxc3 Nb4	27. Re3 Qd5	39. Nxf4 Bc6
4. Bd3 Nf6	16. Bxb4 Bxb4	28. Qxd5 Bxd5	40. Ne2 Rh1+
5. Qe2 e6	17. Rac1 Qb6	29. Nc3 Rc8	41. Kd2 Rh2
6. a4 c5	18. Be4 O–O	30. Ne2 g5	42. g3 Bf3
7. dxc5 Bxc5	19. Ng5 h6	31. h4 Kg7	43. Rg8 Rg2
8. Nbd2 b4	20. Bh7+ Kh8	32. hxg5 hxg5	44. Ke1 Bxe2
9. e5 Nd5	21. Bb1 Be7	33. Bd3 a5	45. Bxe2 Rxg3
10. Ne4 Be7	22. Ne4 Rac8	34. Rg3 Kf6	46. Ra8 and
11. O–O Nc6	23. Qd3 Rxc1	35. Rg4 Bd6	White resigns
12. Bd2 Qc7	24. Rxc1 Qxb2	36. Kf1 Be5	

54. Korchnoi–Kasparov, Lucerne Olympiad, 1982. Modern Benoni
Kasparov is prepared to risk unfathomable complications on his way to the full point in a headline-grabbing encounter.

1. d4 Nf6	11. Nd2 Nbd7	21. Qe2 Qb6	31. Ra2 Qf5
2. c4 g6	12. h3 Rb8	22. Na3 Rbe8	32. Nxd7 Nd3
3. g3 Bg7	13. Nc4 Ne5	23. Bd2 Qxb2	33. Bh6 Qxd7
4. Bg2 c5	14. Na3 Nh5	24. fxe5 Bxe5	34. Ra8+ Kf7
5. d5 d6	15. e4 Rf8	25. Nc4 Nxg3	35. Rh8 Kf6
6. Nc3 O–O	16. Kh2 f5	26. Rxf8+ Rxf8	36. Kf3 Qxh3+
7. Nf3 e6	17. f4 b5	27. Qe1 Nxe4+	White resigns
8. O–O exd5	18. axb5 axb5	28. Kg2 Qc2	
9. cxd5 a6	19. Naxb5 fxe4	29. Nxe5 Rf2+	
10. a4 Re8	20. Bxe4 Bd7	30. Qxf2 Nxf2	

55. Kasparov–Portisch, Nikšić, 1983. Queen's Indian Defence
Regicide in 1980s style – Kasparov produces one of the most brilliant games of recent years.

1. d4 Nf6	10. Bd3 c5	19. Bxh7+ Kxh7	28. Qh8+ Kf7
2. c4 e6	11. O–O Nc6	20. Rxd5 Kg8	29. Rd3 Nc4
3. Nf3 b6	12. Bb2 Rc8	21. Bxg7 Kxg7	30. Rfd1 Ne5
4. Nc3 Bb7	13. Qe2 O–O	22. Ne5 Rfd8	31. Qh7+ Ke6
5. a3 d5	14. Rad1 Qc7	23. Qg4+ Kf8	32. Qg8+ Kf5
6. cxd5 Nxd5	15. c4 cxd4	24. Qf5 f6	33. g4+ Kf4
7. e3 Nxc3	16. exd4 Na5	25. Nd7+ Rxd7	34. Rd4+ Kf3
8. bxc3 Be7	17. d5 exd5	26. Rxd7 Qc5	35. Qb3+ Black
9. Bb5+ c6	18. cxd5 Bxd5	27. Qh7 Rc7	resigns

56. Smyslov–Ribli, Candidates' Semi-Final, 1983. Queen's Gambit Declined
The veteran unleashes a cascade of sacrifices *en route* to a showdown with Kasparov.

1. d4 Nf6	7. Bd3 Be7	13. Bc4 Rd8	19. Bxb5 Qxb5
2. Nf3 e6	8. O–O O–O	14. Ne2 Bd7	20. Ng3 Ng6
3. c4 d5	9. ae cxd4	15. Qe4 Nce7	21. Ne5 Nde7
4. Nc3 c5	10. exd4 Bf6	16. Bd3 Ba4	
5. cxd5 Nxd5	11. Qc2 h6	17. Qh7+ Kf8	
6. e3 Nc6	12. Rd1 Qb6	18. Re1 Bb5	

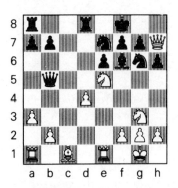

22. B×h6 N×e5	28. R×e6+ f×e6	34. Re1 Rh8	40. f×e5+ Ke6
23. Nh5 Nf3+	29. Q×g7+ Nf7	35. h4 Rhd8	41. Qc4+ Black
24. g×f3 Nf5	30. d6+ R×d6	36. Re4 Nd6	resigns
25. N×f6 N×h6	31. Nd5+ R×d5	37. Qc3+ e5	
26. d5 Q×b2	32. Q×b2 b6	38. R×e5 R×e5	
27. Qh8+ Ke7	33. Qb4+ Kf6	39. f4 Nf7	

57. Beliavsky–Nunn, Wijk aan Zee, 1985. King's Indian Defence
England's John Nunn plays imaginative, aggressive chess, as portrayed here in one of his best games.

1. d4 Nf6	8. d5 Ne5	15. Qc2 Qf4	22. Bg2 N×c4
2. c4 g6	9. h3 Nh5	16. Ne2 R×f2	23. Qf2 Ne3+
3. Nc3 Bg7	10. Bf2 f5	17. N×f2 Nf3+	24. Ke2 Qc4
4. e4 d6	11. e×f5 R×f5	18. Kd1 Qh4	25. Bf3 Rf8
5. f3 O–O	12. g4 R×f3	19. Nd3 Bf5	26. Rg1 Nc2
6. Be3 Nbd7	13. g×h5 Qf8	20. Nec1 Nd2	27. Kd1 B×d3
7. Qd2 c5	14. Ne4 Bh6	21. h×g6 h×g6	White resigns

58. Karpov–Kasparov, 16th Game, World Championship Match, 1985. Sicilian Defence
A stunning (but maybe unsound) pawn sacrifice on move 8 produces a game destined for the anthologies as Gary reduces his opponent to complete helplessness.

1. e4 c5	4. N×d4 Nc6	7. N1c3 a6	10. e×d5 Nb4
2. Nf3 e6	5. Nb5 d6	8. Na3 d5	11. Be2 Bc5
3. d4 c×d4	6. c4 Nf6	9. c×d5 e×d5	12. O–O O–O

13. Bf3 Bf5	21. b3 g5	29. Qd2 Kg7	37. Rxd3 Rc1
14. Bg5 Re8	22. Bxd6 Qxd6	30. f3 Qxd6	38. Nb2 Qf2
15. Qd2 b5	23. g3 Nd7	31. fxg4 Qd4+	39. Nd2 Rxd1+
16. Rad1 Nd3	24. Bg2 Qf6	32. Kh1 Nf6	40. Nxd1 Re1+
17. Nab1 h6	25. a3 a5	33. Rf4 Ne4	White resigns
18. Bh4 b4	26. axb4 axb4	34. Qxd3 Nf2+	
19. Na4 Bd6	27. Qa2 Bg6	35. Rxf2 Bxd3	
20. Bg3 Rc8	28. d6 g4	36. Rfd2 Qe3	

59. Kasparov–Karpov, 16th Game, World Championship Match, 1986. Ruy López

The best game of the 1986 match, according to Kasparov – the commentators were sceptical but Gary claims he had it all worked out from move 32.

1. e4 e5	9. h3 Bb7	17. Ra3 c4	25. Nxe5 Nbd3
2. Nf3 Nc6	10. d4 Re8	18. Nd4 Qf6	26. Ng4 Qb6
3. Bb5 a6	11. Nbd2 Bf8	19. N2f3 Nc5	27. Rg3 g6
4. Ba4 Nf6	12. a4 h6	20. axb5 axb5	28. Bxh6 Qxb2
5. O–O Be7	13. Bc2 exd4	21. Nxb5 Rxa3	29. Qf3 Nd7
6. Re1 b5	14. cxd4 Nb4	22. Nxa3 Ba6	30. Bxf8 Kxf8
7. Bb3 d6	15. Bb1 c5	23. Re3 Rb8	31. Kh2 Rb3
8. c3 O–O	16. d5 Nd7	24. e5 dxe5	

32. Bxd3 cxd3	35. Rxg6 Qe5	38. Re8+ Kd5	41. Nxf7
33. Qf4 Qxa3	36. Rg8+ Ke7	39. Rxe5+ Nxe5	Black resigns
34. Nh6 Qe7	37. d6+ Ke6	40. d7 Rb8	

60. Short–Kasparov, Brussels (OHRA), 1986. Sicilian Defence
Nigel scores a sensational win over the World Champion – will it prove portentous?

1. e4 c5	12. Rhe1 Rc8	24. Nc2 a5	36. Qxb7 Qxd3+
2. Nf3 d6	13. Kb1 Be7	25. Ba7 Kf8	37. Nc2 Rh2
3. d4 cxd4	14. h4 b4	26. Ne3 Qe6	38. Qc8+ Nf8
4. Nxd4 Nf6	15. Na4 Qa5	27. Nc4 Kg8	39. Rxe5 Rh1+
5. Nc3 a6	16. b3 Nfd7	28. Nxd6 Qxd6	40. Kb2 Qd2
6. Be3 e6	17. g5 g6	29. Nb2 Rc3	41. Re8 Qd6
7. Qd2 b5	18. f4 Nxd3	30. Nc4 Qd5	42. Rd8 Qe5+
8. f3 Nbd7	19. cxd3 hxg5	31. Ne3 Qe6	43. Ka3 Kh7
9. g4 h6	20. hxg5 d5	32. Rc1 Qa6	44. Rxf8 Qd6+
10. O–O–O Bb7	21. f5 e5	33. Rxc3 bxc3	45. b4
11. Bd3 Ne5	22. exd5 Qxd5	34. Qxc3 Qxa7	Black resigns
	23. f6 Bd6	35. Qc7 Qd4	

(only the fourth time this century a British player has beaten the world champion.)

61. Kasparov–Karpov, 2nd Game, World Championship Match, 1990. Ruy López
This brilliant win in the second game of the 1990 World Championship match proved that Kasparov was on form to retain his title.

1. e4 e5	13. Bc2 exd4	25. Bxh6 Bxh6	37. Qd4 Ng8
2. Nf3 Nc6	14. cxd4 Nb4	26. Nxh6 Nxh6	38. e5 Nd5
3. Bb5 a6	15. Bb1 bxa4	27. Nxd6 Qb6	39. fxg6+ fxg6
4. Ba4 Nf6	16. Rxa4 a5	28. Nxe8 Qxd4+	40. Rxc6 Qxd8
5. O–O Be7	17. Ra3 Ra6	29. Kh1 Qd8	41. Qxa7+ Nde7
6. Re1 b5	18. Nh2 g6	30. Rd1 Qxe8	42. Rxa6 Qd1+
7. Bb3 d6	19. f3 Qd7	31. Qg5 Ra7	43. Qg1 Qd2
8. c3 O–O	20. Nc4 Qb5	32. Rd8 Qe6	44. Qf1 Black
9. h3 Bb7	21. Rc3 Bc8	33. f4 Ba6	resigns
10. d4 Re8	22. Be3 Kh7	34. f5 Qe7	
11. Nbd2 Bf8	23. Qc1 c6	35. Qd2 Qe5	
12. a4 h6	24. Ng4 Ng8	36. Qf2 Qe7	

62. Ivanchuk–Yusupov, 9th Game, Candidates' Quarter-final Match, Brussels, 1991. King's Indian Defence
The first game of a rapid play-off: although he only has forty-five minutes on the clock Yusupov produces one of the most spectacular games on record.

1. c4 e5	11. Ba3 e4	21. Bxd6 Ng6	31. Nce7+ Kh7
2. g3 d6	12. Ng5 e3	22. Nd5 Qh5	32. Nxg6 fxg6
3. Bg2 g6	13. f4 Nf8	23. h4 Nxh4	33. Nxg7 Nf2
4. d4 Nd7	14. b4 Bf5	24. gxh4 Qxh4	34. Bxf4 Qxf4
5. Nc3 Bg7	15. Qb3 h6	25. Nde7+ Kh8	35. Ne6 Qh2
6. Nf3 Ngf6	16. Nf3 Ng4	26. Nxf5 Qh2+	36. Rdb1 Nh3
7. O–O O–O	17. b5 g5	27. Kf1 Re6	37. Rb7+ Kh8
8. Qc2 Re8	18. bxc6 bxc6	28. Qb7 Rg6	38. Rb8+ Qxb8
9. Rd1 c6	19. Ne5 gxf4	29. Qxa8+ Kh7	39. Bxh3 Qg3
10. b3 Qe7	20. Nxc6 Qg5	30. Qg8+ Kxg8	White resigns

63. Short–Timman, Tilburg, 1991. Alekhine's Defence
Against his eventual Candidates' Final opponent Short stages an extraordinary finish, with his king marching up the board to join in the mating attack.

1. e4 Nf6	10. a4 dxe5	19. bxc4 Re8	28. R1d4 Rae8
2. e5 Nd5	11. dxe5 Nd4	20. Rd1 Qc5	29. Qf6+ Kg8
3. d4 d6	12. Nxd4 Qxd4	21. Qh4 b6	30. h4 h5
4. Nf3 g6	13. Re1 e6	22. Be3 Qc6	31. Kh2 Rc8
5. Bc4 Nb6	14. Nd2 Nd5	23. Bh6 Bh8	32. Kg3 Rce8
6. Bb3 Bg7	15. Nf3 Qc5	24. Rd8 Bb7	33. Kf4 Bc8
7. Qe2 Nc6	16. Qe4 Qb4	25. Rad1 Bg7	34. Kg5 Black
8. O–O O–O	17. Bc4 Nb6	26. R8d7 Rf8	resigns
9. h3 a5	18. b3 Nxc4	27. Bxg7 Kxg7	

64. Fischer–Spassky, 1st Match Game, Sveti Stefan, 1992. Ruy López
After twenty years and one day away from the chessboard Bobby returns for a repeat 'World Championship' match and plays as if he'd never been away.

1. e4 e5	4. Ba4 Nf6	7. Bb3 d6	10. d4 Nbd7
2. Nf3 Nc6	5. O–O Be7	8. c3 O–O	11. Nbd2 Bb7
3. Bb5 a6	6. Re1 b5	9. h3 Nb8	12. Bc2 Re8

13. Nf1 Bf8	23. Rea1 Qd7	33. Ra7 Kf6	43. Qxf4 Kd7
14. Ng3 g6	24. R1a2 Rfc8	34. Nbd2 Rxa7	44. Nd4 Qe1+
15. Bg5 h6	25. Qc1 Bf8	35. Rxa7 Ra8	45. Kg2 Bd5+
16. Bd2 Bg7	26. Qa1 Qe8	36. g4 hxg4	46. Be4 Bxe4+
17. a4 c5	27. Nf1 Be7	37. hxg4 Rxa7	47. Nxe4 Be7
18. d5 c4	28. N1d2 Kg7	38. Qxa7 f4	48. Nxb5 Nf8
19. b4 Nh7	29. Nb1 Nxe4	39. Bxf4 exf4	49. Nbxd6 Ne6
20. Be3 h5	30. Bxe4 f5	40. Nh4 Bf7	and
21. Qd2 Rf8	31. Bc2 Bxd5	41. Qd4+ Ke6	Black
22. Ra3 Ndf6	32. axb5 axb5	42. Nf5 Bf8	resigns

Postscript: if you'd like a flavour of game 3, pop into Simpsons in the Strand, London, formerly Simpson's Divan. This is where Anderssen played his Immortal Game; and behind a glass case in the entrance you'll see a splendid old board on which Morphy, Lasker, Steinitz, Zukertort, Chigorin and others worked their magic.

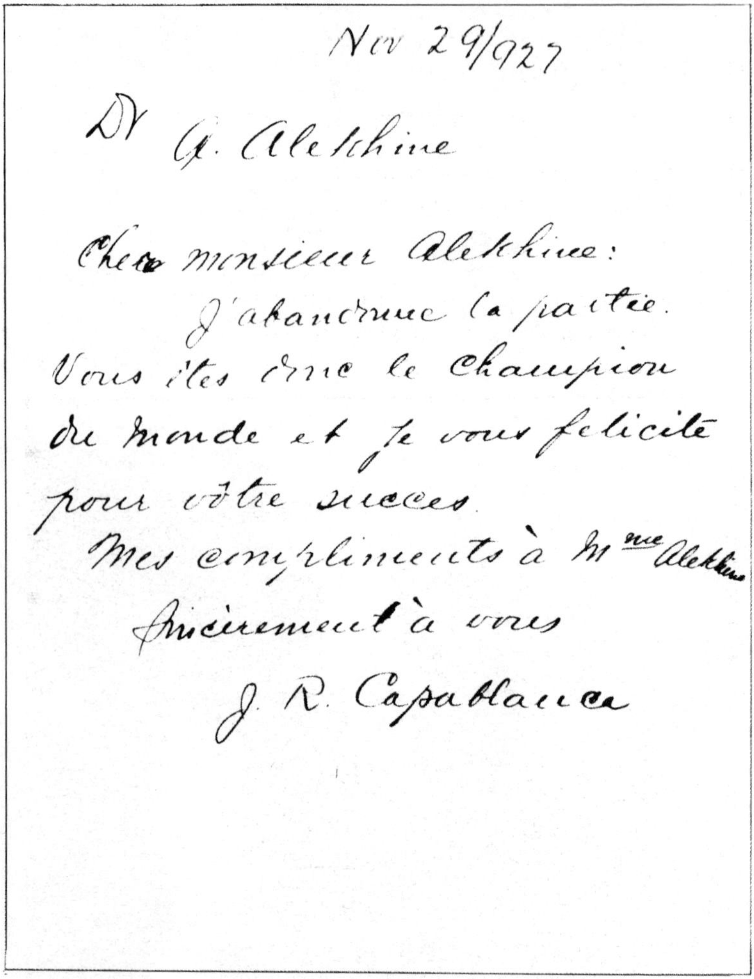

Nov 29/927

Dr. G. Alekhine

Cher monsieur Alekhine:
J'abandonne la partie.
Vous êtes donc le Champion
du monde et je vous félicite
pour votre succès.
Mes compliments à Mme Alekhine
Sincèrement à vous
J. R. Capablanca

Dear Mr Alekhine,
I resign the game.
You are hence the World Champion.
I congratulate you on your success.
Best regards to Mrs Alekhine.
Yours sincerely
J. R. Capablanca

III *The Frightful*

We might escape, ah me! how many a pain,
Could we recall bad moves and play again.
                                    Goethe

'Tell me, how long did it take you to learn to play chess so badly?'
   'Sir, it's been nights of study and self-denial.'
                                    Apocryphal

The greatest

Philidor   Morphy   Lasker

Capablanca   Alekhine

Botvinnik   Fischer

Karpov   Kasparov

'By most standards I'm OK.'
Steve Davis

Pot Black for reds
(Karpov *v.* Sevastianov)

Boris signs for the Blues
(Spassky in Chelsea strip)

Ardiles attacking down the right wing

The Stars Swap Sports

World champs Tal and Petrosian
(note the pawn in Tal's hand – he was
playing a chess and table tennis simul!)

Britain's best-known fireman leads with
his right (Terry Marsh)

'You can always hear the King's call.'
Phil Lynott

The King of bop blows it (D. Gillespie)

Was he or wasn't he?
(W. Sickert)

Did he or didn't he?
(W. H. Wallace)

Does he or doesn't he?
(K. Wojtyła)

Was he or was she?
(C.G.L.A.A.T.D'Éon)

Vera Menchik

Pia Cramling

The Polgárs

The monstrous regiment

Maya Chiburdanidze

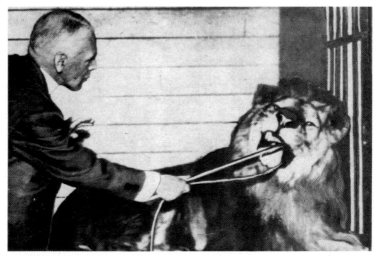

Freddy eyes his lunch (H. Davidson on 28 July 1937)

The Great Beast; vice-captain of the
sinners A. Crowley

Arthur Daley *v*. Inspector Cockrill
(The young George Cole plays Alastair
Sim)

Tolstoy (l.) unwinds after the Tour de France

Maxim Gorky watching Lenin getting peeved and depressed

Tito, in his mountain hideout, takes a break from beating up the Nazis

The Child's Problem by R. Dadd (Position: white king h1, queen a8, rook e5, pawns f4, b6; black king d6, knight d7, pawn e6. Solution: Qd8.)

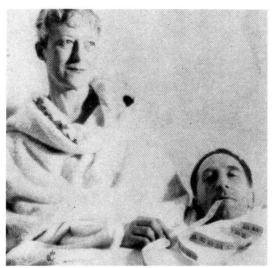

Painting by numbers: chess freak Duchamp and a bad case of tape worm

This is the pits. The worst blunders, the quickest losses, the least successful team, the most ghastly tournament results. And as a bonus, the silliest advice ever given, the worst chess commentary, the rottenest chess opening ever devised, and a dozen other assorted clangers. It's the chapter to cheer you up after yet one more disaster. Lost on time? Read how a grandmaster did it thirteen times in the same tournament. Left a knight *en prise* to the club idiot? See how a future world champion left a whole queen dangling. Sealed a stinker? One world-class player forgot to put his move in the envelope. As the man said: 'The mistakes are all there, waiting to be made.' And here they are.

♖

Picking the worst player of all time is even more difficult than picking the best. In 1958, one of the authors, after playing ten minutes of what he thought was a serious game, was jolted by a query from his Italian opponent: 'Excuse me sir, which is the queen?'

♖

Or there's the strange case, reported in *Chess* 1937, of the Sheffield *v*. Stocksbridge match. Both teams, unbeknownst to the other, were a man short. Both resorted to the last desperate expedient of a team captain: rather than lose a game by default they each picked up a stranger in a pub, gave him a quick refresher course in the moves and stuck him on bottom board. At the end of the match the teams gathered round to gaze in awe at a position unique in 1400 years of chess: both sides were in checkmate.

♖

And Alekhine is said to have watched amused as two café players carried on playing with only kings left on the board. He leaves them to discover the error of their ways; returns to find one jubilant, one crestfallen. 'Draw?' asks the grandmaster. 'No,' he's told. 'I got my king to the eighth rank and made it a queen.'

But we all have to learn, so maybe these don't count.

♖

Of players who've entered chess history, perhaps the strongest claimant for the all-time grandpatzer title is George Hatfeild Dingley Gossip (1841–1907). George had a worse record in major tournaments than anyone in history (last at Breslau 1889, London 1889, Manchester 1890, London 1892, and New York 1893: a total of just 4 wins, 52 losses and 21 draws). This didn't prevent him from promoting himself as a great player; nor did it inhibit him from writing a series of instructional books on the game. These contained a number of flashy (and entirely fictitious) wins he'd scored against famous players; and in one of them he proudly published the summit of his achievement: third prize in the Melbourne Chess Club Handicap Tournament 1885.

Isolating the worst tournament performances of all time is a little easier than picking the world's worst player. We'll announce our finalists, Miss World fashion, in reverse order.[1]

In third spot, an Irishman and part-time magician: Bartholomew O'Sullivan. At the 1947 Zonal Tournament in Hilversum, Mr O'Sullivan managed twelve zeros. A solitary draw spoiled his bid for perfection. What clinches the bronze medal, though, was chess sage Harry Golombek's post-tournament epitaph on the Irishman's chess ability: 'O'Sullivan's play was rather worse than his score.'

Here's O'Sullivan up against a grandmaster and judo brown belt, Rossolimo (France):

B. O.'Sullivan–N. Rossolimo, Hilversum, 1947. Queen's Indian Defence

1. d4 Nf6	4. Bg2 e6	7. Nc3 Ne4	10. Qxe2 Bxg2
2. Nf3 b6	5. O–O Be7	8. Qc2 Nxc3	Resigns
3. g3 Bb7	6. c4 O–O	9. Ng5 Nxe2+	

In the silver-medal position comes Nicholas Menelaus MacLeod, who at the New York tournament of 1889 fought like a tiger to set a

[1] Among the contenders were: Breyev, 0/18, Kiev, 1903; McCord, 0/17, US Open, 1944; Didier, who after a 1/16 in Paris 1900, sank to a unique score of $\frac{1}{4}$/13 in Monte Carlo 1901 (they had a weird scoring system that year); and Trenchard, who collected 27 zeros at Vienna, 1898 (but kept himself out of the records with one win and eight draws).

mark that will last for ages. Despite a few thoughtless wins (two against, guess who, G. H. D. Gossip) and a draw along the way, he still managed to earn his place in the books with a world record – thirty-one losses in a single tournament: particularly gutsy considering he had to sit there each day and watch Chigorin, on board one, score the *most* wins ever in a major tournament: twenty-seven. MacLeod had plenty of time to reflect on his performance: he died seventy-six years later, aged ninety-five, his record still intact (1965).

♜

But for sheer perfection, the gold goes to the gallant Colonel Moreau. At the 1903 Monte Carlo tournament, Moreau racked up an achievement so magnificent, we reproduce it here in full:

C. Moreau: ooooooooooooooooooooooooooooo.

Twenty-six games, twenty-six duck eggs; a world record. For dogged persistence, it's a landmark; you or we would have feigned a headache or beriberi or a sick uncle after maybe ten of those noughts. So Colonel Moreau gets our palm for the gamest of good losers.

F. J. Marshall–C. Moreau, Monte Carlo, 1903. King's Gambit

1. e4 e5	10. Kh1 Bh6	19. Na3 Kd7	25. Qd6+ Ke8
2. f4 exf4	11. Bd2 Qg7	20. Nc4 f3 and	26. Re1+ Kf7
3. Nf3 g5	12. Bb3 Nc6	Marshall	27. Ne5+ Ke8
4. Bc4 g4	13. Bc3 Ne5	announced	28. Ng6+ Be3
5. O–O gxf3	14. Qd5 d6	mate in 11:	29. Rxe3+ Qe6
6. Qxf3 Qf6	15. Rd1 Bd7	21. Rxd6+ cxd6	30. Qxe6+ Kd8
7. e5 Qxe5	16. Ba4 Bc6	22. Qxd6+ Kc8	31. Ba5 mate
8. Bxf7+ Kd8	17. Bxc6 bxc6	23. Qxc6+ Kd8	
9. d4 Qxd4+	18. Qxe5 Qg4	24. Rd1+ Ke7	

♜

Worse even than what happened to Colonel Moreau was the fate of Geoffrey Hosking, an English student at Moscow University in 1965. A beginner at chess, he played a game against a Russian fellow student while they were both legless on vodka. The Russian, a candidate master, was perhaps the more susceptible to alcohol, for he lost. Shortly after, the Soviet Chess Federation cabled Moscow University, asking them to send a foreign master to a tournament at

Baku. Geoffrey was asked, protested, but was eventually persuaded to go (doubtless he fancied a free trip to Baku). What he found when he got there was a dozen international masters out for blood. Geoffrey's was spilled in considerable quantities. He scored a creditable (given his zero rating) nought out of twelve. (Third Programme talk.)

♖

The worst-ever performance by a chess team? You'd have to go a long way to beat the Cypriot team's effort in the 1962 Olympiad. Twenty matches, twenty losses. Sixteen matches they lost by the maximum: four–nil. And out of eighty individual games they scored just three points. Their third board Ioannidis put himself alongside Colonel Moreau with an unbeatable Olympic record of twenty games, twenty zeros. (In the next Olympiad, Ioannidis was at it again: four noughts in his first four games. At this point the Cypriot team selectors decided they'd had enough, and Ioannidis was dropped for ever.)

In this game (from Cyprus *v.* Bulgaria B 1962), Ioannidis, in his customary self-destruct mode, runs into a Chipev cheapo.

Chipev–Ioannidis, Varna, 1962. Pirc Defence

1. e4 d6	6. f3 O–O	11. O–O–O Qc7	16. R x h7 +
2. d4 g6	7. g4 c5	12. Ng3 a6	Black resigns
3. Nc3 Bg7	8. Nge2 b6	13. g5 Nd7	
4. Be3 Nd7	9. h4 Ne8	14. h x g6 f x g6	
5. Qd2 Ngf6	10. h5 Ndf6	15. Bc4 + Kh8	

♖

Messrs O'Sullivan, MacLeod, Moreau and Ioannidis were, to put it kindly, not first-class players. What about the worst performance by the masters? Here are four to cheer you up, starting with an if-at-first-you-don't-succeed story for the fainthearted. At the Vienna tournament of 1908, Richard Réti put himself in the O'Sullivan class with sixteen zeros and just three draws. Undeterred he went on to become one of the most famous chess-masters in history. (He was the chap who broke Capablanca's eight-year no-loss spell.)

♖

British IM Bob Wade has done more for British chess than most, so it seems a little harsh to publish his most embarrassing moment; but while in Moscow in 1951, he took on a simultaneous display against thirty Russian schoolboys. The result – twenty losses, ten draws, no wins. It couldn't have happened to a nicer guy. (This isn't a record by any means, as you'll see later in this chapter.)

♖

The worst tournament performance by an international master (with a contender for the Worst Game Prize thrown in as a bonus) was perpetrated by Kamran Shirazi in the US championships, 1984. He managed just half a point out of seventeen games; *en route* he tossed off this shambles:

Shirazi–Peters. Sicilian Defence

| 1. e4 c5 | 3. a3 d5 | 5. axb4 Qe5+ and |
| 2. b4 cxb4 | 4. exd5 Qxd5 | White resigns |

There's hope for us all. (Next year Shirazi won a brilliancy prize in the same tournament.)

♖

Another one for the record books happened at the Linköping tournament of 1969. A German player scored zero out of thirteen. Not in the Moreau class, you're saying – but what puts it on a pinnacle of awfulness is this: all thirteen were lost by exceeding the time limit. The hero of this exploit wasn't a patzer either: Fritz Sämisch was a noted German grandmaster. He also set the record for the briefest-ever loss on time: after just twelve thoughtful moves, his flag fell. Fritz (who once thought for an hour about his fourth (!) move) had one of the longest thinks on his first move too. His opponent played 1. d4. *Twenty-seven* minutes later, after apparently deep thought, Sämisch came up with the unoriginal Nf6.[1] On another occasion, he thought for forty-five minutes on his first move with white.

♖

The two shortest ever losses on time: (a) from an American junior tournament: 1. e4 e5 2. Nf3 Nf6 3. d3 and white lost on time (he forgot to press his clock); (b) even shorter was Vizhmanavin *v.*

---

[1]Grandmaster Bronstein was similarly relaxed about the clock: he sometimes took up to thirty minutes over his first move.

Utyemov, which went: 1. d4, lost on time because Utyemov decided he had no chance.

♜

All of which brings us to the subject of brevities and some encouraging examples of how the mighty occasionally tread on banana skins. Here's Karpov, choked at losing his role of world-title challenger to Short, playing the most horrid loss of his career:

Christiansen–Karpov, Wijk aan Zee, 1993. Queen's Indian Defence

1. d4 Nf6	5. Qc2 Bb7	9. Nxc6 Bxc6
2. c4 e6	6. Nc3 c5	10. Bf4 Nh5
3. Nf3 b6	7. e4 cxd4	11. Be3 Bd6??
4. a3 Ba6	8. Nxd4 Nc6	12. Qd1 Black
		resigns

♜

Here's what happened when the great Boris Spassky's brain went into neutral against an unknown in Munich in 1979:

Lieb–Spassky. Vienna Game

1. e4 e5	3. Bc4 Nc6	5. f4 d6	7. Rxg1 Ng4
2. Nc3 Nf6	4. d3 Bc5	6. Na4 Bxg1	8. g3 exf4

9. Bxf4 Nxh2?? (a move your granny would be ashamed of)
10. Qh5 and if Black wishes to stop the most ancient checkmate of them all, the knight goes. So the former world champion sheepishly resigned.

♜

Just as bad was what happened to a world champion in 1924. Capablanca (the chess machine) was giving a simul in Brooklyn when one of the rabbits bit him on the ankle:

Capablanca–Kevitz. Orang Utan Opening

1. b4 d5	5. Nf3 Bxb4	9. h3 Nc5	12. Qf3 Nxe3
2. Bb2 Bf5	6. Nc3 Nbd7	(threatening mate)	13. Qf2 Nxf1
3. e3 e6	7. Ne2 Ng4	10. Ng3 Bh4	and
4. f4 Nf6	8. c3 Be7	11. Nxh4 Qxh4	White resigns

One of Capa's quickest losses[1] (though to be fair to him and his opponent, Kevitz was a good deal better than your average simul fodder).

Capa was less than machine-like in his game against Sämisch:

Sämisch–Capablanca, Karlsbad, 1929. Nimzo-Indian Defence

1. d4 Nf6	4. a3 Bxc3+	7. e4 Nc6	10. Qa4
2. c4 e6	5. bxc3 d6	8. Be3 b6	
3. Nc3 Bb4	6. f3 e5	9. Bd3 Ba6??	

He struggled on heroically, a piece down, for sixty-three moves before calling it a day.

♖

One of the shortest losses in a game between world-class players is the horrible:

Marshall–Chigorin, Monte Carlo, 1902. Queen's Gambit Chigorin Defence

1. d4 d5	4. d5 Na5	7. dxe6 fxe6??
2. c4 Nc6	5. Bf4 Bd7	8. Qh5+ (winning
3. Nc3 dxc4	6. e4 e6	a knight) Black resigns

Shorter, but not quite so world class, was:

Tarrasch–Alapin, Breslau, 1889. Petroff Defence

1. e4 e5
2. Nf3 Nf6
3. Nxe5 d6
4. Nf3 Nxe4

---

[1]The record for beating Capablanca in a simul seems to belong to Mary Bain (USA) who nailed the greatest natural player the game has ever seen in just eleven moves.

Capablanca–Mary Bain, Simultaneous Display, Hollywood, 1933. Four Knights' Opening

1. e4 e5	4. Bb5 Bc5	7. Nd3 Bd4	10. Ba4 Ne2+
2. Nf3 Nc6	5. O–O O–O	8. Ne2 Rxe4	11. Kh1 Nxc1
3. Nc3 Nf6	6. Nxe5 Re8	9. Nxd4 Nxd4	White resigns

At this point, Capa resigned. His generous opponent said: 'Let's call it a draw.' Mary was a 1937 Women's World Championship qualifier.

5. d3 and an overhasty Alapin, thinking Tarrasch had played the more
usual 5. d4 picked up his bishop. After 5 ... Be7 6. dxe4 Alapin
gloomily turned over his king.

Similar, and a modern contender for the title, was Zapata *v.* rising
star Anand[1]:

Zapata–Anand, Biel, 1988. Petroff Defence

1. e4 e5	4. Nf3 Nxe4
2. Nf3 Nf6	5. Nc3 Bf5?
3. Nxe5 d6	6. Qe2 Black resigns

At a less august level, the most embarrassing loss of recent years
was IM Andrew Whiteley's game in the London League against a
reserve, A. M. Dunn. A Budapest Defence, it went 1. d4 Nf6 2. c4 e5
3. dxe5 Ne4 4. a3 Qh4 5. Be3 Bc5 6. Qd3 Nxf2 resigns.

♜

Shortest loss by a reigning world champion was:

Liberzon–Petrosian, Moscow, 1964. French Defence

1. e4 e6	5. a3 Bxc3+	9. Qg3 Qa5	13. Nf3 Bd7
2. d4 d5	6. bxc3 c5	10. Bd2 Nc6	14. O–O Bb5?
3. Nc3 Bb4	7. Qg4 Ng6	11. Bd3 Nce7	15. Be3 Black
4. e5 Ne7	8. h4 h5	12.dxc5 Qxc5	resigns??

(He thought he was losing a piece; in fact he's only losing a
pawn.)

♜

Even more embarrassing was a world championship contender's
knightmare against an unknown.

Borochow–Fine. Pasadena, 1932. Alekhine's Defence

1. e4 Nf6	3. c4 Nb6	5. d5 Nxe5	7. f4
2. e5 Nd5	4. d4 Nc6?	6. c5 Nbc4	Black resigns

This is how most authorities quote the game. According to Andy
Soltis, Fine staggered on with 7. ... e6 8. Qd4! Qh4+ 9. g3 Qh6 10.
Nc3 exd5 11. fxe5 Black resigns.

[1] See Chapter VII 'The Future'.

♖

Of course, in postal play you have oodles of time to make sure disasters like the above never happen. Well, mostly never. Here is an Irish correspondence player in action:

Warren–Selman, correspondence game, 1930. Budapest Defence

1. d4 Nf6	4. a3 d6	and White	the queen is a
2. c4 e5	5. exd6 Bxd6	resigns (after	goner.)
3. dxe5 Ne4	6. g3 Nxf2	7. Kxf2 Bxg3 +	

An even shorter correspondence game from *Chess*, 1944:

Ellinger–Revd Durrant. Sicilian Defence

1. e4 c5	3. e5 Nd5	5. Nbc3 Nd3 mate
2. Ne2 Nf6	4. c4 Nb4	

♖

And there's worse. B. H. Wood tells of this débâcle in a postal tournament. After 1. e4, Black replied: '. . . b6. 2. Any, Bb7.' Now 'any' is a useful postal chess time-saver; it's shorthand for 'any move you care to make'. So White replied with the diabolical '2. Ba6, Bb7 3. Bxb7' (and wins the rook as well).

♖

For five centuries, bright schoolkids have been zapping their elders with variations on this sucker punch:

1. e4 e5	3. Bc4 Nf6??
2. Qh5 Nc6 (if White's lucky, 2. . . . g6	4. Qxf7 mate
losing a rook, is often played)	

The Scholar's Mate; certainly the most played quickie[1] of all time. See any under-tens tournament for half a dozen examples. But does anyone ever try it in an adult tournament? And worse, does anyone fall for it? Watch:

---

[1] Another much played quickie is worth knowing: the Blackburne Shilling Gambit, presumably so named because Blackburne used to win shillings with it. Try it on the next sucker you meet. 1. e4 e5. 2. Nf3 Nc6 3. Bc4 Nd4?! 4. Nxe5 Qg5 5. Nxf7? Qxg2 6. Rf1 Qxe4+ 7. Be2 Nf3 mate. This came off twice in successive rounds in a Blackpool tournament in 1987.

Amillano–Loeffler, Mar del Plata, 1972

1. e4 e5	3. Bc4 g6	5. Qxf7 mate
2. Qh5 Nc6	4. Qf3 Nd4	

♖

The shortest loss by a master was, for decades, supposed to be this much publicized gem played at a café in Paris in 1924. A waiter is said to have dropped a tray of plates when Lazard made his winning move.

Gibaud–Lazard

1. d4 Nf6	3. dxe5 Ng4
2. Nd2 e5	4. h3? . . .

and now, if you haven't seen it before, try to spot the crusher.

What made the history books was 4. . . . Ne3! If the knight is taken, it's mate by Qh4 + .

Sadly, Gibaud later denied it ever happened like that (well, he would wouldn't he?).[1] So into the record book went a much less diverting game. It happened to a tired future British champion, in the Chess Olympiad, 1933. Robert Combe, playing for Scotland, had had a tough twelve-hour game the day before, and doubtless sat down hoping for something shorter against a Latvian. That's exactly what he got:

Combe–Hasenfuss, Folkestone, 1933. English Opening (by transposition)

1. d4 c5	4. Nxe5? Qa5 +
2. c4 cxd4	(forking king and
3. Nf3 e5	knight) White resigns[2]

Combe's pained comment: 'The positional layout was perfect: it was unfortunately spoiled by a tactical circumstance.' (Some sources say e4 was white's second move.)

[1] To be fair, modern authorities accept his denial.

[2] The Olympiads seem to bring out the worst in people. Here's the Dutch Antilles versus Wales. White should have quit on move 3, but struggled on for two more moves to avoid erasing Combe's name from the record books:

Rigaud–Cooper, Nice, 1974. Falkbeer Counter-gambit

1. e4 e5	3. fxe5 Qh4 +	5. Kf2 Bc5 +
2. f4 d5	4. g3 Qxe4 +	White resigns

🜲

Topping even Combe's effort is this modern version of the same lemon:

Z. Djordjević–M. Kovačević, Bela Crkva, 1984. Trompowsky Attack

1. d4	Nf6	3. e3?	Qa5 +
2. Bg5	c6		and White resigns

🜲

There is, of course, a still shorter possibility:

Fool's mate: 1. f3 e5   2. g4?? Qh4 mate

But nobody ever played that in a real game, did they? Probably. Look, for example, at this gem (Masefield–Trinka, 1959 US Open Championship): 1. e4 g5 2. Nc3 f5 3. Qh5 mate.

🜲

Finegold seemed to lack the old will to win in his game against Wells, Ostend 1990. It went: 1. d4 d5 (draw offered and refused) 2. c4 resigns.

🜲

And still we haven't reached the limits. Here are two that come close.

Blackburne, in a simultaneous display, was confronted by an old gentleman who replied 1 . . . e6 to Blackburne's 1. e4. Blackburne, the strongest British player for decades, said jokingly, 'I resign.' The oldie held him to it.

🜲

And shorter still: Bobby Fischer, just before he became world champion, played 1. c4 against grandmaster Panno. Panno's reply was original: Resigns.

John Watson's analysis of Panno's move in his 'English: Franco, Slav and Flank Defences' is worthy of record:

1. c4 Resigns

. . . fails to further black's development, but does have a certain surprise value; and one may argue further that you can save a lot of energy by employing the demure approach . . . Those disinclined to the rigors of tournament play may find much of interest here.

🛡

Opening theoreticians may be interested in an improvement on Panno's idea found by Ken Rogoff, a US master, against grandmaster Hübner. It goes:

Hübner–Rogoff, World Student Team Championship, Graz, 1972

1. c4 Draw

🛡

But R. J. Fischer (who else?) holds the ultimate, unsurpassable record. Many others share it; nobody but Bobby played it at such a stratospheric level. In the second game of his world-title match against Spassky, Bobby, with white, just didn't play any moves at all. In effect, the game went:

Fischer–Spassky, Reykjavik, 1972

1. Resigns[1]

🛡

Here too, midnight oil has produced improvements even on Fischer's play. Miles *v*. Reuben, Luton, 1975 (don't blink or you'll miss it):

1. Draw

A more arduous path to the same idea was taken by Van der Sterren and Povah in the Lloyds Bank Masters, 1978:

1. e4 e5   2. Draw

🛡

Losing an important game in five moves or less is pretty depressing – but it's not the worst thing in the world. Imagine how grandmaster Vlastimil Hort (Czechoslovakia) must have felt at Reykjavik in 1977. It's the World Championship Quarter-Finals. Hort has been trying for a decade to get this far. He's level with the great Spassky and only two more games to go. He (black) has this position:

---

[1] To be strictly accurate, Bobby just didn't show up.

– and less than a minute to make five moves. Tough, but no problem for Vlastimil, for he's seen a sure win. 35. . . . Qg4. If 36. g3 Qh3 37. Rf2 Rd1 + and wins. Then, inexplicably, the Czech goes into a trance; completely forgetting his clock, he fails to make any moves at all. His flag falls – and ten years of sweat go down the drain. No wonder he called it 'the blackest day of my life'.

You think that's bad? Look what happened to David Bronstein in even more elevated company. It's Moscow, 1951. He's playing world champion Botvinnik for the title. He has oodles of time; and he has white in this position:

Bronstein sees that Ne6 + gets the draw. Fine; but then he slides off into a daydream about how he should have played the opening. After *forty-five* minutes of irrelevant musing he absent-mindedly picks up his king – and after 57. Kc2?? and Black's 57. . . . Kg3, bang goes the draw.[1] 'Blunder of the century' is what he called it. (Mind you, even the iron man of chess – Mikhail Botvinnik – once proved he was human. In a winning position against Smyslov in the World Championship Match of 1958, the most disciplined player in chess history forgot to press his clock.) So did Kasparov in a world title match, Seville 1987.

Five years after his Moscow débâcle, Bronstein was involved in another supershocker. He's black, playing Tigran (the Tiger) Petrosian, a future world champion, and he's in terrible trouble. He also has practically no time left on his clock.

Desperately, he's just banged a knight on f5, but his game is falling apart. Petrosian, with lots more time, calmly plays the awesome 36. Ng5?? and it's thank you and good-night as the incredulous Bronstein takes off the queen.

Then there's the gruesome thing that befell a Yugoslavian grandmaster in Havana.

It's the summer of 1965, and Borislav Ivkov is on top of the world: he's beaten two all-time greats (Smyslov and Fischer) and he's leading a very strong field in the Capablanca Memorial Tournament. If he wins, it'll be the best result of his life. With two

[1]After 57. . . . Kg3 the e pawn queens. But if 57. Ne6 + and Nd4, Black is fighting for the draw.

rounds to go, Boris is expected to clinch first place with an easy win against a tail-ender, the Cuban Gilberto García – a relative unknown.

True to form, Ivkov (black) crushes the local boy in the middle game and reaches a position in which García should resign. But, as they say, you never win a game by resigning . . .

What would you play? Boris chose the move that is still waking him up in the middle of the night: 36. . . . d3??; and after 37. Bc3, it was the ashen-faced Ivkov who had to resign.[1] (Doubtless shattered by this horror story, Ivkov blew his last game too – and finished, a sadder and wiser grandmaster, equal fourth.)

♜

Tarrasch (a doctor) called it *amaurosis schacchistica*.[2] It struck several times in the 1977 Korchnoi–Spassky match. The worst example happened, appropriately enough, in game 13. Korchnoi (white) has outplayed Spassky and has just missed an easy win to reach this position:

---

[1] Anthony Glyn uses this disaster as part of the plot in his absorbing novel *The Dragon Variation* (1969).
[2] Chess blindness.

Then he plays two world-class blunders in a row:

32. B×f5?? R×f5   33. Q×f5?? and loses his queen

But none of this is as agonizing as what happened to one of the greatest players of all time. It's Chigorin versus Steinitz for the world title. The result of the whole match depends on the outcome of one game. Chigorin (white) has this against the World Champion:

Pick a move for Chigorin. It probably wasn't as bad as what happened: imagine his feelings after Bb4?? and it's mate in two.

There are quite a few examples of grandmasters missing mates in two, but here's one of the best players in the world doing what you'd have thought impossible: missing a mate in *one*.[1] We'll leave you to find it. It was at Saltsjöbaden 1948 in a World Championship qualifying tournament: (Gligorić–Böök)

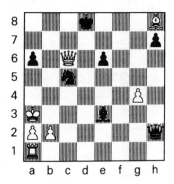

While the spectators reeled back in astonishment, Gligo played Rd1 +. Fortunately for his sanity, he went on to win eighteen moves later.

And here's Britain's world title aspirant at Linares (versus Beliavsky, 1992), allowing a mate in one in a favourable position.

1. Ke6?? Bc8 mate

[1] Other world-class players who missed a mate in one: Smyslov (*v.* Florian), Moscow *v.* Budapest 1950 (Smyslov picked a mate in three instead). Bronstein (*v.* Gligorić!) Moscow 1967. (From *Chess Notes*)

And, yet again, Timman *v.* Yusupov (Candidates' Match, 1992):

1. . . . Qe4?? – and resigned before 2. Q x f8 mate

Here's Karpov (black) playing Short for the right to meet Kasparov once more, making one of the worst moves of his career (Candidates' Match, 1992):

1. . . . Q x d3?   2. Rd2 skewers the rook

A promising young grandmaster blows it against The Man (Kasparov–Anand, Dortmund, 1992):

1. .... f5? 2. exd5 Black resigns (his intended 2. .... exd5 is met by Be2, keeping the piece).

♖

Even worse is what an obscure Argentinian, Jaime Emma, missed against a great Soviet grandmaster, Leonid Stein, at Mar del Plata, 1966.

Leonid (black), incomprehensibly, and after a twenty-minute think, put his queen *en prise* (34. .... Qc2??). Señor Emma, to his everlasting regret, didn't spot it (35. Rd7??). The game was drawn.

♖

You read above about the blunder of the century. Here's what Bronstein (an expert on such things) called the blunder of five centuries. Once again we're in the chess stratosphere: the 1973

Interzonal Tournament at Petropolis, Brazil. A good result in this means you qualify for the final stages of the world championship.

American grandmaster Sammy Reshevsky has white against the Soviet star Savon.

He has half a minute on his clock; he has one move to make before time control; and he also has a forced win. Instead of playing it, Sammy, a wizard of time trouble, chose what he thought was checkmate: 40. Q×g6 + ??? (mate) B×g6 and white resigns. (40. g5 + would have been mate in three.)

■

Poor Reshevsky played his shocker in time trouble. Given enough time, a grandmaster would never make the kind of blunders we make, would he? Well, Bogoljubow, world title contender of the twenties, broke the world record for long thinks by taking one hour fifty-seven minutes over a move. After all that sweat he played something that wouldn't look good on board six of your club second team. (It lost a whole knight.)[1]

■

Instances of masters resigning won games are not unknown. Here's Marco doing it against von Popiel in perhaps the best-known blunder of all:

[1]For a longer think, see Chapter V.

As is well known, Marco delighted generations of chess-players with the unenterprising . . . Resigns, instead of winning with . . . Bg1.

♖

More recent, and more entertaining, was what happened between Sztern and Lundquist in Australia, 1983. Sztern was offered a draw; he chose instead: Resigns. It happened like this:

Black offers the draw. White asks him to make a move first. Black plays 28. . . . Q x b2 + , to which White, stunned, replies 29. Resigns?? This was considered ingenious enough to be awarded the 1983–4 Blunder of the Year award by seven assorted masters and grandmasters. (Legally of course, he could still have taken the draw.)

♖

Just as nutty was what happened in Motwani–Chandler (British Isles Zonal, 1990):

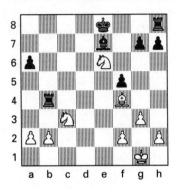

In this position, Motwani, in time trouble, played a check, 30. Nxg7 + . Then Black replied, illegally, 30. . . . . Rxf4?!? White resigned (??).

Just to demonstrate that nobody's perfect, here's Kasparov in a world title match missing something any run-of-the-mill computer would have leapt on in seconds.

It's 1986, London, and Kasparov is once again battling with Karpov for the world title. Gary, white in the second game, has miraculously squeezed something from nothing to reach this:

He played 39. Ne3? and a dozen moves later regretfully accepted a draw. But what Kasparov and some masters on the spot missed was the winning 39. Rc7 (threatening Rxd7 + or Nxe5).

♜

You can of course chuck away the win without making a bad move. Such was the horrid fate of Tringov in the Chess Olympiad of 1972. In a quite respectable position, against Korchnoi, the Bulgarian grandmaster sealed (he thought) his move, and adjourned for a night of analysis. Next day he found what he'd got was an empty envelope. The day after, after an agonizing search, he found the errant score sheet tucked in a jacket pocket. Understandably, he was too embarrassed to tell his team mates.

Woman grandmaster Marta Shul blew a key game in the Soviet championship with the same trick. Result, in both cases: a possible win turned in to a zero.

♜

Up to now the booboos have all been committed under the tension of match play. For a change, here's a most respected master tripping up in the quiet of his study. It's the Grand Old Man of British chess, Harry Golombek, annotating an Alekhine quickie, back in 1956.

Alekhine–Evensson, Kiev 1918. Vienna Game

1. e4 e5	3. Bc4 Bb4	5. dxc3 Nxe4	7. Qd5 + Ke8
2. Nc3 Nf6	4. f4 Bxc3	6. Bxf7 + Kxf7	8. Qxe4 Nc6

(at which point Golombek's note in *British Chess Magazine* says 'Even more vigorous is 8. . . . Castles') (?)

9. fxe5 Qe7	11. Bg5 Qe6	13. Nxe5 a6?
10. Nf3 d6	12. O–O–O dxe5	

and Harry (a world championship arbiter) repeats the blunder: 'Correct was

13. . . . Castles' (??)

14. Qxc6 + Black resigns

As scores of delighted readers pointed out – you can't castle if you've moved the king.

♜

Next, the worst display of ignorance by a grandmaster.

At world championship level, you figure that both players know the rules of chess. Imagine umpire O'Kelly's[1] emotions in the

---

[1]See Chapter VI for his full name.

Korchnoi–Karpov match (Moscow, 1974) when Korchnoi strolled over to him in one game and posed a beginner's query: can I castle if my rook is attacked? Answer: Yes. Korchnoi's explanation: 'It had never come up before.'

🨅

Here's what rising star Gata Kamsky did in 1990 at the Manila Interzonal.

Illescas–Kamsky, Manila Interzonal, 1990. Caro-Kann Defence

1. e4 c6	9. Ne5 e6	16. Nxf7 Kxf7	21. Rc1+ Bc5
2. c4 d5	10. Ne4 Be7	17. Ng5+ Ke8	22. Bg5 Qf7
3. cxd5 cxd5	11. d4 Bxb5	18. Qxe6+ Qe7	23. Qd6 Nb8
4. exd5 Nf6	12. Qxb5+	19. Qxd5	24. Rxc5+ Nc6
5. Nc3 Nxd5	N8d7	O–O–O?!,	25. Be7 Black
6. Nf3 g6	13. Bh6 a6	replaced by	resigns
7. Qb3 Nb6	14. Qe2 Bb4+	19. . . . Kd8	
8. Bb5+ Bd7	15. Kf1 Nd5	20. Ne6+ Kc8	

On move 19 Illescas pointed out that Kamsky's king had already moved. So the embarrassed Gata played Kd8, which lost immediately to 20. Ne6 + . For more on Gata see our Chapter VII, 'The Future'.

🨅

In the France–Hungary match, 1983, Kouatly (France), against Sax played 24. . . . O–O–O, although fourteen moves earlier he'd moved his rook to d8 and then back to a8. No one noticed until the game was published.

🨅

And in Ireland in 1973, a player castled twice in the same game – and got away with it. Heidenfeld (a strong player), playing Kerins in a club match, castled king-side. Subsequently, under attack, he moved his king back to the king's square; then, forgetfully, he castled queen-side. No one noticed. (He lost the game, but entered the record books.)

🨅

More worsts:

Worst simultaneous performances on record:

In August 1977, Joe Hayden, aged seventeen, tried to set an

American record by challenging 180 people to a simultaneous chess display in a shopping centre in Cardiff, New Jersey. Only twenty showed up. His score – eighteen losses (including one to a seven-year-old) and two wins. One win happened because his opponent got tired of waiting and drifted away. Joe's other win was scored against his mum.

♖

In the early years of this century, according to *Chess*, the Viennese master Josef Krejcik got the worst birthday present in chess history. Having reached his twenty-fifth birthday, he took on twenty-five players in a simul. The result was immaculate: 0–25.

♖

Daftest use of chess in English literature: the romantic novelist Ouïda, in her novel *Strathmore*, has one of her female characters 'castling her adversary's Queen, and nestling herself in her chaise to await his next move' (disinterred by Norman Knight – see our bibliography).

♖

Another entrant in this category: Gilbert Frankau in *Experiments in Crime* has a character playing 'King's pawn to king one'.

♖

A parallel award for television goes to Anthony Aloysius Hancock, none other. In *The Radio Ham*, the champion of Railway Cuttings sent the following improbable move zinging into the ether: 'King's pawn to queen's bishop three.' His Yugoslavian opponent replied with the equally implausible: 'Queen's pawn to king's rook two, checkmate.' (!)

And on Channel 4's *Lost in Space* a robot chess-player accepted the TN Bc1–g4.

♖

The most boring tournament of all time: Beersheva, Israel, in 1990. Out of eighteen games played, seventeen were draws.

♖

Most boring tournament performance: grandmaster István Bilek agreed ten short draws out of ten, the games taking a mere nine to seventeen moves each (125 moves in 109 minutes) at Słupsk in 1979.

191

♖

The worst chess book ever written? The entries are too numerous and the laws of libel too inhibiting for us to declare an outright winner. Among the contenders, two of the most unintelligible writers on the game: the impenetrable Franklin K. Young, and the downright loopy Cho-Yo. For a flavour of Young's style, here he is describing checkmate: 'Given a Geometric Symbol Positive or a combination of Geometric Symbols Positive which is coincident with the Objective Plane; then if the Prime Tactical Factor can be posted at the Point of Command, the adverse King may be checkmated' (*The Grand Tactics of Chess*, 1896). Got it?

Cho-Yo wrote a book called *Japanese Chess* (Press Club of Chicago, 1905) but in it he had much to say about chess in general. Like: 'Queening a pawn would be a ridiculous performance if we do not understand it chessonymously by esoteric connotations of the meaning on trans-modifications of force or vitality. There is in exotery literally no Queening a pawn in the Science and art of War – nay! – all kinds of struggles.'

♖

Competing for the Prince Dadian of Mingrelia award for plagiarism are two problemists: *100 Published Chess Problems* by Percy Wenman (you can still find it in second-hand bookshops) was notable for containing a quantity of problems by just about anybody but Percy Wenman. While of *100 Chess Problems* by B. Scriven, B. H. Wood said: 'The few problems that are sound are plagiarized.'

♖

Finalists for the *Grauniad* award include V. Ravikumar's *Timman's Selected Games*. This is well worth buying if only for the record number of typos. A few examples: 'Timman's technique is Hawless' (capital letters invade the text quite randomly) and he frequently gets into 'tactical skirimishes', Nikolić 'resings since his Queen side pawns crumbles and there is absolutely no counterpaly'. Even the name of the proofreader is spelled wrongly.

In the same league as Ravikumar's opus is the second edition of Keene and Levy's *An Opening Repertoire for the Attacking Player*. The preface proudly announces a massive campaign to eliminate printing errors. This is followed by thirty or so assorted clangers (biship, Tatakover) and a contents list that bears no relation to the actual contents of the book. A collector's item.

♖

Worst spelling of a major opening: in an interview with chess-playing folk-singer Nic Jones (see 'The Entertainers') the magazine *Folk Roots* (November 1988) refers to Bobby Fischer's favourite opening as the Ryall Opus.

♖

The worst opening is called, gaelophobically, the Irish Gambit; it has been dignified by inclusion in Hooper and Whyld's admirable book *The Oxford Companion to Chess*.

It goes (unbelievably):

1. e4 e5   3. Nxe5
2. Nf3 Nc6

The inventor of this opening was asked on his deathbed what possessed him to take the pawn. 'I didn't see it was defended' he gasped, and expired.

♖

The worst advice – 'Great players never castle' – was given in *Kort Afhandling* by Königstedt, the oldest Swedish textbook on chess (1784). A subsequent edition improved this to: 'Good players seldom castle.'

♖

Worst equipment in a national event: in a section of the 1946–7 Hastings tournament, one of the competitors complained that his clock was going backwards.

♖

Worst tournament conditions of all time: the 1979 US Open was played in a hall next to a thousand screaming fans attending 'Beatlefest '79'. GM Andy Soltis tells of struggling to win against Gildardo García while the hall rocked to the high amp strains of 'Can't Buy Me Love'. (And see our chapter 'The Bizarre' for what happened at Hastings a few Christmases ago.)

♖

The worst decision by a referee? Up there among the shoals of contenders must be the arbiter supervising Denker *v.* Reshevsky in an American tournament. Sammy Reshevsky overstepped the time limit. The referee picked up the clock, turned it towards him and in doing so, reversed it. (It's easily done.) So Denker was given a loss instead of Sammy. Uproar: but the result stood.

The worst bit of psychoanalysis: 'To checkmate the opponent's King in chess is equivalent to castrating him and devouring him, becoming one with him in a ritual of symbolic homosexualism and cannibalistic communion, thus responding to the remnants of the infantile Oedipus complex' (from a 1960 paper by Dr Felix Martí Ibañez, and reprinted, courtesy of William Hartston, in *Chess Notes*).

Stuff like this prompted the comment (on Grandmaster Fine's giving up chess for psychoanalysis): 'a great loss for chess, at best a draw for psychoanalysis'.

The worst commentary on a chess game may have happened in London in 1986. It's the first game of the world championship. Kasparov and Karpov are playing a pretty boring Grünfeld Defence and the masters in the commentary box are having a bad time thinking of anything interesting to say to the audience, listening on headphones. Suddenly there's a flurry of exchanges which the masters miss entirely. To the bewilderment of their listeners, they start analysing a totally irrelevant position. By the time they realize their goof the game has moved on too far for them to reconstruct the moves. Their panic is allayed by the arrival of one of the most respected chess pundits in Britain. You can hear the relief as they announce: 'Here is International Master Blank straight from the press room; he'll bring us right up to date. Over to you, Blank.' Blank's reply was memorable: 'I'm so pissed I can't stand up.'

The Tony Blackburn award for naffest chess compère: our vote goes to Tony Bastable of Thames TV, not least for his habit of interrupt-ing Kasparov's fascinating post-mortem analysis with dumb questions.[1] In the words of *The Times*' Andrew Hislop: 'He approaches chess like a Brut salesman at a miners' conference . . .'

♖

Three contenders for the Colemanballs award: chess journalist David Spanier on the 1989 world championship: 'I am inclined to think that whoever makes the fewer blunders will lose'; current-affairs pundit Anthony Howard on today's political scene: 'It's like a game of chess; all the cards are thrown up in the air and it's a whole new ball game'; or John Monie on a Rugby League fixture: 'It was a bit like a game of chess: they kicked the ball from one end to the other.'

♖

The most boring games of all time? We turn to the London tournament of 1851, and the interminable encounters between Elijah (the Bristol Sloth) Williams and the deservedly unknown James Mucklow ('a player from the country' says the tournament book sniffily). Elijah introduced the concept of *Sitzkrieg* into chess: he'd sit there, taking two and a half hours or more on a single move until his opponent dropped from boredom. The tournament book records games in excess of twenty hours (one was adjourned after a whole day, at the twenty-ninth move). Mucklow (a much worse player) was no swifter, and when they got together it must have been like watching an oil painting. ('Both players nearly asleep,' recorded a drowsy secretary midway through one mind-grinding marathon.) Howard Staunton's commentary says it all: 'Each . . . exhibits the same want of depth and inventive power in his combinations, and the same tiresome prolixity in manoeuvring his men. It need hardly be said that the games, from first to last, are remarkable only for their unvarying and unexampled dullness.'[2]

♖

Another contender for the slowest player award might be Louis Paulsen; (according to some editions of *The Guinness Book of Records* he once took *eleven* hours over one move). In mitigation, he was one of the greatest players of the nineteenth century. Still, he's

[1] e.g. 'How you think so far ahead?'
[2] For even slower games, see Chapter VI.

worthy of note if only for an anecdote that made Bobby Fischer laugh for days. He was playing Morphy (one of the quickest players in history), and taking aeons over his move. Many leaden hours of silent cerebration ticked slowly by. Even Morphy, normally the acme of politeness, was constrained to remark: 'Excuse me, but why don't you make a move?' Paulsen came to with a jerk: 'Oh, is it really my move?' No wonder Morphy gave up chess.

The most long-winded notation: that in the fifteenth-century book by Lucena, *Repetición de Amores e Arte de Axedrez*: 'Jugar del peon del rey a IIII casas, que se entiende contando de donde está el rey.' Nowadays they write e4.

Before we conclude this collection of supergoofs, you may like to have our choice for the all-time rock bottom: the worst blunder of all. There are five contenders for the title, quite different in kind, but each of epic proportions. You choose.

Number one is from the master with the hardest name to pronounce: Przepiórka. He's playing Ahues (Black) in an important tournament (Kecskemét) 1927. This is the position:

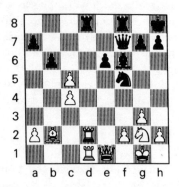

Black played ... R×d2. After much thought, White picked up Black's rook and *captured his own bishop* (on b2). Ahues, getting the flavour of the thing, carried on by capturing the pawn on a2. Przepiórka had lost three pieces in one and a half moves: a world record. Sadly for our story, the tournament director, a spoilsport, stepped in and made them play the moves again. (P.S. Pronounce it Pshe-purer-ka.)

♖

Number two is what German chess-players call a Fingerfehler. It's what happens when the brain sends out an instruction to the hand – and gets number unobtainable.

The protagonists are Herr Lindemann and Herr Echtermayer, and they're playing in a tournament in Kiel in 1893. On move 3, Lindemann, wishing to move a knight, touches his queen's bishop by mistake. According to the rules of the time, he must move his king. The result is this sparkler:

Lindemann–Echtermayer. Scandinavian Defence

1. e4 d5	3. Ke2?? Qe4 mate
2. exd5 Qxd5	

♖

Number three is much simpler. It's New York 1963, the last round of the American championship. Bisguier and Fischer are equal first. Fischer doesn't make a move for a long time. Bisguier looks up and sees his opponent is fast asleep. In another half-hour the great Bobby's clock will fall, making Bisguier the champ. That's where we come to the most gracious blunder of all. In Bisguier's words: 'I made a bad move. I woke up Bobby Fischer.' And of course Bobby, after a couple of yawns, went on to collect his fifth US title.

♖

Our fourth example is the most encouraging of all. Here are two of the greatest masters who ever lived, both missing something we ordinary mortals wouldn't.

It's Rubinstein–Nimzowitsch, San Sebastián, 1912.

Rubinstein is threatening Qxf7+ followed by Qxf8. Nimzo 'prevents' it by Bc5?? and Rubinstein plays Bd4?? instead of . . . well, you tell us.

And at the Interpolis tournament (1992) one of the greats blew a play-off game in spectacular fashion. Karpov (white) has reached this position against Chernin.

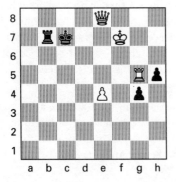

Karpov, winning easily, but in a hurry, has just played 53. e8 = Q. The game continues: 53 ... Kd6+ 54. Qe6+?!? Rxf7!!. Uproar. Then the arbiter steps in and asks the former champ to play a legal 54th move with his queen. So Karpov, rattled, blunders a second time: 54. Qe7+?? (54. Qd7+ Rxd7 55. Kg6 gets the draw) and after a few more moves, a doleful Anatoly is out of the tournament.

To be fair to the sixth[1] greatest player ever, this happened with ten seconds on Karpov's clock. At that speed, even you might have blundered.

[1] Or second if you believe Keene and Divinsky.

First Adjournment: The Unorthodox

'Well, I sort of made it up,' said Pooh ... 'it comes to me sometimes.'

A. A. Milne

'At chess, before gunpowder, The Queen took only Diagonal steps.'

W. H. Auden

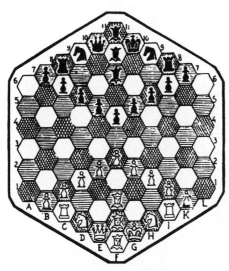

Hexagonal chess

What kind of chess did Aladdin play? You'll find it here, along with the enchanting games of Kriegspiel, Alice chess, snooker chess, alcoholic chess, and even chess as played on Mars.

It's a therapy session for those poor souls who've become bored with chess: a collection of the other games playable on a chessboard (and a few, including two of the best, that aren't).

To give the rules of each one would be too space-consuming – but if you want to pursue the matter, you'll find help in our bibliography.

Shaṭranj (or Arabian Chess)

The form of chess played by Aladdin, and an excellent game, if rather slower than the modern variety. The queen is replaced by a *firzān*, which moves one square at a time diagonally. The bishops are replaced by *fīls* (or *alfīls*), which can jump two squares diagonally (e.g. from f1 to h3). Pawns move one square at a time only and may only be promoted to *firzāns*. Castling is not permitted. A player can win by checkmate, baring the enemy king or stalemating the enemy king. The problem attributed to Aladdin in our frontispiece follows these rules.[1]

Here's a reconstructed game of Shaṭranj, dating from the tenth century. The position after White's 24th move was published by as-Sūlī, the greatest player of his time, and may have arisen from one of his games. We use the letters F for *firzān* and A for *fīl*. Black has the first move:

1. . . . . f6	3. f4 Nf6	5. e3 c5	7. Nh4 e6
2. f3 f5	4. Nf3 c6	6. Ah3 g6	8. b3 Fe7

---

[1] The Aladdin problem (frontispiece) is Shaṭranj: White to play and win.
Solution: 1. Rg7 + Kd6 2. c5 + Kd5 3. Rd7 + Ke4 4. Re3 + ! Kxe3 5. Ac1 + Ke4 6. Fd3 + Kxf5 7. Ng7 mate. Or 4. . . . dxc3 5. Fd3 + Kxf5 7. Ng7 mate. Or 4. . . . Kxf5 5. Ng7 mate.

9. Fe2 Ah6	15. d3 b6	21. Fd3 Rac8	27. Axd3 Nxd3+
10. g3 Kf7	16. e4 fxe4	22. Nc3 Nb4	28. Kf1 Rf2+
11. Nf3 Rd8	17. dxe4 d5	23. Na4 Rxc2	29. Kg1 Nd2
12. Ne5+ Kg8	18. Fd3 c4	24. Af1 Ac4	30. any Nf3
13. Nd3 d6	19. bxc4 dxc4	25. Nd1 Nxe4	mate
14. Nf2 Nc6	20. Fxc4 Aa6	26. N1c3 Rxd3	

And now part of a game between as-Sūlī (White) and his pupil al-Lajlāj (The Stammerer), again from the first half of the tenth century. This is the oldest recorded game of chess:

1. f3 f6	10. fxg5 hxg5	19. Nd2 Nd7	28. Axc5+ Ke8
2. f4 f5	11. d3 d6	20. Fc2 Fc7	29. dxe5 Nxe5
3. Nf3 Nf6	12. e4 e5	21. Fd3 Fd6	30. Nxe6 Rxg1
4. g3 g6	13. Ae3 Ae6	22. Ndf3 Ndf6	31. Rxg1 Nxf3
5. Rg1 Rg8	14. Nxg5 Ke7	23. Ah3 Ah6	32. Kxf3 with
6. h3 h6	15. c3 Nxg4	24. Af5 Af4	advantage to
7. e3 e6	16. Ke2 c6	25. Rac1 a6	White
8. g4 fxg4	17. d4 d5	26. c4 Rac8	
9. hxg4 g5	18. b3 b6	27. c5 bxc5	

Great Chess

Innumerable other versions of chess can be played simply by assigning new powers to existing pieces. Forms of chess played on larger boards with extra pieces are known as 'Great Chess'. Among the most famous devotees have been Aladdin and Tamerlane (see Chapter I), and the third Duke of Rutland, whose variant was played by Philidor and his circle. An eighteenth-century Duke of Brunswick played a mind-boggling version called Helwig Chess on a board of 1414 squares. And, even more boggling, the Count of Firmis-Periés invented a game of Military Chess on a board of 2640 squares with 940 men a side! (Paris *c.* 1815).

There's a fascinating game, Capablanca–Maróczy at double chess (at the RAC Club in London), in Edward Winter's book on Capablanca (see bibliography).

Fairy Chess

Non-orthodox pieces are known by problemists as fairy pieces. Here are a few:

The *Amazon* (or *Terror*) combines queen and knight; *Empress* (or *Chancellor*) combines rook and knight; *Princess* (or *Cardinal*) combines bishop and knight (a version of chess on a 10 × 8 board, with the addition of Chancellor and Cardinal, was invented by Bird in the nineteenth century and more or less re-invented by Capablanca fifty years later – Capa thought it vastly superior to chess); *Mann* moves like a king but is captured, not mated; *Dabbabba* is a 2 × 0 leaper (cf. the knight a 2 × 1 leaper); *Camel* (3 × 1 leaper); *Zebra* (3 × 2 leaper); *Giraffe* (4 × 1 leaper); *Wazir* (*Vizier*) moves one square orthogonally; *Nightrider* moves like a knight but may make a sequence of moves in the same geometrical direction; *Mao*, a non-jumping knight (moves one square orthogonally, one diagonally); *Berolina pawns* move one square diagonally forwards (two on first move), capture by moving one square forwards. A game played using Berolina pawns:

C. F. Snooks–K. M. Oliff, Correspondence, 1957

1. c2–e4 f7–d5	6. Qxd8+ Kxd8	11. h2–g3 Bf5	16. e2–g4 c4–d3
2. Nf3 Nc6	7. Nbd4 Nxd4	12. f2–e3 c5–d4	17. Ke1 c3–d2
3. Nc3 d5–c4	8. Nxd4 f5xf4	13. Ng5 Bb4+	18. Rc1 d3–c2
4. Nb5 d7–f5	9. Bxf4 b7–d5	14. Kd1 d4–c3	White resigns
5. d2–f4 a7–b6	10. Nf3 e7–c5	15. e3–d4 d5xd4	

Barasi Chess

Named after a friend of one of the authors, David Barasi (who has mysteriously changed his name to Paul since our first edition). Pawns are Berolina pawns, but may also move and capture backwards. They are barred from the back ranks and may always move two squares between their own second and fourth ranks (or vice versa). Pieces, on the other hand, can only move forwards. A bishop or knight on the back rank is dead, and a king, queen or rook may only move along the back rank. The current World Champion is Jon Speelman.

Progressive (or Scottish) Chess

An excellent quick game. White makes one move, Black replies with two moves, then White plays three moves, and so on. The game below was played under the Italian rules, in which a check may only be made on the nth move of an n move sequence. Black loses because he can only escape mate by checking on his first move. The Italians are crazy about it and have codified openings.

Dipilato–Leoncini, Correspondence, 1986. Orthodox Defence

1. d4	5. Nc3, Nxe4, Ke2, f4, Nc5 +
2. Nf6, d5	6. Kc7, Bf5, Bxc2, f5, b6, Bxd1 +
3. e4, e5, Bb5 +	7. Kd2, Kc3, Kb4, Na4, Nxb6, Ka5,
4. c6, Ne4, Kd7, cxb5	Nxa8 mate

Protean or Frankfurter Chess

A piece (except a king) mutates into the piece it has just captured.

Marseillaise (or Double-move) Chess

Each player makes two moves on his turn. (In another version White starts with one move only.) Check may only be given on the second of two moves. A player must move out of check on the first move of his pair. Alekhine once played Three-move Chess. He considered that White should always win. Here he is, playing the Marseillaise version:

A. Fortis–A. Alekhine, Paris, 1925

1. b3, Bb2	4. Bxb5, Be2	7. Kxf2, d4	10. Rxg3, Nc3
b6, Bb7	Bxg2, Bc6	Qxg5, Qf5 +	f5, f4
2. e4, Be2	5. Nh3, Rg1	8. Ke1, Bd3	11. Rg1, Re1 +
Bxe4, Bc6	e5, Nf6	Qxd3, Qxd1 +	Kd8, Bf3 +
3. a4, a5	6. Bxe5, Ng5	9. Kxd1, Bg3	12. Kd2, Kd3
a6, b5	Ng4, Nxf2	Bd6, Bxg3	Bg2, f3

13. Ke3, Kf2	15. Rad1, R x d4	17. Rf2, Kd2
Nc6, N x d4	Re8, R x e1	g5, Rd6 +
14. Ne2, N x d4	16. K x e1, Rd2	18. Ke3, c3
c5, c x d4	Rc8, Rc6	h5, Re6 +
		White resigns

Cylindrical Chess

The board is considered to be a cylinder joined at the a and h files. Thus 1. e4 f6 2. B x h7 R x h7 3. c3 + and mate in two.

Snooker Chess

Line-pieces may bounce off the side of the board at an angle of 90°. For example. 1. e4 e5 2. Bc4 Nf6 3. Qd1 x f7 (via h5) is checkmate. Also known as Billiards Chess, but we prefer snooker. The pieces are sometimes referred to as reflecting bishops etc.

Reverso

The positions of knights and bishops are reversed; then proceed as normal. All opening theory goes out of the window. Try it against your club theoretician and watch him flounder! Several tournaments under these rules were held in the late nineteenth century. During the forties, Lord Brabazon (see Chapter I), in the interests of brighter chess, proposed reversing the position of White's king and queen in the initial set-up. Bobby Fischer has advocated this as a way to slow down the domination of chess by opening theory.

Varied Baseline Chess

There are two versions of this.
(i) White chooses a random piece and places it on a1. Black places a similar piece on a8. White chooses a random piece for b1, and so on,

with the provision that the bishops must start on opposite coloured squares. This is also known as 'Randomized Chess'. There are 2,880 possible starting positions.

A game from a 1953 match between Combined Universities and Hampstead featuring two strong players. (The other games in the match were of orthodox chess.)

I. J. Good–M. Blaine, 1953
White baseline: Na1, Rb1, Kc1, Bd1, Be1, Nf1, Rg1, Qh1
Black baseline: Na8, Rb8, Kc8, Bd8, Be8, Nf8, Rg8, Qh8

1. e4 e5	6. Nxe8+ Rxe8	11. Be2 Nb6	16. Ra1 Qxb3+
2. Ne3 c6	7. Nb3 Bg5	12. Kc2 a5	17. Kb1 Nba4
3. Nf5 Ne6	8. Bg4 Rbd8	13. a4 Qb4	18. Ra3 Nxc3+
4. g3 g6	9. c4 Qf8	14. d3 Qxa4	19. Ka1 Qa2+
5. Nd6+ Kc7	10. h4 Bh6	15. Bc3 Nc5	White resigns

(ii) a screen is placed across the board while the players arrange their back rank pieces. A tournament under these rules was held in Brighton in 1976. Also known as 'Screen Chess'. Here's a game between two players of county strength:

T. J. Gluckman– G. H. James, Brighton, 1976
White baseline: Ra1, Bb1, Bc1, Qd1, Ke1, Nf1, Ng1, Rh1
Black baseline: Qa8, Bb8, Rc8, Rd8, Be8, Nf8, Ng8, Kh8

1. c4 c5	9. Nh4 Nh6	17. Nf2 Nd4	25. fxg4 Qxg4+
2. Nf3 b6	10. f3 Bg3+	18. Bxd4 cxd4	26. Ng3 Bd2
3. b3 d5	11. Kf1 Bxb1	19. Qb2 Rc6	27. Reh1 Bb4
4. cxd5 Qxd5	12. Rxb1 Qd7	20. Qa3 Rdc8	28. Ng6+ Kg8
5. Ne3 Qb7	13. d3 e5	21. g4 Be3	29. Qxb4 Rxe2+
6. Bb2 f6	14. Qc2 Ne6	22. Kg2 Rc2	White resigns
7. h4 Bg6	15. Rh3 Bf4	23. Re1 a5	
8. h5 Be4	16. Nd1 b5	24. Ne4 Nxg4	

Losing Chess

The object of the game is to lose all your pieces or to be stalemated. A player who can make a capture must do so. If he has more than one capture he may choose which one to make. The king has no royal powers and may be captured just as any other piece. Here's a quick 'win' for White:

1. e3 d6??	the bishop	6. a4 ...	12. h3 ...
2. Qg4 (from	– as they're	7. b3 ...	13. g4 ...
now we omit	obvious	8. g3 ...	14. f3 ...
all Black's	3. Kd1	9. Bb5 ...	15. e4 ...
moves –	4. a3 ...	10. Ne2 ...	16. d3 ...
mainly by	5. Ra2 ...	11. Rf1 ...	17. Bh6 ...

Burmese Chess

Adapted from the way they play chess in Burma. At the start of the game each player alternately places a piece anywhere in his first three ranks, until all the pieces are in position. Then away you go.

Rifle Chess

When a capture is made, the capturing piece does not actually move. For example, after 1. e4 e5 2. Nf3, Nc6 does not defend the e-pawn as after Nxe5 the white knight remains on f3.

Pocket Knight Chess

Each player has a spare knight which, on any occasion during the game, he may place on the board instead of making a move. In this Pocket Knight game played by post, Black is a grandmaster of correspondence chess.

G. Buckley–K. B. Richardson, Ruy López

1. e4 e5	5. Nxe4 d5	9. g3 Nd7	13. Be8 + Kg8
2. Nf3 Nc6	6. Nxe5 dxe4	10. PNe6 Qg6	14. Bxg6 Nd3 +
3. Bb5 f5	7. Nxc6 Qg5	11. Nxc7 + Kf7	15. Kf1 Bh3 +
4. Nc3 fxe4	8. c4 Nf6	12. Ne5 + Nxe5	16. Kg1 hxg6

| 17. Nxa8 PNe5 | 19. Bb2 Bc5 | 21. Qxf3 exf3 | White resigns |
| 18. b4 Bxb4 | 20. Qe2 Nf3+ | 22. Rf1 Nf4 | (PN = Pocket Knight.) |

Rejection Chess

At any move a player may reject his opponent's move. He must accept the alternative chosen by his opponent.

1. e4 e5	4. Qxf7 mate	White mates	Black's only
2. Bc4 Nc6	(if Black	with 4. Bxf7	king move)
3. Qh5 Nf6	refuses,	and refuses	

Canadian (or Madhouse) Chess

When a player makes a capture he must replace the captured piece on the board, on any square he chooses. Pawns may not be replaced on the back rank.

Alice Chess

Invented in 1954 by an Englishman called V. R. Parton and named after Lewis Carroll's eponymous heroine. Two boards and one set of pieces are required. The game starts with all the pieces on one board. When a piece is moved it is transferred 'through the looking-glass' on to the other board. A move has to be legal only on the board on which the piece starts its move. Pieces on the other board may not be captured. An example: 1. e4 d5 2. Be2 dxe4 3. Bb5 mate. The bishop has reappeared on the first board. The black king has no legal move and any piece that tries to interpose disappears at once on to the second board. A very confusing game.

Leapfrog Chess

Invented in 1992 by England junior Patrick Finglass. Your pieces may jump enemy pieces (only one at a time). So a white bishop on h3 can jump a black pawn on f5 to take a rook on c8; a white pawn on f2 can jump a black one on f3. And 1. e4 b6 2. Qh5 is check.

Avalanche Chess

Invented by Ralph Betza, 1977. After each normal move the player must advance an opponent's pawn of his choice one square (but no two square advance, no *en passant*, no capturing). If no pawn move is possible, no penalty. If in moving an opponent's pawn you give check to your king, you've lost. If you promote your opponent's pawn, he nominates which piece it becomes.

Triplets

Invented by Adam Sobey in the 1970s. Both players start with a pawn move; on their second move, they move a pawn and a piece (not the king) in any order; thereafter each player moves a pawn, a piece and the king – in any order (even if the king is in check). You lose if you get mated, or if you can't make any part of your triple move (NB: you can play O–O, but you can't play O–O–O).

Incidentally, both the above games feature in the second Heterochess Olympiad by Correspondence. Now there's a recherché event.

Knight Relay Chess

Invented by Manis Charosh, 1972. Normal chess except: (1) any man except a king that's a knight's move away from a friendly knight acquires the power of a knight in addition to its own power. A 'knighted' man can't pass on its powers, and loses them when no longer guarded by a friendly knight; (2) a knighted pawn cannot move as a knight to the first or eighth rank; if it returns to the second rank, it regains the right to a two-step move; (3) no *en passant* capture; (4) knights and promoted knights can't capture, check, or be captured. One of the most exotic variants.

Shogi Chess

Picks up one of the rules that make Shogi (Japanese Chess) such a fascinating game. Any captured piece goes into store, and can be returned to the board (instead of a move) with its colour changed. No pawns on the first or eighth ranks.

Kriegspiel

One of the best and best-known variants. Three sets and boards are required, two players and one umpire. The rules that follow are the house rules used by Richmond Junior Chess Club: various minor amendments are possible.

The players sit back to back at separate boards and move as in chess. The umpire, who can see both games, has another board placed between the players so that they cannot see it. The basic idea is that neither player knows what his opponent is doing. The umpire monitors the game and announces when a player has made a move. He also announces when a capture has been made, and on which square ('white has captured on e5'). Checks are announced as being on the rank, file, long diagonal, short diagonal or from a knight. He also informs a player if he tries to make an impossible move. On any turn a player may ask if there are any pawn captures ('Any?'). If there are, the umpire replies 'Try'. In our version a player may make three attempts to find the pawn capture, but this rule is not standard. If he is unsuccessful he must make another move. The game is tremendous fun, especially for the umpire.

Jetan

Edgar Rice Burroughs, in *The Chessmen of Mars*, describes a chess variant he calls 'Jetan' or 'Martian Chess' played on a 10 × 10 board. This game is complex but playable. See our bibliography for further information.

Exchange Chess

A very popular pastime among young players. Four players in teams of two, and two boards. The partners sit next to each other, one playing white, the other black. Checkmate on one board ends the game. When a player captures a piece he passes it to his partner. The player to move may, instead of moving a piece, place a man captured by his partner on the board. A captured piece may not be placed so as to put the opponent in check, and pawns may not be placed on the first or eighth ranks. When a pawn queens it is placed on its side, and, on capture, reverts to being a pawn. The game is best played with a clock at a fast time limit (usually five minutes per player) to prevent stalling.

Alcoholic Chess

Each piece contains an alcoholic drink, the strength of which corresponds to the strength of the piece. If you capture a piece, you drink its contents. Lasker (it is said) once played Alcoholic Chess, winning by sacrificing his queen at an early stage. Also known as Spirited Chess.[1]

Confusion Chess (or, Baffle the Kibitzers)

All you need is a good memory. Stick the pieces and pawns on the first two ranks in random order. Wherever a man is initially placed, it takes on the power of the piece normally starting the game on that square. So a king on f2 is a white pawn; and a pawn on d8 is (and remains) a black queen. If you really want to drive the spectators barmy, shuffle the colours too. Even more confusing is . . .

Continuum Chess

David Pritchard (the generous source of much in this chapter) told us

[1] A San Francisco liquor store used to, and maybe still does, sell hollow glass chess-sets which you fill with red or white wine.

about this. Invented by some boffins in Suffolk, it's in five dimensions and requires a knowledge of pure mathematics up to PhD standard. Fortunately David didn't have the rules to hand.

❧

Lack of space forbids more than a brief mention of the existence of various forms of three- and four-handed chess, three-dimensional chess and hexagonal chess. A four-handed chess club was in existence for about fifty years up to the Second World War. In 1992 Cambridge University beat a London team at four-handed chess. Kieseritzky invented Baltic four-handed chess, played on a board shaped like an eight-pointed star, and is supposed to have shown Anderssen a form of 3D chess in 1851.[1] In an episode of *Batman*, 'The Perfect Crime', Bruce Wayne and Dick Grayson are playing 3D chess on four layers. Dick says, 'Holy Reshevsky, Bruce! I think I'll stick to doing crosswords in Latin.' A variation of hexagonal chess invented by a London-based Pole named Wladyslaw Glinski has recently become sufficiently popular for World Championships to be held.

❧

We have omitted from this necessarily brief survey games played on a chessboard with non-chess pieces, such as draughts and reversi (or Othello, not to be confused with Reverso). We have also omitted Chinese Chess and Shogi (Japanese Chess), claimed by its devotees to be even better than chess. In one version of Shogi the pieces include a Drunk Elephant and a Horrible Panther. Regretfully, we have also had to leave out the superb Japanese game of Go,[2] perhaps the most subtle and difficult of all board games, Mancala,[3] a most delightful and demanding board game played throughout Africa, and the excellent Hnaftafl, a fascinating Anglo-Saxon board game that was pushed out by chess in the Middle Ages; you can occasionally find a set (called The Anglo-Saxon game) in games shops. Buy it. And Diplomacy, a wicked twentieth-century game that has broken up more friendships than bridge.

[1] A 3D chess game was on sale in New York in the seventies.
[2] Try any Japanese shop.
[3] or Wari. Spear's Games used to sell Mancala. Maybe still do.

IV *The Unacceptable*

You may knock your opponent down with a chessboard but that does not prove you are a better player. *Proverb*

'If you ain't cheatin' you ain't tryin'. *James Coburn*

You should be nice at all times but there is a lot to be said for an elbow in the chops when all else fails. This is forceful psychology. *Bill Russell, basketball star*

You can't play chess if you're kind-hearted. *French proverb*

Sports do not build character; they reveal it. *Heywood Broun*

A bad loser (see p. 218)

Next time you kick the board over, this is the chapter to make you feel better. It's a monument to sore losers; a collection of the baddest of bad scenes; and an instructive guide by some of the world's leading exponents of how not to behave around a chessboard.

'We are all one people' is the International Chess Federation's peaceful motto;[1] but now and again the agony of losing becomes insupportable (or the craving for victory at any price becomes overwhelming), and the quiet game gets rough. So in this chapter, we unflinchingly present behaviour that would not be out of place in Madison Square Garden – or on the Centre Court at Wimbledon.

It also takes in such side-issues as cheating, bribery, murder, and drunkenness in charge of a chessboard.

Welcome to the Chamber of Horrors.

The Caliph al-Walīd the First, shouting 'Woe be unto you', cracked open a courtier's head for throwing a game in about AD 690; not much later another Caliph (al-Ma'mūn) became the first person in history to knock the board over;[2] and a thousand years ago Ibn al-Mu'tazz wrote complaining of chess-players swearing, squabbling, making excuses and generally behaving badly.

Things didn't improve as chess spread to Europe. Swearing, for example (the more delicately nurtured of our readers should skip the next couple of paragraphs):

We have already seen ('The Royals'), the Dauphin of France, after

---

[1]*Gens Una Sumus*, actually.
[2]But not the last. The long list of people who've sent the chessmen flying includes Napoleon, Lenin, Alekhine, John Wayne and the sixteen-year-old Bobby Fischer. Bobby is normally impeccably behaved at the board, but after losing a game to Pachman at Mar del Plata in 1959 he was sufficiently miffed to hit the pieces. In 1987, 'Korchnoi scatters the pieces in chess walkout' said *The Times* headline. In a drawn position he'd touched the wrong piece accidentally, against Karpov (SWIFT Tournament, Brussels 1987). Bam! went the chessmen, and out stormed old Vik. And, allegedly, G M Ivanchuk is also prone to this form of self-expression.

losing a series of games to Prince Henry of England, 'called him the fonne of a Baftard, and threw the Cheffe in his face'.

This was mild stuff compared to that recorded in *The Noble and Puissant Galyen Rethore*, an ancient tale of chivalry. Galyen having mated his uncle Thibert one evening after supper got the old board-over-the-head treatment; and then, adding ins. to inj., Thibert called the noble and puissant Galyen 'Baftardly fonne of a whore'. (It's no excuse that Uncle Thibert's curse later turned out to have been at least partly true; Galyen's mother was bedded fifteen times in one night by a passing count for a bet – but we digreff).

♘

Our gold medal for cursing, however, goes to an Icelandic priest. Here's Father Stefan Olafsson getting it off his chest after losing a piece circa 1650:

'My malediction I utter – may Steini's men fall in heaps! May my fearful incantation bewitch him, so that peril shall beset two or three of his pieces at once! May the Old One [the queen] lose her life! May the wee pawns grow fewer and fewer on the squares and may he be mated both with the low and high mates!' Nasty.

♘

The Harvey Smith award for silent profanity goes to the ingenious designer of a handcarved chess-set in the Bavarian National Museum in Munich. It's eighteenth century, probably Flemish, and particularly interesting is the king. The upper part is decorated with a gay acanthus design; if you lose, you press a button and out pops a little man, baring his bottom at your opponent (see illustration at the beginning of the chapter).

♘

We should, *en passant*, mention a twentieth-century entrant who might have challenged Father Stefan for the gold: woman grandmaster Alla Kushnir of Israel (and ex-USSR). In a famous telegram sent to Viktor Korchnoi after his thirteenth match game against Boris Spassky in 1977, Alla called Boris (who we always thought was Mr Nice Guy) a ****, a ****, and a ****. But since the book of the match[1] refused to

---

[1]*Korchnoi vs. Spassky, Chess Crisis*, by Raymond Keene.

translate the asterisks because of the laws of libel, Ms Kushnir's entry must be *hors concours*.

Turning from bad-mouthing to bad sports, we nominate three outstanding contenders for the title of worst loser in chess history.

In third place, former World Champion Alexander Alekhine, a notoriously temperamental loser. At Vienna in 1922, Alekhine resigned spectacularly against Grünfeld by hurling his king across the room.[1]

In the silver-medal position, another famous loser – a world title contender of the twenties, Aron Nimzowitsch. At a lightning chess tournament in Berlin, he said out loud what all of us have at one time felt. Instead of quietly turning over his king, Nimzo leapt on to his chair and bellowed across the tournament hall: 'Why must I lose to this idiot?' Not nice, but one knows the feeling.

But the gold medal, plus the John McEnroe Award for bad behaviour at a tournament, goes to the lesser-known Danish player (reported in *The Chess Scene*) who lost as a result of fingerslip involving his queen. Unable to contain his despair, he snuck back into the tournament hall at dead of night, and cut the heads off all the queens.

All of which goes to confirm that depressing chess adage: the pain of losing is greater than the joy of winning. We'd sooner not name him, but in 1977 an American player certainly felt that way. After a particularly hurtful loss he tried to end it all. Unsuccessfully, we're happy to relate.

Murder and chess are, happily, infrequent companions these days, but as you saw in 'The Royals' section, it wasn't always thus. The London Law Rolls contain a couple of thirteenth-century examples (e.g. William of Wendene stabbed his opponent to death during a chesse quarrel in 1254 and had to seek sanctuary in a nearby church); and according to some sources, at least two world-class players met

---

[1] Or so it is said. These stories grow in the telling – like the one of Alekhine 'reducing the furniture in his hotel room to matchwood' after a particularly galling loss to Yates (or, according to some authorities, Spielmann).

their death by poison: Paolo Boi and Leonardo da Cutri, probably the two best players in the world in 1575.

Boi's life reads like an adventure story from the *Boys' Own Paper*. He travelled to Spain where he carved up the best players of the day at the Spanish court. On his way back to Italy (having netted a life pension from King Philip for his skill) he was captured by Algerian pirates, sold into slavery, and earned his freedom through his chess skill (he made his master a fortune in side-bets). He later travelled to Hungary where he beat the best Turkish players the hard way – on horseback. Paolo ended up in Naples in 1598, poisoned, it is said, by a jealous rival.

Leonardo da Cutri's end, according to one source, was straight out of Hammer Films. He, having been thoughtless enough to upset the Borgias, had a terminal interview with a Borgia hit man. Death by forcible poisoning was the verdict; the gruesome part is that when they removed the gag from around his mouth, a pawn was found clenched between Leonardo's teeth.[1]

♘

The next murder at the chessboard is more reliably documented. It's New York City 1960. A seaman goes into a Greenwich Village bar and throws out the challenge that John L. Sullivan made famous: 'I can lick any man in the house.' Unlike the great John L., however, the matelot didn't make it stick: he lost. In the animated post-game debate a spectator, one Clinton Curtis, was struck in the jugular vein with a broken beer bottle. The sailor was lucky: 'accidental death' was the jury's verdict.

♘

And happily for chess, a murder-at-the-board attempt during the last round of the great interzonal tournament at Saltsjöbaden, 1948, failed. The intended victim was one of the outstanding geniuses of modern chess, USSR grandmaster David Bronstein; the assailant, a political nutter, was removed by the local constabulary. David was shaken, but hung on to win the game and the tournament.

---

[1] The great authority on these matters, Murray, says of the main source for stories about Boi and Da Cutri (Salvio's *Il Puttino*): 'It is not easy to distinguish the basis of truth from the superstructure of fable.'

♘

In December 1992 chess was scarcely ever out of the headlines. If it wasn't Nigel, it was Bobby, and if it wasn't Bobby, it was Robert and Matthew. Robert Bryan (55) made the front pages when he shot male model Matthew Hay (22) over a game of chess. Their strange custom had been that Robert (the stronger player) allowed Matthew to win every game. But relations had deteriorated to such an extent (earlier unpleasantness between the two had featured a crossbow and a medieval mace) that the older man decided to deny his friend the usual win. Matthew hit the roof, Robert reached into his armoury, came up with a sawn-off shotgun, and is now doing a ten-stretch.

♘

Finally, before we leave this macabre section, there is the story of Alekhine's terrible confession. Alekhine, near the end of his life, lonely and sick, but still world champion, told a friend of the amazing happenings at the great St Petersburg tournament of 1914. One night, in mid-tournament, there's a knock on Alekhine's hotel room door. A ragged old Russian peasant demands entrance, saying he has found a chess secret of great importance. Impatiently Alekhine lets him enter. 'I have found a way for white to checkmate in nineteen from the starting position,' claims the old man. Alekhine starts to throw him out, but the peasant is insistent. To end matters, Alekhine sets up the board. Nineteen moves later, the future world champion, white-faced, turns his king over. 'Do that again,' he says. The old man does. And again. Aghast, Alekhine hustles the old man along the corridor, to the room of his great colleague Capablanca. The same sequence of events happens. Capablanca thinks first it's a bad joke: he ends up beaten again and again in nineteen no matter what defence he tries.

As Alekhine concludes his sensational account, the friend leans forward eagerly and asks the question you are now asking yourself: 'Then what did you do?' Alekhine's devastating reply: 'Why, we killed him of course.'

Before you throw this book in the fire in disbelief, we'd better come clean. The above (very roughly) is the plot of a terrific short story by Vincent Fotre 'Mate in Nineteen'.

♘

Our next section covers grievous bodily harm, i.e. chess acrimony stopping short of actually eliminating your opponent.

Here's a letter from the Revd Sydney Smith, Canon of St Paul's, London, to the Canon of Worcester in 1837, about someone who should have known better:

'I was at school with the Archbishop of Canterbury. Forty-three years ago he knocked me down with a chessboard for checkmating him, and now he is attempting to take away my patronage.'

How different from the life of our own Archbishop Carey (who, as we've observed, doesn't play chess).

♘

Physical violence around the board seems on the wane in modern chess, although both authors were present at a Thames Valley League match in the seventies when the Richmond board four, in animated discussion with Hammersmith's team captain, threw a right hook that wouldn't have disgraced Mike Tyson.

♘

At a more elevated level, the most notable bit of aggro in modern chess happened at a London club (Purssell's) in 1867. World champion Steinitz, a pretty irascible character at the best of times, fell out with the great English master, Joseph Henry Blackburne (nicknamed The Black Death). The way Steinitz told it, Blackburne assaulted him, and gave him a black eye – so the world champion spat at him. Other versions have Steinitz spitting first and Blackburne knocking him through a window in retaliation. We shall never know. What we do know is that the same pugnacious pair were at it again in Paris some years later.

♘

GMs Reshevsky and Najdorf were involved in a post-game scuffle at the Amsterdam tournament of 1950.

♘

The most trivial reason for whacking your opponent happened in the French championships, 1989. Jean-Luc Seret was contemplating a mate in one against Gilles Andruet. Andruet hastily wrote down '*Abandonne*' as Seret played the winning move, then hit the clock to end the game. This wasn't the only thing that was hit, for a huge row then broke out over whether Andruet had suffered the ignominy of checkmate before he resigned. Gilles needed eight stitches after the gendarmes removed his opponent.

♘

A notorious post-prandial post-mortem involving a strong Irish player erupted during a recent British championship. The after-game analysis, continued in a local restaurant, got physical when the irate Gael smashed one of those lamps made out of wine bottles, and assaulted his opponent with it. The damage was serious enough for the Irishman to flee the country. If he's still playing, it's under an assumed name.

♘

The most tension-packed match of modern times was a world title eliminator. Korchnoi–Petrosian (1977) was billed as the Match of Hate; it featured more aggro than the Stretford end on a Saturday afternoon and culminated in the organizers having to put a board under the table to stop the two grandmasters kicking each other.

♘

Petrosian was no stranger to g.b.h. at the chessboard. When he lost his famous match against Fischer in 1971, his wife, noted for her excessive partisanship, slapped the face of grandmaster Alexei Suetin – her husband's second.

Mrs Petrosian also features in our next section – gamesmanship, not to say downright cheating.

♘

Sharp practice at the chessboard has a long and doleful history. Not quite cheating, but teetering on the extreme limits of gamesmanship was Lucena's advice in his famous textbook (1497): 'Try to play after your opponent has eaten or drunk freely' and Ruy López's suggestion that you place the board 'so that the sun is in your opponent's eyes' (unhelpful to modern English club players).

♘

More modern examples of gamesmanship include Lasker and his

famous mephitic cigars;[1] Alekhine and his cats (one called 'Chess', another 'Checkmate'), which he used to put on the board before an important game – tough if you were allergic;[2] and a trio of world champions who were not above using music as a weapon. Steinitz would quietly hum *Tannhäuser* during games (Wagner, on receiving this information, expressed the hope that Steinitz's humming ability was better than his own chess ability); Bobby Fischer (in casual games) used to whistle the *Bridge on the River Kwai* theme ('Colonel Bogey') when in a winning position; and Bourdonnais used to sing at the chessboard (and 'swore tolerably round oaths' when things weren't going so well).

We draw a veil over some of the more extreme forms of bad behaviour, pausing briefly to mention Mason's spitting and an allegation that a late world champion used the corner of a tournament hall as a urinal during a simul (anticipating the behaviour of TV's most colourful snooker player by several decades) and we move hurriedly on to plain cheating.

The first example of downright crookedness we have is also a leading contender for the all-time bad sportsmanship award. The Sultan Suleiman (Suleiman the Rotter, they should have called him) was playing a blind chap in 1557. Feeling the need for a little extra help, the Sultan nicked a rook from his opponent's side of the board. As the sightless one remarked afterwards – if anyone else had done it, he would have complained to the Sultan.

In modern times, cheating is generally less obvious, but just as appalling.

　　Take Mrs Petrosian (again). In 1962 she 'won' a world title shot for her husband by organizing a night of grandmaster analysis to help a relative outsider, US grandmaster Benko, find a winning line against Paul Keres (Petrosian's fellow Soviet grandmaster and his

---

[1] It is at this point we omit the over-used story of Nimzowitsch complaining that his opponent, Vidmar, was threatening to smoke.
[2] He used this ploy against Euwe in a world-title match.

main rival for the title shot). The result: Petrosian won the tournament, and eventually the title. Worse, at Zagreb in 1970, Mrs P. is
not best pleased to see Bobby Fischer walking away with the tournament. In the middle of Bobby's game against the unfancied Yugoslav
Kovačević, her husband and Korchnoi spot a Fischer trap. To Korchnoi's horror, Mrs Petrosian oils across to the game and whispers the
news to Kovačević. The result – one of the shocks of the tournament
– a rare loss for Fischer.

R. J. Fischer–V. Kovačević, Rovinj/Zagreb, 1970. French Defence

1. e4 e6	9. Ne2 b6	17. Qg5 Rdg8	25. Nf1 Rxg2+
2. d4 d5	10. Bg5 Qe7	18. f3¹ e3	26. Ke1 Qh4+
3. Nc3 Bb4	11. Qh4 Bb7	19. Bxe3 Nf8	27. Kd2 Ng6
4. a3 Bxc3+	12. Ng3 h6	20. Qb5 Nd5	28. Re1 Ngf4
5. bxc3 dxe4	13. Bd2 O–O–O	21. Kf2 a6	29. Bxf4 Nxf4
6. Qg4 Nf6	14. Be2 Nf8	22. Qd3 Rxh2	30. Qe3 Rf2
7. Qxg7 Rg8	15. O–O Ng6	23. Rh1 Qh4	White resigns
8. Qh6 Nbd7	16. Qxh6 Rh8	24. Rxh2 Qxh2	

There's a happy ending, though. Bobby, despite all, strolled to a
great tournament win. Mrs Petrosian's favourite grandmaster finished
sixth.

But if Mrs Petrosian has a dodgy form card, how about Yugoslav
grandmaster Milan Matulovic? Golombek's *Encyclopedia of Chess*
accuses him euphemistically of 'extravagant behaviour'. What this
means is that Milan has more than once been caught trying to get
away with stuff that would get him thrown off any primary school
chess team. Against Bilek at Sousse in 1967 he, not liking his
position, *took a move back*, saying as he did so, '*J'adoube.*'² Bilek's
jaw dropped, but the arbiter hadn't seen the outrage and Matulović
went on to win. According to David Levy and Stewart Reuben (*The
Chess Scene*) the sneaky Slav repeated the same horror in the same

---

¹The trap: black can win the queen by 18. Nh4 but after 19. fxe4 Rxg5 20. Bxg5
white is on top.
²See glossary.

year – against the same opponent. Which is why, for a while, Matulović was known on the tournament circuit as J'adoubovich.[1]

And in 1970, the experts reckon Matulović threw his last-round game to help Taimanov qualify for the next round of world title matches (he arrived fifteen minutes late, and spent most of the game wandering round the tournament room, chatting to spectators). The game was played by M., say Wade and Blackstock in the tournament book, 'at colossal speed'.

For this sad effort, our hero is rumoured to have received $400 under the table. It is some comfort to know that the 'winner', as a result of this game, went on to play Bobby Fischer – and was terminally crushed 6–0.

For more Matulović beastliness see 'The Bizarre'.

It's the 1986 Chess Olympiad; England, who were silver medallists in 1984, are doing even better – they're leading the field, the unbeatable Soviets are in third place and a sensational upset is on. England are due to play Spain (who are not in the top dozen rated teams) and expect an easy win. But before the match, the Russians lend the Spaniards their precious dossiers on each member of the English team. Now this, while not exactly ethical, isn't crooked either. But what followed was: in the middle of the match, Georgadze, the Spanish team trainer (a USSR grandmaster), 'discussed' the Illescas–Nunn game loudly enough for Illescas to hear his suggestion. The result – Nunn lost, and the English team went down $3\frac{1}{2}$–$\frac{1}{2}$. England's final result in the Olympiad was a notable silver medal – but half a point more would have meant gold for them instead of USSR.

As in many sports, the Chinese look set to become a major factor in world chess. Sadly, some of them have already picked up some of the shadier habits of the occidentals: in a zonal tournament (1987), it was alleged that the Chinese player Qi threw games to his teammates Li and Xu.

---

[1] A more eminent practitioner of this tactic may have been a former world champion. Alekhine was accused of having touched a rook *before* saying '*J'adoube*', against Schmidt in 1941.

The best player Brazil ever produced was Henrique Mecking, one of the giants of the seventies. His career was interrupted by illness (see 'The Holy'); but in the seventies he was a fearsome opponent and not just because of his chess skill. When he played a match with Korchnoi he fidgeted so much the table shook; and during the Hastings tournament of 1971–72 he tried a novel tactic against future Welsh international George Botterill: when they were both in time trouble, Henrique pressed his clock, then kept it pressed down so poor old George couldn't stop *his* ticking. The result – a loss on time for Botterill, and third place for the (if you'll excuse the expression) irrepressible Brazilian.

Grandmaster Mikhail Gurevich stunned the chess world in 1991 by his allegations that Karpov had tried to bribe him to quit Kasparov's squad of assistants, and sell him the secrets of the World Champion's opening preparation. Whether true or not (it was never proved) this pales into insignificance by the side of Bobby Fischer's allegations (1992) that Kasp, Karp, and Korch had been fixing whole matches in advance. Frankly we doubt it; but we await with interest Bobby's promised evidence.

Since the first edition of this book, the Kamsky family, *père et fils*, have seemed determined to write a whole new chapter on unpleasant-ness in chess. Space doesn't permit us to give you all the unsavoury details, but you'll get the general idea from this brief smattering: Rustam Kamsky (daddy) smacks Gata K. (the promising young GM) at a party thrown by their sponsors (the sponsor pulled out); Gata mumbles opening variations audibly and off-puttingly at the board ('Everyone does it,' says dad): Rustam verbally assaults players and officials during the US Championship (1991) and is barred from hall; Rustam accuses innocent spectators of 'obvious cheating' and orders them out of playing area; Gata and Rustam refuse to hand over score-sheets (they claim they can get $700 for the set in New York) at Linares and Gata is fined one point (subsequently retracted after protests from other players); at the same tournament Gata accuses Kasparov of poisoning his orange juice (Kasparov replied that if he was going to poison anybody he'd have picked Ivanchuk, who won the tournament); at their next tournament Britain's Nigel Short sticks a 'poison' sign on the o.j. jug when Kamsky plays Kasparov. And so on and so on. For more palatable aspects of young Kamsky, see Chapter VII, 'The Future'.

♘

The contemplative world of correspondence chess is not often hit by scandal, but in 1987 it was rocked by the strange Leigh Strange saga. Leigh Strange, a reclusive woman player, too diffident to take part in over-the-board tournaments, was nonetheless strong enough to win the British Ladies' Correspondence Championship. She collected the handsome Lady Herbert trophy, and went on to represent Britain in the postal Olympiad. But for correspondence organizer Keith Escott, something didn't quite add up. Ms Strange was just too self-effacing to be true: nobody had ever laid eyes on her. Suspicion fell on a Cambridge undergraduate, one Nick Down, a former British Junior Correspondence Chess Champion. Keith confronted the unfortunate youth, who eventually confessed all. There was no Leigh Strange; the whole thing, phoney handwriting, false addresses and the rest, had been cooked up by a group of undergraduates. The Lady Herbert cup was handed back, and Britain fielded a late sub. in the Olympics. Young Down got a two-year ban, and quite right too.

♘

We leave the best bit of skulduggery to the last.

George Treysman, king of New York coffee-house players, was a legendary win-at-all-costs tactician. Playing in the smoke, noise and confusion of New York cafés, he is said to have got away with murder. His most brilliant improvisation was in the heat of a blitz game: Treysman, a rook down, managed successfully to castle with another rook from an adjacent game. He won, collected his dime, and speedily set up the pieces for a fresh game, while three other confused chess-players tried to figure out what had happened.

It is also said – but you don't have to believe it – that Treysman once managed to castle with a salt cellar from the tray of a passing waiter. Treysman never opened a chess book and rarely played outside New York cafés – but on one memorable occasion, in his first major tournament, he finished equal third with grandmaster Fine in the first modern US Championship.

A tacky postscript: unacceptable in a different sense was King Farouk's chess-set. Farouk, King of Egypt, an awesomely self-indulgent man (he once ordered a custom-built Bentley; by the time it arrived he was too fat to get in) owned the largest collection of erotica ever assembled. One of his most treasured possessions was an ivory chess-set of flawless workmanship and disgusting design. The pawns, we blush to tell, were willies; and the pieces were up to the kind of sexual gymnastics that would have raised eyebrows at the court of the Emperor Tiberius. The whole appalling thing was auctioned at Bonham's in 1988 (it went for a very reasonable four grand). If you are sufficiently depraved to want pictures, flip through your back copies of *The Sport*. The date you're after is 24 July 1991.

V *The Awesome*

Wait a minute, wait a minute, you ain't heard nothing yet, folks!

Al Jolson

The Monster: the score-sheets of the longest game, dated 17.02.89
(continued overleaf)

Warning: over-indulgence in the material in this section could very easily turn you into the club bore. (On the other hand, judicious use of it could win you quite a few bets down the pub.) It's a collection of somewhat technical facts of the type that are normally preceded by the words 'Not a lot of people know this but . . .'

It's also your opportunity to break a world record. If you have the score of a game played under match conditions which lasted longer than 269 moves, or in which you castled later than the forty-sixth, or if you can better any other of the arcane feats mentioned below, you're in with a chance. Drop us a line, care of Faber and Faber.

♟

One of the many legends about the invention of chess goes like this. Many centuries ago in India there lived a Brahmin called Sissa (or possibly Sassa). The ruler of his province was a tyrant and in order to teach him a lesson the crafty Brahmin invented the game of chess. This demonstrated to the ruler that a king can only succeed with the help of his subjects. Enlightened by this revelation he offered Sissa a reward: anything in the kingdom he asked for would be his. 'I am a humble man,' replied the Brahmin. 'I only want a modest reward. Just give me one grain of rice on the first square of the chessboard, two on the second, double the number, four on the third, and so on up to the sixty-fourth square.' 'Surely you'd like something better than that,' entreated the king. 'Look at all these nubile serving girls, this fine jewellery, gold and diamonds. Whatever you want, it shall be yours.' 'No, no. just give me the rice,' insisted Sissa. So the king got out the rice sacks. The more mathematically inclined among our readers will already have realized that the total number of grains of rice Sissa asked for was $2^{64} - 1$, or 18,446,744,073,709,551,615 grains of rice. This would cover England to a depth of 10 metres, or sow the entire land mass of the planet 76 times. (In some versions of the story, Sissa got his head chopped off for being a smartyboots.)[1]

---

[1] The truth about the origin of chess is unclear. Most people's favourite authority, H. J. R. Murray, in his monumental *History of Chess* (1913), reckons that the game didn't evolve, but was invented by an inhabitant of north-west India, 'round about AD

♟

A few more large numbers. The number of different legal positions on a chessboard is 10×2^{43}. The number of different games of 40 moves or less has been estimated as 25×10^{115}. This is considerably larger than: the total number of words spoken by everyone (including Ben Elton) since the beginning of human speech (Kasner and Newman estimate 10^{16}); or the number of words printed since the Gutenberg Bible (including the complete works of Jeffrey Archer), estimated at 10^{18}; or the number of seconds since the birth of the universe: 10^{18}; or even the estimated number of electrons in the universe: 10^{79}.

For a truly large number involving chess, we paraphrase the mathematician G. H. Hardy: imagine the entire universe is a chessboard and that every atomic particle within it is a chess piece. If you imagine every particle is to change places with every other particle and you call each one of such interchanges a 'move', the total number of possible moves in this mega-galactic game would be 10 to the 10th to the 10th to the 34th. By coincidence, this is equal to Skewes's number (used in the calculation of primes) which the *Guinness Book of Records* used to list as the largest number used in science.

♟

In the starting array, white has a choice of 20 moves, and black a choice of 20 replies, making a total of 400 possible positions after one move by each side. After two moves by each side the number is 71,852. In 232 of these positions white will have the option of making an *en passant* capture, so, theoretically speaking, the number should be 72,084, which may be reached in about 200,000 different ways. After three moves the number of possible positions is somewhat over nine million. If you wanted to reach every possible position after four moves, taking one minute for each one, it would take you a matter of 600,000 years.

570'. A much more recent suggestion is that of Russian GM Yuri Averbakh, who believes that chess evolved from a combination of an old Indian race game played with dice and the ancient Greek war game Petteia in the fifth century. There is no conclusive evidence for or against this theory. Personally, we'll stick with Murray.

♟

The longest possible game in which neither player claims a draw until he or she is legally able to do so would conclude on white's 5,899th move. Before the law changes agreed at the 1984 FIDE Congress this game would have lasted 5,949 moves, but a player can now claim a draw with king against king. Because of various extensions to the 50-move rule, which have now been dropped, the longest possible game would have finished on black's 6,098th move between 1985 and 1989 and on black's 6,053rd move between 1 March 1989 and 31 December 1992. However, organizers may impose their own extensions to the 50-move rule if an announcement is made at the start of the tournament (they might, for instance, choose to allow 250 moves for rook and bishop against two knights: see Chapter VIII).

♟

The longest game actually played (excluding deliberate record-creating attempts) was I. Nikolić–Arsović, played in Belgrade in 1989. The game was agreed drawn on black's 269th move, smashing all previous records out of sight, after reaching the dreaded rook and bishop against rook. It took 20 hours 15 minutes and seven scoresheets. Masochists who wish to play through the whole thing, see the illustration at the start of our chapter.

♟

Other whoppers are Chekhov–Stavrinov (Riga Championship, 1988), drawn in 209 moves, and Meier–Rausis (Latvian Championship, 1989), drawn in 200 moves. There must be something about the air in Latvia. Previous record-holders were Martinovsky–Jansa (Gausdal, 1987), drawn in 194 moves and Stepak–Mashian (Israel, 1980), a win for white in 193 moves and 24 hours 30 minutes. This game is still, to the best of our knowledge, the longest decisive game and the game with the longest duration.

♟

Other length records: Longest game ending in stalemate: 191 moves in Seirawan–Xu (1988 Olympiad). Longest game between 2600+ players; 162 moves in Salov–Short (Linares, 1990), won by black. Longest game between women: 150 moves in Arkell–Makropoulou (1990 Olympiad), drawn. Longest British game: 163 moves in Miller–Uber (Cheltenham, 1913), won by white.

🨾

We award a special prize for *Sitzfleisch* to the Romanian international master Drimer. The only titled player at Whitby, 1967, he duly won with 10 out of 11. What makes his performance remarkable was that three of his games, including his two draws, exceeded 100 moves (one lasting 132 moves and another 125 moves).

🨾

Also worth a mention is the longest game in a world championship match. This is Korchnoi–Karpov, the fifth game of their 1978 match, where white delivered stalemate on move 124. It was, incidentally, the only world championship game to have ended in stalemate.

🨾

For the longest game without a capture (and a candidate for the most boring game of all time) we offer Filipowicz–Smederavac. This was a 70-move game in which white claimed a draw by the 50-move rule, having had several previous draw offers turned down. Here's their narcoleptic effort.

Filipowicz–Smederavac, Polanica Zdrój, 1966. King's Indian Attack

1. e4 e6	17. Bd2 Rfd8	33. Ne1 Bc7	49. Nc4 Nd5
2. d3 Ne7	18. Ng1 Bf8	34. Nf3 Rh8	50. Nf2 Bb7
3. g3 c5	19. Nf3 Be7	35. Ng5 Bd8	51. Nh3 Bc6
4. Bg2 Nbc6	20. h4 h5	36. Nf3 Be7	52. Qg2 Rhc8
5. Be3 b6	21. Qe2 Ncb4	37. Qg1 Bb7	53. Re1 Rc7
6. Ne2 d5	22. Rfc1 Bb7	38. Nb5 Raa8	54. Re2 Ra7
7. O-O d4	23. Kh2 Bc6	39. Na3 Ba6	55. Ree1 Ra6
8. Bc1 g6	24. Na3 Ra8	40. Qf1 Rab8	56. Re2 Rba8
9. Nd2 Bg7	25. Qe1 Rdb8	41. Nc4 Bd8	57. Ree1 R8a7
10. f4 f5	26. Qg1 Qb7	42. Qd1 Ne7	58. Na3 Ra8
11. a3 O-O	27. Qf1 Kg7	43. Nd6 Bc7	59. Nc4 Nh6
12. e5 a5	28. Qh1 Qd7	44. Qe2 Ng8	60. Na3 Nf7
13. a4 Ba6	29. Ne1 Ra7	45. Ng5 Nh6	61. Nf2 Rd8
14. b3 Rb8	30. Nf3 Rba8	46. Bf3 Bd8	62. Nc4 Rb8
15. Nc4 Qc7	31. Ne1 Bd8	47. Nh3 Ng4+	63. Nh3 Bd8
16. Kh1 Nd5	32. Nf3 Rb8	48. Kg1 Be7	64. Na3 Ra7

65. Qh1 Bc7	67. Qh1 Nh6	69. Nh3 Qe8	Drawn by the
66. Qg2 Rg8	68. Ng5 Nf7	70. Kh2 Rd7[1]	50-move rule
			(Zzzzzzzz)

♟

Soviet grandmaster David Bronstein was in the habit of thinking half an hour or more over his first move. In a game played in 1982 Viktor Korchnoi thought for well over an hour and a half on his sixth move in a Ruy López opening. But the record 'longest think' since the introduction of chess clocks currently belongs to Brazilian IM Trois, who, against Santos at Vigo 1980, thought for two hours twenty minutes over his seventh move! The time limit for the tournament was (presumably) 40 moves in two and a half hours. The opening was 1. c4 e5 2. Nc3 Nf6 3. Nf3 Nc6 4. e4 Bc5 5. Nxe5 Bxf2+ 6. Kxf2 Nxe5 7. d4 and . . . eventually . . . Ng6.

♟

The records for latest castling have been tabulated, like much else in this section, by the indefatigable Tim Krabbé and published in *New In Chess* (a terrific English-language magazine for the real enthusiast) and his wonderful book *Chess Curiosities*. The record-holders at the time of writing look like this:

– Latest castling: Bobotsov–Ivkov, Beverwijk, 1966 (46. O–O).

– Latest castling by black: Soeterboek–Van der Heijden, Netherlands, 1981 (44. . . . O–O).

– Latest queen-side castling: Popovych–I. Ivanov, New York, 1983 (43. . . . O–O–O).

– Latest queen-side castling by white: Pupols–Myers, Lone Pine, 1976 (40. O–O–O). This game also holds the record for castling with the fewest pieces on the board – eight.

– Latest castling as sealed move: Magrin–Rosenblatt, Biel, 1972 (42. O–O), just half a move better than the previous, hitherto unpublished, record, James–Mozoomdar, Twickenham, 1971 (41.

[1] In our first edition we omitted two moves from near the end of this game; interestingly, nobody noticed.

... O–O). As this game was won by black, we shan't give the score.
- The record total of castling move numbers in one game is still held by Yates–Alekhine, San Remo, 1930, with a total of 60 (24. ... O–O, 36. O–O). This looks very beatable to us.

♟

The greatest number of queens on the board at once – a controversial one, this. The well-known five-queens 'game', Alekhine–Grigoriev, is actually only Alekhine's analysis of a Grigoriev–A. game. (Alekhine was also notorious for doctoring the finishes to his games to make them look more brilliant than they really were.) Hoax games with six and seven queens on the board have also been published. But we only know of two genuine games with five queens on the board at once: Tresling–Benima (Winschoten, 1896) and Vondung–Lamprecht (Correspondence: West Germany, 1972) – see below. Black had three queens against one in Williams–Ginsburg, (New York, 1982–3) and in Dely–F. Portisch (Budapest, 1968) black resigned on seeing white's third queen appear on the board. (This record excludes the many thousands of games in kiddie tournaments where one player tries to queen as many pawns as possible, so don't write and tell us that your seven-year-old son got five queens in a school game.) The greatest number of queens to appear at any time in one game is seven, this record standing to Konopleva–Schmidke (1968): black scoring four queens to three and winning the game.

Tresling–Benima, Winschoten, 1896. Ruy López

1. e4 e5	13. axb3 e4	25. Qd1 c5	37. Be5 Bxe5
2. Nf3 Nc6	14. Nd2 O–O	26. dxc5 Bxb2	38. Qxe5 a2
3. Bb5 a6	15. c4 Rfe8	27. Rf4 Qe7	39. d7 Qa3
4. Ba4 Nf6	16. Nxe4 Nxe4	28. Qxh5 Bf6	40. c7 b3
5. Nc3 Be7	17. Qxe4 Bf6	29. cxd6 Qxd6	41. d8 = Q b2
6. O–O b5	18. Qd3 Qg4	30. Qf3 Re5	42. c8 = Q b1 = Q
7. Bb3 d6	19. Be3 b4	31. Re4 Rxe4	(and there we
8. d3 Be6	20. f4 h5	32. Qxe4 Qg3	are – five
9. Qe2 Qd7	21. h3 Qd7	33. Bf4 Qxb3	queens)
10. Nd5 Bxd5	22. f5 Qe7	34. d6 Rf8	
11. exd5 Na5	23. Rae1 a5	35. c5 a4	
12. d4 Nxb3	24. Kh1 Qe4	36. c6 a3	

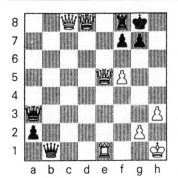

Position after black's 42nd move.

43. Qxf8+ Qxf8 44. Qxf8+ Kxf8 45. Qe8 mate

In the game, Vondung–Lamprecht, played, appropriately enough, between two women, two queens proved better than three. White had just queened on b8 (see diagram), but Black's next postcard announced mate in 4: 54. .... Qeg1+ 55. Kh3 Qf5+ 56. g4 Qxg4+ 57. Qxg4 hxg4 mate.

♟

We also have one game with five knights on the board at once – Szabó–Ivkov, Belgrade, 1964. Black's three horsepower proved better than white's two and he triumphed in 93 moves. Underpromotion to a knight is relatively common as the knight has properties denied to a queen, but a unique case arose in the Yugoslav Ladies' Championship in 1985 where white had to promote to a knight to avoid a fork, leaving the first practical example of an ending with three knights against one (a win for the three knights as it happens).

Forced underpromotions (that is excluding trivial or facetious examples) to rook or bishop are very rare: Tim Krabbé only gives six examples. We are still awaiting the first game in which one player has three rooks or bishops on the board at once.

The record for the piece making the longest series of moves goes to the black queen belonging to James Mason, which made 73 consecutive moves (from move 72 to 144) before the point was shared in the second match game Mackenzie–Mason, London, 1882.

The record for the longest unmoved piece goes to the black f-pawn in the game Seirawan–Xu (see above), which was captured on f7 at move 172.

In Britton–Crouch (Phillips & Drew Knights, London, 1984), black made 43 checks in succession, another record.

46. ... R xe3 +	55. Kg1 Qe1 +	64. Kc2 Qc1 +	73. Ka3 Qa5 +
47. R xe3 R xe3 +	56. Kg2 Qg3 +	65. Kb3 Qd1 +	74. Kb3 Qb5 +
48. K xe3 Q xc5 +	57. Kf1 Q xh3 +	66. Kb4 Bd6 +	75. Kc2 Qb2 +
49. Kd3 Qa3 +	58. Ke1 Qe3 +	67. Kc3 Be5 +	76. Kd1 Qb1 +
50. Ke4 Qb4 +	59. Kd1 Qd3 +	68. Kc4 Qc2 +	77. Kd2 Bf4 +
51. Kd3 Qb1 +	60. Kc1 Bf4 +	69. Kb4 Qb2 +	78. Kc3 Qc1 +
52. Ke2 Qc2 +	61. Kb2 Be5 +	70. Ka4 Qb5 +	79. Kb3 Qd1 +
53. Kf3 Qd3 +	62. Kc1 Qf1 +	71. Ka3 Qa5 +	80. Kb4 Bd2 +
54. Kg2 Qe2 +	63. Kd2 Bf4 +	72. Kb3 Q xb6 +	81. Kc5 Qc2 +

82. Kb6 Be3 +	85. Kb7 Qb5 +	88. Ka7 Qc7 +	White resigns
83. Kb7 Qe4 +	86. Ka8 Qc6 +	89. Qxc7 Bxc7	
84. Kc7 Qe5 +	87. Kb8 Bf4 +	90. Kxa6 h3	

♟

A record for the longest sequence of moves without a capture (100 moves) is claimed by the player of the white pieces in the game M. Thornton–M. Walker (BCF Major Open, Plymouth, 1992). After a capture on black's 65th move an ending of queen and h-pawn against queen was reached. The end came when black resigned on move 165, an exchange of queens being forced. Only a blunder on his 164th move prevented the previous British length record (see above) being broken.

♟

In a game Clawson–Fletcher, USA, 1983, black made nine successive captures, which he claims as a record.

♟

The record for the longest series of mutual captures is 13, shared between Heidenfeld–Littleton, Dublin, 1964 and Suttles–Yepez, Nice Olympiad, 1974.

Heidenfeld–Littleton, Dublin, 1964. Bird's Opening

1. f4 Nf6	10. Qe1 Nc6	19. Nxb5 Ra2	(end of
2. Nf3 g6	11. Qh4 e6	20. d3 (and here	sequence)
3. b3 Bg7	12. Ng5 h6	goes) . . . Nxc2	27. Ke2 Kf6
4. Bb2 O–O	13. Nf3 Nb4	21. dxe4 Nxe3	28. Ned3 Rh4
5. e3 b6	14. Rad1 Ne4	22. Rxd6 Rxd6	29. h3 Ke7
6. Be2 Bb7	15. Qxd8 Rfxd8	23. Nxd6 Rxe2	30. b4 Kd6
7. O–O c5	16. Bxg7 Kxg7	24. Nxb7 Nxf1	31. Kf3 Rc4
8. a4 a6	17. Ne1 b5	25. Kxf1 Rxe4	32. Ke3 f5
9. Na3 d6	18. axb5 axb5	26. Nxc5 Rxf4 +	Draw agreed

Suttles–Yepez, Nice Olympiad, 1974. English Opening

1. d3 e5	6. Nf3 Be7	11. Ba3 e4	(Here we
2. c4 d6	7. O–O Na6	12. Nd4 d5	go again)
3. Nc3 f5	8. Rb1 O–O	13. bxc6 bxc6	16. Bxd7 Nxd4
4. g3 Nf6	9. b4 Qe8	14. cxd5 cxd5	17. Rxd5 Nxe2 +
5. Bg2 c6	10. b5 Nc5	15. Rb5 Ne6	18. Qxe2 Qxe7

19. dxe4 fxe4	25. Ra4 Rf7	31. Kf2 Rd3	37. h5 Rbe7
20. Bxe4 Nxe4	26. Rc1 g6	32. Re2 Rf7	38. hxg6 hxg6
21. Qxe4 Qxe4	27. Rc2 Rbb7	33. Re3 Rd2+	39. R3a5 Kh7
22. Nxe4 Bb7	28. Ra6 Kg7	34. Kf3 Rdd7	40. Kg5
23. Re5 Bxe4	29. h4 Rf5	35. Rea3 Rc7	Black resigns
24. Rxe4 Rab8	30. f4 Rd5	36. Kg4 Rb7	

One other possible record that deserves mention if only for the stratospheric nature of both the contestants and circumstances was provided by the 32nd game of the notorious 1984 Karpov–Kasparov match. In this game both kings remained unmoved until white's 34th move, at which point there were only eleven pieces left on the board.

The 1984 K–K match, of course, holds a number of other records. The longest world championship match (forty-eight games), the highest number of draws in a match (forty), the most consecutive draws in a match (seventeen), the only world championship match to be abandoned without a result. It is a little-known fact, however, that the dreaded Campo considered abandoning the 1978 Karpov–Korchnoi match in similar circumstances, at the point when Viktor was catching up on his rival. (This was reported in the Filipino book of the match.)

The longest master tournament concerns our friends Mason and Mackenzie. In New York, January 1869, the forty-eight competitors had to meet each other twice. Unsurprisingly, not all the games were completed, the leading scores being Mackenzie (+82, −8). Delmar (+69 −13) and Mason (+69 −17).

The esoteric field of chess problems has its own records. Lack of space prevents more than a brief mention of a few of the longest direct mate problems. This effort, published back in 1889 by Ottó Bláthy, requires white to force mate in 290 moves. One of the black bishops is a promoted pawn. The solution starts with 1. Rd1 + Bd4 2. c4+ Kd6 3. Rxg1, and involves a 16-move manoeuvre repeated 17 times.

Vielzügige Schachaufgaben, 1889

Problem, 1969

The Bláthy problem is, of course, illegal (look at the pawns and white bishops). The longest direct mate problem in a legal position is shown in the second diagram, composed by one of the most remarkable of contemporary composers, Nenad Petrović (Yugoslavia), in 1969. White is to play and mate in 270 moves. Again there is a promoted bishop on the board. The solution runs:

1. Bb1 h4 2. Ka4 Ka8 (from here to move 231 the black king moves between b7 and a8 except when he moves a pawn)

3. Ka3	11. Bb1	19. Ka1
4. Ka2	12. Kf1	20. Bb1
5. Ka1	13. Kf2	21. Ka2
6. Ba2	14. Ke1	22. Ka3
7. Kb1	15. Kd1	23. Ka4
8. Kc1	16. Kc1	Kb7
9. Kd1	17. Ba2	24. Ka5
10. Ke1	18. Kb1	f5

White now repeats moves 2 to 24 nine times, with black moving a pawn at the end, namely:

47.... f4	208.... h4	257. b8=Q f1=Q	264. Bxf4 Ke2
70.... f6	231.... h3	258. Qxe5 Qxh1	265. b6 d3
93.... f5	and then	259. Qg7+ Ke6	266. cxd3 Kf2
116.... h3	we reach	260. Qg6+ Ke5	267. Bc2 Ke2
139.... h2	254. Ka5 Kc8	261. Bb8+ Ke4	268. Bd1+ Kf2
162.... h6	255. Ka6 f2	262. Qc6+ Ke3	269. Qf3+ Kg1
185.... h5	256. b7+ Kd7	263. Qxh1 Kf2	270. Be3 mate

The longest direct mate problem without promoted pieces was composed by Jim Hetherington and Sir Jeremy Morse, and is a mate in 226.

The solution starts with 1. Bh2+ and involves a sequence of five queen checks repeated thirty-five times.

Readers interested in further exploration of records in the world of problems should consult Sir Jeremy Morse's authoritative work on the subject, *Chess Problems* (Faber and Faber).

Sir Jeremy, by the way, apart from being the former chairman of Lloyds Bank, is probably the only problemist to have given his name to a TV detective. Like Colin Dexter, the author of the Inspector Morse books, Sir Jeremy is a devotee of the *Observer* Crossword. All the characters in the first Morse book were named after fellow *Observer* Crossword freaks.

Our next diagram is a composition by J. N. Babson, dated 1882. White is to mate in 1220(!) moves, with the condition that the black knight makes three successive complete tours of the board. The authors regret that they do not have the solution to this problem. You may nevertheless try to solve it. Lots of luck.

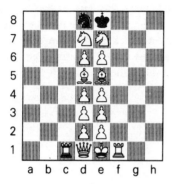

The award for the longest announced mate goes to Liverpool Chess Club, who, in the appended diagram from a correspondence game against Edinburgh Chess Club in 1901, announced mate in 45 moves.

The analysis starts

53. .... Bxf4	56. Kd4 c5+	60. Kb5 Kd6	64. cxb5 c4
(best)	57. Kc3 Kd7	61. f7 Ke7	65. b6
54. Kxf4 Kd6	58. Kb3 Kd6	62. Kc6 Kxf7	
55. Ke4 Ke6	59. Ka4 Kd7	63. Kb7 b5	

when White queens first and apparently mates on move 98.

Mrs Ellen Gilbert, an American correspondence player, certainly deserves an honourable mention here. In 1879 she played a correspondence match between Britain and the USA against the egregious and hapless George Gossip, whom we met in Chapter III. In one game she announced mate in 21 moves, and in another mate in 35. From the diagrammed position in the latter game she analysed.

42. ... g5	51. Kc3 g1 = Q	60. Kc4 Ke5	69. Kxc6 a1 = Q
43. hxg5 hxg5	52. Bxg1 Kxg1	61. Kc3 Ke4	70. Kd7 Ka3
44. Bd8 Kf4	53. Kd3 Kf2	62. Kc4 Ke3	71. c6 b2
45. e5 g4	54. Kd2 Kf3	63. Kc3 Ke2	72. c7 b1 = Q
46. Bxc7 g3	55. Kd3 Kf4	64. Kb4 Kd2	73. c8 = Q Qd4 +
47. e6 + Kf3	56. Kc4 Ke5	65. Ka3 Kc2	74. Ke7 Qh7 +
48. Be5 g2	57. Kb4 Ke6	66. Kb4 Kxb2	75. Ke6 Qg6 +
49. Bd4 Ke2	58. Kc4 Kxe7	67. Ka5 a3	76. Ke7 Qdd6
50. e7 Kf1	59. Kb4 Ke6	68. Kb6 a2	mate

This diagram shows a position in which Blackburne announced mate in 16 as follows:

1. R x e6 + Kh7	5. Be6 + Kf8	9. R x a7 + Kb8	13. Rf7 + Kd8
2. Qd3 + Rg6	6. Rf7 + Ke8	10. Nd7 + Kc8	14. Nb7 + Ke8
3. Q x g6 + f x g6	7. Nf6 + Kd8	11. Nc5 + Kd8	15. N x d6 + Kd8
4. Re7 + Kg8	8. Rd7 + Kc8	12. Rd7 + Kc8	16. Bb6 mate

Alternatives throughout lead to quicker mates. Nothing so remarkable about that, you may think; but no, it wasn't a correspondence game, and yes, this was one of eight games played simultaneously blindfold.

♟

Finally we present the oldest recorded game of modern chess. (For the oldest recorded game of any form of chess see our First Adjournment) It comes from an allegorical poem published in Spain towards the end of the fifteenth century, shortly after the moves of the queen and bishop were changed. According to Murray it may well have been played over the board, but in a recent article in *New in Chess* magazine, Spanish IM and historian Ricardo Calvo suggests that it was an invention. Francisco de Castellvi took the red pieces and Narciso Viñoles the green.

F. de Castellvi–N. Viñoles, *c.* 1476. Scandinavian Defence

1. e4 d5	5. Nf3 Bg4	9. Nb5 Rc8	13. Bb5 + N x b5
2. e x d5 Q x d5	6. h3 B x f3	10. N x a7 Nb6	14. Q x b5 + Nd7
3. Nc3 Qd8	7. Q x f3 e6	11. N x c8 N x c8	15. d5 e x d5
4. Bc4 Nf6	8. Q x b7 Nbd7	12. d4 Nd6	16. Be3 Bd6

17. Rd1 Qf6	19. Bf4 Bxf4	21. Qd8 mate
18. Rxd5 Qg6	20. Qxd7 + Kf8	

♟

For your delectation, we spell out in non-indexed notation the number of different games of chess of 40 moves or fewer. It is:

250,000,000,000,000,000,000,000,000,000,000,000,000,000,000,000,
000,000,000,000,000,000,000,000,000,000,000,000,000,000,000,000,
000,000,000,000,000,000,000.

VI The Bizarre

We are all born mad. Some remain so.   *Samuel Beckett*

A useful invention   *P. H. Williams* 1909

You're not going to believe this, but a dog once played on board eight for Brighton third team. Honest. The details are in this chapter, together with the chess-playing monkey, the revolting habits of certain Indians and what your favourite chess-masters do when they aren't playing chess.

If you're a Trivial Pursuit addict, or if you find unputdownable all those mind-numbing collections of useless information that regularly appear in the *Sun* newspaper ('Twenty things you didn't know about Prince Charles's bald patch') you'll love what follows.

♜

Up to a few years ago the annual Hastings Christmas Congress took place beneath a concert hall which was staging a pantomime. As reported by Ray Keene in the *Spectator*, one of the players sent a spy to watch the panto. At one point a clown asked the children to stamp their feet loudly on the floor to disturb the chess-players below. Later, they were encouraged to stamp especially loudly because a Russian was winning the tournament.

♜

The 1876 Customs Act was introduced to prevent the import of indecent chess-pieces which were being sent to a girls' boarding school.

♜

The Dutch for 'resigns' is '*Geef het op*' and the Swedish is '*Upgivet*'. The Swedish for 'good move' is '*bra drag*'.

♜

If you're sufficiently desperate for a reason to believe in the superiority of homo sapiens over other animals you may alight on the fact that only humans can play chess. But wait. Here's Baldasare Castiglione, the early sixteenth-century Italian author of a perfectly serious tome entitled *The Book of the Courtier*. Doubtless a man whose veracity is to be trusted. He tells us how the Portuguese brought a chess-playing ape back with them from the Indies. On one occasion the ape played the fellow who brought her back with him. The ape, needless to say, soon forced checkmate, whereupon her victim, understandably miffed by this development, took the king and cuffed her about the ear with it. He then demanded his revenge and the ape, reluctantly, agreed. As the ape was about to play the winning move she took a cushion from under her opponent's arm and held it against her head with one hand while delivering checkmate with the other.

♖

Among the members of Brighton Chess Club in the 1930s was Mrs Sidney, an aristocratic old lady whose inseparable companion was her dog, Mick. At that time the club met in the splendid Royal Pavilion, built for George IV when he was Prince Regent. There was a strict rule: No Dogs Allowed, but the club secretary, not wishing to incur the fearsome old crone's wrath, pretended not to notice her canine companion. Then a new club secretary was appointed, who asked Mrs S. not to bring her dog in future. A tirade of angry words from Mrs S. and eventually a compromise was reached. Mick was to be elected a full member of the club, his owner paying the subscription. Some time later, the third team played a friendly match. The team captain, noticing a new name on the Members' List, decided that he should be given some match experience, so the name of Mr Mick went on to the match sheet. The result? He lost on time. Persistent rumour has it that the opening was the Collie System. (Unless he was a paw to king four player.)[1]

♖

Before the 1990 World Championship match, former champion Karpov played a game against a Teenage Mutant Ninja Turtle (Donatello). The Turtle, says the *Daily Mirror*, was more than a match for Anatoly, but generously conceded that Karp. was 'one mean dude'.

♖

Chess magazine, in 1976, reviewed a volume entitled *Sex Mates of a Chess Mistress*. Quite apart from the rather dubious delights you might expect from the title ('nauseating to the point of hilarity') it

[1] One of the world's strongest grandmasters, Vasily Ivanchuk, confided to spectators at the Tilburg 1990 tournament that he often plays chess with his dog.

features a chess-playing kangaroo. 'NOT available from stock,' they added. (This was not the first example of soft pawn. A pornographic novel published in 1968 called *The Pushers*,[1] whose author hid under the alias of Kenneth Harding – actually Paul Hugo Little – featured lookalikes of leading contemporary players.)

Chess Openings and Variations with Zoological Names

– Bird's Opening (1. f4, also known as Bird's Bastard)

– Orang-Utan Opening (1. b4)

– Döry Defence (1. d4 Nf6 2. c4 e6 3. Nf3 Ne4)

– Dragon Variation (Sicilian Defence with Black Bishop on g7)

– Pelikán Variation (Another variation of The Sicilian)

– The Rat (Canadian name for 1. . . . g6 2. . . . Bg7)

– The Hippopotamus (Putting most of your pawns on the 3rd rank)[2]

– The Krazy Kat (American version of The Hippo)

– The Hedgehog (More sophisticated modern form of Hippo)

– The Monkey's Bum (1. e4 g6 2. Bc4 Bg7 3. Qf3)

– The Vulture (1. d4 Nf6 2. c4 c5 3. d5 Ne4)

– The Pterodactyl (Canadian name for The Rat with 3. . . . c5)

– The Elephant Gambit (1. e4 e5 2. Nf3 d5)

– The Benoni Snake (Benoni with Bd6)

– The Great Snake (1. c4 g6)

– The Canard (1. d4 2. f4)

– The Double Duck (1. f4 f5 2. d4 d5)

---

[1] No connection with Haroun al-Rashid (see Chapter I).
[2] The most persistent devotee of this opening, J. C. Thompson, was noted for wearing boots and no socks.

– The Lemming (1. e4 Na6)

– The Wild Bull (1. Nc3)

The Monkey's Bum was analysed and practised by members of Streatham Chess Club in London in the mid-seventies. When one of them was shown the idea his first reaction was 'If that works, then I'm a monkey's bum!'

Other chess openings with strange names

– Fried Liver Attack (Variation of Two Knights Defence)

– Long Whip Variation (Variation of King's Gambit)

– Horny Defence (Another variation of King's Gambit)

– Stone-Ware Defence (Variation of Evans Gambit)

– Corkscrew Counter-Gambit (Variation of Greco Counter-Gambit)

– The Spike (Another name for Grob's Opening, 1. g4)

– Bayonet Attack (Line in Giuoco Piano)

– Siesta Variation (Variation of Ruy López)

– Meadow Hay Opening (1. a4)

– The Corn Stalk Defence (1. . . . a5)

– Lolli Gambit (Another King's Gambit line)

– Fingerslip Variation (French Defence line accidentally played by Alekhine)

– Frankenstein-Dracula Variation (Variation of Vienna Opening)

– The Fred (1. e4 f5 2. exf5 Kf7)

– The Woozle (1. d4 c5 2. d5 Nf6 3. Nc3 Qa5)

– The Gotcha[1] (1. d4 c5 2. d5 Nf6 3. Nf3 c4)

– The Borg (a name invented by R. James; a reversed Grob)

[1]Our translation from the German.

– The Nescafé Frappé Attack (Line in Benko Gambit)

– The Scud (Another line in Benko)

– The Battambang (1. Nc3 2. a3)

– The Hammerschlag (1. f3 e5 2. Kf7)

– The English Spike (1. c4 f5 2. g4)

– The English Queen (1. c4 e5 2. Qa4)

– The Sicilian Fred (1. e4 c5 2. Nf3 g6 3. d4 f6)

– The Neo-Mongoloid Defence (1. e4 Nc6 2. d4 f6)

– The Beefeater (Benoni line played by Djin. See page 259. Get it?)

– The Paleface Attack (1. d4 Nf6 2. f3)

– The Gloria (Line in the English played during Hurricane Gloria)

Note: The names of chess openings are subject to whim; many names in the above lists are taken from a much-criticized book: *Unorthodox Openings* by Benjamin and Schiller (Batsford, 1987).

♖

The names of chess openings may seem strange to non-aficionados. What, for instance, would the man on the Clapham omnibus make of books with titles like *Sicilian–Accelerated Dragons*, *Play the Bogo-Indian* or the sadistic *Beating the Sicilian*?

♖

Especially revolting were the habits of certain Indians as reported by one al-Maṣʿūdī, an Arabian historian, in about AD 950. It seems that they wagered parts of the body on the result of chess games. After a defeat they would cut a finger with a dagger, cauterizing the wound with a reddish ointment boiled over a fire. When they ran out of fingers they moved on to hands, forearms, elbows and 'other parts of the body'. At which point it must have been rather difficult for them to move the pieces.

♖

A continental tournament shortly after the Second World War was interrupted when one of the spectators, overcome by the excitement of the moment, started to remove all his clothes. The clocks were stopped while he was hustled out into the next room. But shortly afterwards he was back again doing the same thing. Again play was halted, and this time he was forcibly dragged back to his hotel room, while the local constabulary was called. A few minutes later he could be seen again, performing in his hotel window. At this point Dr Tartakower, wittiest of grandmasters, claimed a draw by three-fold repetition.

♖

A strong candidate for the least successful simul-giver of all time (his rivals may be found in Chapter III) is one Leon Roper. Claiming to be an international player, he gave a simultaneous display at Dane Court School, Broadstairs, Kent. Against seven young boys he lost five games and drew two. His £20 fee was refused. Dover College, where he had arranged to give a talk on 'the finer points of the game', was warned, and his lecture was cancelled. It was later revealed in court that Roper had previous convictions for theft, burglary, assault and attempted fraud, and that he lived with a woman named Countess Racquel von Kruger (né Christopher Collins).

♖

Oscar Tenner, for many years a well-known figure on the American chess scene, was at one time in the habit of eating his chess pieces. As a prisoner during the First World War he did not have access to a chess-set, so pieces were constructed out of the daily bread ration. (Dr B. in Stefan Zweig's famous short story 'The Royal Game' ate his chess-pieces for the same reason.)

♖

The most extraordinary World Championship Match was undoubt-edly that between Karpov and Korchnoi held in Baguio City in 1978. During the second game Karpov had a yoghurt delivered. This triggered off the Great Yoghurt Controversy. The Korchnoi camp, including English GMs Ray Keene and Michael Stean, protested that this could constitute a coded message. 'Thus a yoghurt after move 20 could signify "we instruct you to offer a draw"; or a sliced mango could mean "we order you to decline a draw". A dish of marinated quails' eggs could mean "play Ng5 at once", and so on.' This was intended as a parody of previous protests but was taken seriously at the time. Eventually it was agreed that Karpov could be served with a bilberry yoghurt at a specific time by a specific waiter. Later diversions included the mysterious Soviet hypnotist (or whatever) Dr Zhukar and assorted parapsychologists, mystics and gurus. These included Dada and Didi, a.k.a. Stephen Dwyer and Victoria Shepherd, two members of a mystical sect called Ananda Marga who had apparently been convicted of attempted assassination. These two characters joined the Korchnoi camp and soon had Viktor and his colleagues standing on their heads, meditating and chanting mantras.

In 1982 Batsford published a book called *The Amazing Adventures of Dan the Pawn*, by Simon Garrow. It aimed to teach the moves of chess to young children by weaving a story around a short game, which, as it happened, was won by white. The editor of the official magazine of the National Union of Teachers wrote: 'It would have been more symbolically exciting if the blacks had been allowed to win. Racist stereotypes and assumptions permeate our culture in many subtle ways.'

The life expectancy of leading chess players (from Philidor to Alekhine) has been calculated at 60, according to a Pittsburgh University study, while that of twenty-four other occupations comes out between 64 (British authors) and 71 (US presidential advisers). Another American study has estimated that the strain of a five-hour game of tournament chess is equivalent to ten rounds of boxing or five sets of tennis. Capablanca lost eleven pounds in weight in winning the world championship from Lasker; and Petrosian nearly a stone (fourteen pounds) in winning the title from Botvinnik.

Some chess players have met their end in bizarre fashion. Here are three.

Alonzo Morphy, father of the legendary Paul, was killed by a Panama hat. A cut above the eye from a Panama hat worn by a friend led to congestion of the brain, causing Judge Morphy's untimely demise.

W. R. Henry (William Henry Russ) (1833–66), was a pioneer American chess archivist. When his girl-friend declined his hand in marriage he shot her four times in the head and jumped off the nearest bridge into the river. Alas for his calculations, the tide was out, so he climbed out and shot himself twice in the head. Again he failed to end it all, was arrested and taken to hospital. But, broken-hearted from the loss of his beloved, he lacked the will to live and died ten days later. He was evidently not a very good shot. His girl-friend survived.

♖

Thomas Barnes, one of the leading English players of the same era, was the Cyril Smith of chess. He dieted so successfuly that he lost 130 pounds in less than a year. Too successfully, as it turned out. His body was unable to accept the sudden change and he died.

♖

From the dead to the quick, and US master Sidney Bernstein who, in 1931, turned up one hour $59\frac{1}{2}$ minutes late for a match. This left him just 30 seconds for 40 moves, which he negotiated successfully, drawing the game. This was, however, the only half-point dropped by his college team all season (Reuben Fine was on top board).

♖

At the opposite extreme are Glaswegian Lawrence B. Grant and Dr J. Munro MacLennan from Ottawa. When last heard of in 1975 they had been playing a correspondence game for forty-nine years at the rate of about one move a year. As Mr Grant said, 'Ye cannae hurry these things.'[1]

♖

Chess Players with Impressive Names

Abu'l Faraj bin al-Muzaffar bin Saʿ-īd al-Lajlāj ('The Stammerer')[2]
Don Scipione del Grotto

[1]B. H. Wood and W. Ritson Morry engaged in a consultation correspondence game with two Londoners that dragged on from the mid-thirties to the mid-fifties.
[2]See Chapter II.

Prince Dadian of Mingrelia[1]
Count Alberic O'Kelly de Galway
Marquis Stefano Rosselli del Turco
Count Jean de Villeneuve Esclapon
Baron Tassilo von Heydebrand und der Lasa
Alexander Markovich Konstantinopolsky
Alexander Feodorovich Iljin-Genevsky
Mikhail Alexandrovich Bonch-Osmolovsky
Feodor Ivanovich Duz-Khotimirsky
Eugene Alexandrovich Znosko-Borovsky
Roman Yakovlevich Dzindzichashvili
Octavio Siqueiro F. Trompowsky de Almeida[2]
Kornelis Dirk Mulder van Leens Dijkstra
Conel Hugh O'Donel Alexander
Wellington Pulling
Lionel Adelberto Bagration Felix Kieseritzky[3]

♖

David Spanier tells a haunting story in his fascinating book *Total Chess*. Björn Palsson Kalman, a schoolboy chess prodigy in Iceland in the early years of the century, was, because of his chess prowess, invited to study at Harvard University. On the boat crossing the Atlantic he beat two chessmasters simultaneously blindfold. But on reaching Harvard he discovered to his chagrin that he was not allowed to play for the university until he had been in residence a year. To console himself he immersed himself totally in chess until he feared he was going mad. He gave up chess, dropped out of university, and eventually surfaced in Winnipeg, working as a bricklayer. Several years later he was persuaded to play in a simul against Frank Marshall, the leading American player of the time. He won and was challenged to a return game, but declined and was never heard from again.

♖

[1]See 'The Aristocrats'.
[2]Does anyone know what the 'F' stands for ?
[3]For our schoolboy readers we have an Austrian called Titz, a Dutchman called Messemaker, a Pole called Fux and Yugoslavs called Manić and Panić. Also Karl Willy and two Russians, Frog and Basin (who may one day play Sick, of Germany)). And see also our section on the longest game.

Some Bobby Fischer quotes (mainly from his notorious 1961 interview with Ralph Ginzburg)[1]

On women: 'They're all weak, all women. They're stupid compared to men. They shouldn't play chess, you know. They're like beginners. They lose every single game against a man.'

On chess clubs: 'When they used to have the clubs, like no women were allowed and everybody went in dressed in a suit, a tie, like gentlemen, you know. Now, kids come running in in their sneakers – even in the best chess club – and they got women in there.'

On Jews: 'Yeh, there are too many Jews in chess. They seem to have taken away the class of the game. They don't seem to dress so nicely, you know.'

On school: 'You don't learn anything in school.' 'You shouldn't be doing homework.' 'The teachers are stupid. They shouldn't have any women in there. They don't know how to teach. And they shouldn't make anyone go to school.'

On his mother: 'She keeps in my hair and I don't like people in my hair you know so I had to get rid of her.'

On Kennedy: 'Besides, he doesn't have any class. He puts his hands in his coat pockets. God, that's horrible.'

On becoming World Champion: 'First of all, I'll make a tour of the whole world giving exhibitions.' 'I'll have my own club. The Bobby Fischer ... uh, the Robert J. Fischer Chess Club. It'll be class. Tournaments in full dress. No bums in there. You're gonna have to be over eighteen to get in, unless like you have special permission because you have like special talent.' 'I got strong ideas about my house. I'm going to hire the best architect and have him build it in the shape of a rook. Yeh, that's for me. Class. Spiral staircases, parapets, everything. I want to live the rest of my life in a house built exactly like a rook.'

Fischer again from another 1961 interview: 'I would not marry an

---

[1] To be fair to one of the strongest players who ever lived, Bobby later denied having said some of the things attributed to him by Ginzburg.

American girl. With a foreigner would be much better. First you get her without customs, second, if you don't like her you can send her back home.'

And again, on the same subject: 'Chess is better.'

And, it seems, a lifetime ago: 'All I want to do, ever, is play chess.' Alas.

After winning the world championship, Bobby didn't push a pawn in anger for twenty years (!).[1] He lived in Pasadena, California, moving from one cheap hotel to another, hiding behind a red beard and the alias of Robert D. James (no relation).

The story of his sensational comeback has been too well documented to need repeating here; suffice it to say he was certainly back to his old form: spitting on faxes from the US Treasury, accusing Kasparov, Karpov and Korchnoi of fixing matches, claiming he was the real World Champion, dancing the conga, attacking Israel and generally providing grateful journalists with their daily bread. For more on The Match, see our Chapter VII 'The Future'; meanwhile, a historical curiosity, his only published game against a woman, who happens to be a former pupil of both your authors:

C. Forbes–R. Fischer, Offhand Game. Sveti Stefan, 1992. Pirc Defence (by transposition)

1. d4 Nf6	9. Bd3 a6	17. Nd2 Nh5	25. Nd5 Bxd5
2. Nf3 g6	10. a4 b6	18. Bh2 Nf4	26. exd5 Nc4
3. Bf4 Bg7	11. O–O Bb7	19. Bxf4 exf4	27. Qd3 and
4. Nc3 d6	12. Re1 Nbd7	20. Nb3 Nd7	White
5. e4 O–O	13. Be3 Qc7	21. Qd2 f3	resigns without
6. h3 c5	14. Qe2 e6	22. g3 Ne5	waiting
7. dxc5 Qa5	15. Bf4 e5	23. Bf1 h5	for Nxb2
8. Bd2 Qxc5	16. Bg3 Nc5	24. Rad1 Rad8	

---

[1] He played friendly games against Campomanes, ex-President Marcos and MAC HACK (see Chapter VIII); and around 1981, one of the authors, in the Manhattan Chess Club, heard that Bobby had played around a hundred blitz games with Canadian GM Peter Biyiasis. Fischer drew one and won the rest.

Tsk, tsk, Cathy. That's not how we taught you to play. Still, it must have been a pretty awesome occasion.

Incidentally Fischer still seems biased against women players. He expressed himself as sceptical about Judith Polgár's prospects for improvement. Ironic if, as seems possible, he ends up playing a match against her.

As we go to press the bad news for Bobby is that, on his fiftieth birthday, Jezdimir Vasiljević, the entrepreneur behind Fischer *v.* Spassky II, fled from Serbia to Israel leaving thousands of creditors (including possibly Fischer) gnashing their teeth.[1]

♖

Another World Champion who may have shared Fischer's anti-semitism was Alexander Alekhine. In 1941 a series of articles was published under his name claiming the superiority of Aryan attacking chess to Jewish defensive chess. Alekhine later denied authorship, but the original manuscript in his handwriting was found after his wife's death.

♖

Alekhine holds the record for the World Champion with the most wives. He was married four times, and three of his wives were much older than him. But, unlike Capablanca, he was much more interested in chess than women. During the London Tournament in 1922 he and Capa were taken to a show. It was reported that Alekhine never took his eyes off his pocket chess-set, while Capa never took his eyes off the chorus line.

♖

Runner up to Alekhine in the marriage stakes is Boris Spassky, who has so far been married three times. After divorcing his first wife he described their relationship as 'like bishops of opposite colours'.

♖

Gary Kasparov seems to share Alekhine's preference for older women. In his mid-twenties he fell for an actress in her late thirties. His great rival, Karpov, married an attractive young secretary several

---

[1]An astonishing (and ridiculous) footnote to the Fischer saga: on 13 March 1986 the United States House of Representatives passed a resolution recognizing Bobby Fischer as still the official World Chess Champion.

years ago. A few months later she produced a son; shortly afterwards they were divorced.

♖

For the chess groupies amongst our readers we have two suggestions. Filipino GM Eugenio Torre was once voted one of the ten sexiest sportsmen in the Philippines, and featured in a film entitled *Basta't Isipin Mong Mahal Kita* (Always Remember That I Love You) along with a couple of local starlets. Or you may prefer US Number One Yasser (Yaz) Seirawan, who, after being featured as *Cosmopolitan* magazine's Bachelor of the Month ('I love snorkelling, tennis, dancing till dawn. Also women with lustrous hair and twinkling honest eyes – a direct gaze is *all*') was inundated with marriage proposals. Yaz elaborated on his preferences in a recent interview with Ms Forbes: 'I also like the Gillette Sensor Razor, and one absolutely must wear Royal Copenhagen Musk Oil.'

♖

A romance that never blossomed was that between Bobby Fischer and Barbra Streisand. Yes, really. Bobby and Barbra were fellow students at Erasmus High, Brooklyn. Imagine being the teacher in charge of those two gigantic egos. They used to swap *MAD* comics, and, it is reported, Barbra had a crush on the future champion. Friends said they looked good together: even their noses matched. (A few years later, in the 1959 Candidates' Tournament, Bent Larsen's main duty as Bobby's second was to read him Tarzan stories.)

♖

Other leading players have had more healthy interests. Botvinnik, for example, was good at skittles and reached championship standard at dancing the Charleston and foxtrot.[1] Spassky, in his youth, was a 5' $11\frac{3}{4}''$ high-jumper. Euwe was a boxer, Capablanca was good at baseball and basketball, Keres excelled at tennis and Reshevsky at table-tennis. Alekhine listed canoeing among his interests. The Graeco-Russo-Franco-American GM Nicholas Rossolimo was a brown belt at judo. Thirties' women's World Champion Vera Menchik once beat English master F. D. Yates at billiards. American

---

[1] He also won an award for designing a trench mortar.

grandmaster Arnold Denker won three successive Golden Gloves bouts; he also played pro baseball and American football.

♖

Just as many musicians, as we have seen, are keen on chess, so many chess-players have an interest in music. Most notably, Philidor. Smyslov has a fine baritone voice and in 1950 just missed a place in the Bolshoi Opera. During tournaments he frequently gave recitals, often accompanied by fellow grandmaster Taimanov, a concert pianist. Julius du Mont, a prominent chess author and editor of the *British Chess Magazine*, was also a concert pianist. Rudolf Loman, a Dutch master, was organist of the Dutch Church in London for many years. On the other hand, the versatile Rossolimo played the concertina and made a record of Russian folk songs. Fischer once considered a career as a pop singer. Korchnoi sang a heavily accented version of 'There is a Tavern in the Town' at a banquet during one of his matches with Karpov. Nigel Short was a member of a group called The Urge which appeard on BBC TV's popular children's show *Blue Peter*. (He had originally wanted to call his band Pelvic Thrust but this was vetoed by the other members. Probably just as well.) Hungarian supergrandmaster Lajos Portisch once gave a recital of songs on Hungarian radio; and at the Wijk aan Zee 1990 tournament sang Schubert's '*Winterreise*', accompanied by IM Bouwmeester. At the close of the Subotica tournament former world champ Tal led the assembled company in a chorus of 'When the Saints Go Marching In' (with GMs Daniel King and Nigel Short on guitars).

♖

Other masters have also had artistic leanings. Alekhine was a pupil at Moscow's first school for film actors, but failed. Howard Staunton, the Englishman who was unofficial World Champion between 1843 and 1851 was, before he took up chess, an actor who appeared alongside Edmund Kean, and later edited the works of Shakespeare. Max Harmonist, a minor Berlin master in the late 1880s, was a dancer in the Royal Ballet. The Swiss international master Henry Grob, who gave his name to the eccentric début 1. g4, was a celebrated portrait painter.

♖

It is only to be expected that many chess-players also have an interest in bridge. Capablanca and Alekhine played. Emanuel Lasker was good enough to represent Germany.[1] The Swedish grandmaster Ståhlberg was a very strong player. The Soviet woman grandmaster Irina Levitina won an award in 1986 for the best-played hand of the year. Karpov and Korchnoi are also amongst the many contemporary stars who play (sometimes as partners!).

♖

Nearly as many masters were addicted to gambling, notably Tartakower, Janowsky and Marshall. At one tournament, held in a casino, the craving overcame Tartakower to such an extent that he was seen placing bets at roulette between moves. Janowsky regularly lost his prize money at the gaming tables. In his later years Marshall became addicted to, of all things, bingo.

♖

The most boring World Champion must surely be Anatoly Karpov. On one occasion he gave his interests as 'stamp-collecting and Marxism'. Later, he admitted to reading the detective novels of Dame Agatha Christie; and in 'The Sportsmen' section you can read of his unlikely relationship with snooker champion Steve Davis, who has also been (unkindly) called boring. Anatoly's list of favourite musicians includes James Last (and Judith Polgár's, Richard Clayderman).

♖

One of the most versatile chess masters was Alexandre Louis Honoré Lebreton Deschapelles, perhaps the world's strongest player between Philidor and Bourdonnais. He learned, so he said, all he needed to know about chess in three days, and soon became the best player in France, giving odds of at least pawn and two moves to even his strongest rivals. Finding no serious opposition he took up whist instead, rapidly becoming expert at that game as well. (He is remembered among bridge-players even today as the originator of the Deschapelles Coup – perhaps he should be board one for our Sportsmen's team.) He was also an expert billiards player, using the stump of his right arm which he had lost fighting for Napoleon, and grew the best melons in Paris.

[1] But opinions differ on how good he was. Gerald Abrahams, an authority, says he wasn't so hot.

♜

Even Deschapelles would have seemed modest compared with Johannes Zukertort, the loser of the first official World Championship Match. He claimed fluency in nine languages, had studied theology, philology and social science, was an expert swordsman, dominoplayer, whist-player and pistol shot, a musician and music critic, a military veteran of over a dozen battles, twice dangerously wounded and once left for dead, entitled to wear seven medals, the orders of the Red Eagle and the Iron Cross, a student of chemistry (under Prof. Bunsen) and physiology to degree level, and editor of a political journal. To the best of our knowledge, no one believed him.

♜

Alexander Iljin-Genevsky played a major part in the shaping of modern chess. One of the leading early Soviet players, he was also a friend of Lenin, doing much to popularize chess in the Soviet Union. The remarkable thing about I-G was that he had to learn chess twice. Shell-shocked during the First World War, he suffered amnesia as a result and had to learn again how to play chess. (See Podola in 'The Sinners' section.)

Drink like a Grandmaster

Chess and alcohol, we find, go very well together.[1] Provided, that is, you exercise a certain degree of restraint. We certainly don't recommend downing six pints of Old Peculier just before your decisive last-round game in the club championship. Here are some players noted for their fondness for the bottle:

1. *Alexander Alekhine*, whose penchant for drink cost him his World Championship title to Max Euwe in 1935. His Dutch hosts thoughtfully provided him with free champagne. Stunned by his defeat he renounced alcohol in favour of milk, and, two years later, regained his title.

2. *Joseph Blackburne.* Fond of the Scotch Game, and also the Scotch bottle, which he placed at strategic locations while giving simuls,

[1]'Chess and wine are born brothers.' (Russian proverb)

frequently with amusing consequences,[1] though it didn't seem to affect his results. He even penned a testimonial to the powers of whisky for a trade journal, much to the chagrin of The Temperance Society.

3. *James Mason*, one of the leading players of his day, who, it is claimed, frequently lost games in a 'hilarious condition'. During a game in the London Tournament, 1899, he was discovered asleep in the fireplace.

4. *Charles Stanley*, American Champion before Morphy, was an incurable alcoholic who was confined to an institution for his last twenty years. Morphy played a match against him, sending his winnings to Mrs Stanley.

5. *Jacques-François Mouret*, one of the operators of The Turk (see Chapter VIII), a great-nephew of Philidor. Another alcoholic, in 1834 he sold the secret of how the automaton worked to keep himself in drink.

6. *Georg Marco*, a Viennese master rated one of the best annotators of all time. During a tournament he complained to Frank Marshall, a fellow competitor, of stomach-ache. Marshall poured him a drink and took one himself. Marco felt no better so they had another. And another. And another. The next day they played in the tournament. 'He beat me like a child,' said Frank, ruefully.

7. *Efim Bogoljubow*. Originally Russian but later a naturalized German, he developed a taste for beer. It is said that 'beer' was the only word of English he knew. Once he gave a blindfold simul in a small town in Spain. The local press photographer came along to record the event for posterity, but when the picture appeared Bogol wasn't there. 'Oh, you mean the fat little fellow with the glass of beer? I took him out of the photo: he didn't seem to fit in,' he explained.

8. *Mikhail Chigorin*, founder of the Russian school of chess, was particularly fond of drink. During his World Championship matches

---

[1] We omit here the oft-told tale of Blackburne taking his opponent's glass of whisky *en passant*.

with Steinitz a sponsor provided him with free brandy (while Steinitz preferred champagne).

9. *Cecil De Vere*, first British Champion in 1886 at the age of twenty-one but dead of tuberculosis before his thirtieth birthday. He turned to drink on learning of what was to be his fatal disease, never approaching the fulfilment of his tremendous natural talent.

10. *Frank Marshall*, a couple of years before his death, played a series of ten lightning games against Reuben Fine, one of the best players in the world at that time. Frank was drunk, Reuben sober. The result: 10–0 in Marshall's favour.

At the concluding banquet of an International Team Tournament, says Fine, Frank was so overcome with emotion that when he was asked to make a speech on behalf of the victorious Americans, he could only wave the Stars and Stripes and shout 'Hip-hip-hoorah!'

11. *Florencio Campomanes*. Yes, the man who aborted the first K–K match. A surprising entrant perhaps, but US master Tony Santasiere tells how he once played Campo in New York State Championship. Campo 'arrived fifteen minutes late, and rather intoxicated, carrying six bottles of beer which he put carefully on the floor. After play began, he suddenly burst into tears, and nursed this outburst by consuming bottle after bottle of the beer, all the while making some very good chess moves.' The game was drawn. (*Essay on Chess*)

12. *Mikhail Tal*, who, on being told that the Soviet state was launching a campaign against alcoholism, commented, 'The state against vodka? I'll be on the side of vodka.' We'll drink to that.

13. *Michael Adams*, who in 1990 chose 9 as his number in the draw to decide which of three tied players should go through to the Interzonal. According to some reports, this was on the basis that he'd drunk nine pints the previous evening. Adams was lucky – 9 came out of the bingo machine first.

14. *Igor Ivanov*, who had a game postponed in the 1989 US Championships because of alcoholic poisoning; and later, during a game, poured hot chicken soup into a hand he mistakenly thought was holding a thermos. He lost the game (*v.* Dzindzichashvili) after setting a bizarre record – seven draw offers in twenty-three moves.

We have one example of an alternative approach. Canadian IM Lawrence Day played in the 1972 Toronto Championship while stoned on grass. 'Really it was a disaster, result-wise,' he says.

Clink for a Grandmaster

From masters who like propping up bars to those who have spent time behind bars. Some for a variety of crimes, but others on matters of principle, or as victims of oppressive regimes. (We exclude from this list wartime internees.)

1. *Norman Whitaker.* American international master and professional confidence trickster, whose exploits are recounted in Chapter I.

2. *Raymond Weinstein.* American international master and murderer, another refugee from our Sinners' team in Chapter I.

3. *Milan Matulović*, star of Chapter IV, got nine months' porridge after a car crash in which a woman was killed. 'The sentence was too long,' complained the errant grandmaster, 'she was only a Bosnian.' Perhaps he should have shouted '*J'adoube*' first.

4. *William Winter*, an English International Master of bohemian outlook and communist sympathies, and a nephew of J. M. Barrie. He served a six-month sentence, which, he said, he rather enjoyed, for sedition in 1921.[1] Winter was responsible for what must have been one of the most hilarious simuls of all time, against Winchester Conservative Club. No doubt Willie tried extra hard in this display, winning all fifteen games.

5. *Alexandre Deschapelles*, who was incarcerated for his part in the insurrection of June 1832. Despite his well-known republican sympathies he pleaded with the king for his release on the grounds that he was too old, too ill, and innocent.

6. *James Mortimer*, a late-nineteenth-century rabbit who usually

---

[1] Willie once set up a provisional communist government of Britain in Bristol. It was rather less popular than Screaming Lord Sutch's Official Monster Raving Loony Party is now.

managed to finish just above our friend Mr Gossip, but at the age of seventy-four was still able to beat the likes of Tartakower and Blackburne. He was by profession a playwright, who wrote a success-ful series of farces, and a newspaper editor. His crime, for which he was imprisoned, was to refuse to reveal the author of an article which was sued for libel. While inside he taught his fellow inmates how to play chess.

7. *Ludek Pachman*, Czech-born grandmaster and author, was a sup-porter of the Dubček regime during the 'Prague Spring' of 1968. After the Russian tanks had moved in he was gaoled twice between 1969 and 1970 and again in 1972. He was then granted permission to leave his country and settled in West Germany.

8. *Alexander Alekhine*, who told Reuben Fine that he spent some time in prison during the Russian Revolution accused of passing on secret information.

9. *Alex Wojtkiewicz*, the Latvian/Polish GM, spent a year in a Soviet labour camp for political dissidence.

10. *Vladimir Petrov*, the Latvian master, was imprisoned (and died) in a Russian labour camp during the Second World War for objecting to the Russian annexation of the Baltic republics.

And a couple of World Champions who were victims of false allega-tions.

1. *Wilhelm Steinitz*, who was arrested and accused of spying when the moves of some correspondence games against Chigorin were intercepted. The authorities suspected that the moves were coded military secrets (cf. Graham Mitchell, Chapter I).

2. *Bobby Fischer* was arrested in Pasadena in May 1981 under suspicion of being a bank robber. Two years later he published a pamphlet entitled 'I was tortured in the Pasadena Jailhouse', in which he claims he was held for two days, the first twenty-four hours without food or drink, stripped and beaten up before being released on bail. He was later charged with damaging gaol property: to wit one mattress.

Perchance to Dream

What do chess-players dream about? Why, chess, of course. Some players even dream complete games, and problemists compose problems in their sleep.

This game was dreamed up by David Bronstein in 1961, and an instructive and entertaining one it is too:

Nimzo–Indian Defence

1. d4 Nf6	6. Nf3 d6	11. dxc6 O–O	16. Qb3 Be6
2. c4 e6	7. Qa4+ Nc6	12. a3 Ng4	17. Qa3 Ne3+
3. Nc3 Bb4	8. d5 exd5	13. g3 Qf6	18. Kc1 Qe1+
4. Bg5 h6	9. cxd5 Qe4	14. axb4 Qxf2+	19. Nd1 Qxd1
5. Bh4 Qe7	10. Nd2 Qxh4	15. Kd1 b5	mate

And, twenty years later, a contribution from American IM Anthony Saidy:

French Defence (by transposition)

1. Nf3 Nf6	6. e5 Nfd7	11. exf6 Qxf4	16. Nc7+ Kd8
2. Nc3 d5	7. Bd3 Nc6	12. fxg7 Rg8	17. Ngxe6 mate
3. d4 c5	8. Qe2 a6	13. Qxe6+ Ne7	
4. dxc5 e6	9. O–O Qc7	14. Nxd5 Qd6	
5. e4 Bxc5	10. Bf4 f6	15. Ng5 Qxe6	

This dream chess problem was composed by US problemist William Spackman. It's pretty easy. You should be able to solve it with your eyes closed.

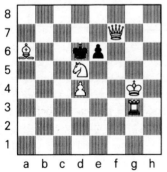

Mate in 2.

Blithe Spirits

The composers of one of the most celebrated problems acknowledged assistance from the other side in creating their masterpiece. Two problemists, A. J. Fink, of San Francisco, and J. Frank Stimson, who lived in Tahiti where he went by the local name of Ua Tane, were interested in composing a record-breaking problem. Stimson contacted his friend Lewis White Fox, of San Diego, to ask his wife, who was a medium, to contact the 'entities'. The next night, Fink received the problem in his sleep, but the white king was in check, which is not acceptable in problem circles. He sent the problem to Stimson, who, a few days later, dreamed an improved version. You'll see the result for yourself in the 'Second Adjournment' below (question 13 (xiii)).

Fox's wife was in contact with the shade of the Anglo-Irish master James Mason (1849–1905), who played a series of games against LWF. In the climactic game, Mason made a succession of brilliant sacrifices, then blew the game, claiming (via Mrs Fox) that he could no longer see the board. 'Playing chess through a medium is like playing a violin standing on your head,' said the spooky master.

A more recent game with, it is claimed, the other side, was one between Korchnoi and Maróczy, which started in 1985, the moves being transmitted through a Swiss medium, Robert Rollans. The last we heard of the game, in 1987, Young Vik was a pawn up in a rook ending against his 117-year-old opponent.

Maróczy–Korchnoi, Astral Correspondence, 1985–7. French Defence

1. e4 e6	8. Qxg7 Rg8	15. Bxe7 Kxe7	22. Rd3 Kf7
2. d4 d5	9. Qxh7 Qc7	16. Qh4+ Ke8	23. Rg3 Rg6
3. Nc3 Bb4	10. Kd1 dxc3	17. Ke2 Bxf3+	24. Rhg1 Rag8
4. e5 c5	11. Nf3 Nbc6	18. gxf3 Qxe5+	25. a4 Rxg3
5. a3 Bxc3+	12. Bb5 Bd7	19. Qe4 Qxe4+	26. fxg3 b6
6. bxc3 Ne7	13. Bxc6 Bxc6	20. fxe4 f6	27. h4 a6 ...
7. Qg4 cxd4	14. Bg5 d4	21. Rad1 e5	

You read in Chapter I about W. B. Yeats playing against a spirit. Another celeb who may have had a ghostly opponent was Humphrey Bogart. Bogie, it was reported, had agreed to play against the shade of Prince Kutuzov, Napoleon's Russian adversary, through a medium.

The game that never was

Alas, the famous and astonishing Adams–Torre game, with its witty offer of a queen sacrifice on six consecutive moves, is now widely believed to have been a paste diamond. It was partly manufactured by Torre, says Dale Brandreth, as a present for Torre's friend E. Z. Adams. Still, it's well worth a look:

E. Z. Adams (?)–C. Torre (?), New Orleans, 1920 (?). Philidor Defence

1. e4 e5	7. Nc3 Nf6	13. cxd5 Re8	19. Qc4! Qd7
2. Nf3 d6	8. O–O Be7	14. Rfe1 a5	20. Qc7! Qb5
3. d4 exd4	9. Nd5 Bxd5	15. Re2 Rc8	21. a4! Qxa4
4. Qxd4 Nc6	10. exd5 O–O	16. Rae1 Qd7	22. Re4! Qb5
5. Bb5 Bd7	11. Bg5 c6	17. Bxf6 Bxf6	23. Qxb7
6. Bxc6 Bxc6	12. c4 cxd5	18. Qg4! Qb5	Black resigns

For other mythical games, see pp. 89, 175, and 238.

The stars' stars

We conducted a survey into the birth signs of 851 prominent chess-players. The results look something like this:

Capricorn	63	(Lasker, Keres, Chiburdanidze)
Aquarius	79	(Spassky, Bronstein)
Pisces	101	(Fischer, Tarrasch, Geller, Larsen)
Aries	76	(Smyslov, Kasparov, Korchnoi, Portisch)
Taurus	77	(Miles, Nunn, Steinitz)
Gemini	67	(Petrosian, Karpov, Short, Euwe)
Cancer	54	(Morphy, Anderssen)
Leo	67	(Botvinnik)
Virgo	63	(Philidor)
Libra	69	(Rubinstein, Fine)

Scorpio   71 (Capablanca, Alekhine, Nimzowitsch, Tal)
Sagittarius   64 (Reshevsky, Pillsbury)

So players born under Pisces are clearly no fish. And it seems that the best time of year for chess-players to be born is in the spring. Interestingly, astrologers claim that those born under the sign of Pisces have no interest in things logical or rational, whereas those born under Cancer, the worst sign in our survey, are just the opposite. What this proves we're not quite sure.

♖

The largest chess piece in the world is reputed to be the giant knight guarding the entrance to the Dubai Trade Centre for the 1986 Chess Olympiad. It is ten metres high. For the smallest, see 'The Entertainers'.

Postscript

Too bizarre even for us, but worth a mention are various loony stories appearing in publications like *The Sport*:

'CHESS ROBOT TURNS KILLER' (about a supercomputer that was on trial in Russia for electrocuting its opponent, one Nikolai Gudkov).

'RANDY ROMEO GOES PAWN CRAZY' (about Robert Thompson, who fell in love with a black pawn. 'I don't want to go into the nitty-gritty of it, but it wasn't feasible to have sex,' said Robert, who'd previously taken the pawn for a ride round Tesco in a shopping trolley.

'ESKIMO SEAL HUNTER BEATS TOP RUSSIAN CHESS CHAMPS' (about Uki Derzhal, a fifty-seven-year-old Eskimo, who, a few days after learning the game, crushed an international master in six moves, and grandmasters in less than ten. Not surprisingly, the GMs described Uki as 'a crude savage'. See 'Mate in Nineteen' story in Chapter IV, 'The Unacceptable'.)

Dream solution: Kf3

Second Adjournment: Desert Island Chess

It is a riddle wrapped in a mystery inside an enigma: but perhaps there is a key.

W. S. Churchill

Hell, says Sartre, is other people. If he'd been a chess-player,[1] he would have known better. Hell is being stuck somewhere with a chessboard and men, and no opponent. Should this ever happen to you, the next section will serve as a pain-killer. It's a collection of solitary pursuits you can enjoy on a chessboard.

Some of them shouldn't tax the intelligence of the average vole; most of the remainder will detain you for not more than a couple of hours; but for those of our readers who are in Antarctic research stations, or Wormwood Scrubs, or lost up the Amazon, we've put in a few killer-dillers that should make the time race past.

Answers, where necessary, are at the end of this section.

1. The knight's tour

A most ancient puzzle. A thousand years ago the Hindu Rudrata was writing about it. Stick the knight on any square, and then tour the board, touching each square once only.

There are billions of solutions. Many of them make pretty patterns.

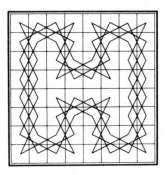

[1] Maybe he was. Before the twentieth game of the 1978 Karpov–Korchnoi match a telegram ('Avec vous en coeur') arrived, addressed to Korchnoi, and bearing the names of four literary eminences – Sartre, Beckett, Arrabal and Ionesco. We know the last three were chess-players.

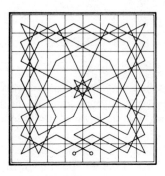

The first one is a re-entrant (the knight is able to reach the first square after its 64th move). There are 122 million like that.

This version (expressed in figures) was invented by Euler, the great mathematician. It almost makes a magic square: each rank and file adds up to 260.

63	14	37	24	51	26	35	10
22	39	62	13	36	11	50	27
15	64	23	38	25	52	09	34
40	21	16	61	12	33	28	49
17	60	01	44	29	48	53	08
02	41	20	57	06	55	32	47
59	18	43	04	45	30	07	54
42	03	58	19	56	05	46	31

Now you try.

2. The eight queens

Put eight queens on the board so that none commands a square occupied by another

This problem fascinated the prince of mathematicians, Karl Gauss. He demonstrated that there are only 12 basic solutions. With rotations of the board, this gives 92 possible ways of doing it (and, roughly, four and a half thousand million ways of doing it wrong).

3. The five queens

Place five queens so that they control all 64 squares (there are 4,860 ways of doing this).

4. The eight chess pieces

Place the eight white chess pieces on the board (keeping the bishops on opposite coloured squares) so that

(i) the maximum number of squares are guarded, including the squares on which the pieces are placed
(ii) the minimum number of squares are guarded, including the squares on which the pieces are placed

5. The student's breakthrough

(i) Every Russian schoolboy knows it.

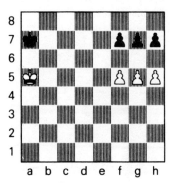

White to play and win.

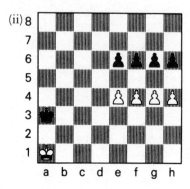

(ii) Slightly more difficult.
White to play and win.

6. Constructions

(i) Construct a game in which Black delivers mate by discovered check on move 4; (S. Loyd, Le Sphinx, 1866)

(ii)

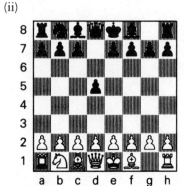

Construct a game to reach this position after Black's fourth move; (E.C. Mortimer)

(iii) Construct a game to reach this position after White's sixteenth move.

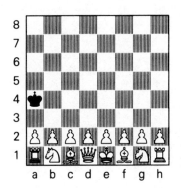

(K. Fabel)

7. Reconstruction

White's king has fallen off the board. On which square must it be replaced?

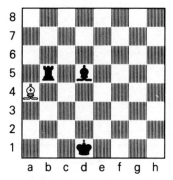

R. Smullyan,
Manchester Guardian, 1957

8. The Réti study

This seeming impossibility gets our vote as the bestest, simplest chess composition of all. Richard Réti created it in 1921.

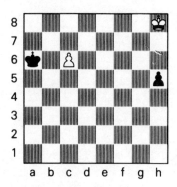

R. Réti, *Deutschösterreichische
Tages-Zeitung*, 1921

White to play and draw.

9. *The Saavedra position*

The most famous chess study of all (and one of the most elegant) was named after a Spanish priest living in Glasgow in 1895. Maybe he should be in the holy team. Fernando de Saavedra was a duff chess-player, but found immortality when he spotted a win in a position that was thought to be a draw. The result, this gem (composed by Barbier, improved by Saavedra):

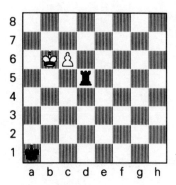

G. Barbier & F. Saavedra,
Glasgow Weekly Citizen, 1895

White to play and win

10. *The ten-move stalemate*

A genius called Sam Loyd invented this. From the starting position, reach a stalemate in just ten moves. This could take you years. Unless you're on a desert island, consult the solution immediately.

11. *Just how good are you?*

Older, less talented, players may find this depressing. It was used by the Czechs as a test of young chess talent. You need a stop-watch, and a friend to time you.

You put black pawns on c3, f3, c6 and f6. You put a white knight on a1, then you move to b1 (via c2, a3) c1 and through to h1 and then h2, and so on to a8 – without going to a square occupied by or attacked by a pawn (ten seconds' penalty each time you do).

According to C. H. O'D. Alexander, ten to fifteen minutes is respectable, under seven minutes is good, and below two minutes is young grandmaster standard. One of us took six and a half minutes. If you care to try a second time, a 25 per cent improvement means you have good learning ability. We got worse.

12. *Fourteen more studies*

You've already (8 and 9 above) seen two of the most famous studies; here are fourteen more well-known ones:

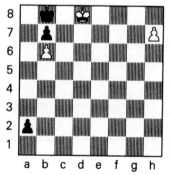

D. Joseph, *Hackney Review*, 1922

White to play and win

(ii)

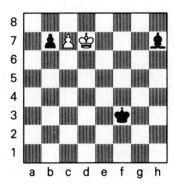

A. & K. Sarychev commended
Shakhmatny Listok, 1928
(Version)

White to play and draw

(iii)

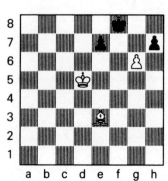

A Troitsky, *Novoye Vremya*,
1895

White to play and win

(iv)

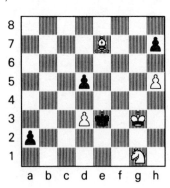

V. & M. Platov, First Prize,
Rigaer Tageblatt, 1909

White to play and win

(v)

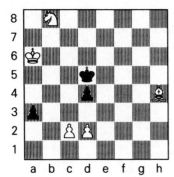

L. Kubbel, *Shakhmatny Listok*, 1922

White to play and win

(vi)

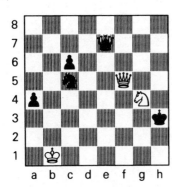

L. Kubbel, *150 Chess Studies*, 1925

White to play and win

(vii)

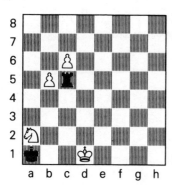

M. Liburkin, Second Prize, *Shakhmaty v. SSSR*, 1931

White to play and win

(viii)

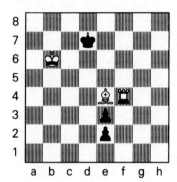

R. Réti, corrected by H. Rinck, *Bohemia*, 1935

White to play and win

(ix)

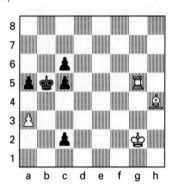

H. Mattison, *Rigaer Tageblatt*, 1913

White to play and draw

(x)

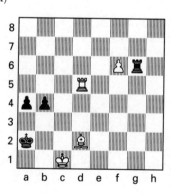

G. Kasparian, First Prize, *Shakhmaty v. SSSR*, 1939

White to play and win

(xi)

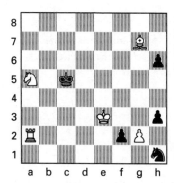

A. Gurvich & G. Kasparian,
First Prize, All-Union
Physical Culture and
Sport Tournament, 1955

White to play and win

(xii)

A. Seletsky, 1933

White to play and win

(xiii)

A. Kazantsev,
Equal First Prize,
Olympic Study Tourney, 1964

White to play and win

(xiv)

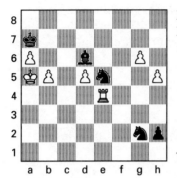

L. Mitrofanov, First Prize,
Rustaveli Tournament,
1967 (version)

White to play and win

13. And sixteen problems

In case you're wondering, a *study* has no fixed limit of moves attached to it, and generally looks like something that might happen in a game. A *problem* has a fixed number of moves as a condition, and is often artificial in its appearance. We're no experts, but here are sixteen of the most famous:

(i)

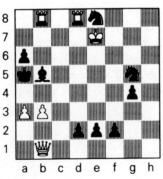

A. Anderssen, *Illustrated London News*, 1846

Mate in 5

(ii)

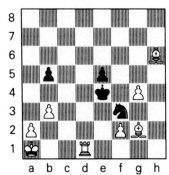

H. A. Loveday, *Chess Players' Chronicle*, 1845 (version)

Mate in 3

(iii)

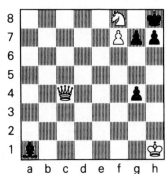

S. Loyd, *Leipziger Illustrierte Zeitung*, 1869

Mate in 3

(iv)

S. Loyd, 1858.
Loyd was fond of asking friends to guess which piece delivered mate in the main variation of this problem. They were always wrong. Go ahead, have a guess.

Mate in 5

(v)

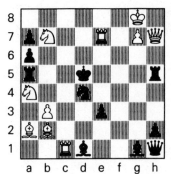

G. Heathcote, First Prize
Hampstead and Highgate Express,
1905

Mate in 2

(vi)

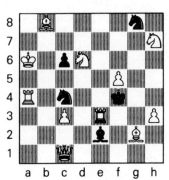

C. Mansfield, First Prize *Good
Companions*, March 1917

Mate in 2

(vii)

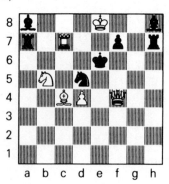

L. Loshinsky, Commended
Tijdschrift v.d. N.S.B., 1930

Mate in 2

(viii)

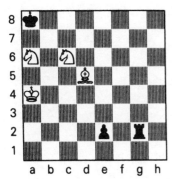

C. S. Kipping, *Manchester City News*, 1911

Mate in 3

(ix)

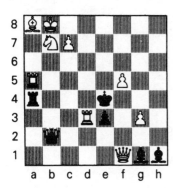

A. Ellerman, First Prize Guidelli Memorial Tourney, 1925

Mate in 2

(x)

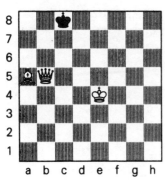

W. A. Shinkman *Offiziers-Schachzeitung*, 1905

Mate in 3

(xi)

C. Bayer, *Era*, 1856

Mate in 9

(xii)

S. Loyd, First Prize,
Checkmate Tourney, 1903

Mate in 3

(xiii)

A. J. Fink & Ua Tane,
First Prize, *Good Companions*,
July 1920

Mate in 2

(xiv)

C. Mansfield, First Prize,
Die Schwalbe, 1956

Mate in 2

(xv)

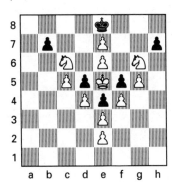

T. Dawson,
Falkirk Herald, 1914

Mate in 2

(xvi)

L. Yarosh, First Prize,
Shakhmaty, 1983

Mate in 4

14. Three jokes

(i)

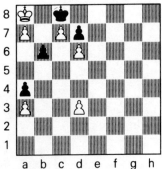

V. Røpke
The easiest problem of all.

Find someone who claims to be no good at chess problems. Bet him he can solve this one no matter how hard he doesn't try.

Mate in 6

(ii)

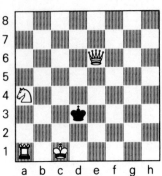

Deliver mate in half a move

(iii)

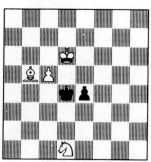

Deliver mate in no moves

15. The most difficult position of all

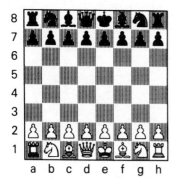

White to play, what result?

16. The Dudeney problem

This, invented by the English genius Henry Ernest Dudeney, has been called the best puzzle ever devised. You don't need to know the rules of chess to tackle it.

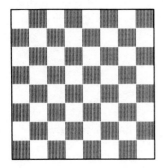

Two people have a perfectly constructed chessboard, and an unlimited supply of white pawns of exactly the same dimensions. The first person places a pawn anywhere on the board (not necessarily in the middle of a square – *anywhere*); the second does the same. And so on until one person can't fit another pawn on the board. He's the loser.

With perfect play, who wins?

Solutions

1 James Mason (*Elements of Chess*) says where two apparently equal
  routes lie open choose that which leads the furthest outward, or to
  the square whence the knight will have less scope for action.

2 One answer is: a6, b4, c1, d5, e8, f2, g7, h3

3 One answer is: h1, f3, e4, d5, b7

4
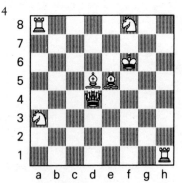

63 squares controlled (all except e2. This is one of over 80 solutions)

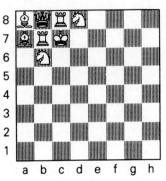

16 squares controlled (including the ones on which the pieces stand)

5 (i)   1. g6 fxg6 2. h6 gxh6 3. f6 and wins, or 1. ... hxg6 2. f6
         gxf6 3. h6.
   (ii) 1. h5 gxh5 2. e5 fxe5 3. f5 and white promotes with check.

6 (i)   1. f3 e5 2. Kf2 h5 3. Kg3 h4+ 4. Kg4 d5 mate.
   (ii) 1. Nf3 d5 2. Ne5 Nf6 3. Nc6 Nfd7 4. Nxb8 Nxb8
   (iii) 1. Nc3 b5 2. Nxb5 Nf6 3. Nxa7 Ne4 4. Nxc8 Nc3
         5. Nxe7 c6 6. Nxc6 Nb1 7. Nxb8 Ra3 8. Nxd7 g5 9. Nxf8

Qd6 10. Nxh7 Kd7 11. Nxg5 Rh4 12. Nxf7 Rc4 13. Nxd6
Kc6 14. Nxc4 Kb5 15. Nxa3 + Ka4 16. Nxb1.

7   K on c3. (− 1. c2–c4 b4xc3 e.p. o. Kxc3 must have been
the previous moves)

8   1. Kg7 h4 2. Kf6 Kb6 3. Ke5 Kxc6 4. Kf4 and draws

9   1. c7 Rd6 + 2. Kb5 Rd5 + 3. Kb4 Rd4 + 4. Kb3 Rd3 +
5. Kc2 Rd4 6. c8 = R Ra4 7. Kb3 and wins

10   1. e3 a5 2. Qh5 Ra6 3. Qxa5 h5 4. Qxc7 Rh6 5. h4 f6
6. Qxd7 + Kf7 7. Qxb7 Qe3 8. Qxb8 Qh7 9. Qxc8 Kg6
10. Qe6.

12   (i)   1. h8 = Q a1 = Q 2. Qg8 Qa2 3. Qe8 Qa4 4. Qe5 + Ka8
5. Qh8 and wins

     (ii)   1. Kc8 b5 2. Kd7 Bf5 + 3. Kd6 b4 4. Ke5 Kg4 5. Kd4 and
draws

     (iii) 1. Bh6 + Kg8 2. g7 Kf7 3. g8 = Q + Kxg8 4. Ke6 Kh8
5. Kf7 e5 6. Bg7 mate (or 2. . . . e6 + 3. Kd6 Kf7 4. Ke5 Kg8
5. Kf6 and wins, or 2. . . . e5 3. Ke6 e4 4. Kf6 and wins)

     (iv)   1. Bf6 d4 2. Ne2 a1 = Q 3. Nc1 Qa5 4. Bxd4 + and
5. Nb3 + wins (or 3. . . . h6 4. Be5 wins). This was Lenin's
favourite study.

     (v)   1. Nc6 Kxc6 2. Bf6 Kd5 3. d3 a2 4. c4 + Kc5 5. Kb7 a1 = Q
6. Be7 mate

     (vi)   1. Ne3 + Kg3 2. Qg4 + Kf2 3. Qf4 + Ke2 4. Qf1 + Kd2
5. Qd1 + Kc3 6. Qc2 + Kb4 7. Qb2 + Nb3 8. Qa3 + Kxa3
9. Nc2 mate

     (vii) 1. Nc1 Rxb5 2. c7 Rd5 + 3. Nd3 Rxd3 + 4. Kc2 Rd4
5. c8 = R Ra4 6. Kb3 and wins (compare 9) (or 1. . . .
Rd5 + 2. Kc2 Rc5 + 3. Kd3 Rxb5 4. c7 Rb8 5. cxb8 = B
and wins)

     (viii) 1. Bf5 + Kd6 2. Rd4 + Ke7 3. Re4 + Kd8 4. Bd7 e1 = Q
5. Bb5 and 6. Re8 mate

     (ix)   1. a4 + Kb6 2. Bf2 c1 = Q 3. Rxc5 Qxc5 4. Kh1 Qxf2 stale-
mate

     (x)   1. Bg5 b3 2. Rd2 + Ka1 3. f7 Rxg5 4. f8 = Q Rg1 + 5. Rd1
Rg2 6. Qa3 + Ra2 7. Rd2 Rxa3 8. Rb2 Ra2 9. Rb1 mate

     (xi)   1. Bd4 + Kd5 2. Ke2 h2 3. Ra1 f1 = Q + 4. Kxf1 Kxd4 5. g4
Ng3 + 6. Kg2 h1 = Q + 7. Kxg3 Qxa1 8. Nb3 + Ke5
9. Nxa1 Kf6 10. Kh4 and wins

(xii) 1. Qg5 Ke6 + 2. Kg1 Kxd7 3. Nc5 + Kc8 4. Ba6 + Kb8 5. Qg3 + Ka8 6. Bb7 + Bxb7 7. Nd7 Qd8 8. Qb8 + Qxb8 9. Nb6 mate

(xiii) 1. e7 Qa3 + 2. Rb4 Qa7 + 3. Kxc4 Qxe7 4. Nxg6 + fxg6 5. Bf6 + Qxf6 6. Kd5 + Kg5 7. h4 + Kf5 8. g4 + hxg4 9. Rf4 + Bxf4 10. e4 mate

(xiv) 1. b6 + Ka8 2. Re1 Nxe1 3. g7 h1 = Q 4. g8 = Q + Bb8 5. a7 Nc6 + 6. dxc6 Qxh5 + 7. Qg5 Qxg5 + 8. Ka6 bxa7 9. c7 Qa5 + 10. Kxa5 Bxb6 + 11. Kxb6 and mate next move

13 (i) 1. Qe1 dxe1 = Q 2. Rd4 f1 = Q 3. Ra4 + Bxa4 4. b4 + Qxb4 5. axb4 mate

(ii) 1. Bc1 b4 2. Rd2 Kf4 3. Rd4 mate

(iii) 1. Qf1 Bb2 2. Qb1 and mate next move, or if 1. . . . Bc3 or Bd4, 2. Qd3, or if 1. . . . Be5 or Bf6, 2. Qf5, or if 1. . . . g6 2. Ng6 +

(iv) 1. b4 Rc5 + 2. bxc5 a2 3. c6 Bc7 4. cxb7 any 5. bxa8 = Q mate

(v) 1. Rcc7 threatening Nc3 mate. After every move of the black knight on d4 a different mate occurs

(vi) 1. Be4 threatening Nxc4 mate. If 1. . . . Ne5 2. Rd3 mate, or 1. . . . Nxd6 + 2. Bd3 mate, or 1. . . . Nxe3 + 2. Nb5 mate, or 1. . . . Nd2 + 2. Nc4 mate

(vii) 1. Bb3, no threat. All twenty-three of black's replies allow mate. Note the interferences on b7, g7 and f6.

(viii) 1. Ka5 d1 = Q + 2. Kb6 and mate next move. Or 1. . . . Rg8 2. Nd4 + Ka7 3. Nb5 mate, or 1. . . . Kb7 2. Ne7 + Ka7 3. Nc8 mate. But not 1. Kb5 because of Rg8.

(ix) 1. Rd7 threatening Qf4. If 1. . . . Qd4, 2. Nd6, or if 1. . . . Qe5, 2. Nc5, or if 1. . . . Qh8 +, 2. Nc8, or if 1. . . . Bf2, 2. Qxh1, or if 1. . . . Bf3, 2. Qd3, or if 1. . . . Rd4, 2. Re7

(x) 1. Qb2 Kd7 2. Qe5 Kc8 3. Qc7 mate or 2. . . . Kc6 Qd5 mate

(xi) 1. Rb7 Qxb7 2. Bxg6 + Kxg6 3. Qg8 + Kxf5 4. Qg4 + Ke5 5. Qh5 + Rf5 6. f4 + Bxf4 7. Qxe2 + Bxe2 8. Re4 + dxe4 9. d4 mate. Compare 12 (xiii).

(xii) 1. Ke2 f1 = Q + 2. Ke3 and mate next move, or 1. . . . f1 = N 2. Rf2 + and mate next move.

(xiii) 1. Rc8. Eight of Black's possible moves block a flight-square for his king, each allowing a different mate (see if you can find them): a record. The curious circumstances surrounding its composition were revealed in Chapter VI.

(xiv) Black's rooks and bishops each prevent a different mate. White's four moves with his f and g pawns each interfere with two of these pieces, so threatening two mates. But 1. g3? fails to ... Nc2!, 1. g4? fails to ... Nxf2! and 1. f4 fails to e3! The only move to work is 1. f3!, threatening Qe3 and Qd1. 1. ... Kd4 is met by 2. Qxc3. Black can also meet both threats with either Bf4, which interferes with the rook and allows Qxe4, or Rf4, which interferes with the bishop and allows Bxb3.

(xv) White has made ten pawn captures, balancing Black's missing men, so Black must have moved his d-pawn long ago to release the bishop. Therefore, Black's only possible last move was f7–f5. So white can mate in 2 with exf6 e.p.

(xvi) This is the famous Babson Task: matching white and black promotions to all four pieces. It had defeated problemists for nearly sixty years, until in 1983 a previously unknown soccer coach named Lev Yarosh came up with no less than three four-movers. This is one of them.

The solution is 1. a7 when the Babson variations run: 1. ... axb1=Q 2. axb8=Q Qxb2 3. Qxb3 (or 2. ... Qe4 3. Qxf4), 1. ... axb1=R 2. axb8=R Rxb2 3. Rxb3, 1. ... axb1=B 2. axb8=B Be4 3. Bxf4 and 1. ... axb1=N 2. axb8=N Nxd2. 3. Qc1, in each case mating next move. Miraculous! We'll leave you to work out the other variations for yourself. For more information see *Chess Curiosities* (Krabbé).

14 (i) If you can't solve this, you really do have a problem.

(ii) Rd1 (i.e. white completes the second half of castling queen side. He's already played the other half: Kc1).

(iii) Just turn the board round. Now the white pawn is giving mate.

15 Crack this one and you'll become immortal (and rich).

16 The first player. He puts a pawn in the exact geometric centre of the board; then whatever move his opponent makes, he matches it symmetrically, until there are no more spaces left for the second player. (As far as we recall this problem was originally set with cigars and a large table as the props – but it has appeared in many guises.)

VII *The Future*

For I dipt into the future, far as human eye could see,
Saw the Vision of the world, and all the wonder that would be.

Alfred, Lord Tennyson

We are passing from the sphere of history to the sphere of the present and partly to the sphere of the future.

V. I. Lenin

The Future?

These are exciting times for chess fans. Since the first edition of this book a whole new generation of colourful players has emerged on to the world stage, coming not just from Eastern Europe but from countries such as India and China. The fragmentation of the former Soviet Union and Yugoslavia has made team tournaments more competitive: Uzbekistan, which most of its rivals would be hard pressed to locate in an atlas, took the silver medals in the 1992 Olympiad. Tournament organizers are experimenting with ways of making chess more spectator-friendly: knock-out tournaments, faster time limits and spectacular settings all combine to increase both publicity and interest. Judith Polgár and her sisters are proving that sex is no barrier to success, younger and younger children are playing better and better, while computers are challenging even the best players in the world.

In this chapter we introduce you to some of the players who will be making the chess headlines as the century draws to its close.

The Dinosaurs

In a year in which chess made the front pages of British newspapers on no less than three occasions, the most remarkable story of all was the return of Bobby Fischer. After two decades in the wilderness the eccentric American was back for another encounter with his old rival Boris Spassky, complete with a beard, a new chess-clock and, it was reported, a fiancée. Well, the fiancée bit turned out to be something of an exaggeration. The lady in question was one Zita Rajcsanyi, a nineteen-year-old Hungarian. Zita had written Bobby a fan letter after reading *My Sixty Memorable Games*, and, to her surprise, Bobby phoned, inviting her to Los Angeles where he expressed an interest in returning to chess competition. Zita contacted a friend who had helped organize the 1990 Novi Sad Olympiad, a sponsor was found and the match arranged. And so, on 1 September 1992, twenty years to the day after Bobby became World Champion,

Bobby Fischer and Boris Spassky sat down together to face the world's press.

The next day they were off and running, for a total purse of $5 million. Fischer pushed his e-pawn two squares forward with the result you will already have seen in Chapter II. The winner of the match was to be the first to ten wins, with Fischer retaining his title of 'World Champion' if the tally of wins reached 9–9. Play started on the island of Sveti Stefan, with a transfer to Belgrade after one player had won five games. The match started with a bang: Fischer won the first game. Spassky went into the lead with wins in games 4 and 5, Fischer struck decisively, taking the full point in games 7, 8, 9 and 11, at which point they moved to Belgrade. Spassky immediately pulled one back in game 12, after which the pace slowed, and it was not until the 30th game that Fischer scored his tenth victory, retaining his 'title' by ten wins to five.

The games reveal that, at his best, Bobby is almost as good as ever. In the 25th game, Fischer demonstrates his familiarity with a modern opening line popular with Nigel Short. The main point of the game is his imaginative 15th move. If instead 15. Q x b4, Bc6 gives Spassky excellent play for the pawn. After 15. Nb6 N x b6, 16. Q x b4 would regain the piece leaving Fischer a safe pawn ahead. The exchange of knights in the game slows down Spassky's attack and the white pawns touch down first.

Fischer–Spassky, 25th Match Game, Belgrade, 1992. Sicilian Defence

1. e4 c5	10. g4 Nxd4	19. h5 e5	28. Rxg7 Qf6
2. Nc3 Nc6	11. Bxd4 b5	20. Be3 Be6	29. h6 a4
3. Nge2 d6	12. g5 Nd7	21. Rdg1 a5	30. b3 axb3
4. d4 cxd4	13. h4 b4	22. g6 Bf6	31. axb3 Rfd8
5. Nxd4 e6	14. Na4 Bb7	23. gxh7+ Kh8	32. Qg2 Rf8
6. Be3 Nf6	15. Nb6! Rb8	24. Bg5 Qe7	33. Rg8+ Kxh7
7. Qd2 Be7	16. Nxd7 Qxd7	25. Rg3 Bxg5	34. Rg7+ Kh8
8. f3 a6	17. Kb1 Qc7	26. Rxg5 Qf6	35. h7 Black
9. O–O–O O–O	18. Bd3 Bc8	27. Rhg1 Qxf3	resigns

But, as is only to be expected after twenty years' absence, Fischer is much more prone to carelessness and outright blunder. The 4th game is one of Spassky's best efforts. Boris starts slowly but catches Bobby off guard with a fine positional exchange sacrifice on move

20. The tactical sequence between moves 35 and 38 forces Fischer to return the exchange leaving Spassky a pawn up. Fischer's quote after the game: 'That's chess, you know. One day you give a lesson, the next day your opponent gives you a lesson.'

Spassky–Fischer, 4th Match Game, Sveti Stefan, 1992. Queen's Gambit Accepted

1. d4 d5	14. f3 b5	27. Nc2 Rb8	40. Kxd3 Nf6
2. c4 dxc4	15. Be2 Bc5	28. Ba3 h5	41. Bd6 Rc8
3. Nf3 Nf6	16. Kf1 Ke7	29. Rg1 Kf6	42. Rg5+ Kh7
4. e3 e6	17. e4 g5	30. Ke3 a5	43. Be5 Ne8
5. Bxc4 c5	18. Nb1 g4	31. Rg5 a4	44. Rxh5+ Kg6
6. O–O a6	19. Ba3 b4	32. b4 Nb7	45. Rg5+ Kh7
7. dxc5 Qxd1	20. Rxc5! Nxc5	33. b5 Nbc5	46. Bf4 f6
8. Rxd1 Bxc5	21. Bxb4 Rhd8	34. Nd4 e5	47. Rf5 Kg6
9. b3 Nbd7	22. Na3 gxf3	35. Nxe5! Nxe5	48. b6 Rd8
10. Bb2 b6	23. gxf3 Nfd7	36. Rf5+ Kg7	49. Ra5 Bxf3
11. Nc3 Bb7	24. Nc4 Ba8	37. Rxe5 Nxe4	50. h5+ Black
12. Rac1 Be7	25. Kf2 Rg8	38. Bd3! Rc3	resigns
13. Nd4 Rc8	26. h4 Rc7	39. Bb4 Rxd3+	

What next for the two combatants? 'Bobby has saved me from oblivion,' said a grateful Boris, who was in danger of becoming the forgotten man of world chess. Spassky, who has represented France since 1984, had dropped well down the world rankings, all too often happy to agree a quick draw and adjourn to the tennis court. But now, thanks to Fischer, he is, perhaps only for a short time, able to command big money again.

In the nineteenth century Paul Morphy was dubbed the 'pride and sorrow of chess'. The same description could equally well be applied to Fischer. Just think of all the wonderful Fischer–Karpov and Fischer–Kasparov games that might have happened over the past twenty years. But maybe, just maybe ... Will Fischer play more matches, against more demanding opponents? Or will he disappear again, perhaps doomed to replay those ghostly reminders of the glories of Reykjavik every twenty years into eternity? Whatever happens, we're sure to hear a lot more of Bobby over the next few years. As we write these lines (June 1993) he's still in Eastern

Europe. He's been indicted by the US government for breaking economic sanctions and faces a heavy fine and possibly imprisonment on his return. Following the collapse of match sponsor Jezdimir Vasiljević's Jugoskandic Bank, it is unclear whether Bobby will ever get his hands on all the prize money. We surely haven't heard the last of his clock, which seeks to eliminate both time trouble and adjournments. Enterprising tournament organizers will certainly be trying this out in future. And, fascinatingly, a film of Fischer's life based on Frank Brady's biography is scheduled for release. Once again, the world awaits Bobby's next move.

The Rivals

'I know him so well,' sang Elaine Paige and Barbara Dickson in their 1985 hit from the musical *Chess*. This could easily be the theme song for Gary Kasparov and the man he calls his 'perpetual opponent', Anatoly Karpov. Their seemingly interminable series of matches between 1984 and 1990 somehow failed to catch the imagination of the general public or the media, who saw the matches simply as being between two Russians with similar names.

Similar names, yes, but they could hardly be more different in style, personality or appearance. Karpov the cautious minimalist, short and slight, with auburn hair and squeaky voice, fond of philately and James Last, polite and pleasant but rather dull. A sportsman in the same category as Steve Davis, Ivan Lendl or Geoff Boycott. Kasparov the aggressive maximalist, darkly handsome, charming when courting the media but arrogant and opinionated. Imagine a sober Alex Higgins, a well-behaved John McEnroe or an intellectual Ian Botham.

It was with an enormous sigh of relief, not least from Kasparov himself, that the news of Short's win over Karpov was received. At last Gazza would face a challenger whose name didn't begin with K and who wasn't Russian. Nevertheless, the two Ks have produced some magnificent and memorable chess over the past decade. We present two more examples here.

Inevitably, their tournament games have received less publicity than the Kasparov–Karpov World Championship encounters. Here's one of Kasparov's best efforts, from Linares, 1992. Note Kasparov's highly original use of his rook.

Kasparov–Karpov, Linares, 1992. Caro-Kann Defence

1. e4 c6	12. dxc5 Bxc5	23. Rh4! Kb8	34. Nxb7 Kxb7
2. d4 d5	13. Ne5 Bd7	24. a4 Be7	35. Qa6+ Kc6
3. Nd2 dxe4	14. Ngf3 Nh5	25. a5 Nd5	36. Ba4+ Kd6
4. Nxe4 Nd7	15. O-O-O Nxg3	26. Kb1 Bd8	37. Qd3+ Nd5
5. Ng5 Ngf6	16. hxg3 O-O-O	27. a6 Qa5	38. Qg3+ Qe5
6. Bc4 e6	17. Rh5! Be8	28. Qe2 Nb6	39. Qa3+ Kc7
7. Qe2 Nb6	18. Rxd8+ Kxd8	29. axb7 Bxg5	40. Qc5+ Kd8
8. Bb3 h6	19. Qd2+ Bd6	30. Nxg5 Qxg5	41. Rxa7 Black
9. N5f3 c5	20. Nd3 Qc7	31. Rh5! Qf6	resigns
10. Bf4 Bd6	21. g4 Kc8	32. Ra5 Bc6	
11. Bg3 Qe7	22. g5 Bf8	33. Nc5 Bxb7	

Karpov's best game from the 1990 World Championship was a smooth positional victory in the style of Capablanca. Kasparov never gets to grips with the Karpov pawn centre. Will he ever play the Grunfeld Defence again?

Karpov–Kasparov, 17th Match Game, Lyons, 1990. Grünfeld Defence

1. d4 Nf6	12. h3 Bd7	23. d5 Nc4	34. Bc7 Ba1
2. c4 g6	13. Rb1 Rc8	24. Nd2 Nxd2	35. Bf4 Qd7
3. Nc3 d5	14. Nf3 Na5	25. Bxd2 Rc8	36. Rc7 Qd8
4. cxd5 Nxd5	15. Bd3 Be6	26. Rc6! Be5	37. d6 g5
5. e4 Nxc3	16. O-O Bc4	27. Bc3 Bb8	38. d7 Rf8
6. bxc3 Bg7	17. Rfd1 b5	28. Qd4 f6	39. Bd2 Be5
7. Be3 c5	18. Bg5 a6	29. Ba5 Bd6	40. Rb7 Black
8. Qd2 O-O	19. Rbc1 Bxd3	30. Qc3 Re8	resigns
9. Nf3 Bg4	20. Rxc8 Qxc8	31. a3 Kg7	
10. Ng5 cxd4	21. Qxd3 Re8	32. g3 Be5	
11. cxd4 Nc6	22. Rc1 Qb7	33. Qc5 h5	

At the beginning of 1993 Karpov is still rated number two in the world, despite having been briefly overtaken by Ivanchuk in 1992. But the great little man is by no means as infallible as a few years ago. Time trouble has become more prevalent in his games and he has developed an alarming tendency to blunder at critical moments.

You'll have seen some of the more grisly examples of this in Chapter III. Even so, he'll be pretty near the top for a good few years yet. We don't seen him as a realistic future challenger though: the younger generation will have too much hunger. But a match against Fischer: now that really would be something. Get on the phone to Bobby now, Tolya, agree to all his demands and make our dreams come true.

Kasparov has been firmly established at number one since winning the world title, but in the last couple of years he has no longer had things quite his own way in tournaments. Ivanchuk, Anand and Kamsky have all taken individual games off him in impressive fashion. By the time this book appears he'll be playing Nigel Short, a match he really ought to win fairly comfortably. According to the January 1993 rating list he would be expected to win by an overwhelming $12\frac{1}{2}$–$5\frac{1}{2}$ (but our prediction is that the match will be closer: $12\frac{1}{2}$–$8\frac{1}{2}$). If the World Championship cycle remains the same (which is open to doubt), and if Gary avoids getting too heavily involved in politics, he should have too much experience for his 1996 challenger, and perhaps also in 1999. If we had to make a prediction we'd speculate on a possible defeat in 2002. We'll reveal the identity of his successor in a few pages' time.

The Brits

It was August 1972. A seven-year-old boy, just developing an interest in chess, was on holiday with his parents in the Isle of Wight. The Fischer–Spassky match was on the front page of all the papers and the youngster amused himself on the long journey home to Manchester playing through the games on his pocket set. The seed was sown. But the lad and his parents could hardly have imagined that twenty-one years later young Nigel would himself be playing a match against the World Champion.

The rest of the story is well known: Nigel Short's emergence as a prodigy and ascent to the ranks of super grandmasters. His results over the past few years have been somewhat erratic. A weakness, which, incidentally, he shares with his victim in the Candidates'

Final, Jan Timman, is a tendency to lose his nerve or his interest when things start to go wrong in tournaments. This has led to some fluctuation in his rating. But he has recently made two excellent moves. His marriage to Rea, a drama therapist from Athens (they have a daughter exotically named Kyveli) has given him an extra stability. And his appointment of Czech-born US Grandmaster Lubosh Kavalek as his trainer has improved both his opening preparation and his mental approach.

♛

'I played like God' was Nigel's reaction after the eighth match game against Karpov, restoring his lead at a critical point in his Candidates' Semi-final match. *Chess Informant*'s panel of grandmasters couldn't agree on the best game of the period February–May 1992. Kasparov's win against the same opponent at the same venue (see above) scored the same number of points as Short's win. Judge for yourself.

Short–Karpov, 8th Match Game, Linares, 1992. Ruy López

1. e4 e5	11. cxd4 d5	21. Bc6 Qb6	31. exf7+ Kh8
2. Nf3 Nc6	12. e5 Ne4	22. Bxd5 Rxb2	32. Re1 Bg6
3. Bb5 a6	13. a4 bxa4	23. Qc4 Rc2	33. Re8 Rxe8
4. Ba4 Nf6	14. Bxa4 Nb4	24. Qg4 Qc7	34. fxe8=Q Bxe8
5. O–O Be7	15. h3 Bh5	25. Nd4 Rc3	35. Bxc5 Bxc5
6. Qe2 b5	16. Nc3 Bg6	26. Nc6 Re8	36. Qe6 Black
7. Bb3 O–O	17. Be3 Rb8	27. Bd4 Rc2	resigns
8. c3 d6	18. Na2! c5	28. Nb4! Rd8	
9. d4 Bg4	19. dxc5 Nxc5	29. Nxc2 Bxc2	
10. Rd1 exd4	20. Nxb4 Rxb4	30. e6 Bf8	

A further successful match, against Holland's Jan Timman, in early 1993, set Nigel up for a crack at Gary Kasparov. At the time of writing we're expecting Kasparov to win without too much difficulty, but he will have to be careful not to underestimate his opponent. Under Kavalek's tutelage Short has developed into a formidable match player, and, like Lasker, he has always had the ability to win critical games. Gary may not find the match quite as Short as he predicted.

♛

Another young Englishman has recently joined Nigel Short in the chess superleague. The quiet young Cornishman, Michael Adams, hit the big time towards the end of 1992 with victories in two major knock-out tournaments, the SWIFT Rapidplay in Brussels, followed by the Interpolis in Tilburg. Adams's strengths and weaknesses are clear: superb middle-game play, speed of thought, excellent temperament but inadequate openings and lack of endgame technique. Just what you would expect from a player who has done a lot more playing than studying. If he chooses to follow Short's example and find himself a trainer anything is possible. But for the moment Mickey, a laid-back easy-going character, has declared a singular lack of ambition. Will the twin temptations of fame and fortune induce a change of mind?

At the same time as the Short–Karpov match, Michael Adams was undergoing a baptism of fire in his first mega-GM tournament at Dortmund. Adams only won one game, against Russia's Valery Salov, but it was a good one. Salov's opening system gives him weaknesses on the d-file. Watch how Mickey uses d5 for his minor pieces and wins the pawn on d6.

Adams–Salov, Dortmund, 1992. Sicilian Defence

1. e4 c5	11. c3 f5	21. Nc2! Qd7	31. Bc2 e4
2. Nf3 Nc6	12. exf5 Bxf5	22. Ra6 Bh3	32. Qd4+ Qf6
3. d4 cxd4	13. Nc2 O-O	23. Re1 Bg5	33. Qa7 Qh6
4. Nxd4 Nf6	14. Nce3 Be6	24. Nb4 Bd8	34. Ra1 b4
5. Nc3 e5	15. g3 Ne7	25. Be4 Bb6	35. Qd4+ Qf6
6. Ndb5 d6	16. Bg2 Rb8	26. Nd5 f5	36. Raa7 Qxd4
7. Bg5 a6	17. O-O Nxd5	27. Nxb6 Qd8	37. cxd4 Black
8. Na3 b5	18. Bxd5 Kh8	28. Nd7 Qxd7	resigns
9. Bxf6 gxf6	19. a4 Bh6	29. Rxd6 Qe7	
10. Nd5 Bg7	20. axb5 axb5	30. Rd7 Qg5	

The next British candidate for superstardom could well be Matthew Sadler, from Kent. Matthew's career has been fairly quiet for a few years while he's been completing his education, but now he's playing full time and starting to move up the rankings. Sadler seems more studious than players such as Adams, but does he have the ability and determination to reach the top? Only time will tell.

The Stakhanovites

The two leading representatives of the generation now in its early twenties from the former Soviet Union are Vasily Ivanchuk, from the Ukraine, and Boris Gelfand, from Belarus (Byelorussia). Both have been ranked among the top half-dozen in the world for the past few years. As of 1 January 1993 they occupy third and fifth place respectively. What chance do they have of becoming World Champion?

Ivanchuk and Gelfand are two players comparable in age, strength and background. Both attended a chess school from an early age, and worked closely with a top trainer. Both, especially Ivanchuk, are noted for their nervous mannerisms. Both, too, will have learned a lot from the Candidates' Quarter-final defeats at the hands of, respectively, Yusupov and Short.

Gelfand seems a highly competent player, but perhaps lacking in that extra spark to take him to the top. Ivanchuk, if he can overcome his nerves, could well be a credible World Championship challenger in 1996 or 1999 if the following game is anything to go by.

Here, Kasparov suffers a humiliating defeat, with his pieces ending up cowering in the corner. An impressive win for the Ukrainian, who went on to win the tournament by half a point and, temporarily, oust Karpov from the number 2 spot in the world rankings.

Ivanchuk–Kasparov, Linares, 1991. Sicilian Defence

1. e4 c5	11. Nc3 Rc8	21. Ref1 b6	31. Nc8 Bf8
2. Nf3 d6	12. Kh1 h5	22. Ne2 Qh6	32. Qd8 Qg6
3. Bb5+ Nd7	13. a4 h4	23. c5!? Rxc5	33. f5 Qh6
4. d4 Nf6	14. h3 Be7	24. Nc4 Kf8	34. g5 Qh5
5. O–O cxd4	15. b4 a5	25. Nxd6 Be8	35. Rg4 exf5
6. Qxd4 a6	16. b5 Qc7	26. f4 f5	36. Nf4 Qh8
7. Bxd7+ Bxd7	17. Nd2 Qc5	27. exf5 Rxf5	37. Qf6+ Kh7
8. Bg5 h6	18. Qd3 Rg8	28. Rc1! Kg7	38. Rxh4+ Black
9. Bxf6 gxf6	19. Rae1 Qg5	29. g4 Rc5	resigns
10. c4 e6	20. Rg1 Qf4	30. Rxc5 bxc5	

Gelfand, too, is capable of fine chess. This game displays all the hallmarks of the modern grandmaster: opening preparation, calculation and judgement. When the Byelorussian takes the rook on move 24 he has to calculate that he must give up his queen to avoid the draw, and judge that the resulting position is winning owing to Black's exposed king and undeveloped queen side.

Gelfand–Ftáčnik, Debrecen, 1989. Grünfeld Defence

1. d4 Nf6	11. Nxe5 Bxe5	21. Qd2 Bxh2 +	31. Rg3 + Kf7
2. c4 g6	12. Qd2 b6	22. Kh1 Be5	32. Rf1 h5
3. Nc3 d5	13. f4 Bg7	23. Qg5 + Qg6	33. Bxf5 h4
4. cxd5 Nxd5	14. c4 e5	24. Qxe7 Qh6 +	34. Bg6 + Kg8
5. e4 Nxc3	15. O–O f5	25. Kg1 Qe3 +	35. Bh7 + ! Kxh7
6. bxc3 c5	16. Bb2 Qd6	26. Kh1 Qh6 +	36. Rf7 + Kh6
7. Nf3 Bg7	17. Qc3 Re8	27. Kg1 Qe3 +	37. Bc1 + Black
8. Rb1 O–O	18. Bd3 Re7	28. Rf2! Bh2 +	resigns
9. Be2 Nc6	19. exf5 gxf5	29. Kxh2 Qxe7	
10. d5 Ne5	20. fxe5 Bxe5	30. Rf3 Qd6 +	

The Eastern Connection

One of the most fascinating developments on the international chess scene in recent years has been the rise of Asian chess. The Women's World Champion at the time of writing is a Chinese girl, Xie Jun. She took the title off long-time champ Maia Chiburdanidze, of Georgia, in October 1991, just before her twenty-first birthday. She also led the Chinese women's team to the bronze medals in the 1990 and 1992 Olympiads.

The Chinese men have yet to match these achievements, but, although their top players are as yet little known in the West, they still provide tough opposition (for instance sharing 5th to 7th place in the 1990 Olympiad). But one Asian player who has made a name for himself in pretty spectacular fashion is Viswanathan Anand, known to his friends as Vishy. Anand, who was World Junior Champion in 1987 and has the reputation of being the fastest player on the grandmaster circuit, was ranked equal third in the world in January 1993. He lost rather unluckily to Karpov in the 1991 Candidates' Quarter-finals and is certainly a highly plausible contender for the world title in 1996 or 1999. Anand, a modest and popular young man, is already a national hero in his home country. His success will surely see an explosion of interest in the land where the game is believed to have originated about two thousand years ago.

Reggio Emilia, 1991–2, was billed as the strongest tournament ever held. Nine of the ten participants were born in the former Soviet Union, but the odd man out came home the winner. Vishy Anand finished half a point ahead of Kasparov and Gelfand, and a point clear of Karpov. This was the game that did the trick: it's not very often that the World Champion is outcalculated.

Kasparov–Anand, Reggio Emilia, 1991–2. French Defence

1. e4 e6	14. Be5 Nxd3+	27. c3 Kg7	40. Qh2 Qf5
2. d4 d5	15. Rxd3 Qc4	28. Rhh4 Qe5	41. Qg3 Qd7
3. Nd2 c5	16. Nd4 Be4!	29. g3 Qe1+	42. Qe1 b4
4. exd5 Qxd5	17. Re3 Qxa2	30. Kc2 Rcd8	43. cxb4 Qa4+
5. dxc5 Bxc5	18. Bxf6 Bg6!	31. Rd4 Qe5	44. b3 Qa2+
6. Ngf3 Nf6	19. Ra3 Qd5	32. Rhf4 Qc7	45. Kc3 a4
7. Bd3 O–O	20. h4 gxf6	33. Qe3 e5	46. bxa4 Qa3+
8. Qe2 Nbd7	21. h5 Qxd4	34. Rxd8 Rxd8	47. Kc2 Qxa4+
9. Ne4 b6	22. hxg6 hxg6	35. Re4 Rd5	48. Kc3 Qa3+
10. Nxc5 Qxc5	23. Rah3 f5	36. g4 b5	49. Kc2 Rd3
11. Be3 Qc7	24. Rh4 f4	37. g5 Qd6	White resigns
12. Bd4 Bb7	25. Qf3 Rac8	38. f3 a5	
13. O–O–O Nc5	26. Rxf4 Qc5	39. Qe2 Qe6	

Another country which could well produce a future World Champion is, surprisingly, Vietnam. Fourteen-year-old Dao Thien Hai already has a phenomenally high rating of 2560, and John Nunn's unpleasant experience at the hands of a twelve-year-old girl from the same country was recounted in Chapter II.

The one major power yet to make its mark in international chess is Japan, where the development of western chess has been held back by the popularity of Shogi (Japanese Chess) and Go. But another of today's young stars does have a Japanese connection. Frenchman Joël Lautier was born in Canada in 1973, the son of a French father and a Japanese mother. In 1978 he succeeded Anand as World Junior Champion, winning on tie-break from Ivanchuk, Gelfand and Serper (who now represents Uzbekistan), with Adams well down the field. In January 1993 Lautier was ranked 14th in the world, and as a (later maturing) western player can be expected to improve on this. It's not inconceivable that he could one day challenge for the world title. What effect would that have on chess in Japan?

Lautier made the fine score of 9/12 on top board for France in the 1992 Olympiad in Manila. The following game from the match against Moldova (it's a republic of the former USSR somewhere near Romania since you asked) features a remarkable *tour de force* by the white knights.

Lautier–Bologan, Manila Olympiad, 1992. King's Indian Defence

1. c4 Nf6	12. Rd1 Qa5	23. Na4 axb4	34. Ng4 Kg8
2. Nc3 g6	13. a3 bxc4	24. axb4 Ra8	35. Nef6+ Kh8
3. e4 d6	14. Bxc4 d5	25. Bb3 Nf8	36. Ne8 Rxe8
4. d4 Bg7	15. Ba2 Bb7	26. Be5! Qc8	37. Rxe8 Qf7
5. f3 O–O	16. O–O Qc7	27. Rxf6! Bxf6	38. Qe5 h5
6. Be3 Nbd7	17. Rfe1 Rad8	28. Bxf6 Rxf6	39. Nh6 Qd7
7. Nh3 c6	18. e5 Ne8	29. Nc5! Rf7	40. Rxf8+ Kh7
8. Qd2 e5	19. e6 fxe6	30. Ng4 Qc7	41. Nf7 Black
9. Be2 a6	20. Rxe6 Nef6	31. Qb2 Rg7	resigns
10. Nf2 exd4	21. Rde1 Rf7	32. Nf6+ Kf7	
11. Bxd4 b5	22. b4 a5	33. Nce4! h6	

The Young Russians

Two more young players from the former Soviet Union are hot in pursuit of Ivanchuk and Gelfand: Alexei Shirov and Vladimir Kramnik. In January 1993 they occupied seventh and sixth place respectively in the world rankings. Over the last few years they've worked together on a regular basis. Another thing they have in common is that they are two of the tallest grandmasters on the circuit.

Alexei Shirov is a Latvian of Russian descent, fair-haired and gangling, a bundle of nervous energy. Like his compatriot Mikhail Tal he is a highly original attacking player, but sometimes his sense of fantasy gets the better of him. A tendency to stick to dubious opening variations has also led to trouble.

In this game from the last ever Soviet Championship, Shirov gives up material for a mind-bogglingly complicated attack in the style of Tal. Nikolenko, not surprisingly, fails to thread his way through the complications.

Shirov–Nikolenko, USSR Championship, 1991. French Defence

1. e4 e6	9. Nf3 b4	17. Nxd5!? Bxh2+	25. d5 Rg8
2. d4 d5	10. axb4 cxb4	18. Kxh2 Qxd5	26. Qc7+ Kg6
3. Nc3 Nf6	11. f5!? exf5	19. c4! Nxc4	27. dxc6 Bc8
4. e5 Nfd7	12. Nf4 Nb6	20. Ng5+ Kg6	28. Nf4+ Kf6
5. Nce2 c5	13. Bb5 Bb7	21. Bxc4 Qxc4	29. Qd6+ Kf7
6. c3 Nc6	14. e6 Bd6	22. Qf3 Rf8	30. Qd5+ Kf8
7. f4 b5	15. exf7+ Kxf7	23. Qg3! Qxf1	31. Be3 Black
8. a3 a5	16. O–O Re8	24. Ne6+ Kf7	resigns

'He's the only player I have ever seen who does not play worse than I did when I was sixteen. He's a chess-player. Many players, they're not playing chess, they're playing moves.' That was Gary Kasparov, quoted in *New in Chess* magazine about the player he thinks will be his likely successor, Vladimir Kramnik. Kramnik, who was born on 25 June 1975, first came into prominence in the 1992 Olympiad when, as first reserve in the Russian team, he won eight and drew one of his nine games. He will probably still be too young to mount a challenge in 1996. If forced to make a prediction we'd speculate on a losing World Championship match against Kasparov in 1999, followed by victory in 2002.

Kramnik's reputation is that of a positional player; but you'll see from the following game, played when he was fifteen, that he is equally at home in tactical situations. The beautiful point of 18. . . . Bh6! is 19. Qxh6? Rxc2+! and mate next move. You can see why Kasparov has tipped him as the next World Champion.

Brodsky–Kramnik, Herson, 1991. Sicilian Defence

1. e4 c5	4. Nxd4 Nf6	7. Bg5 a6	10. Nd5 f5
2. Nf3 Nc6	5. Nc3 e5	8. Na3 b5	11. Bd3 Be6
3. d4 cxd4	6. Ndb5 d6	9. Bxf6 gxf6	12. Qh5 Rg8!?

13. O–O–O Rxg2	18. Nxb5 Bh6!	23. Bd3 Qb6	28. Qxd4 Ra1+
14. f4 Nd4	19. Rhe1 axb5!	24. Be4 Ra2	29. Kc2 Rxd1
15. Ne3 Rf2	20. Bxb5+ Ke7	25. c4 Bxc4	30. Qxd1 Qa4+
16. exf5 Bxa2	21. Qh4+ f6	26. Kb1 Qa5	31. Kc3 and
17. fxe5 dxe5	22. Qxf2 Bf7	27. Nd5+ Bxd5	White resigns

The Hothouse Flowers

Increasingly large prizes in top-level tournaments, combined with the global recession, high unemployment and difficult economic conditions, especially in Eastern Europe, may well make the idea of hothousing children to become chess champions attractive to ambitious parents. They will also be inspired by the remarkable successes achieved by Gata Kamsky and the Polgár sisters.

The behaviour of Kamsky and his father, as reported in Chapter IV, would not inspire anyone, but behind the paranoia lurks a strong player. Gata Kamsky was born in Siberia of Tartar parentage and won the Soviet Junior Championship at the age of twelve. In 1989 Gata and his father left Leningrad for New York, and the following year, at the age of sixteen, he shared first place with Ivanchuk in the Category 16 Tilburg tournament. Kamsky's results are inconsistent; he's had a couple of real disasters, but at his age there's still plenty of improvement to come.

At Dortmund, 1992, Kamsky only won two games. One was against Kasparov; this was the other. Shirov mistakenly exchanges off his knight (missing 11. . . . Nd6! heading for f5 and g7 to defend the king), and finds he has, literally, caught a Tartar. Gata launches a whirlwind attack to which there is no defence. Alexei does the best he can but at the end Kamsky regains the sacrificed piece with a winning ending.

Kamsky–Shirov, Dortmund, 1992. Queen's Gambit Declined

1. d4 d5	6. Bg5 Be7	11. Bd3 Nxc3	16. Bg6! Be6
2. c4 c6	7. Qc2 g6	12. bxc3 c5	17. Nxd4 Qc8
3. Nf3 Nf6	8. e4 O–O	13. h4 cxd4	18. Qd2! fxg6
4. Nc3 e6	9. e5 Ne4	14. h5 g5	19. hxg6 Kg8
5. cxd5 exd5	10. Bh6 Re8	15. Bxh7+ Kh8	20. Rc1 Nc6

21. Bxg5 Qc7	24. Re1 Rg7	27. Qh8+ Rg8	30. gxf7 Black
22. Bxe7! Rxe7	25. Qh6 Kf8	28. Qf6+ Bf7	resigns
23. Kf1 Rae8	26. Rh4 Nxd4	29. Qxf7+ Qxf7	

The story of the Polgár sisters has been related in brief in Chapter II. With a rating of 2630 at 1 July 1993, sixteen-year-old Judith is the strongest woman player of all time, with only big sister Susan within reach. She has no interest in becoming Women's World Champion; only the ultimate accolade will do. What are her chances? In spite of her achievements so far we'd bet against her ever playing a World Championship match, but we'd love to be proved wrong. Judith's results to date show that, given the right environment, women can play just as well as men, and girls perhaps better than boys.

Like many young players, Judith is at her best when attacking. Here, in a live television game with each player having one hour on the clock, she deliberately walks into a combination, offering her opponent a choice of rooks. The point of her play is revealed on move 28, where if Black defends the bishop with Kf7, 29. Rxe6 is winning. So he has to submit to loss of material, after which the result is never in doubt.

J. Polgár–Knaak, Television Game, Cologne, 1990. French Defence

1. e4 e6	12. cxd4 h5	23. f4 Nxe5	34. Bxc2 Qxc2+
2. d4 d5	13. Qh4 Qc7	24. fxe5! Qxe5+	35. Ke1 Qb1+
3. Nc3 Bb4	14. Bf4 Qa5+	25. Kf2 Qxg7	36. Kd2 Qa2+
4. e5 c5	15. Bd2 Qd8	26. Rg1 Qb2	37. Kd1 Qb1+
5. a3 Bxc3+	16. g4 e5	27. Bb4 f6	38. Ke2 Qc2+
6. bxc3 Ne7	17. dxe5 Bxg4	28. Re1! O–O–O	39. Bd2 Rf8
7. Qg4 Qc7	18. Rg1 Qd7	29. Rxe6 Kb8	40. Qxd5 and
8. Bd3 cxd4	19. f3! Be6	30. Qxf6 Qa2	Black lost
9. Ne2 Qxe5?!	20. Nd4 Nbc6	31. Qd4 Rc8	on time
10. Bf4 Qf6	21. Nxc6 Nxc6	32. Bd2 Ka8	
11. Bg5 Qe5	22. Rxg7 Qc7	33. Be3 Rxc2+	

The Kiddies

And still they come. In the 1990s, masters are getting younger and younger, and children stronger and stronger. The leader of the generation following Kamsky and Judith Polgár is at present Peter Lékó, another Hungarian. Like the Polgárs, Peter is educated at home, only attending school to take exams, and spends five to six hours a day studying chess. He was born in 1979 and became an International Master in 1992 at the age of twelve. Coming into 1993, his results are becoming even more impressive. As we go to press he has already secured two GM norms, and without doubt he will shortly become the youngest grandmaster in the game's history. Certainly Peter is a player who will be making waves in the chess scene as we move into the twenty-first century.

Here's one of the games that helped Peter Lékó become an International Master. If any other twelve-year-old played 3. Bc4 against the Sicilian it would be excused by ignorance, but Peter has a subtle build-up in mind which he executes to perfection.

Lékó–Moiseev, Nettetal, 1992. Sicilian Defence

1. e4 c5	10. Nbd2 Rc8	19. h4 b5	28. f3 f5
2. Nf3 d6	11. Nf1 Ba6	20. h5 b4	29. Bxd3! fxg4
3. Bc4 e6	12. Ng3 Nd7	21. Ne2 bxc3	30. fxg4 Qxg4
4. Qe2 Be7	13. Bc2 Re8	22. bxc3 Nde5	31. Bc2 Bg7
5. O–O Nf6	14. Bd2 Bf8	23. Nh2 c4	32. Rf3 Rf8
6. c3 O–O	15. Rad1 g6	24. d4 Nd3	33. Rg3 Qh4
7. Bb3 b6	16. Bg5 Qc7	25. Rf1 Qa5	34. Bg5 Qh5
8. Re1 Bb7	17. Qd2 Bg7	26. hxg6 hxg6	35. Rh3 Black
9. d3 Nc6	18. Bh6 Bh8	27. Ng4 Qh5	resigns

Here in England we are still producing young talents to follow in the footsteps of Nigel Short and Michael Adams. Londoner Dharshan Kumaran, World Under-Twelve Champion in 1986 and World Under-Sixteen Champion in 1991, is just one of a number of fine prospects. Looking at just one year, there were at least five potential world-class players born between September 1980 and August 1981:

Adam Hunt, from Oxford, Karl Mah, from Essex, Joseph Conlon, from Reading, and twins Richard and Nicholas Pert,[1] from Ipswich.

In the 1992 World Junior Championships, English players took three medals. It was particularly pleasing to see the girls doing well: Harriet Hunt (Adam's sister) took the bronze medal in the Under-Fourteen Girls' Championship and Ruth Sheldon, from Manchester, won the silver medal in the Under-Twelve Girls' Championship. An even younger girl, Siobhan O'Neill, from Cambridgeshire, is already doing well against adult opposition at the age of seven. Siobhan is the oldest of three sisters and educated at home. Sounds familiar?

England's 1992 gold medallist was Luke McShane, from London, who won the World Under-Ten Boys' Championship at the age of eight against opponents up to two years older. Fittingly, we leave the last words in the book to Luke.

Meanwhile, take a look at the last-round game which won Luke the World Under-Ten title. Luke chooses a pawn sacrifice prepared with his coach, GM Daniel King, and his Azerbaijani opponent rapidly finds himself out of his depth.

Kuliev–McShane, World Under-Ten Championship (Boys'), Duisburg, 1992. King's Indian Defence

1. d4 Nf6	9. Be2 Qa5	17. Nf3? Neg4+!	25. Kf1 Rxd5!
2. c4 g6	10. Be3 Nb4	18. hxg4 Nxg4+	26. b4 Rxd1+
3. Nc3 Bg7	11. a3 Rd8	19. Kg1 Nxe3	27. Bxd1 Qxc4+
4. e4 d6	12. Qb1 Nc6	20. Qc1 Ng4	28. Be2 Qxe4
5. f3 O-O	13. Kf2 Qe5	21. Nd5 Bf8	29. Ne1 Be6
6. Be3 c5	14. f4 Qb8	22. Qg5 Qd6	30. Bf3 Qe3
7. dxc5 dxc5	15. h3 e5	23. Qh4 h5	31. Bxb7 Bc4+
8. Bxc5 Nc6	16. fxe5 Nxe5	24. Rd1 Qc5+	White resigns

[1] The 1993 European Boys' Under-12 bronze medallist.

VIII *The End?*

'The Eighth Square at last!' she cried ... 'Oh how glad I am to get here! And what *is* this on my head?'

Lewis Carroll, Through the Looking Glass

The Turk

Gary Kasparov recently admitted to having lost some informal blitz games against something called FRITZ 2, a piece of computer software available for under £80. Things have come a long way since 1968, when David Levy, a Scottish International Master, first made his famous bet that he could beat any chess computer in the world. Voltaire said that chess 'reflects most honour on human wit'. Perhaps these days the developers and programmers of the iron monsters deserve as much honour as that accredited to Kasparov and Fischer.

In fact the history of chess machines goes back over two hundred years. The first chess automaton was built as long ago as 1769. It revolutionized the world of magic, inspired the invention of Cartwright's power mill and indirectly furthered the career of Edgar Allan Poe. The astounding history of The Turk and its successors is related in this chapter.

Read also about the world's first genuine chess-playing machine, created, would you believe it, back in 1890, and about how Britain's leading chess-players helped win the Second World War and, in so doing, helped sow the seeds of the computer revolution.

Finally, we feature the triumphs and disasters of today's silicon superstars, from programs running on the world's most powerful computers to those micro marvels without which any civilized home is assuredly incomplete.

♛

The first chess automaton, known as The Turk, was designed by the Hungarian inventor and engineer Wolfgang von Kempelen in 1769 to entertain the Empress Maria Theresa. The empress and her court saw a figure dressed in Turkish costume, slightly larger than life, seated at a wooden cabinet. The figure would take on all-comers at chess, and beat them, perform the knight's tour starting from any square designated by one of the audience, and finally answer questions by pointing to letters on a board. The Turk was the first of the great cabinet illusions which have delighted audiences at magic shows for the past two hundred years.

♛

Between 1781 and 1838 The Turk toured Europe and then, in the ownership of Johann Nepomuk Maelzel, of metronome fame, America, amazing and delighting its opponents, who included many celebrities.

♛

Ben Franklin played The Turk at the Café de la Régence in Paris. According to his grandson he was 'pleased with the Automaton'.

♛

The Revd Edmund Cartwright, an obscure country clergyman and poet, visited The Turk in London. Inspired by the thought that, if it were possible to construct a machine to play chess, a weaving mill would present few problems, he set about creating his power loom, changing the face of the clothing industry and playing a major part in the Industrial Revolution.

♛

Napoleon played against The Turk in 1809. As we have seen in Chapter I, the general was one of the world's worst losers, and, true to form, he tried to cheat the machine by making illegal moves. According to some versions of the story he also tried the effect of placing an enormous magnet on the board, or covering the android's head with a shawl. Despite these efforts he was still soundly beaten, and, it is reported, threw the chessmen off the board and stormed out of the room shouting 'Bagatelle.'

♛

Amongst The Turk's visitors in America was a young journalist named Edgar Allan Poe who in 1836 published an essay speculating, for the most part correctly, on how the machine worked.[1] This has been claimed by his biographers to be the first example in Poe's writings of purely logical reasoning, and may have encouraged his later forays into detective fiction.

♛

The Turk was finally retired to the Chinese Museum in Philadelphia, where it perished in a fire in 1854.

---

[1] If you haven't already guessed: it had a man inside.

The next celebrated chess automaton was built by an Englishman, Charles Alfred Hooper, in the 1860s, and was later to be known as Ajeeb. It was first exhibited in 1868 at the Polytechnic in Regent Street.

A few months later the Automaton was moved to Crystal Palace, where it remained for another seven years. It was operated either by Hooper or his son. The son, who had aspirations to become a chess-master, had to give up operating the Automaton when he became too fat to enter the machine.

One of the Crystal Palace Automaton's most persistent opponents was the artist and critic John Ruskin, who wrote to a friend in 1874: 'I shall play some games of chess with the automaton chessplayer. I get quite fond of him, and he gives me the most lovely lessons in chess. I say I shall play him some games, for I never keep him waiting for moves and he crushes me down steadily.'

In January 1876 the Automaton moved to the Royal Aquarium in Westminster, London. Among its visitors there were the Prince (later King Edward VII) and Princess of Wales, and Prince Leopold, who, the previous year, had been President of the Oxford University Chess Club.

For thirty years from 1885 to 1915 the original Crystal Palace Ajeeb (there was by now at least one imitation) was exhibited at the Eden Musée, New York's answer to Madame Tussaud's. In 1889 Hooper decided to hire masters to operate his automaton. The most famous of these was the brilliant and tragic Harry Nelson Pillsbury. It has often been speculated whether operating Ajeeb contributed to Pillsbury's early death.

One of Ajeeb's New York operators, Peter J. Hill, was twice attacked by dissatisfied customers. On one occasion Ajeeb was stabbed by a lady with a hatpin, who was clearly upset at just having had her bishop taken. Even more painful: when an angry Westerner with a six-gun shot the Automaton, wounding Hill in the shoulder.

♛

Another operator had the habit of falling asleep during games. When this happened a flunky from the museum was called in to make repairs. This consisted of banging loudly until the operator woke up again.

♛

Among the celebrities who played Ajeeb at the Eden Musée were Admiral Dewey, Teddy Roosevelt, Houdini, Sarah Bernhardt and O. Henry.

♛

Twenty years after the closure of the Eden Musée, Ajeeb was bought by Frank Frain and Jesse Hanson, who had been its last draughts operator at the museum; and it toured the country playing draughts. The following year they signed a contract with RCA to advertise Magic Brain radios, and Ajeeb's turbaned head was transformed into a Magic Brain.

♛

Ajeeb was last heard of dumped in a Cadillac in a parking lot in 1943.

♛

The third of the famous chess automata (there were many others), called Mephisto, was constructed by Charles Godfrey Gumpel, a manufacturer of artificial limbs and surgical appliances, and first exhibited in 1878. Unlike Ajeeb and The Turk, the operator was not hidden inside the machine but in an adjacent room. The moves were transmitted to the operator electro-mechanically. The operator when it was displayed in London was Isidor Gunsberg, a young Hungarian who was later to put up a good show in a World Championship match against Wilhelm Steinitz.

♛

In August 1878 Mephisto entered the Counties Chess Association Knock-out Handicap Tournament. In the first round it was paired against the Revd George Alcock MacDonnell,[1] who promptly with-

[1] See 'The Holy'.

drew from the event in protest – not because he refused to play against the Devil, but for more practical reasons. There was no guarantee that the operator could not consult books or move the pieces around, or indeed that he would be the same player in every game. Mephisto had no difficulty in winning the tournament, our favourite rabbit G. H. D. Gossip being amongst the also-rans.

In 1879 Mephisto founded his own chess club, and from 1881 to 1890 edited a chess column in a popular scientific magazine called *Knowledge*.

Mephisto was exhibited in London and Brighton sporadically for ten years after its construction, but public interest gradually waned. Although it was a much more impressive device than The Turk or Ajeeb, Gumpel was not so much of a showman as Maelzel or Hooper. It made its last appearance at the 1889 Paris Exposition, when the operator was the Franco-Polish master Jean Taubenhaus.

The concept of a chess-playing machine has always proved fascinating to those in the forefront of computer development. In 1864 the computer pioneer Charles Babbage considered using his Analytical Engine, a prototype computer which, sadly, he was never able to develop very far, to play chess.

The first genuine chess-playing robot was invented, believe it or not, back in 1890. This was a machine designed to play the ending of king and rook against king, and was invented, appropriately, by a Spaniard named Leonardo Torres y Quevedo (*torre* is the Spanish word for rook). Among his other inventions were a machine for solving algebraic equations and the Astro-Torres airship, which was used by France in the First World War. The Torres machine, of course, pre-dated the electrical age and consisted of a series of pulleys, weights and wires, which caused moves to be made on a small chessboard according to a simple algorithm. It was first demonstrated to the public at the Sorbonne in 1915 and can be seen today, still in working order, at the Polytechnic Museum in Madrid.

In the early months of the Second World War the Government Code and Cipher School was set up at Bletchley Park to break the machine-generated German Enigma codes. Many of the best brains in the country were recruited, including the best young British chess-players. Two of the earliest recruits were the late Hugh Alexander and Stuart (now Sir Stuart) Milner-Barry, and they were later to be joined by Harry Golombek. Among the mathematicians at Bletchley Park were Donald Michie, whom we shall meet again later in the chapter, and Alan Turing. Turing, who was to die tragically and far too young, was the most brilliant of the lot. He could well be described as the father of the modern electronic computer, as the machine he designed to break the Enigma codes was in effect the prototype of the computers we know and love today. But, genius though he was, Turing was, as we have seen in Chapter I, a complete rabbit at chess. The success of the Bletchley Park team was recognized by no less a person than Churchill himself, who maintained that they played a major part in winning the war.

In the late 1940s both Alan Turing and Donald Michie produced sets of instructions which simulated computer chess, called respectively TUROCHAMP and MACHIAVELLI. Turing started to program both TUROCHAMP and MACHIAVELLI but never completed the task. In 1951, though, TUROCHAMP 'played' a game against Alick Glennie, a Manchester University student. TUROCHAMP had White and was doing well until blundering on move 29.

TUROCHAMP–Glennie, Manchester, 1951. Three Knights' Opening

1. e4 e5	9. gxf3 Bh5	17. Bb5 Nxb7	25. Bb3 Qa6
2. Nc3 Nf6	10. Bb5 + c6	18. O–O–O Nc5	26. Bc4 Bh5
3. d4 Bb4	11. dxc6 O–O	19. Bc6 Rfc8	27. Rg3 Qa4
4. Nf3 d6	12. cxb7 Rb8	20. Bd5 Bxc3	28. Bxb5 Qxb5
5. Bd2 Nc6	13. Ba6 Qa5	21. Bxc3 Qxa4	29. Qxd6? Rd8
6. d5 Nd4	14. Qe2 Nd7	22. Kd2 Ne6	White resigns
7. h4 Bg4	15. Rg1 Nc5	23. Rg4 Nd4	
8. a4 Nxf3 +	16. Rg5 Bg6	24. Qd3 Nb5	

The boffins at the Los Alamos Scientific Laboratory in New Mexico spent most of their time developing the atomic bomb, but in 1956 they came up with a rather more constructive project. They programmed their MANIAC computer (not an inappropriate name considering its main function) to play a game of mini-chess with no bishops on a 6 × 6 board. A strong player gave it queen odds and won but a young woman who had just been taught chess contrived to lose to it, thus going down in history as the first human to lose to a computer at chess.

The first genuine chess-playing program was written in 1958 by an American named Alex Bernstein. Here it takes on a strongish human opponent and soon runs into trouble, dropping its queen.

IBM 704 (Bernstein's program)–Human. Bishop's Opening

1. e4 e5	7. O–O d5	13. Ng5 Qg6	19. g3 exd1 = Q
2. Bc4 b6	8. exd5 cxd5	14. Nh3 e3	20. Nxd1 Qc2
3. d3 Nf6	9. Bb5 + Nc6	15. f3 Bc5	21. b3 Rad8
4. Bg5 Bb7	10. c4 dxc4	16. Re1 O–O	22. h4? Rxd1
5. Bxf6 Qxf6	11. Bxc6 + Qxc6	17. Nc3? e2 +	White resigns
6. Nf3 c6	12. dxc4 e4	18. Nf2 Bxf3	

In 1966–7 a four-game match was played between Russian and American computers. The Soviet program won two games and conceded draws in favourable positions in the others. Here's one of the wins:

USSR Program–USA Program. Three Knights' Opening

1. e4 e5	6. dxe5 Bxe5	11. Qd5 Ne6	16. Rxg7 c6
2. Nf3 Nc6	7. f4 Bxc3 +	12. f5 Ng5	17. Qd6 Rxf5
3. Nc3 Bc5	8. bxc3 Nf6	13. h4 f6	18. Rg8 + Rf8
4. Nxe5 Nxe5	9. e5 Ne4	14. hxg5 fxg5	19. Qxf8 mate
5. d4 Bd6	10. Qd3 Nc5	15. Rxh7 Rf8	

The first computer to enter a tournament was MAC HACK VI, programmed by Richard Greenblatt, a student at Massachusetts

Institute of Technology. Its first tournament was in February 1967, where it scored one draw from five games. The following month it managed one win from five games, scoring its first victory with a queen sacrifice in the style of Morphy.

MAC HACK VI–Human, Massachusetts State Championship, 1967. Sicilian Defence

1. e4 c5	7. Bf4 e5	13. Bh4 Bg7	19. Nxe5 Be6
2. d4 cxd4	8. Bg3 a6	14. Nd5 Nxe4	20. Qxc6 + Rxc6
3. Qxd4 Nc6	9. O–O–O b5	15. Nc7 + Qxc7	21. Rd8 mate
4. Qd3 Nf6	10. a4 Bh6 +	16. Qxc7 Nc5	
5. Nc3 g6	11. Kb1 b4	17. Qd6 Bf8	
6. Nf3 d6	12. Qxd6 Bd7	18. Qd5 Rc8	

MAC continued to play in tournaments and hacked quite a few more opponents before retiring from competitive chess in the early 1970s. A few years later he provided the opposition for Bobby Fischer's last published games before his comeback, which show how an early computer program compared with a galactic megastar of the (almost) human variety.

Fischer–MAC HACK, Cambridge, 1977. King's Gambit

1. e4 e5	7. O–O Nxd5	13. dxe5 c6	19. Rc1 Kg7
2. f4 exf4	8. Nxd5 Bd6	14. Bxf4 Qg7	20. Rg3 Rh8
3. Bc4 d5	9. d4 g5	15. Nf6 + Kh8	21. Qh6 mate
4. Bxd5 Nf6	10. Nxg5 Qxg5	16. Qh5 Rd8	
5. Nc3 Bb4	11. e5 Bh3	17. Qxh3 Na6	
6. Nf3 O–O	12. Rf2 Bxe5	18. Rf3 Qg6	

♛

'COMPUTER LOSES GAME IN KING-SIZE BLUNDER' trumpeted the *New York Times* after the first round of the first-ever computer chess tournament in 1970. One of the programs, named MARSLAND after its programmer, had developed a bug which caused it to choose fairly randomly between its best and worst moves. Its opponent in this game was J. BIIT (Just Because It Is There), programmed by Hans Berliner, a man destined to play a large part in the history of computer chess.

MARSLAND—J. BIIT, New York, 1970. Queen's Pawn Game

1. c4 Nf6	4. Nf3 d5	7. Bd2 Bxd2 +	White resigns
2. d4 e6	5. Ne5 dxc4	8. Kxd2?? Nxe5	
3. Qd3 Nc6	6. Qxc4 Bb4 +	9. Qc5??? Ne4 +	

The 1971 United States Computer Championship witnessed what USCF Computer Chess Committee Chairman David Welsh has described as an 'all-time classic of computer ineptitude'. Strangely enough, it also showed how far ahead some of the early programs were capable of calculating. On the morning of this game, Ed Kozdrowicki of Bell Telephone Laboratories had joined the consortium betting that David Levy would lose to a computer by 1978.

Here is Kozdrowicki's program, COKO III, a queen up after twenty-seven moves against GENIE. COKO has seen a forced mate so kicks off with . . .

28. c5 + Kxc5 29. Qd4 + Kb5 30. Kd1 + Ka5 31. b4 + Ka4 32. Qc3 Red8 + 33. Kc2 Rd2 + GENIE sacs its rooks to delay the inevitable. 34. Kxd2 Rd8 + 35. Kc2 Rd2 + 36. Qxd2 Ka3 37. Qc3 + Kxa2. White has a choice of two mates in one but now COKO starts clowning around. 38. Kc1? f5 39. Kc2?? f4 40. Kc1??? g4 41. Kc2???? f3 42. Kc1????? fxg2 43. Kc2?????? gxh1 = Q COKO's last chance for mate. 44. Kc1??????? Qxf1 + 45. Kd2 Qxf2 + 46. Kc1 Qg1 + 47. Kc2 Qxh2 + 48. Kc1 Qh1 + 49. Kc2 Qb1 + 50. Kd2 g3 51. Qc4 + Qb3 52. Qxb3 + Kxb3 53. e4 Kxb4 54. e5 g2. Aladdin rubs his magic lamp and GENIE produces a new queen. COKO's

masters had had enough and resigned on its behalf at this point. Observers reported that Kozdrowicki was heard mumbling something about a 'dam' fool bet'[1] after the game.

You remember what happened to poor Vlastimil Hort in his Candidates' Match against Spassky? In a winning position he 'froze' and lost on time. You might think that this couldn't happen to a computer, but you'd be wrong.

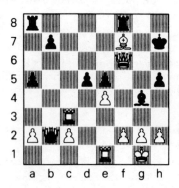

Here's TECH II with White against something called RIBBIT, again in the 1974 US Computer Championship. TECH II has forty-five minutes to go to the time control and, amongst other goodies, a simple mate in two. But TECH II fell alseep and RIBBIT unsportingly claimed a win on time.

The First European Computer Chess Championship, held in Amsterdam in 1976, matched ORWELL, from England, against TELL, from Switzerland. ORWELL, two rooks up, pushed a pawn to the end of the board and ... left it there. TELL had no objection to this so arbiter David Levy decided that the game should continue. George pushed another pawn to the eighth rank, again left it there, and finally mated William with his two rooks.

---

[1]See page 335 for how Kozdrowicki lost his bet. Last time we heard, he hadn't paid up.

The first computer to play in the US Open was one SNEAKY PETE, in 1977. It played very weakly and was annihilated in the first few rounds. Then it came up against an inexperienced young woman player. The word soon spread that SNEAKY PETE was winning and crowds gathered at the board. His opponent, in desperation, set a trap. Pete fell headlong into it and his victorious opponent slammed down the winning move shouting, 'Games for people, not machines! Games for people, not machines!'

Playing against human opposition in the 1982 US Open, CHAOS made a valiant attempt to emulate grandmaster Sämisch,[1] losing four games on time, one of them on move 15. The time control was fifty moves in two hours, so it had another thirty-six moves to go.

OK, it's time to stop sniggering and look at some of the successes of the silicon stars of the sixties and seventies.

In the first diagram old MAC HACK VI, in one of its early tournaments, found a winning combination which some watching US masters apparently failed to spot. Can you find the winning move for black?

The second diagram is from a 1974 World Championship game between CHAOS and CHESS 4.0. Here, white unleashed the first ever positional sacrifice played by a computer. Over to you, maestro.

Finally, here's a position from the Second World Computer Chess Championship, held in Toronto in 1977. The Soviet program KAISSA, black against DUCHESS, from Duke University, caused a sensation by giving up a rook with Re8. What had it seen that had been missed by the masters in the audience?

Don't be outwitted by a computer. Work out your own solutions before looking up the answers at the end of the chapter.

♕

In February 1977, CHESS 4.5 became the first machine (discounting Mephisto) to win a tournament against humans when it took the Minnesota Open with five wins and one loss. How it spent its prize money is not recorded. Later in 1977, CHESS 4.6 became the first computer to beat a grandmaster when taking a five-minute game off English grandmaster Michael Stean.

CHESS 4.6–Stean, Blitz Game, 1977. Owen's Defence

1. e4 b6	11. Rad1 Rd8	22. Ncxe4 Rxf2	33. Qg4 Bxe4
2. d4 Bb7	12. Qc4 Ng6	23. Rxd6[1] Qxd6	34. Qxe6+ Kh8
3. Nc3 c5	13. Rfe1 Be7	24. Nxd6 Rxg2	35. Qxe4 Rf6
4. dxc5 bxc5	14. Qb3 Qc6	25. Nge4 Rg4	36. Qe5 Rb6
5. Be3 d6	15. Kh1 O–O	26. c4 Nf5	37. Qxc5 Rxb3
6. Bb5+ Nd7	16. Bg5 Ba8	27. h3 Ng3+	38. Qc8+ Kh7
7. Nf3 e6	17. Bxe7 Nxe7	28. Kh2 Rxe4	and Black
8. O–O a6	18. a4 Rb8	29. Qf2 h6	resigns
9. Bxd7+	19. Qa2 Rb4	30. Nxe4 Nxe4	
Qxd7	20. b3 f5	31. Qf3 Rb8	
10. Qd3 Ne7	21. Ng5 fxe4	32. Rxe4 Rf8	

In deference to Stean, we must point out that his opponent was, relatively speaking, a very much stronger player at blitz speed than at tournament speed.

The following year, CHESS 4.6 took the Twin City Open with 5/5, and followed up with a win in a simul against grandmaster Walter Browne.

♛

1978 saw the famous challenge match between CHESS 4.7, as it had now become, and international master David Levy. This was the culmination of the first stage of the 'Levy bet'. Among the academics on the side of the machines was Donald Michie, whom you will remember from Bletchley Park days. In the first game Levy weakened his king's side, allowing CHESS 4.7 a stunning sacrifice. Defending desperately, Levy managed to reach an ending three pawns down, which he came close to winning! In the next two games, the human representative took no chances, then, convinced that he could win whenever he wanted, tried a risky opening in game 4. This is what happened:

[1] 'Bloody iron monster!' exclaimed the normally equable Stean at this point.

CHESS 4.7–Levy, Challenge Match, 1978. Greco Counter Gambit

1. e4 e5	13. g4 Nxd3+	28. Rae1 Rg3+	43. Rd8+ Kf7
2. Nf3 f5	14. cxd3 Bc5	29. Kf2 Rhh3	44. Rd7+ Kf8
3. exf5 e4	15. O–O h5	30. Re3 Ba6	45. Rxd4 Rb2
4. Ne5 Nf6	16. Na4 Bd4	31. Ne2 Bxe2	46. Kf3 Bc5
5. Ng4 d5	17. Be3 Be5	32. R1xe2 c5	47. Rd8+ Ke7
6. Nxf6+	18. d4 Bd6	33. f4 Rxe3	48. Bh4+ Kf7
Qxf6	19. h3 b6	34. Rxe3 Rh4	49. g5 g6
7. Qh5+	20. Rfe1 Bd7	35. Kg3 Rh1	50. Rd7+ Kf8
Qf7	21. Nc3 hxg4	36. Bf2 Rd1	51. fxg6 Rxa2
8. Qxf7+	22. hxg4 Rh4	37. Ra3 cxd4	52. f5 Ra3+
Kxf7	23. f3 Rah8	38. Rxa7+ Kf8	53. Kg4 Ra4+
9. Nc3 c6	24. Kf1 Bg3	39. Rd7 Rd3+	54. Kh5 Rd4
10. d3 exd3	25. Re2 Bc8	40. Kg2 Bc5	55. Rc7 Be7
11. Bxd3 Nd7	26. Kg2 Bd6	41. Rxd5 Rd2	56. f6 Black
12. Bf4 Nc5	27. Bg1 Rh3	42. b4 Bxb4	resigns

Levy upheld the honour of the human race by winning the fifth game to clinch his bet.

The first of the 1980s superstars was BELLE, from Bell Telephone Laboratories. Running on specially designed hardware it became computer World Champion in 1980, shared second place in the 1982 US Speed Chess Championship and defeated several masters in the 1983 US Open. Here's one of the games from that event. Black had a USCF rating of 2321 (about a 209 BCF grading).

BELLE–Radke, US Open, Pasadena, 1983. Pirc Defence

1. e4 d6	6. e5 Ng4	11. Ne4 f5	16. O–O–O bxc5
2. d4 Nf6	7. dxc5 dxe5	12. exf6 exf6	17. Bb5 Ne5
3. Nc3 g6	8. Qxd8+ Kxd8	13. Nd6 Ke7	18. Nxe5 fxe5
4. f4 Bg7	9. h3 Nh6	14. Be3 b6	19. Rhf1 Black
5. Nf3 c5	10. fxe5 Nd7	15. Bc4 g5	resigns

Over the past decade. BELLE has been spending her(?) spare time analysing all possible five-man endings. According to Reuben Fine's endgame bible *Basic Chess Endings*, queen against two bishops or two knights is a draw. Not any more it isn't. BELLE has demonstrated that in most positions the queen wins. Many queen and pawn versus queen endings that were thought to be drawn have also been shown to be won. What's more, she'll tell you how many moves the win takes with best play. For instance, the longest win with queen against two bishops is seventy moves (tough luck if you draw under the fifty-move rule). The fruits of BELLE's analysis have recently been made available on two CD-ROMs. Computer buffs will be interested to know that BELLE's programmer, Ken Thompson, is also the brains behind the UNIX operating system.

In 1983 BELLE lost its World Champion title to CRAY BLITZ, running on what was then the world's fastest computer. CRAY BLITZ had already won the Mississippi State Closed Championship with a score of 5/5, achieving a provisional master rating.

The next cybernetic candidate to attempt to conquer humankind over the chessboard was launched in 1985. Named HITECH, it emanates from Carnegie–Mellon University, where its programming team is led by Dr Hans Berliner, and reached a rating of about 2350, close to international master standard. Berliner, a former World Correspondence Chess Champion, had previously written programs called J. BIIT, which we have met before, and PATSOC (Plays A Terrible Sort Of Chess). In its first tournament against human opposition it beat two masters and drew with a grandmaster.

In June 1986 HITECH took on international woman grandmaster Dr Jana Miles in a charity match. The mighty monster had little difficulty in winning both games.

HITECH–Miles, London, 1986. Caro-Kann Defence

1. e4 c6	7. Bb5 + Bd7	13. Qc5 Rc8	19. Rad1 Qf6
2. d4 d5	8. Bxh6 Bxh6	14. O–O e6	20. d5 Bd6
3. Nc3 g6	9. Qe2 O–O	15. Nb6 Rc7	21. b4 a5
4. h3 Bg7	10. Nxd5 Bxb5	16. Qa3 Bf4	22. Qxa5 Qc3
5. Nf3 Nh6	11. Qxb5 Nc6	17. Rfe1 Ne7	23. a3 exd5
6. exd5 cxd5	12. c3 a6	18. c4 Nf5	24. Nxd5 Qxc4

25. Nxc7 Bxc7	28. Red1 b6	31. Kf1 Qh1+	34. Qf6 Black
26. Qc5 Qf4	29. Qxb6 Nh4	32. Ke2 Re8+	resigns
27. Rd7 Bb8	30. Nxh4 Qh2+	33. Kf3 Qh2	

In September 1988, HITECH became the first computer to win a match against a grandmaster when it trounced veteran American GM and Golden Gloves star Arnold Denker 3½–½. Here's the last game.

HITECH–Denker, 4th Match Game, New York, 1988. Sicilian Defence

1. e4 c5	7. Nc3 Qd8	13. Qc4 Nf8	19. Nb5 Qb4
2. c3 d5	8. Bc4 Bg7	14. Nxg7+ Kd8	20. d5! Qxb5
3. exd5 Qxd5	9. Qa4+ Nbd7	15. O–O Bd7	21. dxc6 Qxg5
4. d4 Nf6	10. Bxf7+! Kxf7	16. Re1 Qd6	22. cxd7 N6xd7
5. Nf3 cxd4	11. Ng5+ Ke8	17. Bg5 Rc8	23. Rac1 Black
6. cxd4 g6	12. Ne6 Qb6	18. Qf7 Rc6	resigns

The most recent mainframe megastar to emerge goes by the name of DEEP THOUGHT and comes, like HITECH, from Carnegie–Mellon University in Pittsburgh. Its development team is led by Feng-Hsiung Hsu (a.k.a. Crazy Bird, which is what his name means in Chinese). DT made its tournament début in May 1988. In November of that year it shared first place with Tony Miles in the Software Toolworks Chess Championship in Long Beach, California, scoring 6½/8. Its most illustrious victim, who thus acquired the dubious distinction of becoming the first active grandmaster to lose to a computer under tournament conditions, was none other than the Great Dane, Bent Larsen.

Larsen–DEEP THOUGHT, Long Beach, 1988. English Opening

1. c4 e5	10. Qb3 b6	19. Bb2 Bg6	28. Rhg1 c5
2. g3 Nf6	11. Qa4 O–O	20. Nc4 Nd5	29. fxg4 Nxg4
3. Bg2 c6	12. Nc3 b5	21. O–O–O N7f6	30. Bxg7 Rg6!
4. Nf3 e4	13. Qc2 Bxe3	22. Bh3 Bf5	31. Qd2 Rd7
5. Nd4 d5	14. dxe3 Re8	23. Bxf5 Qxf5	32. Rxg4 Rxg4
6. cxd5 Qxd5	15. a4 b4	24. f3 h5	33. Ne5 Nxe3
7. Nc2 Qh5	16. Nb1 Nbd7	25. Bd4 Rd7	34. Qxd7 Nxd1+
8. h4 Bf5	17. Nd2 Re6	26. Kb2 Rc7	35. Qxd1 Rg3!
9. Ne3 Bc5	18. b3 Rd8	27. g4 hxg4	36. Qd6 Kxg7

37. Nd7 Re3	39. Nf8+ Kh8	41. Ng6+ fxg6	43. Qh7+ Kf6
38. Qh2 Kh7	40. h5 Qd5	42. hxg6+ Kg7	White resigns

DT's FIDE rating for the tournament was 2601, which would have been enough for a GM norm had it played nine games instead of eight and three rather than two grandmasters. In 1989 DEEP THOUGHT took the gold medal in the sixth World Computer Championship with a 100 per cent score, including wins against HITECH and CRAY BLITZ. Later in the same year, DT finally met its match when it came up against a certain G. Kasparov and was twice decisively beaten. Here's the second game.

Kasparov–DEEP THOUGHT, New York, 1989. Queen's Gambit Accepted

1. d4 d5	11. gxf3 Bxf3	21. Ke2 cxd5	31. Qb4 Bd6
2. c4 dxc4	12. Bxc4 Qd6	22. Qg4 Be7	32. Rxd6 Nxd6
3. e4 Nc6	13. Nb5 Qf6	23. Rhc1 Kf8	33. Rb8+ Rxb8
4. Nf3 Bg4	14. Qc5 Qb6	24. Rc7 Bd6	34. Qxb8+ Kh7
5. d5 Ne5	15. Qa3 e6	25. Rb7 Nf6	35. Qxd6 Rc8
6. Nc3 c6	16. Nc7+! Qxc7	26. Qa4 a5	36. a4 Rc4
7. Bf4 Ng6	17. Bb5+ Qc6	27. Rc1 h6	37. Qd7 Black
8. Be3 cxd5	18. Bxc6+ bxc6	28. Rc6 Ne8	resigns
9. exd5 Ne5	19. Bc5 Bxc5	29. b4 Bxh2	
10. Qd4 Nxf3+	20. Qxf3 Bb4+	30. bxa5 Kg8	

After a 4–0 demolition job on David Levy, DT found itself up against another human megabrain in A. Karpov. The mighty monster showed better form in this game, missing a draw in a rook ending before going down to an honourable defeat.

As we go to press, a new and much faster version of DEEP THOUGHT, called DEEP BLUE, has just made its first appearance. Its designers claimed it would be able to see two moves further ahead than DEEP THOUGHT, giving it enough strength to beat Kasparov. DB's début proved rather disappointing: a 2½–1½ loss to its predecessor's victim, Bent Larsen.

A few years ago computer-chess guru David Levy put forward 2014 as the date by which a computer would surpass all humans. But others in the business are optimistic that we will see the first 3000-rated program by the turn of the century. Levy's prediction seems more realistic to us. Brute force alone may not be enough to beat a strong grandmaster on a regular basis: computers will need to brush up their positional and endgame play to reach the summit.

Mainframe computers are continuing to break down barriers in endgame theory. BELLE has now analysed out all five-man endings. Soon, we'll see the same thing happening to six-man positions, seven-man . . . thirty-two man?! A start on six-man endings has been made by Lewis Stiller, of Johns Hopkins University in Baltimore. Using a computer at Los Alamos, Stiller proved that king, rook and bishop can defeat king and two knights in 223 moves from the optimum defensive position.

While developments in the mainframe world have been relatively quiet since the emergence of DEEP THOUGHT, micros have been getting stronger and stronger. Our friend MEPHISTO has been king of the micros for some years, but coming into 1993 its place at the top of the pile is being challenged. You'll meet this ending about once a millennium.

Here's the top-of-range MEPHISTO LYON 68030, playing at 50 MHz, rather than the commercially available 36 MHz, taking the black pieces against the solid Dutch GM Gena Sosonko.

Sosonko–MEPHISTO LYON 68030, Aegon Computers *v.* Humans Tournament, Holland, 1991. Queen's Gambit Accepted

1. d4 d5	8. d5 Ne5	15. Qa4+ c6	22. Qe8+ Kc7
2. Nf3 Nf6	9. Bf4 Bxf3	16. Qxc4 O–O–O	23. Rf1 a6
3. c4 dxc4	10. gxf3 Ng6	17. Rd1 Rxd1+	24. h3 g6
4. Qa4+ Nc6	11. Bg3 e5	18. Kxd1 Qf6	25. a3 Qf6
5. Nc3 Nd5	12. dxe6 Qe7	19. Ke2 Nxf4+	26. Rc1 Bc5
6. e4 Nb6	13. f4 fxe6	20. Bxf4 Qxf4	White resigns
7. Qd1 Bg4	14. Bxc4 Nxc4	21. Qxe6+ Kb8	

Computers playing at well over 200 BCF/2200 ELO strength are now available for a few hundred pounds. PC owners can buy software of the same strength for under £100. And at blitz chess these programs are even stronger, aproaching grandmaster level. One of the best is CHESS GENIUS, programmed by Mephisto's Richard Lang. At the 1993 King's Head Rapidplay, for instance, CG achieved a 2500 (GM strength result). IM Keith Arkell is one of England's best blitz players, but could only manage two draws in a series of four five-minute games.

Rather more expensive is a combination of software and hardware called CHESS MACHINE, potentially even stronger. Watch it in action in a forty-five minutes per player tournament against a Bulgarian IM.

CHESS MACHINE–Danailov, Oviedo, 1992. Philidor Defence

1. d4 d6	9. h3 b6	17. Ng5! bxc4	25. Rxd6 Qe7
2. e4 Nf6	10. Rd1 a6	18. Qxc4 Rf8	26. Qxa8 h6
3. Nc3 e5	11. Be3 Bb7	19. Rxa8 Bxa8	27. Re6 Qg7
4. Nf3 Nbd7	12. dxe5 dxe5	20. Bxf8 Nxf8	28. Nf3 Kh7
5. Bc4 Be7	13. Nh4 g6	21. Nb5 Qb7	29. Rxc6 Black
6. O–O O–O	14. Bh6 Rfd8	22. Qxf7+ Kh8	resigns
7. Qe2 c6	15. Nf3 b5	23. Nd6 Qd7	
8. a4 Qc7	16. axb5 axb5	24. Qa2 Bxd6	

Other rivals to CHESS GENIUS in the same price range include M-CHESS and FRITZ 2. Gary Kasparov himself recently confessed to having lost some blitz games against FRITZ 2. Here's one of them. FRITZ's opening may look unimpressive but not so his middle-game play, where he defends accurately against Gazza's over-speculative attack.

FRITZ 2–Kasparov, Training Game, 1993. Dutch Defence

1. Nf3 d5	11. b3 g4	21. Bxf5 Qf7	31. Ke1 Bg4
2. d4 e6	12. hxg4 Nxg4	22. Bxg4 Bxg4	32. Qg2 Rg8
3. c4 c6	13. Qc2 Rg8	23. Nfd4 h5	33. Nb5 Qe7
4. e3 f5	14. Bc1 Nf8	24. Nf4 O–O–O	34. Nxa7+ Kb8
5. Bd3 Bd6	15. Bb2 Qg6	25. f3 Bd7	35. Bxe5+ Qxe5
6. c5 Bc7	16. g3 Qh6	26. Nxh5 Rdf8	36. Nxc6+ bxc6
7. Nc3 Qf6	17. Ne2 Ng6	27. Nf4 Nxf3	37. Qh2 Black
8. h3 Nh6	18. Kg2 Qg7	28. Kxf3 Rxg3+	resigns
9. Bd2 Nd7	19. Rh1 e5	29. Kxg3 Bxf4+	
10. O–O g5	20. dxe5 N6xe5	30. Kf2 Be5+	

So there you are. An opponent who doesn't complain about the lighting, knock the pieces over when he loses or demand higher prize money when he wins. Who doesn't send coded messages in yoghurt or poison your orange juice. Who doesn't kick you under the table during the game or punch you in the eye during the post-mortem. A grandmaster strength opponent on your living-room table or office desk for a mere fraction of Kasparov's appearance fee. Whatever next?

Answers

1. MAC HACK played 1. ... R x f2 +, and if 2. R x f2 Nh2 + 3. Ke2 Qb2 + 4. Kd1 Qb1 + 5. Ke2 Rb2 mate. White instead tried 2. Kg1 and resigned a couple of moves later.

2. White played 1. N x e6, and after 1. ... f x e6 2. Q x e6 + Be7 3. Re1 CHAOS had an overwhelming position.

3. KAISSA had seen that after Kg7 DUCHESS had a forced mate with the startling 1. Qf8 + K x f8 2. Bh6 + Kg8 (or Bg7) 3. Rc8 + Qd8 4. R x d8 + Re8 5. R x e8 mate.

♛

It's only tenuously related to chess, but since our book is largely for entertainment, we couldn't resist concluding with this story. We found it in an advertisement for Epson computers, so it must be true: Gilbert Bohuslav, a computer wizard from Houston, Texas, programmed his computer (DEC 11/70) to play chess. He was so pleased with its prowess that he decided to introduce DEC 11/70 to the world of literature. He fed into it all the most used words in every Western movie he'd ever seen. Here is the result:

'Tex Doe, the marshal of Harry City, rode into town. He sat hungrily in the saddle, ready for trouble. He knew that his sexy enemy, Alphonse the Kid, was in town.

'The Kid was in love with Texas Horse Marion. Suddenly the Kid came out of the upended Nugget Saloon. "Draw, Tex," he yelled madly. Tex reached for his girl, but before he could get it out of his car, the Kid fired, hitting Tex in the elephant and the tundra.

'As Tex fell, he pulled out his own chess board and shot the Kid 35 times in the King. The Kid dropped in a pool of whisky. "Aha," Tex said, "I hated to do it but he was on the wrong side of the Queen."'

Afterword by the World Champion[1]

I keep going back to the bookshelf to find this book
because I really enjoys it. I like it because it
has loads of fun information.

Little McShane

---

[1] (1992 World Under-10 Boys' Champion)

Bibliography

A much earlier labourer in the same vineyard, Richard Twiss, eighteenth-century collector of chess anecdotes, had this to say: 'It is unnecessary to particularize the number of books, many of them tedious and disgusting, I have waded through, swallowing and execrating to the end.' Here are some of those we consulted that were a pleasure to read.

Magazines and Periodicals

British Chess Magazine (St Leonards-on-Sea, London) *passim*
Chess (Sutton Coldfield, London), *passim*
Chess Informant (Belgrade), *passim*
Chess Notes (Geneva), *passim*
New in Chess (Amsterdam), *passim*
Also various issues of *The Problemist* (Leeds), *Chess Life and Review* (published by USCF), *Kingpin* (Ilford), *Myers Opening Bulletin* (Davenport, Iowa), and other periodicals.

Reference Books

The Oxford Companion To Chess (Hooper and Whyld), OUP, 1984, 1992
Chess: The Records (Whyld), Guinness Books, 1986
The Encyclopedia of Chess (ed. Golombek), Batsford, 1977
The Encyclopaedia of Chess (Sunnucks), Robert Hale, 1970
A Catalog of Chess Players and Problemists (Gaige), privately published, 1971
Chess Personalia: A Biobibliography (Gaige) McFarland, 1987
Hundert Jahre Schachturniere 1851–1950 (Feenstra Kuiper), W. Ten Have, Amsterdam

Chess History

A History of Chess (Murray), OUP, 1913; reprinted Benjamin Press, n.d.
A History of Chess (Golombek), Routledge and Kegan Paul, 1976
Chess: The History of a Game (Eales), Batsford, 1985
History of Chess (Gizycki, ed. Wood), The Abbey Library, 1972; rev. 1977
Grandmasters of Chess (Schonberg), Fontana, 1975
The Kings of Chess (Hartston), Pavilion, 1985
A Century of British Chess (Sergeant), Hutchinson, 1934
The 1851 Chess Tournament (Staunton), Batsford, 1986

Chess and Literature – Compilations

Chess Pieces (Knight), Sampson Low, 1949
King, Queen, Knight (Knight and Guy), Batsford, 1975
Chess (Twiss), 1787
Caissa's Web: The Chess Bedside Book (Harwood), Latimer, 1975
The Poetry of Chess (Waterman), Anvil Press, 1981

Games Collections and Biographies

Oxford Encyclopaedia of Chess Games, Volume I, (ed. Levy and O'Connell), OUP, 1981
The Golden Dozen (Chernev), OUP, 1976
The Golden Treasury of Chess (Wellmuth), Arco, 1958
Die Hypermoderne Schachpartie (Tartakower), Olms, 1981
500 Master Games of Modern Chess (Tartakower and du Mont), Dover, 1975
Warriors of the Mind (Keene and Divinsky), Hardinge Simpole Publishing, 1989
The Polgár Sisters (Forbes), Batsford, 1992
Confessions of a Chess Grandmaster (Soltis), Thinkers' Press, 1990
Capablanca (Winter), McFarland, 1989

A. Alekhine: Agony of a Chess Genius (Moran, ed. Mur), McFarland, 1989
Paul Morphy: The Pride and Sorrow of Chess (Lawson), David McKay, 1976

Computer Chess

Chess: Man vs Machine (Ewart), Barnes/Tantivy, 1980
Chess and Computers (Levy), Batsford, 1976
Computer Chess Compendium (Levy), Batsford, 1988

Endgame Studies and Problems

Test Tube Chess (Roycroft), Faber and Faber, 1972
An ABC of Chess Problems (Rice), Faber and Faber, 1970
Solving in Style (Nunn), Allen and Unwin, 1985
Miniature Chess Problems from Many Countries (Russ), Unwin, 1981, 1987

Chess Variants

100 Other Games to Play on a Chessboard (Addison), Peter Owen, 1983
Chess Variations (Gollon), Tuttle, 1968

Miscellaneous

The World of Chess (Saidy and Lessing), Collins, 1974
Wonders and Curiosities of Chess (Chernev), Dover, 1974
The Chess Companion (Chernev), Faber and Faber, 1970
The Book of Chess Lists (Soltis), McFarland, 1984
Chess Curiosities (Krabbé), George Allen and Unwin, 1985
Total Chess (Spanier), Secker and Warburg, 1984
The Chess Scene (Levy and Reuben), Faber and Faber, 1974

Cabbage Heads and Chess Kings (Hayden), Arco, 1960

Chess Panorama (Lombardy and Daniels), Chilton, 1975

The Adventure of Chess (Edward Lasker), Dover, 1959

Chess and its Stars (Harley), Whitehead and Miller, 1936

The Soviet Chess School (Kotov and Yudovich), Moscow, 1984

The Ratings of Chess Players Past and Present (Elo), Batsford, 1978

Idle Passion: Chess and the Dance of Death (Cockburn), Weidenfeld and Nicolson, 1975

Chessmen for Collectors (Keats), Batsford, 1985.

The Chess Beat (Evans), Pergamon, 1980

Das Spiel der Könige (Diel), Bamberger Schachverlag, 1983

Polygamie auf dem Schachbrett (Müller), Schachverlag Manfred Mädler, 1981

Confessions of Aleister Crowley (Symonds & Grant), Routledge and Kegan Paul, 1979

The Prostitutes' Padre (Cullen), Bodley Head, 1975

If you've enjoyed this book why not join your local chess club?

To find out the address of your nearest club contact:

British Chess Federation, 9a Grand Parade, St Leonards-on-Sea, East Sussex TN38 0DD
Phone: 0424 442500

If you're interested in correspondence chess contact:

R. Gillman, President, British Postal Chess Federation, 85 Hillyard Road, Hanwell, London W7 1BJ

For chess problems:

C. A. H. Russ, Hon. Secretary, British Chess Problem Society, 76 Albany Drive, Herne Bay, Kent CT6 8J

For endgame studies:

A. J. Roycroft, Chess Endgame Study Circle, 17 New Way Road, London NW9 6PL

Finally, and most important of all: teach your children to play chess (see page 102). Buy them a copy of *Move One!* by Richard James, and enrol them in a Junior Chess Club.

Both authors run successful Junior Chess Clubs, Mike Fox in Birmingham and Richard James in Richmond-upon-Thames. If you live within reach of either club, write to Mike or Richard, c/o Faber and Faber. Otherwise, contact the British Chess Federation for information about Junior Chess Clubs in your area.

Le Tout Ensemble

'. . . all the men and women* merely players'

(As You Like It, II viii)

* and children, and machines, and animals

Le Tout Ensemble

Willmers, Rudolf 34
Willy, K. 259
Wilson, Edward 97
Wilson, Lord 83–4
Wilson, Woodrow 79–80
Wimsatt, W.K. Jnr 99
Winawer, S. 127
Winchester, Marquess of 11
Windom, William 56–7, 63
Windsor, Lord Frederick 13
Winter, E. 204
Winter, W. 269
Wittgenstein, Ludwig 77
Wojciechowski, A. 39
Wojtkiewicz, A. 270
Wojtyła, Karel 16–17
Wolsey, Cardinal 20
Wood, B.H. 175, 192
Woods, Donald 97
Woolf, Leonard 38
Wooster, Bertie 60
Worcester, Canon of 222
Wreford Brown, C. 36, 66
Wycliffe, John 14
Wyvill, Marmaduke 80–81

X, Signor 17
Xie Jun 109, 123, 312
Xu Jun 225, 235, 240

Yang Kwei-Fang 4
Yarosh, L. 293, 299
Yates, F. D. 142, 219, 238, 263
Yeats, W. B. 45–6, 272
Yeltsin, Boris xv, 80
Yepez, O. 241–2
Young, F.K. 192
Young, Terence 59
Yusupov, A. 120, 161, 184, 311

Zamora, Jorge 109
Zapata, A. 174
Zartobliwy, Wanda 17
Zatopek, Emil 3, 68–9
Zepler, Prof. Erich 75
Zhukar, Dr V. 257
Znosko-Borovsky, E. 35, 259
Zukertort, J. xxv, 19, 28, 117, 120, 127–8, 136, 162, 266
Zurich F.C. 70
Zweig, Stefan, 52, 256

368

Index of Openings

THE ⬧⬧⬧ TIMES
MEETING OF MINDS

Chess and *The Times* are natural partners. Both challenge the mind and stimulate the intellect. *The Times* has been associated with the game for 200 years and so we are delighted to be sponsoring the biggest event in chess history.

Britain's interest in chess has never been stronger. We had to wait until 1976 for our first Grandmaster, now we have 20. In bringing Nigel Short's challenge to Britain we hope to foster and strengthen this interest in an occupation that encourages brain over brawn.

The Times World Chess Championship prepares the game for the next century, providing a global platform for this thrilling confrontation as well as introducing the latest interactive technology. The backing of *The Times*, and its partners Teleworld Holding BV and Telechess World Promotions Ltd., means that the players will, for the first time, receive the rewards that other top sports people have been enjoying for years.

The Times World Chess Championship has all the elements of an epic - a British challenger for the world crown, staged in the Savoy Theatre, next to Simpson's-in-the-Strand, the historical "home of chess," with innovations in marketing and technology.

That it is happening at all I am very grateful. That it is happening with the backing of *The Times* I am extremely proud.

PETER STOTHARD
Editor of *The Times*

For the best coverage of the Grandmasters, read ours.

RAYMOND KEENE
THE TIMES CHESS CORRESPONDENT

Keene on Kasparov and Short. Every day in The Times.

THE TIMES

THE 🛡️ TIMES

THE TIMES CHESS TRADITION

The Times' tradition of reporting on chess goes back to the 18th Century. *The Times'* first recorded coverage of chess was on September 2nd, 1795; an obituary of the great French Chess Master, Philidor, who died in London.

The Times' first Chess Editor was Samuel Tinsley (1847-1903). Tinsley was a self-educated man who went on to found a publishing firm, Samuel Tinsley & Co. before becoming a professional chess writer. He was a distant relative of the reigning World Draughts Champion, Dr. Marion Tinsley.

By 1922 *The Times* was so synonymous with chess that it was involved with the creation of Capablanca's World Championship Match rules. These rules, which became known as the London Statutes, were in force, with minor modifications, until 1946 when FIDE took over the title for itself.

During the 1930s, *The Times'* chess coverage was conducted by the Chess Master, Sir Stuart Milner-Barry. Sir Stuart was later to become a member of the English Olympic Chess Team and President of the British Chess Federation. At the age of 82, Sir Stuart was instrumental in winning the Counties' Chess Championship for Kent.

The most distinguished incumbent at *The Times* for chess was Grandmaster Harry Golombek, OBE. A brilliant writer who inspired many generations of young players. Chess historian and British Champion, Harry Golombek persuaded *The Times* and *The Sunday Times* to sponsor both the British Schools Chess Championship and, for several years, Britain's Premier Chess Tournament at Hastings.

When Harry Golombek retired in 1985 chess coverage was taken over by Raymond Keene, OBE. The culmination of the paper's support for chess is *The Times* World Chess Championship between Garry Kasparov and Nigel Short, the greatest event in the history of British chess.

MIRROR OF THE WORLD
Chess is war without blood, politics without the rhetoric

Chess is the game of Kings. Its name pro-claims it; the old Persian-Arabic *shah māt*, "the king is dead" , eventually produced the checkmate. But chess is also the king of games and a metaphor for the world outside the chequered board : war without blood, diplomacy without the compromises, and, despite its sometimes petulant internal manoeuvrings, politics without the rhetoric. The World Championship between Gary Kasparov and Nigel Short in London in September promises to be both epic contest and contemporary parable.

As a game this will be a thrilling drama between the two best players in the world, with contrasting styles and psychologies, at the height of their powers. The level of play will be one that ordinary mortals follow in normal times only through a glass darkly. But in September their glass will include a television and a telephone linked to a computer; thanks to plans arranged by *The Times* and its fellow sponsor, Teleworld, millions of international enthusiasts will be able to try to guess the next moves.

As a metaphor, the chess struggles of Short and Kasparov mirror the real world, as chess always has. The two players' breakaway from the international chess federation, Fide, is a reflection of the end of the Cold War and the rise of individualism, freedom and democracy against restrictive ideology and central planning.

The power of the game as an image may recall the days, more than 300 years ago, when Thomas Middleton produced his famous policital play, *A Game at Chess*. In 1624 Middleton took the English and Spanish magnates concerned in the so-called "Spanish marriage affair " and thinly disguised them as the White Knight, the Black King, and so on. It proved as dangerous an idea as any in the chess battles of today. The Spanish ambassador protested, the play was stopped, and dramatist and actors were summoned to answer for it.

For the past generation, since the beginning of the Cold War, Fide has held world chess in a zugzwang, a chess position in which any move makes things worse. It has restricted where it should have been spreading the glory of the game. For more than 20 years, the world championships were always held in Moscow, whereas before the war they were shared around several cities. Bobby Fischer was defaulted and stripped of his title for asking for changes in the rules that were granted without a murmur two years later, when a Soviet champion wanted them. In 1985 Florencio Campomanes stopped Kasparov's first world challenge against Anatoly Karpov at a crucial point, after Kasparov had won several games in a row, claiming that the players were tired.

The dash for freedom by Kasparov and Short will encourage millions around the world to follow and play the game of kings and commoners. Chess can be ludic sublimation for their aggression and boredom. Nobody yet said "checkmate" in tones that did not sound to the opposition bitter, boastful and aggressive. But nobody is harmed. Chess champions can become heroes, as exemplary in their cerebral sport as tennis and golf players, who show that a game can be hard but sporting. Chess will continue to be the metaphor on a board for a more hopeful and rational world.

1st April 1993

THE ❦ TIMES

CHESS BY RAYMOND KEENE

THIS COLUMN gives games which have been decisive or important in the history of chess or the development of chess ideas. This week's game goes further. It was a crunch and grudge match. Played at the world's highest-ranked tournament, at Linares in February, it pitted those two great rivals, Gary Kasparov and Anatoly Karpov, against each other.

Kasparov was racing ahead in the tournament, but a win by Karpov at this stage, playing with the advantage of White, would have meant that he caught up. To add fuel to the flames, Kasparov had just declared that he would break away from Fide, the World Chess Federation, to defend his title against Nigel Short under the auspices of the newly formed Professional Chess Association. Karpov, conversely, was about to announce that he would be prepared to take the Fide title by default and play a match for the Fide championship with Short's vanquished opponent, the Dutchman Jan Timman.

The stage was set for a cliffhanger which could decide the fate of world chess. I have published this game before in The Times, but this is a special treat, the notes to this crucial encounter are Kasparov's own.

White: Karpov; Black: Kasparov. Linares, 1993. King's Indian.

1 d4 Nf6 **2** c4 g6 **3** Nc3 Bg7 **4** e4 d6 **5** f3 0-0 **6** Be3 e5 **7** Nge2 c6 **8** Qd2 Nbd7 **9** Rd1 a6 **10** dxe5 Nxe5

This move dooms the d6 pawn, but what true King's Indian player would be held back by such a trifle? It is much more important to create piece play.
11 b3 b5 **12** cxb5 axb5 **13** Qxd6 Nfd7

This position is extremely hard to analyse, because both sides have an alternative to almost every move in almost every line.
14 f4

Here, one of Karpov's greatest assets, his sense of danger, lets him down. 14 Bg1 was preferable.
14 .... b4!

The essence of Black's idea is as simple as it is effective. This is illustrated by the variations 15 Qxb4

c5! 16 Bxc5 Nxc5 17 Rxd8 Ned3+ and 15 Na4 Rxa4 16 bxa4 Nc4 17 Qd3 Nb2 18 Qc2 Nxd1 19 Qxd1 Qa5 with a clear advantage in both cases.
15 Nb1?

This move is the decisive mistake. This may seem somewhat radical, but the almost forced variations that follow dispel all doubts. White had to try 15 fxe5 bxc3 16 Nxc3 but then after 16...Qa5, Black has the better of the complications.
15 .... Ng4 **16** Bd4 Bxd4 **17** Qxd4 Rxa2 **18** h3 c5 **19** Qg1 Ngf6 **20** e5 Ne4 **21** h4 c4 **22** Nc1

How often do you see a sizable White army huddled on the first rank after only 22 moves? Now I realised it was possible to ignore the attack on the rook.
22 .... c3!!! **23** Nxa2 c2 **24** Qd4

Karpov avoids the beautiful loss which is inevitable after 24 Rc1 Nxe5! The following variations are examples, 25 Rxc2 Bg4 and now:
a) 26 Be2 Nd3+ 27 Bxd3 Qxd3;
b) 26 Rd2 Nxd2 27 Nxd2 Re8 28 fxe5 Rxe5+ 29 Kf2 Qxd2+ 30 Kg3 Re3+ 31 Kh2 Rh3 checkmate; or
c) 26 Nd2 Nd3+ 27 Bxd3 Qxd3 28 Nxe4 Qxe4+ 29 Kd2 Qxf4+, with an elementary win in all variations.
24 .... cxd1Q+ **25** Kxd1 Ndc5 **26** Qxd8 Rxd8+ **27** Kc2 Nf2

In this position White lost on time, thus saving himself the choice between 28 Rg1 Bf5+ 29 Kb2 Nd1+ 30 Ka1 Nxb3 mate or 30 Kc1 Nxb3 mate. So, Kasparov had triumphed dramatically and reasserted his right at a most critical moment to be regarded as the strongest chess-player in the world.

10th July 1993